THE POLITICIAN

BY

JACK LUCHSINGER

THE POLITICIAN

Cover Design by Robert Shamus Mulholland

Library of Congress Catalog Card Number: 96-69944
ISBN#: 0-9648622-8-X

Forward

Politics has been a national pastime since the days of the American Revolution. But few really understand its true meaning and all that it involves.

The Politician is an in-depth look at the behind-the-scenes activities of people involved in politics. Their emotions, prejudices, preconceived ideas, needs, wants, and strategies are all revealed in this novel based upon the real life experiences of the author.

The characters are composites of people who work in and out of politics. The story is the unfolding of a race for the State Senate in Upstate New York. Two candidates, one an incumbent Democratic Senator and the other a Republican businessman, vie for votes, money, power, and the right to be called The Politician.

If you ever wanted to know what politics is really about, or ever considered entering the political arena yourself, *The Politician* is must reading. Be it local, state, or national elections, the only thing that really changes in a political race is the magnitude of involvement. The effort, the work, the agony, and the triumphs are all there. Names change, but the characters do not.

Politics is the last great adventure, the last frontier for change, and a power game that reaches out and touches all of our lives. It needs to be understood. But to understand politics, you must know the players. Above all else, you must know The Politician!

TABLE OF CONTENTS

Forward

Chapter I

Introduction

It was summer and New York City was always a hot, dirty town in the summer. The heat was magnified by the pavement. The buildings walled off any hopes of a breeze. Temple had worked his way from air-conditioned building to taxi to airport. He was waiting for his flight when he spotted a familiar face amidst the hustling masses.

She was hurrying to catch the same plane. Both were "Upstaters." Both had graduated from college ready to change the world. Both had climbed into the political arena; one a Democrat, and the other a Republican.

She had worked her way through college as a dancer in a local bar. After graduation she spent a short time in city government as a councilwoman. Then, in an unprecedented move, she ran against an entrenched Republican State Senator and won. It was a close race. Her next two races became her proving grounds. She won both handily. The Republicans had tried a businesswoman and then a county District Attorney. Neither could handle her fiery style nor her unorthodox tactics.

Temple had gone on to law school after college. He worked at a Wall Street law firm during the summers and then in private practice on Long Island. Eventually, his practice of law brought him to Syracuse, New York. There he was elected to the school board and became active in a number of community activities.

When the Republican Congressman in Temple's district retired, Temple had tried to gain the nomination. Eventually, the son of a former State Senator received the nomination, but Temple had laid the groundwork for a future run. Three years later, he would receive the nomination to run for the State Senate. His opponent would be the maverick Democratic State Senator who had caught the old Republican guard by surprise.

Temple had a longstanding interest in politics. His dad had been active in Long Island politics, working on Eisenhower's Presidential race and managing campaigns for Congressman Wainwright and Assembly Leader Duryea. He had been at his father's heels every step of the way.

While in law school, Temple had worked as a coordinator for John Lindsay's campaign for mayor of New York City. He had seen politics at its best and at its worst. He spent a brief time working on Robert Kennedy's campaign for the Presidency in the late '60s. He had met Kennedy as an undergraduate, then again while with the Lindsay campaign staff. But the Kennedy campaign had been cut short by a gunshot in California.

After his move to Syracuse, Temple had coordinated the efforts of his father's old friend in the State Assembly, Assemblyman Duryea, as he ran for Governor of New York. That race ended in defeat, but again Temple had been able to see politics from the inside out. The game intrigued him. He still had not lost that desire to make a difference in the world, a desire shared by all those he had seen and worked with over the years.

There were needs out there that called out for answers. He thought he had them. There were those around him who thought that he did too.

She checked her luggage, and as she turned, their eyes met, locked, and for an instant the old bruises surfaced for both. It was only momentary though, because above all else, they were the politicians.

She walked directly over to Temple as he stood up and started toward her. "It's been a while, Laura Ann. How are you?"

She made it a point never to allow anyone to address her other than as "Senator Mann," but with Temple she had always made the exception. Her name had been an issue of sorts during the campaign. The fact that he now called her Laura Ann was a victory for her. Even small victories have meaning to politicians.

She smiled, "I'm fine, busy but fine. How are you?"

The conversation was casual and polite. Neither gave it much thought although, to a few who recognized the former antagonists, it was a sight that would be talked about afterward.

Both were going back in time. Remembering bits and pieces of a part of each of their lives that had been both a time of great expectation and of great disappointment.

USAir announced the boarding of Flight 787. Temple picked up his brief case. He and Laura Ann Mann walked down the ramp for their flight back. . .back to Syracuse.

Chapter II

Prelude to a Campaign

Congressman Wales sat back in his chair, smoking his cigar and looking questioningly, first at his campaign manager, and then at his public relations director. "Who is my most likely opponent in next year's election?"

They all knew the answer. Laura Ann Mann. She had beaten the veteran Republican State Senator and two thought-to-be tough candidates to retain her Senate seat in a strongly Republican district.

The manager spoke first. "Laura Ann Mann. That bitch can't wait to get out of the Republican–controlled Senate. She's about as effective there as. . .."

The Congressman cut in. "Yeah, yeah, but the voters in her district keep sending her back! A farmer I know once told me that he doesn't agree with everything she says but when she comes to his farm and flings her legs up over his fence, he's all eyes and ears!"

The PR man chuckled, then turned serious. "What we need is someone who will give her a run for her money. Someone who can take her on and not be intimidated. Someone who doesn't need to win to have a job."

"Where are we going to find someone like that?" The manager wasn't disagreeing, he just couldn't think of any politician stupid enough to take on Laura Ann Mann. Deep inside, he was concerned that his Congressman might have a tough race against the maverick Democratic Senator.

The PR man smiled. "I think I know just the person we

4

need." He waited as both his boss and the manager looked to him for the answer. "Temple."

Wales turned in his chair to gaze out the window. He remembered Temple well. It had been a four-way primary of sorts. He had gotten the delegates committed before it even began. The party bosses had thought that a primary would give him some added exposure. It was to be easy. A bureaucrat, a little known county legislator, and a lawyer with virtually no political experience, were to be his opponents. The debates would be in a format that would showcase the Congressman. He would be given briefings before each of the debates and be ready for fielding the questions as they were presented to each of the candidates. It seemed simple but Temple had turned out to be more formidable than the party bosses had expected.

The Congressman watched a father cross the street with his son as he sat there thinking about Temple. Temple with his facts and figures. . .his off the cuff humor. . .his easygoing style. He'd made inroads with the committee people. In the end, the Congressman had prevailed and Temple had finished fourth in the four-man race. But, had the Congressman not won, his supporters would have backed Temple, and Temple would be in Washington.

"He'd give her a run for her money!" The manager liked the idea. "I think he could debate her and not look like a shithead like some others we've seen."

The PR man pressed his point. "We could give him some of our people to help him get started and you could have a news conference to announce your support for him." The PR man hoped the Congressman was going for his idea. "That would get him some publicity and legitimize his candidacy."

"He did come on board and help us after his loss to you in the primary. If you help him now, he'll be indebted, win or lose. We won't have to worry about facing him later." The manager was always figuring the angles and trying to foresee future pitfalls.

The Congressman turned back to his two cronies. "I

don't think that Jay would ever run against me, but I like the idea of putting him up against Laura Ann Mann. It'll make a race of it, and if he wins, he could be a useful ally in the State Senate. How do we get him?"

The manager smiled. "Let me take care of that."

* * *

Temple had been appointed to the Community College board after his first foray into politics. It was a job he enjoyed. He was part of a group of community leaders who were committed to giving young people a chance for continuing their education at an affordable price.

Temple had just taken his seat at the trustees' meeting when his friend Rick Handon pulled up a chair next to him.

Rick had once been the County Chairman of the Republican Party and had known Temple for a long time. He had moderated the debates when Temple had sought the congressional nomination and as always, thought that Temple had shown something not seen in a lot of political hopefuls.

"Mr. Temple, how are we today?" It was Rick's usual way of saying hello.

"We are fine, Mr. Handon, Esquire. What's up?" Temple smiled at his old friend.

"Jay, I have a proposition for you to consider. I don't need or necessarily want an answer from you today. But I want you to think about it. What would you say to your running for the New York State Senate?"

Temple half turned in his seat. "The New York State Senate! Against whom?"

"Laura Mann."

"Why me?"

"Well, you know that several of us were impressed with the way you handled yourself in the Congressional primary. The Congressman also appreciated your willingness to help him with his campaign after you lost. I've talked to our county leader and

6

he thinks you'd be a good candidate. In fact, there is no one that I have discussed the possibility with who has had anything but good comments to make."

Temple smiled. "I have never really thought about New York State politics. I kind of had this picture of me involved with national issues. That's really where my interests lie."

Handon picked up on this. "You know New York has a lot of the same problems the country has only on a different scale. Central New York needs an effective Senator. Laura Mann has no support in the Senate and is useless when it comes to big issues that effect this community. She's all show but no go!"

"What about Senator Lansing? He carries some weight in Albany."

"Senator Lansing is not going to be around much longer. He's already talking about this next term being his last. When he steps down, there will be a big void in the Upstate delegation. We need a businessman and lawyer in Albany who can get things done. Think about it. It's a chance to run for a fairly high position without the normal progression up the ladder."

Temple did think about it. He read every newspaper and magazine article that he could get his hands on that in any way related to the State Legislature and the needs of the community.

About one week had gone by when Temple received a call from his friend, Ken Mathews. Mathews was a successful entrepreneur who had taken a local printing concern and made it a nationwide operation. He had ties to the Republican Party locally, statewide and even nationally. He was one of the key fund raisers in the Upstate area.

"Jay, this is Ken. Tom Mosby and I would like to take you out for lunch today. Are you free?"

Temple had a good idea about what was in store for him. Tom Mosby was a successful lawyer/lobbyist in Albany. He had a lot of important connections statewide. He had known Mosby but not well. Unlike Mathews who was both a business and social friend, Mosby was strictly a business acquaintance. "I'd

7

be glad to have lunch with you, Ken. Where and when?"

Three hours later, the three men sat around a table eating lunch and talking.

Mathews initiated the conversation that was the main reason for the lunch. "Jay, some of us in the Republican Party have been talking about mounting a credible challenge to Laura Mann. She has been absolutely ineffective for the six years that she has spent in the Senate. She hates business. She refuses to meet with our manufacturer's group unless we agree, up front, to finance her next campaign. She harasses Senator Lansing every chance she gets, and she can't even muster support on her own side of the aisle. We need to put up a viable candidate. We think that you are that candidate."

Mosby joined in. "Jay, I know you, and you are well thought of by everyone in this community. After a few years in Albany, you will enjoy that same influence there. Albany needs good people like you. People who understand business and that understand the needs of their local communities. As a Republican in a Republican-controlled Senate, you could do a lot."

Temple was interested. From all that he had read, he recognized that there were a lot of problems that could be solved at the state level. He had concluded that the State government had set the wrong priorities. When thousands of workers were out of jobs, when businesses were leaving the state, when education had fallen behind other states, when one out of every twenty workers was on a government payroll, when people in the state were hungry, homeless, the targets of increasing crime, and when drugs could be purchased on any street corner in rural or urban communities, yes, good people were needed in Albany.

Temple looked at Mathews and Mosby. "What you have said about Laura Mann may be true, but she has tremendous support from her constituents and from the press. I think that she is probably the toughest elected official anyone could try to unseat."

Mathews spoke up. "Don't worry about the press. We

8

have some heavy hitters who can see to it that you get good coverage."

Mosby added, "Her constituents never really had much of a choice. With you in the race that will be different."

Temple sat back in his chair. "It will take a lot of money to run in this race. I understand that the county party is broke, or worse, that it owes about $80,000."

Mathews smiled. "If you run, we will get you the money."

Mosby leaned forward. "There are a lot of people out there who would be willing to give to a campaign that stood for the things that they believe in. There are also some people out there who would support you just to get rid of Senator Mann."

Temple looked at Mathews and Mosby. "One thing needs to be made clear right from the start. I will not make any deals. This is going to be a tough race, and I want to do it my way, with my positions on the issues. People, especially contributors, have got to understand that."

Mosby and Mathews looked at one another and both spoke at the same time, "Agreed."

Mosby then asked, "Does that mean you'll run?"

"Yes."

Less than an hour later the Congressman received a call from his manager. "Temple is going to run against Mann."

Temple had discussed the race with his wife, Pat. He valued her opinion and rarely did he do anything without at least getting her input. More often than not, she gave another view of the matter at hand that he had not seen.

His major concern had been the time the campaign would take away from his family. They had gone over this when he had entered the Congressional primary, but this was going to be a race for the long haul.

Pat told him that she knew this was something that was in his blood, and that he should do it or he would never be happy. She said, "I knew when I married you that some day you would run for public office. You have no choice. You were

9

meant to run."

He had talked it over with the people with whom he worked and they, too, thought that it was a good idea. "Good publicity and a way to get your name out there!"

He was asked what he thought his chances of really winning were.

"40 - 60," Temple had replied.

"That good?" was the reaction.

Chapter III

January: Month One
The Campaign Manager

It was January and the election was a little over ten months away. A lot of work was needed before Temple was ready to hit the campaign trail in earnest.

Mathews, Mosby, and Handon agreed to be on the campaign team. They brought in Bob Berry, a professional PR man who had worked on the Congressional race, and Dr. Richard Carey, a heavy contributor to the Republican Party.

Temple had turned to two old friends to add stability to the campaign: Kevin Roth, a CPA who served on a number of community boards with Temple, and Jim Summers, an attorney who had successfully started his own law firm.

The group met at Temple's home one snowy evening to map out a game plan, one that would take them to the first week in November and their date with destiny.

Berry offered his consultations without a fee but said that any work would be billed. He reviewed the campaign strategy used by the Congressman and made it clear that to win, you had to really "hate the guts" of your opponent. Temple chuckled to himself at that one.

Mathews then said that the important thing to do at this point was to raise money. "The more money we raise now, the better our chances will be in the fall."

Loans were discussed and ruled out by Temple. "I don't want to finish this race in debt."

Mosby said that every campaign is run on credit and that

the party would help to offset any losses. Temple knew that the party was having trouble paying off the County Executive's indebtedness for his race last year, and the Executive had won. He wasn't about to accept the idea that the party would be there for him, especially with a 60 - 40 chance of losing.

Temple listened as each person around the dining room table offered their thoughts on fund raising. Finally Bob Berry said, "To be taken seriously as a candidate against Laura Mann, we'll need about $27,000 seed money up front. My suggestion is that Jay and a few of you go to the bank and co-sign for a loan."

Temple thought to himself, 'the consultation is free, but the work is $27,000.' He stood up. "I guess I haven't made myself clear. I am not going to spend more than I can raise and neither my friends nor I are going to co-sign any notes."

There was silence around the table as eyes shifted back and forth. Temple continued, "Ken, Tom, and the good Doctor know how to raise money, and I have confidence that they will raise what we need when we need it. If it's truly time for a change in government, let's start right now and not be tied to old ideas and old ways of doing things." He paused. A few eyes were now looking his way. "You all believe I can make a race of this. If not, you shouldn't be here wasting your time and mine. As I see it, there are two races to be won: the Senate seat and the pocketbook. Let's go after both."

They did. By November, when all the pocketbook votes were tallied up, Temple had raised over $400,000. Mann had raised almost $200,000.

Before breaking up for the night, a discussion of a campaign manager was undertaken. It was agreed that Jay would find a manager with whom he could work closely, trust, and who had the time needed to devote to the campaign. Those present excluded themselves due to heavy workloads, family, and lack of experience.

* * * *

12

CANDIDATE

SCHEDULER

CAMPAIGN MANAGER

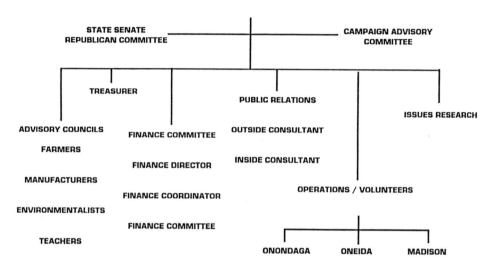

| STATE SENATE REPUBLICAN COMMITTEE | | CAMPAIGN ADVISORY COMMITTEE |

TREASURER

PUBLIC RELATIONS

ISSUES RESEARCH

ADVISORY COUNCILS

FARMERS

MANUFACTURERS

ENVIRONMENTALISTS

TEACHERS

FINANCE COMMITTEE

FINANCE DIRECTOR

FINANCE COORDINATOR

FINANCE COMMITTEE

OUTSIDE CONSULTANT

INSIDE CONSULTANT

OPERATIONS / VOLUNTEERS

ONONDAGA   **ONEIDA**   **MADISON**

FUND RAISING

MAJOR EVENTS

PRIVATE PARTIES

SENATORIAL SERIES

CEO LUNCHEONS

SPECIAL EVENTS

SIGN COMMITTEE

PHONE BANK

MAILINGS

NEWSLETTER

BROCHURE

DOOR TO DOOR

DO ME A FAVOR

Temple had been impressed by Congressman Wales' campaign team. They were close friends who had grown up together, and above all else, were loyal to the Congressman. He hoped to be able to put together a similar team for his race.

He and Pat sat down the following evening and ran through a list of potential candidates for manager. They finally narrowed the list to three good friends: Joel Blankstaff, a former reporter turned successful stockbroker; Allen Benair, a manufacturer's representative who was the godfather of Temple's son; and Robert Anderson, owner of a successful manufacturing company and politically active in the business community.

Temple met with Blankstaff at his home. It was a cold Sunday afternoon and Blankstaff's wife had made tea for the little group assembled in their living room.

Temple turned to Blankstaff, "Joel, I have decided to run for the New York State Senate, and I would like you to be in this race with me."

Blankstaff was taken by surprise. "Who are you going to run against?"

"Laura Mann."

"You're kidding?"

"No. I have decided to run, and I am putting together a team so that we can do this right. I want you to be the campaign manager."

Blankstaff was having a hard time comprehending all this. "Me? The campaign manager? I have never done that in my life!"

Temple laughed. "That's perfect, because I have never run for the State Senate in my life."

As they talked, Temple pointed out that Joel's experience as a reporter was a real plus because he knew the media people and could relate to them. He also reviewed the initial organizational meeting he had with the others and said that he needed someone who understood numbers and could keep the campaign in the black. Finally, he needed someone he could trust. He and Joel had been friends, business associates, and tennis partners, and Temple trusted him.

Blankstaff said, "It's an interesting offer. Let me check with my boss, and I will call you tomorrow."

Temple felt good about his choice until the next day when Blankstaff called.

"Jay, this is Joel. I can't do it. My boss says that we have too many connections with the State and that if I ran your campaign, he's afraid that Senator Mann would make our lives miserable. I'm really sorry, but he's the boss."

Temple knew that Joel was uneasy, and he appreciated the fact that Joel at least didn't waste time getting back to him.

"Joel, I can appreciate what you are saying although I can't imagine Senator Mann using her office for something like that."

Blankstaff had been around and knew a lot about the inner workings of the community. "Jay, check out the power company some time and then tell me what the Senator will or won't do. Anyway, I will help you financially. Send me a pledge card, and I'll get a check out to you."

Temple was disappointed. He and Blankstaff had played tennis together, had frequently had lunch together, gone out socially with their wives, and had done business with each other over the years. He would have been a great manager, but now it was time to turn to his next candidate, Allen Benair.

Temple and Benair attended the same church and often would take their families out together after the Sunday service. The following Sunday Benair and Temple were sitting in their normal Sunday haunt when Temple made the announcement. "Well, I want to tell you something. I've decided to run for the New York State Senate, and I would like to have Allen be my campaign manager."

Benair sat back and laughed. "Are you serious? I hate politics, politicians, and I'm not even a Republican!"

Temple smiled. "I know, but you are a close friend. I need someone I can trust and who will give me 150%. If you agree, I know that the rest will fall into place."

14

Benair looked at his friend. He had known Temple for a long time and knew of Temple's keen interest in politics. They had kidded one another over the years about politics and politicians. Benair had even suggested on more than one occasion that Temple should run for office. But now his friend was serious.

Temple said, "Look, Allen, if nothing else happens, we can have a great time!"

Benair thought for a moment about it, but then turned to Jay, "If you are really going to do this, you need someone who knows what is going on. That's not me. You know I'd help you any way that I can, but I'm not the right person for this. If you want money, I'll be glad to write a check out right now. You name the amount. But you really need a professional for the campaign, and that's not me."

Benair pulled out his checkbook and wrote out a check for $1,000. Temple knew he felt badly about not being able to say yes, but he also knew that he was asking for a big sacrifice from whomever took on the task.

Two days later, Temple was having lunch with Robert Anderson at Reilly's. Reilly's was an Irish pub with good food, great atmosphere, and a history of political wheeling and dealing.

"So, you want to run for the Senate. Well, how can I help?"

Temple thought that at least Anderson was not peddling backwards. Temple liked Anderson's direct approach to life in general. He was a no–nonsense businessman, straightforward, and willing to give you his right arm if you were a friend.

"I want you to be my campaign manager."

Anderson smiled. "You know, I know Laura Ann Mann?"

Temple said, "That doesn't change things. You know me too."

Anderson gave a quick laugh. "A month ago Laura Ann's brother-in-law stayed with us at our house. Paul and his wife Nancy are friends of ours going back to high school."

15

Anderson looked at Temple for a reaction. Temple thought about this for a moment. "If you feel you can't do this, just say so, Robert. I didn't know you were a family friend."

Anderson laughed again. "No, no, wait a minute. This is great. Paul would get a real kick out of this. I'd love to see his face when I told him that I was going to work for the guy who is running against his sister-in-law!"

Temple wasn't sure he followed all this, but he wasn't going to argue. Anderson would be a great choice for campaign manager.

Anderson finally turned serious. "Let me do some homework before I give you an answer. You don't need to know right away, do you?"

"No, but I would like to have an answer by next week."

"That will be fine. There are a few people I want to talk to about your candidacy before I say 'yes' or 'no.'"

Temple wondered about the few people and his candidacy but waited out the week.

On Friday, Temple received a call from Anderson asking that they meet for lunch. Temple hoped this was a good sign. They could start going over strategy.

Anderson showed Temple into his office. "Jay, the bottom line is that you can't win. I've talked with some very smart people, and they say you haven't got a chance against Laura Ann. Nobody has. It's not you, it's her. She's popular, and she says the things people want to hear. She can't deliver, but she doesn't have to because people know the Republicans won't let her. She knows she can't deliver. That's why she is so outrageous. She can't lose. She's against the system and gets all the benefits from it."

Temple raised his hand. "But isn't that just the point? She can't do anything about the things that people need the most help with because she has no power. Six years in the Senate and all her district has gotten are a few member items which she herself says she is opposed to."

Anderson nodded. "Agreed. But if the people are that

stupid that they continue to elect her, there is nothing you are going to do about it."

"I need to try," Temple told him.

Anderson looked at him. He thought back to a time when he was idealistic and ready to take on windmills. How had Temple kept that flame alive when he had not. Well, he was a realist. "Listen, Jay, I would work for you if I thought you had a chance, but you don't. The pro's are using you to keep her busy so that she won't put her efforts into other campaigns. I have a company to run. This State is going to hell, so I'd be willing to put the time in on your campaign if you had a chance, but I can't justify the sacrifice to my business and my family for a losing effort."

Temple stood up and thanked his friend for his honesty. "I'll pass on the lunch, Robert. I need to think about what you've said."

Back in his office Temple wondered if he was being used by the pros. He'd suspected some of that because he had not worked his way up the ladder, jumping from one political post to another. That was the normal routine before the State Senate. Others in the party would have gone after the seat if it were at all do-able. But the only competition in sight was a news reporter who had lost his job and thought this might hold him over.

No, he was actually using the pro's. He thought that, if given the opportunity and the right timing, the 40-60 odds would be more like 50-50. Moreover, if lightning were to strike, and he were to win, right away he would have statewide recognition for beating a very strong Democratic Senator.

Temple was committed, and he had to press onward.

That evening the Temples went out to dinner with Tony Falo and his wife, Joan. The Falos had been friends of the Temples since college. The women had been sorority sisters, and Falo and Temple had met while double-dating.

During dinner Temple had discussed his decision to run for the Senate seat. Pat had gone into detail about the difficulty

17

of finding a manager. While she was talking, it hit Temple that Tony might be the one for the job. Tony ran a family business with offices around the country. Under his leadership the company had grown and prospered. It was well-organized, and people were well-trained and placed. Maybe this could be translated into a political organization.

Tony was very interested in politics. He was very interested in a lot of things. "Jay, isn't she going to be tough to beat?"

Temple smiled. "That's the $64,000 question. I think so, but that's the appeal of this race. Look. You and I know that New York State is in a real mess in terms of jobs, business, education, and crime. We also know that a newly elected official has little or no power in his first term in office. But if I can knock off a Democrat who has everyone else running for cover, I just might have a little more clout in Albany than normal, and I might just be able to start turning some of New York's negatives into New York's positives."

Tony leaned back. "Wow! That's something I never thought about. Do you really think that is possible?"

"If I didn't, I wouldn't be running."

Joan nudged her husband. "Why don't you help Jay? Pat and I could get rid of you both for the next ten months!"

Tony laughed. "What can I do?"

Temple looked at him, then at Pat, then back at Tony. "Be my campaign manager."

They talked long into the night about what was needed and how campaigns worked. . .at least to the extent that they knew. In the end it became obvious that Tony had too many business commitments to spend the time needed to run a political campaign for a State Senate seat.

Chapter IV

February: Month Two
The Campaign Team

February blew in cold and desolate. The wind from the North Country cut through the hills and valleys of Central New York and snow blanketed the countryside.

Temple called on an old friend from the Perry Duryea days for some advice. Terry Levin had worked in Albany for the legislature as a legislative counsel. He knew upstate politics and politicians. He also had a grasp of what it would take to do what Temple wanted.

"It's been a while, Terry. How has life been treating you?" Temple and Levin liked each other. Levin respected Temple's judgment and fairness. Temple appreciated Levin's insights and interest in politics.

"Life's been good. Better for me than for you. Eh, my friend?"

"How did you know?"

"Word travels fast in a small town. Too fast. You better plan to announce your intention to run the way you want it to be announced or someone else will do it for you."

Good advice as always. Temple got what he expected: the unexpected.

"Seriously, Terry, I'd like to know how you found out?"

"The Congressman told me. He wants to help you. He figures if he helps you, he helps himself. You beat Mann, and he won't have to."

"Does he really think that she would go after him?"

"No question about it. They never got along when they were on the City Council together. The Democrats have no one else with the name recognition that she has. The Congressional District and the Senate District practically overlap, and the numbers show she could win."

"What numbers?"

"A recent poll. She leads all elected officials in positive name recognition. That's a concern for all Republicans. It should be a concern for you."

"Tell me about Senator Mann."

Levin thought for a moment. It wasn't that he had to concentrate to come up with an answer, it was more about where to begin. "She is a great campaigner. Her first run for the Senate, no one gave her a prayer. She was a woman and a City Councilor. We figured she'd get swamped out in the countryside, but while we were figuring, she was knocking on doors all over the district. It was October before we realized we had a race on our hands. By then it was too late. The bar dancer was State Senator."

Temple knew the story. He, too, had been impressed with Mann's victory. She had used her looks, her brains, and her youth all to her advantage and had won on a rhythm and blues jingle. In fact, Temple had hosted a question and answer session with the freshman Senator at his business and had been impressed with how easily Mann had made the transition.

Levin continued, "Mann learned an important lesson. It's not so much what you do as how you come across to the public that counts. And how you come across to the public depends on the media. She is the queen of ten second bytes on radio and television."

"How do you think I can beat her?"

"Be yourself."

The waitress brought their lunch to the table. "Anything else, I can get you gentlemen?" Temple thought to himself, 'Yeah, about 100,000 votes.'

Levin had suggested two public relations firms, Ajax

Consultants, and Berry & Ophidia. Ajax had worked on several local elections, most notably the County Executive's race last year. Berry & Ophidia had worked both local and state-wide races including the Congressman's recent campaign. Temple told Levin that Berry was already helping out, but that he would meet with both.

* * * *

The February weather continued to pound the whole Northeast. Twice during the past week, schools had to be closed and once the State Thruway had been closed between Buffalo and Albany.

Temple pulled his van into the parking lot of the County Republican Headquarters. Snow had drifted up to ten feet high in the lot so that finding a space to park was not an easy task. Temple wore his favorite outback hat and woolen parka to keep out the cold.

Arthur Gaines, the County Republican Chairman, pulled up alongside Temple's van just as Temple was getting out. "Great hat, Jay. Wish I could get away with wearing one of those."

"You can. Just buy one," Temple mused. He didn't know whether Gaines was being serious or trying to be funny. It was too nasty outside to care.

Once both were inside headquarters, Gaines said, "The boys are anxious to meet with you. We should have about twenty committee people here this morning. They want to hear your plans and how you are progressing."

Temple was taking off his parka, "I think I can handle that."

Ten minutes later the small conference room was full. Thirty-two committee people had come out in the snowy, wintry weather to hear what the Senate hopeful had to say.

Gaines smiled at the group. "We have a great Republican candidate who wants to be our State Senator and who

21

we want to be our State Senator. This guy is enthusiastic, smart and is already doing the right things to win this race. Ladies and gentlemen, Jay Temple, our next State Senator."

Temple stood up as all eyes fastened on the attorney/businessman who was going to run against the toughest elected Democrat in Upstate New York. He could just imagine the thoughts these committee people had. 'Who is this guy? How can he beat Laura Mann? Gaines must be losing it.'

Temple decided on the direct approach. "Thank you for coming out on a day like today to meet and talk with me.

"I'm Jay Temple. I have a wife Pat, three great children, Amy, James, and Tyler and a dog, Duke. All of us, especially Duke, plan on spending twenty hours a day for the next eight and a half months campaigning for the New York State Senate. What questions do you have?"

For the next two hours, Temple fielded questions ranging from the state budget to drug related crime. During the two hour session, more committee people filtered into the room along with several elected officials, party contributors, and a couple of people on Temple's steering committee. By the time he had finished, it was a standing room only meeting and all were on their feet to applaud this new candidate with an uncanny ability to cite facts and draw conclusions that made sense.

Temple took a short break in Gaines' private office before going back to meet with the next scheduled group, the party's finance committee.

Charles White was chairman of the Finance Committee and one of the biggest contributors to the party. He had run a multi-billion dollar business with world wide sales and distribution. He now concentrated on two things, his investments and politics.

Other committee members included Joseph DiNagro, attorney and County Legislator; Donald Basney, auto dealer; Thomas Castinetta, commercial construction company president; Roy Swift, department store owner; Ken Mathews, printing company executive; Dr. Richard Carey, physician; John

Turnlow, entrepreneur; and Elaine Bonney, businesswoman and unsuccessful candidate against Mann four years earlier.

White called the meeting to order. "Art, why don't you introduce Mr. Temple to everyone."

Gaines took his cue from White, "Gentlemen and lady." He smiled at Bonney who did not return the smile and apparently did not appreciate the recognition.

"A little while ago, in this same room, I heard a man speak who not only had a command of the issues, but who captivated his audience. I think we have a winner with Jay Temple. Our job now is to raise the money to get his message out to the public. If I were Laura Mann I'd be concerned!" Gaines looked at White.

White turned to Temple, "Would you like to say a few words?"

"Yes. Thank you." Temple again stood up. "Some of you already know me. For those of you who might not, you should know that I always play to win. I've told my campaign team that we have two races to run between now and November: the Senate election and the pocketbook race. I need your help with both but particularly with the fund raising. What do you need from me?"

The committee outlined the work that they needed from Temple, not the least of which were his phone calls to all possible contributors and personal visits to the larger contributors. It was obvious that Temple was going to have to spend as much time raising money as he was campaigning.

The only reservation expressed came from Joseph DiNagro. He wanted to be on record that he did not think that Temple could win. "Nothing against you, Jay, but Laura Ann can't be beaten. A lot of the big contributors know this and won't give you the time of day. Without the big bucks, you're dead in the water."

Temple knew DiNagro from other dealings. DiNagro was a solid politician, abrupt, smart, hardworking, well-organized, and opinionated. He wouldn't work for Temple, but he also wouldn't work against him.

The meeting concluded with the advice that the candidate needed a campaign manager 'yesterday,' a finance chairman, and a public relations firm.

Gaines met with Temple and Mathews after the meeting. "We need to publicly announce your candidacy. The Congressman has agreed to join you here on Thursday to make it official and to endorse your candidacy. We'll notify the press. Now what about a campaign manager? Ken, how about you?"

Mathews sat up. "I'm better at raising money than running a campaign. I can do more good for Jay if I am free to get out there and solicit dollars. He's right. He has two races to win, and I plan to help him win the dollar one."

Gaines looked at Temple. "Let me suggest someone. Ted Cordis is President of the Young Republicans. He's smart, hard working and a comer. They have a good group of young people who could really add to your team. Think about it."

Temple looked at Mathews then Gaines. "I don't know this Cordis, but I'll be happy to talk with him."

"What about the PR?" Gaines was anxious to get everything in place.

"I have a meeting tomorrow with Ajax Consultants at my office and then lunch with Berry and Ophidia."

Mathews spoke up, "You know Bob Berry has already helped out, Jay. He and Ophidia did a great job for the Congressman and have statewide experience. They also know your opponent."

"I know, Ken. It was suggested that I talk with both. For my own satisfaction, I want to at least compare the two and see what they have to offer."

Temple met with the Ajax people in the morning. They had extensive newspaper experience but little radio and television background. They presented an outline of how they thought the campaign ought to proceed, involving a lot of newspaper advertising and a direct mail campaign. Their slogan was to be: "Sow the seeds of success for the future, elect Jay Temple to the

24

Senate." In each direct mail piece there would be a packet of morning glory seeds.

Temple appreciated the work and pride that they had put into the presentation but also realized that this wasn't quite what he had in mind for his campaign. He thanked them and went to lunch with Bob Berry and Arnold Ophidia.

Berry made the introduction. "Jay, this is Arnold Ophidia, one of the most successful political campaign strategists in the State. In the last five years, he has successfully run 32 state and federal campaigns. He is very interested in making your race his 33rd."

Temple looked at the man, half in disbelief. Ophidia was everything you would expect and then some in a professional political public relations man. Hollywood couldn't have typecast him better. He was short and fat, with thick black hair and red cheeks. He was smoking a thick cigar and attempting to blow rings toward the ceiling as Bob Berry spoke. His thumb was jammed behind the suspenders holding up his large checkered pants and he tilted precariously back in his chair till it touched the restaurant wall.

As Berry finished the introduction (written by Ophidia), the man quickly brought his chair down on its four legs. "Temple, Bob here, is my new partner. Together we are going to make you the next New York State Senator." His quick grin showed smoke–stained teeth.

"Yessir. I have heard a lot about you, Temple." Ophidia had a slight twitch which Jay had not noticed at first. "I've talked with the Congressman, with the County Chairman, and a couple of your supporters, and I think we can win this race. It will take money, but with your connections that shouldn't be a problem."

Swinging around in his chair, he picked up a thick file from the floor. "Here it is!" He waited for the question to be asked, so Temple obliged him. "Here what is?"

Ophidia pulled out some sheets of paper. "The goods on Senator Mann. This stuff will be leaked to the press and

BINGO! you are on your way to Albany."

Temple had been amused long enough. "Listen. This is my deal for you. First put your papers back in the file. I am not going to run that kind of a campaign. I am going to make this an issues–oriented campaign. No personal attacks on Mann."

Now it was Ophidia's turn at disbelief. "Are you nuts? Bob, this guy is not being realistic. He wants to run for the Senate against possibly the most popular elected official in Central New York and wants to do it on issues." He turned from Berry to Temple, "You'll never make it out of the gate. Mann will bury you before the campaign is a month old."

Temple didn't like Ophidia, his politics, or his advice. "Arnold, that's the way it is. It's my campaign to win or to lose."

Ophidia shot back, "Oh, you'll lose. You'll lose all right. That bitch made mincemeat of her last two opponents. Now neither one of them has a career that you can blow to hell! Temple, to win you got to go for the throat. The press doesn't want to hear about a milk program for school kids, it wants the dirt on Senator Mann. You've got to give it to them packaged just the way I have it here for you."

Temple stood up. "No!"

Berry jumped to his feet sensing that Temple was going to leave and that an opportunity would be lost. "Jay, Arnold, let's take a look, at least, at the rest of the outline for the campaign and maybe we can reach some understanding."

Temple spoke up, "You fellows came highly recommended. I watched Bob work the Congressman's campaign and so far I have appreciated his work on my campaign. But I will not tolerate any personal attacks on Senator Mann. I've looked at her record in the Senate, and I think we have a good case to go after her on the record, the public record."

Berry said, "Well, let's see what we can come up with," and he outlined a campaign, heavy on radio and television, and light on newspaper coverage. He pointed out the penetration the three local commercial TV stations had within the Senate District and the ample radio coverage. He also had a cost breakdown of the air time. He had even worked out a weekly news conference schedule with tentative topics and site locations. It was a good plan.

Temple concluded that he would use Berry for his PR and would let his partner concentrate on some other race for number 33. "Bob has his office here in Syracuse. I'd like to have him work directly on my campaign. Arnold, your offices are in Albany, so maybe you can keep us up to date on the Albany scene?"

The implications of Temple's comments were clear to all. Ophidia was the senior partner, but it was obvious to him that Temple did not want him directly involved in Temple's campaign. This irked him, but money was money, and he thought, 'a loser's money is just as green as a winner's.' So, Ophidia accepted the deal and wrote off the race.

Berry lost no time in setting up the first news conference. No less than 105 invitations went out to the media. Jay Temple was about to enter a race where no other politician was willing to go.

Temple had his family and friends present for the announcement. He acknowledged that with one very notable exception, no other politician was to be seen. The County Chairman even passed on the opportunity for some media coverage. The exception was the Congressman. He was committed, and he alone stepped to the microphone to introduce Jay Temple to the political arena.

Temple looked around the room. One hundred and five invitations went out and two local TV stations, the local newspaper and four radio stations had shown up for the big day. Berry had told him that this was a good turnout. He'd hate to see a bad one!

The Congressman gripped the podium and glanced down at his notes. Temple sensed that the Congressman was nervous

27

though his voice seemed steady. "Ladies and gentlemen. It is my pleasure to introduce to you today, a man who I believe will be the next State Senator from Central New York. Jay Temple is a knowledgeable, articulate, honest businessman and attorney. He knows the problems of this District and this State. He has some good ideas and a lot of energy. He has my full support and I hope you will give him yours. Jay Temple."

Temple rose to the applause of his family and friends and to the skepticism of the press. He thanked the Congressman for his support and thanked all those who came to hear his announcement for the State Senate. Halfway through his remarks, the cameramen started taking down their equipment and the reporters began giving instructions.

Temple concluded his speech on jobs, education, taxes, and crime. "Any questions?"

Steve Adamson, a local television reporter, raised his hand. "Mr. Congressman. What are the chances of any federal funds coming to us to help clean up Onondaga Lake?"

Wales stood up and answered the question. Yes, the chances were good. Both United States Senators from New York were in favor of funding.

Sally Notholm, another local television reporter, stood. "Mr. Congressman. Wouldn't it be better to spend the billions of dollars it will take to clean up the lake on the homeless?"

The Congressman's face turned red. "Ladies and gentlemen. We are here today for the candidacy of Jay Temple. I'll be happy to answer your questions after this news conference, but for now, let's take advantage of this time to get to know Mr. Temple."

The Congressman sat down. There was a moment of silence, then Adamson spoke. "Mr. Temple. Two questions. You have the Congressman's support, but where are all the other Republican office holders and their endorsements? Second, do you really think that you can seriously challenge Senator Mann?"

Temple thought as he stood up, 'Welcome to politics.'

He looked at Adamson. "In three weeks, the first of

28

three County Republican Committee meetings will be held in Oneida County. I will be seeking their endorsement as well as endorsements from Madison and Onondaga County. Once I have the endorsements, I am sure that all Republicans will work for my campaign.

"As for running against Senator Mann, if I didn't think I could win, I wouldn't be in this race."

George Hague, a newspaper reporter, asked, "Senator Mann is seen as a reformer and not well-liked by the good old boys in Albany? Are you a 'good old boy' too?"

Temple looked directly at Hague. "I'm a candidate for the New York State Senate. I have ideas about what needs to be changed in Albany and about how those changes should take place. New Yorkers need jobs that pay well. Business needs incentives to stay in New York. Our kids need improved education. We all need tax relief. And we need to get drugs out of our society.

"There are no labels for these things, just challenges that are not being met. I'd like to be a part of the change that makes these things happen."

The news conference ended with Temple's family and friends congratulating him and wishing him well. The reporters congregated around the Congressman. Adamson asked, "Off the record, do you really think this guy has a chance against Mann?"

The Congressman looked over at Temple. "Yes."

* * * *

Temple, Berry, Roth, Mathews, Mosby, Carey, and Summers sat around Temple's dining room table planning the next phase of the campaign.

Temple's wife had just provided coffee and cake and was taking her place at the table next to her husband.

"Did I miss anything?" she asked.

"Almost missed some great chocolate cake!" Berry offered.

29

Temple smiled, "We need to put together a campaign team. Kevin has agreed to be the treasurer." Temple looked at Roth. "Thank you, sir."

Temple went on, "I have been given a suggestion for campaign manager from Art Gaines. A fellow named Ted Cordis. He's President of the Young Republicans, and Gaines thinks the whole group might get involved. Any other suggestions or offers?"

Ken Mathews set his coffee cup down. "What about a woman? Running against Mann, a woman campaign manager might be an asset."

Summers asked the question that was on everyone's mind. "Who?"

Mathews said, "Well, how about Liz Connors? She has been active in a number of charities, has the time, and knows a lot of people."

Berry spoke, "She has good credentials, but for the kind of campaign we plan on, we need someone who will sleep, eat and breathe Temple's campaign. This is going to be a very grueling eight months and we need a full-time commitment.

"The other part of this is that the campaign manager and Jay and I are going to be living with each other," Berry chuckled, "We don't want any rumors starting about the campaign manager and the candidate."

It was agreed that Cordis would be interviewed by Berry and Temple.

Next for discussion was the upcoming round of meetings with committee people. Although Temple was the declared candidate, he still needed the endorsements of the Republican Committees in Oneida, Madison, and Onondaga Counties.

There was some talk about a local newsman running, and possibly the Mayor of Rome. The decision was made to get Temple out to Oneida County and Rome as soon as possible. Also, a letter was put together for mailing to all committee people in all three counties, asking for Republican support and outlining the four major issues. It was to be individually signed by the candidate.

It was also decided to go after the Conservative Party endorsement. In a close race, there were enough Conservative votes to swing the election.

Before the group broke up, they again reviewed the finances of the campaign. Dr. Carey agreed to be Finance Chairman. Everyone in the room agreed to serve on the fund raising team and each agreed to kick in a thousand dollars. The race for dollars was underway.

* * *

Temple appeared at a 'Meet The Candidates' forum in Liverpool, New York, two nights later. A crowd of about a hundred and fifty committee people filled the room. Temple was accompanied by his wife, Kevin Roth, and Ed Thatcher, an insurance agent with Temple's company. Thatcher was also a committee person from the east side of the district.

The candidates' forum was hosted by the Young Republicans and Ted Cordis was busy seeing to the last minute details of the evening's event.

The press had run a short feature on Temple after his news conference. Most people in the district hardly took notice, but for those in this room, there was more than just passing interest in this new face. For them, Temple had come out of nowhere to be the front runner for the Republican nomination for the New York State Senate. Politically interested, they wanted to see this Jay Temple first hand. He did not disappoint them.

His speech took no more than fifteen minutes, but it was hard hitting and packed with new ideas. Temple finished by raising his hand, "It's time for a change! We must grasp this moment in time and make a difference. Together, you and I will make a difference."

It was what they came to hear. They were on their feet, clapping, cheering and giving the thumbs up sign. Temple never expected this. He found that as he talked, he warmed, both to the crowd and to the subject. Without a single note, he had covered the political landscape and never lost the attention of those listening.

Ed Thatcher was the first to congratulate him. "That was great! Laura Ann Mann, watch out!"

Pat Temple was next. "Honey, you were terrific. I'm so proud of you."

A stream of Republicans came by offering congratulations, support, and advice.

As the crowd finally thinned out, Ted Cordis walked up to Temple. "Nice job."

Temple acknowledged Cordis, "Thanks. You too. With the arrangements. This was a great forum."

"Yeah. I guess. Listen, I'm President of the Young Republicans. We are having a meeting next Monday and I was wondering if you would come and speak to us?"

Temple said, "I'd be glad to. As a matter of fact, maybe you could join my PR man and me for breakfast on Tuesday."

"Sounds good." Cordis smiled at Temple, his wife, and Thatcher, then left. As Cordis went out the door, Thatcher laughed, "The brown shirts."

"Brown shirts?" asked Temple.

"Yeah, like Mussolini and Hitler," Thatcher replied. "They all had on brown shirts."

Temple caught a glimpse of the last of the Young Republicans as they left the hall. They were all wearing brown shirts.

* * *

The Congressman finished his talk to the Young Republicans (YRs as they prefer to be called), vowing to bring the Russians to their knees before he'd vote for one cut in defense spending. The YRs applauded and shouted their approval.

Cordis thanked Wales for his talk and for reaffirming the

principles 'we all believe in.' The Congressman shook a few hands, and as he was leaving, walked over to Temple and said, "Give 'em hell!"

Cordis then introduced Temple. "The other night, several of us heard Mr. Temple speak at the candidate's forum in Liverpool. Mr. Temple impressed us, and so we invited him to speak to us tonight about his upcoming campaign. He is running against Laura Ann Mann for the New York State Senate. We'd all like to see her out of office. So, I give you Jay Temple."

Temple stood up. "Thank you, Ted," he turned to the audience of young faces, "and thank all of you for being here tonight."

Temple walked around the podium and pulled a chair out to the front of the room. He climbed up on the chair, sitting on the back with his feet on the seat. "I'd like this to be a good exchange of ideas between all of you and myself. I'd like to learn what each of you thinks about jobs, drugs, education, and taxes. . .or anything else that you feel is important. How about it?"

Temple looked at a young woman in the front row. "What bothers you about New York State?"

She didn't hesitate. "Taxes! I just graduated from college last year, and between my college loans, food costs, rent, and other expenses, plus New York's taxes, I'd be as well off if I were on unemployment!"

"Better!" added the young man sitting next to her.

Temple looked at the young woman. "What is your name?"

"Mary. Mary Tarkings."

Temple then looked at the young man. "And what is your name?"

"Patrick Fitzgerald."

Temple turned to the audience. "Mary and Patrick have hit one of the major issues of this campaign right square in the middle. We have a lot of hard working people in this state who cannot get ahead because of the huge tax burden they are required to bear.

"New York State has one employee on a government payroll for every twenty residents. It has a welfare system with one of the highest benefits payments and shortest waiting periods of any state in the Union. And, it has a State Government that knows only how to tax-and-spend and not how to cut-and-save.

"We all have to prioritize our expenditures, the State Legislature needs to do this too. My priorities are straightforward: education, jobs, reduced crime and drug use, and reduced taxes."

Temple and the YRs spent the next three and one half hours running through a host of issues, some of which they agreed on, and others which they did not. Finally at about midnight, Cordis thanked Temple for his straight talk on the issues and wished him success with the campaign..

Less than eight hours later, Temple and Berry were joined by Cordis for breakfast at a TJ's Big Boy restaurant in Fayetteville, New York.

"Bob, this is Ted Cordis. Ted, Bob Berry."

The two men shook hands, each trying to size up the other. Bob opened the conversation. "Jay tells me that you're the President of the Young Republicans?"

"Yes, I am." Cordis looked from Temple to Berry. "I've been President for about three years. I'm also a committeeman and treasurer of the West End Republican Club."

"What do you do for a living?" Berry asked.

"Basically, a stockbroker. I also have several businesses which I run with a group of friends. As a matter of fact, a number of my business friends have gotten involved with the YRs." Cordis moved closer to the table as he warmed to the subject at hand. "The YRs work as a group. I've tried to build an organization that can not only enjoy the political activity, but can also have a social and business relationship as well. It's worked. Both of you will find that whether it's a campaign or a business deal, our people are totally committed."

Berry thought to himself, 'this is just what we need, a built-in organization that is ready to go.' He smiled his best PR smile as he talked to Cordis. "Jay has the battle of the decade on his hands. Laura Ann Mann is well-known, outspoken on women's issues, relates well in the inner city and on the farm, and has in place a political machine that has swamped her last two Republican opponents. We need a group of people to dedicate every available hour of the day to working with Jay to turn the tables on Senator Mann and kick her pretty little ass out of office."

Cordis laughed. "We can do it. Last night, after your meeting with the YRs, we stayed to discuss this year's campaigns. We unanimously agreed that we wanted to work on your campaign. Some thought we ought to work on several campaigns to broaden our political base, but in the end, we all concluded that if we all went in the same direction, we could have a bigger impact and a better experience. We want to commit to Mr. Temple's campaign."

Temple had talked with Berry before their meeting with Cordis. The guy looked good. He fit the profile for a campaign manager. The only hesitation Temple had was that he had not known Cordis and the decision was being made on the recommendations of others.

Temple decided that the direct approach was best. "Ted, we have been talking about having the YRs play a big role in the campaign. We also have been thinking about having you join our campaign team."

Cordis listened with eager interest. Temple went on. "You and I don't know each other so there are some questions I need to ask you."

Cordis nodded, "I understand. Shoot."

Temple took a quick glance at Berry and then asked, "Is there anything on the negative side about you that we need to know? In a campaign, everyone's life is open for public view. If we get into a real race, the press will be digging everywhere

35

and I need to know what they will unearth."

Cordis looked Temple in the eye, "I have nothing in my past that would in any way be a problem. No convictions, no gambling, you name it." He paused, thinking, "One thing. In college, campus security hauled a bunch of us in one night for a drinking party. They took our names but that was all. I haven't had a drink since."

Berry smiled. "If that's the worst they can come up with, we're home free. Hell, that might even get us a few votes."

Temple spoke, "Anything else?"

Cordis knew decision time was at hand. "No. That's it. Except, I want you to know that we won't do anything that will embarrass you in any way. We believe in you. Last night, we saw a candidate that we could relate to. We all hate what Mann did to Senator Ahern and none of us buy her act . We want to help you beat her. Nothing would give me greater pleasure than to personally remove her Senate plates from her car after the election."

Temple needed to get on with the campaign. He needed a campaign manager. He liked the way Cordis had organized the Young Republicans and he had good reports on Cordis from people who should know. He liked his personality, his appearance, his dedication, and his enthusiasm. Temple made the decision. "Ted, I'd like to have you be my Campaign Manager. It's asking a lot. A lot of time and sacrifice. We've got a long way to go and I don't plan on losing. You'll be sleeping, eating and drinking politics from now until November and you'll probably end up hating everything about it. But it will be an exciting trip!"

Cordis smiled. The tension that had been building inside him broke. "That's great! I was hoping you would ask me. We're going to kick butt. . .Ms. Mann's butt!"

The following afternoon, a cadre of YRs filed into Temple's office.

Mary Tarkings was Vice President of the Young

Republicans and a clerk in Cordis' brokerage firm. Tall, dark hair, attractive, and intelligent, she would become the volunteer coordinator for the campaign.

Patrick Fitzgerald was a college student who loved politics and being involved in campaigns. He had worked for the Republican Party in each of the last three years and no job was to be too big or too small for him. Fitzgerald had developed a quiet sense of humor. Temple attributed this to his family background (big and Irish!). He became a campaign assistant and a trusted friend of Temple's.

Fred Childs was a local, newly admitted attorney. He had been a city fireman for eleven years before deciding to return to school and get a law degree. Part of getting ahead professionally was to be active in politics. This desire to get ahead and his feeling that Temple was someone who would not go unnoticed attracted him to the campaign. He would be the campaign coordinator for the cities of Syracuse and Rome.

Mary Price was a close friend of Ted Cordis. She had lost her husband in the closing days of the Vietnam War and had to fend for herself and her two-month-old baby. She had gone to work for a local bank and had moved up the ladder from teller to Vice President of Customer Loans. She was a committeewoman in Cicero and found relief from the pressures of business and family in politics. Mary Price was to become Temple's scheduling coordinator and the detail person for functions and events.

Laney Gardiner was a fashion model. During periods of unemployment as a model, Gardiner had worked for the National Republican Committee in Washington, D.C. She had developed computer skills and knew how to maintain campaign records for volunteers and contributors. She also had good people skills that, when coupled with her striking appearance, gave a campaign office the aura of success. Gardiner would be the campaign office manager for Temple's campaign.

Others present were Donald Tailing, Cordis' best friend and follower; Kerry Heathrow, an ardent conservative who hated everything Laura Ann Mann stood for; Ira Sterling, an admirer of Heathrow who worked with Heathrow on a number of political campaigns; and Larry Malcolm, a former student of Temple's, committeeman, and manager of a local food store. (Temple had taught a course in government at Syracuse University). Malcolm would be Temple's driver during the first phase of the campaign.

After everyone had arrived Cordis, Temple, and Temple's secretary, Gloria Bryan, walked into the meeting room followed by Kevin Roth and Dr. Carey.

Temple thanked the group for assembling and then asked that each person identify him or herself and tell a little about their background.

When this initial ice-breaker was over, Temple outlined the needs of the campaign, the positions that had yet to be filled, and let everyone know that he, Cordis, and Roth would be interviewing all those interested in a major role in the campaign.

For the next week, the three met with interested YRs and others and rounded out the campaign team. While doing this, Temple also had joined the speaking circuit and was making appearances at Rotary Clubs, Kiwanis Clubs, Farm Bureaus, and Republican Clubs throughout the Senate District.

A van had been outfitted with phone, file system, television, and bed for keeping on top of the demands of the campaign. Before the campaign was over, 78,000 miles would be added to the van and countless stories in which "mobile headquarters" would play a part.

In the early days of the campaign, the crew of the van included Cordis, Malcolm, Fitzgerald, the "two Marys," Laney, Kevin, and Temple. Once in a while, they would be joined by Berry, Thatcher, Childs or others interested in finding out what the "road trips" were like.

In these early days, the van would roll into the parking lot of a grocery store or shopping center and everyone would pile out to join the candidate in "pressing the flesh" and meeting the people in the district. Weekends were filled with fairs, bazaars, barbecue chicken dinners, field days, and fund raisers. Every so often a parade would be added to further test the stamina of the "road gang."

These were both fun days and days of exhaustion, but they were also days when Temple really got to know his would-be constituents. He had never realized the extent to which the economy had taken its toll on the people of Central New York. He had known the statistics, but these trips helped him to also see the faces, people's faces, faces that went with the numbers.

Temple never got over a weekend he spent in southeastern Madison County. He had marched in a local parade behind Josh Tobias' Racing Pigs. His "road gang" as always marched along with him handing out brochures to the adults and candy to the kids. They laughed about the racing pigs and having to watch where they stepped along the march.

As Temple was shaking hands along the parade route, he noticed one little boy, five or six years old, barefoot and underdressed for the weather, following along with him. Temple left the parade route and walked through the crowd to where the little boy was standing. The boy wasn't much older than Temple's youngest son. He was clutching a piece of candy that had been thrown to him by one of Temple's people.

Temple knelt down, "Hi. What's your name?"

The little boy looked down at the ground. A girl about ten or eleven years old came over. "He don't say much. He's my brother."

She wasn't dressed much better than the little boy but she was more talkative. "He likes the candy, mister. Me too."

The 'two Marys' had caught up with Temple and had taken this all in. They gave the two children and several others who had now joined the group a handful of the penny candy.

Temple patted the little boy's head and looking at his sister said, "Take care of your brother." He smiled and as he was walking back to the parade he heard a little voice say, "Tyler."

He turned to catch a smile from the little boy. It was his

son's name.

That night, as the "road gang" returned to Syracuse, Temple turned to Cordis, "That's what this campaign is all about."

Cordis looked at Temple. "What?"

Temple was very serious now. "Those children, those people, they haven't got much to live on. In a State as rich in resources as New York, it's a crime that our people should have to live like that. If nothing else, when I get to Albany I'm going to see to it that those kids and their families have the opportunity to get ahead."

Cordis looked back at the rest of the crew in the van and smiled. "That's why we're working for you!"

Chapter V

Rome

Tom Mosby picked up his telephone and called Temple. "Jay, this is Tom. I've lined up somebody I think you should meet. Calvin Wendt. Cal is a good guy. He lives in Rome and wants to meet you. We could use his help. He's well connected in Rome and can get you into the right places." Mosby paused.

Temple responded, "When and where do we meet Mr. Wendt?"

"How about tomorrow?"

"Fine."

"Good. I thought we would invite Berry. What do you think?" Throughout the campaign Mosby would be a big supporter of Berry.

Temple thought for a moment, "Great, if Bob has the time."

Okay, I'll call him and we will pick you up about eleven in the morning." Mosby hung up.

Temple wondered what Wendt would be like. It was a constant source of wonder to him why people that he did not know would be willing to devote time, money, and energy to his campaign. He knew that some did it in the hopes of having political "clout" or patronage after the election. But there were so many in a campaign such as this that there would never be enough patronage to pay them all, yet still they came.

The next morning, Temple had breakfast with Cordis, Dr. Carey and Mathews. They began mapping out fund raising plans and time schedules. Meetings would be set up with prominent contributors, phone calls would be made by the candidate to friends who might support him, and the Congressman would be contacted for his list of contributors as well as the party's. Temple mentioned his noon meeting in Rome. Mathews knew Wendt and suggested that he might be another source for raising money for the campaign. It was decided that the fund raising activity should be extended to include Oneida and Madison Counties. In the previous two races, both counties had been excluded, but in this race Temple intended to represent all three counties so there was no reason not to seek financial support in all three.

A need was also identified to have a full-time fund raiser on the campaign team. Mathews would be a central figure in the fund raising, as would Dr. Carey, but a full-time staff person was needed. Cordis and Temple agreed to find that person.

At eleven a.m. Mosby and Berry picked Temple up at his office. Temple's secretary, Gloria Bryan, had confirmed their appointment with Wendt and Wendt had mentioned that he had set up some meetings for Temple that afternoon. Fortunately, the afternoon was open for the candidate.

Mosby had the full run-down on Wendt. As they drove to Rome, Mosby gave a sketch of a self-made man who had built a small manufacturing empire in Rome. Eventually, he had expanded into real estate investment, then construction, and then into politics. Wendt had run for Mayor of Rome, lost, and then decided to work behind the scenes. Within six years, he had put his hand-picked candidate into City Hall, controlled the City Council, and was highly sought after by would-be State politicians for advice and support.

He had played a prominent role in two gubernatorial elections and been on the Nixon reelection team. Wendt could open almost any door in the Rome area on both sides of the aisle. Democrats as well as Republicans respected his power and prestige. He had been instrumental in bringing and keeping the Rome Air Base in that community. This meant jobs and money for the area and those two commodities transcended party lines.

42

Berry drove the car up to an imposing shopping plaza. This was Wendt's latest project. It was a clean, sleek, glass and brick building located directly across from City Hall.

The three men climbed out of the car and walked into the complex. A life-sized painting of Wendt hung in the lobby. A large information desk was located directly opposite the door and two security guards manned the desk.

Temple walked over to the desk. "Could you tell us where we might find Calvin Wendt?"

The guard looked up. "Yes, sir, Mr Temple. Room 310, a right off the elevator." The other guard stood up. "Follow me, Mr. Temple. Mr. Wendt is waiting for you."

Temple was surprised by the recognition. "How did you know who I am?"

The guards smiled. "It's our job to know."

Temple, Mosby, and Berry were taken to the elevator where they were left to fend for themselves. When the elevator door opened on the third floor, Wendt's secretary was there to greet them. She smiled, "Welcome to Rome."

Dolly Pattersani ran Wendt's enterprises in Rome. Secretary, office manager, bookkeeper, and 'gal Friday,' she was a key player in his businesses. At fifty-five, Ms. Pattersani looked thirty-five and acted it. A quick smile, good figure, shiny black hair, and eyes like coal, she could both charm and intimidate at will. Today, she chose to be charming.

"So, Mr. Temple, you have decided to take on our infamous State Senator this fall?" She smiled over her shoulder at Temple then abruptly stopped and turned. She again took the measure of Temple from his head to his toes and continued, "Yes, you might just be the one to do it."

Pattersani opened the door to Wendt's inner office and stepped aside. "Mr. Wendt, your guests are here."

Wendt was a short, stocky man in his early sixties. His gray hair was cut close to his head, military style, and he wore thin silver-rimmed glasses.

Mosby walked over to Wendt. "Hi, Cal. I've got

43

somebody here that I think you will want to meet."

Wendt wasted no time on introductions. He came around from behind his large mahogany desk, held out his hand to Temple and said, "Jay Temple, our next State Senator. Are you ready to get started here in Rome? I have several meetings planned for you today."

Temple wasn't quite ready for this. "Tom told me a lot about you in preparation for today but he forgot one thing. . .he didn't mention that I'd need a good night's rest!"

Wendt gave a quick laugh then turned to Berry. "Another campaign for you and Ophidia. You guys got a real racket. Temple's a shoo-in, and you guys'll take all the credit. In my next life, I'm coming back as a PR guy."

Berry took this in stride. "Calvin, anytime you want to trade places, let me know."

Wendt ignored the remark as he took Temple in one hand and Mosby in the other. "We got to get Temple down to the Rome Rotary meeting. There are some people there he has to meet."

Wendt looked at Dolly on his way out. "Don't know when I'll be back. Rotary at the Rome Club, newspaper, and probably City Hall. I'll call you."

Dolly winked. "Right."

The Rome Club was a quasi-private club that allowed local groups to hold meetings in its facility. The Rome Rotary Club was part of an international service organization that sponsored many community improvement programs for Rome as well as participating in world-wide service projects. Its members were influential and dedicated.

Wendt, Temple, Mosby, and Berry sat at a round table for eight in the middle of the dining room at the Rome Club. The room filled rapidly just before noon. Although Temple had never met Wendt before today, he did know a number of Rotarians from the Rome area. As the members arrived, a number of them made their way over to say hello to Temple and to wish him good luck.

44

Wendt turned in his seat to look at Temple. "I thought you needed me to introduce you around. Maybe you should be introducing me."

Temple smiled, "No. I'm sure you know a lot more of these people than I do. I just happen to have met some of them at other Rotary functions. About eight years ago, I was District Governor of Rotary and some of the members of your club gave me a lot of help."

Wendt frowned. "Eight years ago was before my time in Rotary. Let's hope a lot of our members will give you a lot of help this year!"

Wendt stood up as a short, well-built man walked up to the table. He was introduced as a golfing buddy of Wendt, Tom Granger. Granger had sandy hair, gray eyes, and stood unnaturally straight, making the most of his 5'7" height. His handshake was firm and his smile genuine.

Granger sat down next to Temple, and for the better part of the lunch, the two men discussed issues involving national defense. Granger told Temple that he worked at the Rome Air Base and that he was concerned about talks of military cutbacks in Washington. Temple had done considerable reading in this area and was aware that Granger's concerns were well-founded.

When Temple had made his short run for Congress a few years earlier, he had met with members of the Trilateral Commission and some military people from the Pentagon. It was evident that, absent a major conflict, the politicians in Washington were ready to scrap military spending to help pay for the ever spiralling costs of domestic programs.

Granger and Temple lost track of the others around them as they got deeper into their conversation.

"My points are these. The United States can ill afford to let down its guard now. At least once a month, the Russians send in a couple of 'bear' bombers into our air space, and we have to scramble our F-14s to escort them along the coast down to Cuba.

"On top of that threat to our security, more and more,

we are being called upon to interdict drug traffickers flying in from Canada. Rome is an important base and needs to be kept operational." It was obvious that this was a subject Granger had a keen interest in.

Wendt interrupted Granger. "Tom should also point out to you that the Rome Air Base is crucial to the local economy. It employs more than fifteen thousand military and civilian personnel and is responsible for at least that many additional people in support services. The Research Center at the base has had a tremendous impact on our community. And the airmen and their families are a part of our community."

Granger nodded. "Jay, what are your plans for tomorrow?"

Temple said, "I'm very flexible at this stage."

Granger grinned, "I like flexible. How about meeting me at the base tomorrow? Say, about 0800, eight o'clock?"

"Great."

"Good. I will arrange for a tour to give you some idea of what we are all about. It will also give you a chance to meet some of the people in your district."

Temple never could get used to the idea of how much people seemed to go out of their way to help him with his efforts to become a State Senator. This was another example of that extra mile that people were going for him.

Visitors and guests were introduced to the Rotary Club as part of their luncheon meeting. Wendt introduced his guests, Temple, Mosby, and Berry. After the program, many former acquaintances of Temple's from his days as District Governor came over to congratulate him on running for the Senate and to offer their support. On the way out of the Rome Club, Wendt leaned over to Temple and said, "Rome's yours in November."

The next stop was the Observer Dispatch, the local daily newspaper. It was a family-run paper, as were most papers in Central New York.

Captain Reynolds was the owner and publisher. He had distinguished himself in World War II and returned to Rome to buy the local paper and build it into a fairly substantial operation serving three counties, two of which were in Temple's Senate District, Madison and Oneida.

Reynolds' wife, Madeline was the power behind the throne. While Reynolds saw to the business aspects of running a newspaper, Madeline concerned herself with its editorial direction. She was a conservative Democrat by her own measurements. She worked as an appointee of Governor Cuomo on several commissions, and both she and her husband were very active in civic organizations in the city of Rome.

Wendt had suggested that Mosby and Berry grab a cup of coffee somewhere while he and Temple paid a visit to the Reynolds.

Wendt and Temple were immediately ushered into Captain Reynolds' office. The room was filled with sailing memorabilia. Boats, navigational equipment, pictures of the Captain's earlier days in the Navy covered the walls and tables. Temple noticed one picture in particular.

"Joe, this is Jay Temple. He'd like to have your support in his bid for the New York State Senate." Wendt certainly wasn't shy about asking the key questions.

Captain Reynolds spoke softly for a big man. He was about six feet tall, in good shape for a man pushing seventy, and very at ease with himself. He had been through all this before. "Nice to meet you, Mr. Temple."

Temple smiled as they shook hands. "The pleasure is mine." And it was. Temple always enjoyed meeting new and interesting people. "I noticed your picture with General Eisenhower."

The Captain looked at the two men in the picture. A smiling Ike and a younger Joe Reynolds. "Ike was quite a guy. I thought of him as a politician even back then."

Temple knew what Reynolds meant. Eisenhower had used his political talents, which were considerable, to maneuver himself into the position of Allied Commander during World War II, over other more flamboyant and perhaps more skillful generals.

Temple looked at the photo one more time then back to the Captain. "My dad ran Eisenhower's first campaign for President down on Long Island."

The Captain was interested. "Did your Dad serve with Ike?"

"No. Dad was a naval pilot during World War II. But he always liked Eisenhower. I remember going with dad to a rally for Eisenhower at Madison Square Garden. Before the rally, we were ushered backstage and introduced to the Eisenhowers. It was pretty exciting stuff for a young boy."

The Captain was enjoying this. "I was at that rally. Ike gave a great speech about the United States and its new role in the world. The responsibility of being the most powerful nation on the face of the earth."

Temple was remembering back. "I was too young to appreciate the speech but the lights, banners, marches, and music all seem pretty clear to me. I remember after the rally, hundreds of Eisenhower supporters marched down Broadway at midnight singing 'we like Ike because Ike is easy to like.' I think that is when my interest in politics first started to take shape."

The Captain sighed as he too was remembering back. "Those were good days. Innocent days."

There was a quick knock on the door and Madeline Reynolds walked in.

She was a very striking woman. Her age was hard to guess. Her hair was dark gray with a slight bit of white showing through at selected spots. She was tall, slender, and well–dressed. Her face was refined with high cheek bones, blue eyes, and a bright smile.

"Good afternoon, gentlemen. How was Rotary?"

Wendt spoke first. "Madeline, I'd like to have you meet Jay Temple."

Madeline Reynolds looked straight at Temple. "Mr. Temple, it is nice to meet you. I was just talking with some friends of yours."

Madeline held out a thin hand for him to shake.

"It's nice to meet you too, Mrs. Reynolds. Who were you talking to?"

"Tom Mosby and Bob Berry. I was having lunch at Capriotti's and thought I recognized the Albany boys."

The Captain spoke up. "Now, Madeline."

Madeline Reynolds waved her hand. "Just having some fun, Joe." She turned to Temple. "You see, Mr. Temple, I am in Albany periodically and get to meet a lot of people. Mosby is a regular in the Senate hallways, and Berry and his partner are always drumming up business there. I surmised that Calvin sent the two of them out walking while you came here to meet with us."

Temple smiled at her. "I'd never want to play poker with you. You work for Governor Cuomo, don't you?"

Madeline looked at Wendt. "Calvin has been briefing you, I see. Yes, the Governor has been kind enough to appoint me to a couple of commissions. One on aging, nothing personal I hope, and the other on drug abuse. It is interesting and challenging work."

Temple knew something about both problems. He had served as a board member of both a local hospital and the Salvation Army and had seen first-hand the problems of the elderly and of those afflicted with drug addiction.

Temple and Mrs. Reynolds talked about their respective experiences while Wendt and the Captain looked on. They agreed that society had a responsibility to assist the aging and the addicted. They also agreed that when you say that society has an obligation, what you really mean is that government has an obligation, because only government has the ability to deal with the large-scale problems of society.

"How can you say that we need to reduce taxes and still agree that government has the responsibility to care for these people?" Madeline pressed.

Temple was quick to reply. "In business we have to set priorities. In government it's time we began operating the same

49

way. There are issues like the aging, drug abuse, education, employment, all of which require State and Federal attention. The problem today is that our elected representatives are more concerned with their reelection than with taking care of those things which really need their attention."

"Give me an example."

"Fifteen thousand dollars was recently given to a marching band in the district to buy uniforms. That was fifteen thousand dollars of taxpayer's money that could have been better spent on issues that affect all of us, not just a small group."

"Band uniforms aren't important?

Temple frowned, "Of course they are, to the group receiving them. But is that a State issue or a local issue? When dollars are hard to come by, when thousands of people are being laid off, and when we have high crime rates, a large homeless population, an increasing use of drugs throughout the state, band uniforms are a lower priority."

Madeline Reynolds smiled, "You are talking about member items. I agree that a lot of money is given out by legislators for local programs but that's not limited to Democrats, and in fact, in the Senate, the Republicans control member item allotments. Are you telling me that you would take away the very thing that gives the Republican Senate power?"

Temple nodded. "And the Democratic Assembly and the Democratic Governor."

The Captain chuckled. "Noble reforms, Mr. Temple. What else would you do to make Albany more accountable?"

"Term limitations. Three four-year terms for all elected officials and you either move on or get out of government. Right now we have professional politicians. Their whole livelihood is living off the public. I think this affects their thinking and their judgment. They are more concerned with what will help them keep their jobs than what will be best for the people they represent. They lose touch with the real world. Those that put together our government envisioned a government by the people, not a government by the governing. Term limitations would get government back where it belongs, with the electorate."

Madeline broke in, "Yes, noble ideals, but ones that won't get you elected. People are selfish. They complain about high taxes and all the rest, but they still want the band uniforms, and they will vote for the uniforms not the ideals. I'm afraid, Mr. Temple, you have more to be concerned about than the popularity of Senator Mann."

Temple looked at Madeline Reynolds. "Then let's make this a noble effort."

An hour and a half later Wendt and Temple joined Mosby and Berry at Capriotti's.

"How did it go?" Mosby asked.

Temple looked at Wendt. "Better ask Cal, I'm new at this."

Wendt gave the thumbs-up sign. "Our candidate showed them that he's got a few cells upstairs. We'll be all right with the Observer."

The next stop was the Mayor's office.

Tony Eiles was a friend of Wendt and a good politician. He had successfully developed ties with both Democrats and Republicans in his efforts to woo benefits for the city of Rome. Most recently he had been working on getting State aid for the Rome Hospital.

Temple noticed that Eiles was a collector of photographs too. The mayor's office walls were lined with pictures of the Mayor and various political celebrities. Governor Rockefeller, Governor Carey, Governor Cuomo and Senator Mann, Senator Robert Kennedy, Senator D'Amato, and Senator Moynihan. The Democrats seemed to out-number the Republicans.

The Mayor stood up to greet his guests. He was dressed in a sweat suit that had 'Princeton' on the front. "Hi guys."

Wendt made the formal introductions and then the business at hand was discussed. Mosby knew Eiles. "Mr. Mayor, you have been struggling to get State aid for Rome Hospital and the holdup is in the Senate."

51

"Yes, Tom. My fellow Republicans won't do for me what the Democratic Assembly has already done: give Rome the right to raise its debt limit to fund the renovations required at the hospital."

Mosby pushed on without hesitation. "You know that in order to get Senate approval, your State Senator must sponsor the amendment. Senator Mann has refused to do that."

The Mayor interrupted. "She doesn't want to be accused of raising taxes in Rome in this upcoming election. That's no surprise."

Mosby again pushed on. "And it's no help, either."

Temple finally entered the conversation. "You mean that the only way the hospital can get these funds is for the local Senator to sponsor the bill?"

"Apparently so," said the Mayor, half disgusted.

"Have you talked with Senator Lansing about this?"

"He's not our Senator, but frankly Laura Ann thinks he'll use her support for it, if she gives it, against her." The Mayor obviously had been in touch with Senator Mann on the subject and knew her feelings.

"Maybe I can help. I'll get in touch with Lansing. I know the Senator fairly well, and he's always been reasonable with me." Temple believed that this was a worthwhile cause and it would give him a chance to pay a visit to the Albany establishment."

The Mayor held up one finger. "One problem. The vote on this is tonight."

Temple thought a moment then said, "We're wasting time, let's go to Albany."

The Mayor wasn't sure about this guy named Jay Temple. It seemed rather rash to him that this stranger to Rome would suddenly champion their cause. But without the funds the hospital would close and Temple couldn't do any worse than the Mayor and his staff had done.

The Mayor told Temple that his assistant, Allan Gant, was in Albany now and would meet him in the Senate chambers.

With that Wendt, Mosby, Berry, and Temple climbed into Wendt's Lincoln and off they went to Albany.

They arrived in Albany two hours later and Mosby immediately took them to Lansing's office. Lansing and the other Senators were on the Senate floor debating a funding bill that should include the Rome Hospital amendment.

The small group made its way up to the Senate anteroom where they met Allan Gant. Eiles had called Gant with some crazy story about this guy from Syracuse who wanted to help Rome. Gant wanted to see this.

Mosby asked a page to get Senator Lansing. In a few minutes the Senator came out, looked around the anteroom and seeing Temple smiled and hurried over. "How's the next State Senator doing?" Lansing shook everyone's hand. "We're really busy so I can't stay out here too long. Budget bill."

Temple broke in, "That's what I wanted to talk with you about. The Rome Hospital amendment. They need that amendment to keep the hospital open. If it closes, Utica and Syracuse are the next closest major medical treatment centers."

Lansing appeared nervous. "That's not my district. We have a standing rule that the Home District Senator must sponsor those bills. Senator Mann knows about the amendment. You have to get her to sponsor it."

"Do you think if I asked her she would?" Temple didn't expect an answer. "Is this home sponsorship a legal requirement?"

Lansing looked back at the Chamber doors. "No. Protocol. We respect it in the Senate."

"What about the patient who doesn't survive the trip from Rome to Utica but who would have lived if she had Rome hospital to go to?" Temple wasn't buying into the protocol idea.

"Good point, Counselor. Get Senator Manto to OK it and I'll give you your amendment." Lansing flashed a brief smile. "I'll be on the floor."

Lansing went back into chambers as Mosby and Temple walked through the anteroom into the outer corridor.

"Do you know Manto?" Mosby asked.

"No, but he's from Long Island, and he might know my dad."

"Here's his office."

As they walked in a young man greeted them. "Can I help you?"

Temple smiled. "Yes. My name is Jay Temple. I'm the Republican nominee for the State Senate in Central New York and I would like to see Senator Manto."

The young man gave Temple a knowing look. "Are you John Temple's son?"

"Yes, I am."

"I'm Mark Fuller. My dad's Jerry Fuller, a friend of your father."

"Sure, Mark. We used to buy paint in your dad's store. Is the Senator in."

"Yeah. And I'm sure he'd be happy to see you."

Manto was a big man with a booming voice and a ruddy complexion. He had been a commercial fisherman before going into politics and still owned a big fishing business on Long Island. "Welcome to Albany, Jay Temple."

"Thank you, Senator."

Manto introduced Temple to the other men in the room. "This is Senator Ryan from Rochester, Senator Giles from Lake George, and Senator Valli from Queens. Gentlemen, this is Jay Temple, our candidate from Syracuse who is going to give Senator Mann a run for her money."

Temple shook hands with everyone then turned to Manto. "I need a favor."

"You've come to the right place. What is it?"

"I need your OK for Senator Lansing to sponsor the Rome Hospital amendment for the budget bill. Rome needs a hospital, and I need Rome."

"Makes sense to me." Manto turned to the others, "What do you fellows think?"

They nodded their approval.

"Go get your first bill, Senator!" Manto said to Temple.

"That easy?" Temple replied.

"This time. There will be others that will be harder." Manto was serious. "But we want to get you going, and we should support the hospital amendment."

"Thanks."

The Senators wished him a hearty "good luck!"

Temple walked out of Manto's office and was again joined by Mosby.

"How did it go?" Mosby asked.

"Almost too easy," Temple replied uneasily.

The Observer Dispatch carried the headline story of the Rome Hospital amendment being approved. Allan Gant had told the reporter that months of hard work by the Mayor's office had paid off. He also mentioned that many people had helped, including Jay Temple.

It had been a late night, but the drive back to Rome and then to Syracuse was a triumphal one. Wendt, Mosby, and Berry each felt that their candidate had met his first test with a degree of success beyond all expectation. Temple was satisfied that if elected, he would be able to work within the system for change. He always believed that most people, given the choice, will do the right thing. Giving Rome its hospital was the right thing.

Mornings come early in a campaign. Temple had gotten home around 2:30 a.m. and was up again at 6:00 to head back to Rome and his meeting with Granger at the air base.

Wendt had told Temple that Granger would meet him at Building 4 around 8:00 a.m. Temple drove up to the air base and stopped at the guardhouse at Gate 2. He identified himself and said, "I have a meeting with Mr. Granger at building 4."

The guard gave Temple a quick look, checked his visitor log, and said, "Yes, sir. Building 4 is the fourth building on your left, about a mile and a third straight ahead. You may park next to the building."

"Thank you." Temple drove down the main road exactly

one and one third miles to Building 4. Temple laughed to himself 'Building 4, fourth building! Made sense.'

As he climbed out of his car, he saw Granger coming out of the building to greet him. To Temple's surprise, Granger was wearing an Air Force Uniform with three stars on the shoulders.

"Welcome to Griffiss," General Granger said. He was accompanied by two aides, Captain Spyke and Lieutenant Duffy. "Jay, this is Captain Spyke with our bomber wing and this is Lieutenant Duffy with our mountain division. They are going to give you a tour of our base and explain our operations to you. I have a couple of meetings to attend, and then I'll meet you at around ten this morning."

"Great!"

Temple was shown the entire base operation. It was impressive. Everything from response time to satellite radar was covered and Temple came away with a renewed respect for the country's military capabilities and the men and women who serve in the Armed Forces.

About ten o'clock, Spyke and Duffy led Temple to a huge hangar at the end of one of the base runways. General Granger was there as promised. "Well, how did you like our tour?" the General asked.

Temple responded. "It's nice to know that our security is in such capable hands. I had no idea of the scope of coverage that Griffiss provides to the northeast."

Granger motioned to Temple. "How would you like to go up in this B-52 for an hour or so?"

"Are you serious?"

"Sure, we're scheduled to do a radar check. We'll be going out over Long Island up to the Cape and then back to Rome."

"Well, General, if nothing else happens in this campaign, it'll be worth the ride," Temple said half–jokingly and half–seriously.

Late that afternoon, Temple arrived home with a lot to tell his wife. It had been a full two days in Rome, New York.

Chapter VI

Back Room Politics

Temple found that once into the campaign there was very little time to sit back and savor the moments. That evening, he was off again, this time to speak to the Madison County Republicans.

As part of the nominating process, Temple had to appear before the Republican Committees of three counties to get their endorsements. Although no other candidates had come forth to challenge Mann, all candidates for nominations are required to make an appearance and become known.

George Calder had been chairman of the Madison County Republican Committee for seventeen years. He was a veteran of many campaigns, and he enjoyed a good political fight. Calder had only just met Temple and liked what he saw. But being the "pro" that he was, he would hold his decision until after the candidate had spoken.

Calder introduced Temple. "Six years ago, Laura Ann Mann forced a good man and a good friend of Madison County out of the New York State Senate. Tonight, I have the privilege of introducing to you the person who is going to force Ms. Mann out of office. Ladies and gentlemen, Jay Temple."

Temple was met with polite applause. Two hundred and fifty-three committee people had come to hear the candidates and were waiting to be convinced. Temple put his notes down and walked around the podium to stand before the Committee. "We are at a crossroads in New York State. One road, Governor Cuomo's road, leads to unemployment, poor educational results, ever increasing crime rates, and higher taxes. Does this affect Madison County? You bet it does!" Temple jabbed his finger in the air, emphasizing each point that he made. He cited specific statistics for Madison County and recalled for all present the list of companies that had left the County for other States where the business climate was healthier.

Temple continued, "The other road is the road that we Republicans in Madison County and throughout the State intend to take. We intend to put New Yorkers back to work through tax incentives. We intend to bring jobs back to New York with a well educated, highly skilled work force. We intend to restore a criminal justice system that will punish criminals and protect our citizens. And we intend to stop the ever increasing tax burdens through prioritizing spending and cutting out pork barrel legislation."

The crowd was becoming responsive. Temple sensed it as he spoke. "For six years, we've had a senator who has been unable to get even one bill passed by the Senate. For six years that same Senator has criticized spending and then voted 96% of the time for those same spending bills that she has criticized," Temple paused. "For the last eight years, we've had a Governor whose tax-and-spend policies have put thousands of people out of work and added thousands more to our welfare rolls. We need jobs not welfare. We need leadership not lip service. We need a Republican Senator to represent our interests in Albany!"

The room exploded with applause and cheering. People stood up yelling their approval and stamping their feet. They began chanting "We want Temple! We want Temple!" Calder smiled as he thought 'This one will be a good fight.'

* * *

Laura Ann Mann returned to her office in the Legislative Office Building in Albany. It had been another frustrating day for the Democratic Senator from Central New York.

As a not so popular member of the minority party, she

58

had gotten little or no support from either side of the aisle for her proposal to allow conjugal visits for inmates in high security penitentiaries.

She had made what she felt were strong arguments for her proposal. Giving inmates such a privilege might reduce the AIDS epidemic by reducing contact among inmates; such a privilege might reduce inmate agitation and related problems; and inmates were still members of the human race with families and friends, and therefore should not be denied normal relations to the extent that those relations do not interfere with society.

'Good arguments but on deaf ears' the Senator thought as she threw her file on the couch in her office. Her secretary Annie Wilson, and her legislative aide, Tork Johns, had followed her into her office.

"You were 100% correct. There is no earthly reason not to let prisoners have conjugal rights. They're nothing but a bunch of backward, conservative. . .." Johns was really worked up but the Senator raised her hand to quiet him.

"I may be 100% correct but I am also 100% without a bill. I didn't even get support from my own party. You'd think at least a couple from our side would support me," Mann sat down heavily in her chair.

She turned to the door as Joel Samuels entered. Samuels was her campaign manager. His job was to keep the Senator advised of what was happening in her district and to keep the district informed about the Senator.

"Any good news, Joel?" Mann was hopeful. Joel wasn't.

"I think we need to take this guy, Temple, seriously."

The Senator sat up straight and concentrated on Samuels. All thoughts of her bill were gone. This was survival and as a politician, she took any challenge seriously. Temple had been dismissed by her advisors early on. She had seen him in action. He had her speak to his company when she was a freshman Senator and again at a business group meeting of which he had been president. He was articulate, intelligent, and savvy. She didn't dismiss the challenger.

"What's going on, Joel?" The Senator wanted to know what led to this change of heart by Samuels. He had initially dismissed Temple as any sort of threat.

"Temple gave a speech to the Madison County Republicans last night. He hit hard and got a standing ovation. Some of our supporters were even standing. Clayton called. He said Temple is better than anyone we've run against." Samuels waited for some response from the Senator.

Mann had respect for Clayton's opinion. He was a reporter for the Madison Daily and had covered every campaign she had been in for the Senate. He had given her good advice on how to win and where the pitfalls were. If he felt Temple was good, he was.

"So what do we do to take him seriously?" she asked.

"We need to get you back to the district. On the speaking circuit. Get some releases out of the Albany office, a couple of mailings. We need to crank up the machine and cement your supporters. Use your member items where it counts and ignore the hell out of this guy." Samuels had it all envisioned. They would take Temple out of the race before it got started.

"Can we ignore him?" the Senator wasn't sure.

"You've got to. Once you recognize him, it's a race. Right now, the press won't give him the time of day. The only publicity he will get is what he pays for and right now he hasn't got the money to pay for anything. We want to keep it that way. Republicans won't contribute to a losing cause. Word has it that Onondaga County Republicans have already written him off."

"How do you know that?" she asked.

"Assemblyman White and Councilman Towns both told Blakesley that he hasn't got a chance. No experience and no money. They both think that you are unbeatable," Samuels smiled. He thought that it was nice that the Senator had so many media people willing to be helpful. Blakesley worked for the Syracuse Gazette and had access to politicians in both parties. He often shared his information with the Senator.

"With all this positive feedback, why are you concerned with one speech?" She was, but she wanted to hear Samuels reasons. He was a seasoned politician, had been in a lot of campaigns, and knew people well.

"Remember your first race against the unbeatable Senator? The Republicans saw this under–funded, little known, young woman from the inner city and said she didn't have a prayer. My guess is that White, Towns, and even Blakesley, were part of the group that drew that conclusion early on. They were wrong. We can't afford to be that wrong!"

Mann looked at Johns and Wilson. They both nodded agreement with this logic.

"Okay, guys. It's back on the campaign trail tomorrow. Tork, find out what I have left in the kitty for handouts and what requests are pending. Annie, get me a list of all our past community gifts. I'll get a reminder letter out to them. Joel set up a speaking schedule for me and some press conferences. We'll work the reform business again."

Johns asked, "What about Temple?"

Mann replied, "Who's he?" They all laughed.

* * *

The morning following the Madison County Republican Committee meeting, Stewart Ropespear called a meeting of his political reporters in his private office. It was six-thirty in the morning and Ropespear had breakfast brought in for the occasion. His reporters knew there was a purpose to the meeting, an important purpose.

Ropespear had started in the business as a reporter. He had worked long hours in his early years and had impressed the publishers of the Syracuse Gazette with his stories and his insight. Eventually he was assigned to the city desk and once there he made a number of important contacts with some very influential people.

Ropespear used his columns to promote the interests of

his new acquaintances and in turn began stockpiling favors from those he had assisted.

In 1947, the Gazette was sold to a group of local investors and upon closure of the deal, Ropespear was named Editor. As Editor, he was in high demand. Politicians seeking favorable coverage, businessmen interested in promoting their concerns, community leaders pushing their causes, all sought the support of the Editor. He became a central figure in every aspect of the community's life and as he did, his power and influence grew.

In 1956, Ropespear led a group of investors in the purchase of one of the three commercial television stations servicing Central New York. He had recognized the added influence that this would provide and thought it to be the perfect compliment to the newspaper. He had amassed a small fortune through the paper and had put most of it up for the television station. It had been a gamble, but it had paid off. He and his partners now controlled a significant share of the media.

Ropespear had always been an active participant in the editorial policy of the newspaper, and he likewise maintained a steady hand on the editorial policy of the television station.

Blakesley and Hague always enjoyed these meetings with the boss. They knew Ropespear was a powerful man, and they each had a sense of their own power through him.

Ropespear smiled at his two reporters. "I hate eggs sunny side up but the name always amuses me so I order them just to test myself." The men laughed.

Ropespear turned to Blakesley. "I read your column on the Madison County Republican meeting held last night." Ropespear sipped his coffee, smiled again at the two reporters, and continued. "You seemed impressed with this Mr. Temple."

It was a statement, but Blakesley knew it was a question too. "The guy gave a pretty good speech and got a pretty good response."

Ropespear nodded. "Yes, but the way you wrote this, it sounded as though we were impressed. I don't think that we should be impressed that easily."

Blakesley's mind was racing through his column. Where had he shown any bias? He had just reported on what he had seen. Then it hit him that this was his editor's way of delivering a message. "You are right. I'm sorry. I'll do a follow–up on Temple with an interview and facts."

Ropespear sat up in his chair. "You will do no such thing. Mr. Temple will have to generate his own publicity. As you know, Senator Mann has supported the newspaper in its drive to save the inner city. I see no good reason to climb aboard this fellow Temple's bandwagon because he can deliver a speech. Let him deliver something of consequence and then we will talk about giving him some ink."

Hague had sat quietly throughout this exchange. A chain smoker, he was dying for a cigarette but knew that the boss frowned on it. Hague had become a survivor. A product of the sixties, he had protested everything from nuclear bombs to bans on topless bathing. He liked being a reporter, and he liked the freedom he had in reporting. Freedom to the point that it didn't cross the boss's preconceptions.

Hague had covered Temple's news conference with the Congressman. He didn't like either of them. Blue suits, short hair and financial success were in stark contrast to his life style. He wore his hair long, boasted a shaggy beard, rarely wore a tie and rode a Harley. He had a built–in dislike for the establishment, and in his mind 'these two boys' were the establishment.

Hague discerned that the boss had the same dislikes even though it was probably for different reasons. His life had been compromised to the point that reasons didn't matter anymore, only results. He knew he'd have his shot at Mr. Temple before the campaign was over.

* * *

Temple knew that he had a lot of work to do before he

63

was ready to go head–to–head with Senator Mann. He also knew that being a politician, Mann's first line of defense would be to totally ignore his candidacy. He figured this was a positive for him because it would give him time to develop issues, become well informed about what had been happening in Albany, and give him time to come to his own stride for the campaign.

Two days after his speech in Madison County, he was standing at a podium in Utica, New York, addressing the Oneida County Republican Committee.

"Ladies and gentlemen, thank you for the opportunity to talk to you about something near and dear to all of us. . .our families." He stepped from behind the podium and walked out onto the convention hall floor with the microphone. "How safe are your children and grandchildren?" He looked around the room. "Crime rose in this state by 27% last year. Albany's answer, reduce the number of State Policemen working to protect the innocent victims of these crimes. Murder rose by 13% last year. Albany's answer, veto the capital punishment bill that might help deter these crimes and at the very least punish those who committed the crimes."

Temple had their attention. "What about jobs? How many of you know of someone who has lost a job within the last two years?" Hands went up around the room. "You know jobs are at risk, we all do. But that message hasn't reached Albany. Last year 160,000 manufacturing jobs left New York State. Those aren't just numbers; they are people, they are friends, neighbors, family. We need people in Albany who are going to represent us and the things that are important to us."

Temple was walking back and forth as he spoke. He kept eye contact with his audience as his voice rose and fell with the emotions of his speech. He stopped in the middle of his audience. "Let me tell you what the issues are this year: jobs, health care, crime, education, affordable housing, the environment, and children at risk. It's the quality of life that affects us all."

Temple was on a roll. "We need to do more in each of

these areas. We need a Senator who will pitch in and work for all of us. A Senator with common sense. A Senator who offers solutions not just problems. I'd like to be that Senator and with your support, I will be!"

A hundred Republicans jumped to their feet applauding and yelling, "Yes! Yes!"

Reporters covering the event were surprised to find their lead story was the neophyte politician from Onondaga County who wanted to represent a portion of Oneida County in the New York State Senate.

As Temple moved through the throng of applauding committee people, reporters rushed forward to get a few direct quotes for their stories.

"Mr. Temple, why are jobs leaving New York?" a radio reporter jammed a mini-microphone in front of Temple.

"New York's tax burden is 137% higher than the National Average and still climbing. Why would business want to stay?" Temple responded.

Another reporter shouted, "Do you support the state's purchase of more land in the Adirondacks?"

"This year's budget showed a deficit of $3 billion. We've had budget deficits for the last six years. The Governor has proposed an environmental bond of $1.9 billion with $800 million going toward the purchase of privately held land. Given our financial position, that cannot have a high priority. We need to end deficit spending. The people want lower taxes, not more spending." Temple was a businessman and the numbers were ingrained.

As Temple neared the exit, spot lights went on and a camera crew from the local Utica station moved in on Temple.

"Mr. Temple. I'm Jim Taggart of WUTC. May I ask you a couple of questions?"

"Sure." Temple turned toward the camera.

"Why are you running for the New York State Senate?" Taggart held the microphone in front of Temple, studying his reaction.

"We all complain about government as if it were some force beyond us. I decided that it was time to step up to the plate and take my best shot at making a difference.

"I'm not happy when I read that child abuse rose to 213,000 cases last year, or that infant mortality in New York State is among the three highest states in the country. Our children deserve more than that.

"I'm not content to shrug off seven years of deficit spending and continued tax hikes resulting in businesses and farms either folding or leaving the state.

"It doesn't make me feel good, when elderly friends of mine have to give up their homes because they can no longer afford to keep them on their fixed incomes.

"When 10% of New York State's population 12 years old or older are on drugs, then I believe we need to take some strong action state-wide to solve these and other problems.

"We cannot afford business as usual. That's why I'm running for the Senate." Temple realized his answer was too long for television, but he also had a lot more that he could have said. There was always that problem of content versus coverage.

Taggart hadn't expected to be hit with so many issues. He quickly regained his composure. "Mr. Temple. Your opponent is on the Senate Agriculture Committee. You mentioned a loss of farming business tonight. What can you tell us about this and do you think that Senator Mann has not represented the farming interests of her district?"

Temple knew that Mann prided herself on her farm connection and that she had strong support among farmers. He also knew that this television station had a heavy viewership in Madison and Oneida Counties, where a large farm population resided.

"Jim, between 1978 and 1987, New York State lost 7,500 farms. 7,500 farms that just went out of business because New York State didn't provide for their needs. 1.2 million acres of valuable farmland went out of production during that same period. You tell me if Albany is doing a good job."

66

Taggart was ready for this and asked, "What can Albany do?"

Temple smiled as he looked into the camera. He was beginning to get the idea of this television business. "I would propose legislation that would stabilize fluctuations in agriculture assessment values so that we don't force farmers off their land. We should also have legislation that would provide for a land management and use plan including development rights and the ability of municipalities to purchase these rights."

Taggart had one final question. "What is your top priority for Albany?"

Temple again looked unflinchingly into the camera. "To develop a plan on how to best utilize our limited resources to provide the best possible quality of living for ourselves and future generations of New Yorkers."

Taggart looked at his cameraman and said, "That's it." He turned back to Temple. "Very well done. Have you done this before?"

Temple smiled as he was turning to talk to another committee woman. "Thanks. First time."

Oneida and Madison County Republicans gave their unanimous support to Temple. The Observer posted the headline in its political column: TEMPLE TO MAKE IT A RACE. Taggart had reported on WUTC that Temple was a well-informed candidate who thought that he could make a difference in State government. The radio stations in Oneida and Madison Counties carried most of Temple's comments in their entirety. Fair coverage was never an issue in these two counties.

Chapter VII

March: Month Three
Conservatives

The months had slipped by all too quickly for a campaign that had too much to do and too little time to do it. Time was proving to be the task master for Temple and his growing number of supporters.

Cordis, Dr. Carey, Mathews, Mosby, and Berry met with Temple to discuss finances. Mathews had raised about $27,000 and had recruited several business people to help raise more. Carey had gone to the Medical Society and had asked for support both at the local and state level. He was waiting for a response. Mosby had sought funds from several business interests and state associations that he thought had compatible views with the candidate. To date only the Auto Dealers Association had responded.

Cordis gave a report on the volunteer effort. "We've got the initial organization put together and just about all positions filled in Onondaga County. We need literature, signs, and a central office for a campaign headquarters. That all takes money."

Berry spoke next. "I've made arrangements to do some TV spots tomorrow. We've hired a crew from Rochester to come in and shoot footage of Jay all day. We have been working on some ideas and some scripts. The camera crew will cost $1500 for the day. Add editing $2000 and voice overlay $1000 and we should be ready to buy some TV time."

Carey asked, "How much is TV time?"

Berry replied, "To do adequate penetration into the market, we are looking at about $25,000 for all three networks for about a three week period."

As Berry was speaking, Kevin Roth arrived at the meeting, doughnuts in hand. "$25,000!! I better take this box of doughnuts back!"

Temple always appreciated, not only Roth's accounting skills, but his humor as well. "Don't do that, we need all these 'fat cats'!" Temple paused long enough for the groans over his attempt at humor to subside. "Bob, hypothetically you've spent $29,500 and to date we only have $27,000 with a lot of other needs."

Mathews interrupted, "Jay, we know that there is more money in the pipeline, it just hasn't arrived yet."

"I hope you're right, Ken, but as I have said before, we are not going to commit dollars that we do not have." Temple looked at Berry.

"Bob, what do you say to doing the filming tomorrow, spend the $4500 to get the tapes ready, but then holding them until we have what we need to do a good job in the marketplace?"

Berry had worked enough campaigns and knew Temple well enough to know that was his only choice. He replied, "We can do that, but I would suggest that we make some radio buys then just to let everyone know that you are for real."

Roth, always interested in the dollars asked, "How much are we talking about for radio?"

"A good penetration, probably seven thousand," Berry answered.

"Does that include production?" Temple was catching on to this part of the campaign too.

"Add $500 for production costs," Berry said.

"What about flyers and posters?" Cordis was thinking of the volunteers and the need to get them up and running.

Mathews leaned forward in his chair. "I may be able to get them donated as a contribution. What do you need to get started? Fifteen, twenty thousand flyers and a couple hundred posters?"

"That would be great," Temple answered. "Bob, why don't you, Ted, and I get together after this meeting to work out the copy."

Carey asked Cordis if any of the volunteers could be used as a solicitor and finance director. He explained that his schedule was such that he could use the help. Cordis said that he didn't feel comfortable with any of the volunteers in that position.

"I have someone in mind that may fit the bill," Temple said. "A friend of mine was the fund raiser for the Heart Association and has since left that organization. He'd be great at this job. I'll call him right after this meeting."

Dave Yondle was at home when Temple called. He was between jobs and had not found anything that came close to the salary level he had while with the Heart Association. Yondle had known Temple for six or seven years, going back to Temple's tenure as President of the Association. Yondle liked Temple and was happy to hear a friendly voice.

Yondle, Cordis, and Temple met at Temple's office that afternoon.

"Dave, I'd like you to join our campaign team as Finance Director. I know your ability to deal with people and you have great contacts that could help us raise some money. I really need your help."

Yondle was excited at the prospect of working on a political campaign in a key position. His only hesitation was that he needed money to help support his family. His wife had a good job but he needed work, paying work for his own ego.

Yondle asked, "Is this a paid position?"

Cordis answered, "No. The campaign doesn't have the money to pay you, but I need help in my business and based upon what Jay has told me about you, you will be perfect for the job."

Yondle and Cordis worked out a business arrangement

70

that allowed both to work on the campaign and also keep Cordis' business operating. Yondle took on the job of Finance Director for the Temple Senate Campaign Committee.

* * *

The Conservative Party in Central New York was an interesting and necessary political organization for any campaign. Temple had been told that he needed to get their endorsement if at all possible. He was also told that they had supported his opponent in the last two of her three races for the Senate.

Dawn Lake worked as secretary for Assemblyman White. She was a registered Conservative. She held a delegate's certification with the State Committee, and she was active with the Onondaga County Conservative Party.

Lake had also been active in several community service activities. She had a son who had been born with cerebral palsy. For fifteen years, she worked with the local organization dedicated to helping these special needs children and their families. Jay Temple had been a board member and active fund raiser for this group. When Dawn learned through the Assemblyman that Temple was running for the Senate, she decided that she would help in any way she could.

Lake called Temple to volunteer. She told him of her involvement with the Conservative Party and agreed to help him secure the nomination.

A week later, Lake met with Temple, Cordis and Mosby. She outlined the process for obtaining the Conservative Party endorsement. "In order to win the Conservative nod, you have to receive the support of the Conservative Party Committees in two of the three counties, Onondaga, Madison, and Oneida."

Temple asked, "How is it that the Conservatives have supported Senator Mann in the last two elections?"

Lake nodded. "Laura Ann has some strong backers in the party, former Democrats. They say that they are conservative but really they are frustrated liberals who couldn't get what they wanted out of the local Democratic Party so they joined us."

Cordis asked, "Don't the others in the party see what you do?"

Again Lake nodded. "Some do, but you have to realize that Laura is very good at what she does. She picks her issues. Last time around, she skunked the D.A. by being anti–gun legislation while he was pro–gun legislation. She knew that a lot of our old timers belonged to the NRA and she got to them. The D.A. didn't have a snowball's chance in hell of winning their support after his gun legislation talk. They couldn't care less about abortion or state spending if it meant that the government would take their guns away. Laura knew that; the D.A. did not."

Mosby wanted to know more about the process of obtaining the endorsement. "Can you outline for us each step necessary to get the Conservative line on the ballot?"

"Sure," Lake said. "Each county committee has a candidates' night and invites all those who have expressed an interest in having their support.

"That evening each candidate is allowed ten minutes to speak, and then they have to take questions from the floor. After all candidates for a particular seat have spoken, the committee goes into a closed door session, and they pick a candidate.

"The name of that candidate is sent to the State Committee and is usually approved for endorsement. In this case, because the district covers three counties, the candidate will have to have support from at least two of the three counties to be approved by the State Committee."

Mosby then said, "Dawn, can you get us the names of the people we need to contact in the other two counties?"

"Yes. The woman from Madison County is on the State Committee with me. Her name is Martha Edwards. Oneida County's chairman is Tony Fitzgerald. He usually isn't interested in nominations outside Oneida County. I'll get phone numbers for both for you."

"And addresses!" Mosby prodded.

"And addresses," Lake agreed.

* * *

Two weeks after that meeting, Temple drove up to Denny's Restaurant in Mattydale, a suburb of Syracuse. Lake had provided names and addresses and, as it turned out, none too soon. Mann's people in the Conservative Party had pushed for early resolution on the candidates. Temple would have been too late to get into the race for the Conservative line had he waited any longer.

Temple climbed out of his van along with his older son, James.

"This should be an interesting experience for you, James," Temple smiled at his son. He was remembering those days with his own father.

"Can I go into the interview with you, dad?" James asked.

"You sure can. I want you to see how these things go and give me your impressions of the people when we are done."

As they entered the restaurant, Senator Mann, her legislative aide Tork Johns, and three or four Conservative Party members were coming out of the back room of the restaurant.

There were the usual awkward moments in the early part of a campaign, when rivals first cross paths.

As the two opponents looked at one another, both groups were silent. Then Temple said, "Hello, Laura."

She looked for a moment longer, then responded nodding, "Jay."

She continued past Temple and his son and went out the door with her contingent trailing behind her.

It was James who spoke up as the last in Mann's group went by, ignoring Temple and his son. "The guys at school want you to kick her butt!"

Temple laughed. "Now there's an idea."

73

Lake came out of the back room to greet Temple. She quickly summarized Mann's presentation. Mann had said that she had opposed any form of gun control for the last four years; that she wanted to open up the closed door sessions of the legislature; and that she was in favor of multi-party elections which would allow Conservatives equal access to the media. She had asked them to continue the good working relationship that her office had with the Conservatives by again designating her as their choice. The abortion issue never came up.

As Lake was finishing, Paul Smith, the Onondaga County Conservative Party chairman, came out. He looked at Temple. "Mr. Temple, won't you come in?"

There were about fifty people in the room. Temple and his son were led to the front of the room while Lake took a chair in the back. Temple noticed that the people who had left with Mann and Johns were now coming into the room.

Smith introduced Temple as the Republican candidate for the Senate seat now held by Senator Mann.

* * *

As Laura Mann walked through the outside door of Denny's restaurant, she felt an uneasiness that she had not experienced in a long time. Something about Jay Temple bothered her. He wasn't like other politicians she had run against or known. He didn't try to avoid or ignore her the way some had. He wasn't condescending because she was a woman. He was always direct when they talked, and his eyes seemed to see right through her. He seemed to sense her thoughts and he acted with empathy as they spoke. He was going to be a formidable opponent.

Tork Johns interrupted her train of thought. "Temple's going to be in for a surprise with that group."

Mann asked, "What was he carrying?"

Johns responded, "Looked like an easel. Maybe he's going to paint them a picture!" Johns laughed.

"That's what I'm afraid of," Mann said.

* * *

Temple thanked Smith for the introduction and asked for a moment to set up some props he had brought for the meeting. Once the easel was in place and his flip charts displayed, he turned to the Conservatives and began his speech.

"I appreciate the opportunity to speak with all of you this evening. My son, James, is with me tonight to carry on a family tradition. My father used to take me with him to political functions when I was a boy. It's a good way to learn how our political system operates and to learn about people."

Temple sensed that his son's presence was having the unexpected effect of relieving some tension in the room.

He continued, "I am here tonight to ask you for your support in my race for the New York State Senate. Why am I running? Let me show you part of the reason."

Temple walked over to the easel he had set up and flipped over the first page on his charts.

"A recent study was done which compared certain key indicators for the year 1960 with the present. The study found that in that 30 year interval, government spending increased from $143.73 billion to $787.0 billion; spending on welfare increased 630%; and spending on pork barrel legislation had increased nearly 950%.

"That study also found that crime had risen by 560%; illegitimate births by 400%; teenage suicide by 200%; and SAT scores had dropped on average 80 points.

"Although the number of people incarcerated for crime is at an all-time high, the punishment rate is at an all-time low. Nearly three out of every four convicted criminals are not sent to jail and fewer than one in ten serious crimes result in imprisonment."

Temple continued to flip chart after chart illustrating the points that he was making.

"In 1976, the first year records were kept of child abuse, there were 669,000 reported cases. This past year that number had climbed to 2,537,000 cases.

"Drug use continues to be a problem. The survey found that last year there were 33,000 drug related emergency room visits, and it is estimated that there are over two million cocaine addicts in this country today. It has been estimated that one out of every five crimes committed today is drug related."

Temple paused and looked around the room. No one spoke. Their eyes were glued to the charts and graphs being displayed and their concern was evident. Temple went on.

"Where does New York State fit into this picture?" He let the question hang in the air for a moment. "Over the last ten years over one million New Yorkers left New York State. New York State has lost 500,000 jobs in the last five years or 34% of all jobs lost in the United States. Why?" Again Temple paused as the Conservatives waited. "One reason is taxation. New York is the second highest taxed State in this country. The other part of that scenario is government spending. Since 1983, New York State has increased government spending by 78.6%. Business can not afford New York's tax and spend philosophy and our people in this state can not afford this state's policies nor the loss in jobs and business."

No one disagreed. There were nods of consent as he spoke, and one stalwart stood up and applauded.

Temple continued with his charts and speech. "Public employment and government jobs fared much better during this same period of time. Sixty-three thousand additional employees were added to government payrolls and today one out of every fifty people work for the State. Whatever happened to private enterprise?

"What about crime? Over the last ten years, reported crimes have increased nearly 200%. FBI statistics show that New York State ranks as one of the top five states in the country for serious felonies. One out of every three crimes is drug related.

"What about drugs? Walk the streets of Syracuse after 9 p.m.. Whatever drug or substance you can name is available right here in our own community. Talk to the social agencies in town and ask about drug abuse. They all know the problem. Go into our public schools. It doesn't matter if we are in a city school or a rural one. Ask the teachers and administrators about the drug problem. They know firsthand what our children are dealing with.

"It's time for a change! It's time for a new direction! It's time for us to send people to Albany who will represent us and get the job done!

"Give me your support and together we will make a difference!"

"Yes! Yes!" Jenny Bloom had been a longtime Conservative. She liked "the cut" of Jay Temple. She stood to applaud as did most of the Conservatives in the room. Only a few gave their reserved applause to Temple.

Smith thanked Temple after a brief question and answer period. Temple shook hands with a number of well-wishers as he left the meeting room. Dawn Lake nodded and mouthed "Good job," as he turned to again acknowledge those still watching him.

Outside Denny's, he and his son laughed at one of his responses regarding the need for a strong military presence at Fort Drum. Temple had jokingly said "To protect the Canadian border." Temple and his son were not sure that they hadn't taken him seriously.

Tork Johns turned to Senator Mann, "Let them laugh now. They won't be laughing election night."

* * *

Temple met with his advisors the next morning. Dawn Lake had joined the group and reported that Temple's speech had gone over very well.

She also reported that there were a few die-hard Mann

77

supporters who felt the Conservatives should support the incumbent in order to have any influence in Albany. Mann's people had argued that even if Temple was the type of candidate that Conservatives could support, realistically he could not win this race and that the Conservatives would be better served supporting the winner.

Ted Cordis was disturbed by this. "Whatever happened to principles?"

Tom Mosby, not looking at anyone directly, answered, "This is politics. But there is more than one way to handle the Conservative endorsement." Tom paused to let this sink in. He continued. "In this Senate District, you need the endorsement of three county organizations or at least two of the three and then designation by the New York State Conservative Party. Line up Madison and Oneida County Conservatives and the State will put you on the ballot on the Conservative Party line."

"Tom's right," Lake said. "I'm on the State Committee, and I don't think that they are as supportive of Senator Mann as the Onondaga Party is."

Mathews asked, "Well then, what do we have to do next to get their support?"

"Martha Edwards runs the Madison County organization. I think she'll support you, Jay," Lake said. "She owns a restaurant and is usually there during the day. It's the 'Drop Inn' in Oneida."

"Tony Fitzgerald runs the Oneida County Conservative Party. I know Tony and will give him a call. But you need to call him too," Mosby said to Temple.

"I'll do more than that, I'll pay him a personal visit. This is one of a number of races the Senator and I are in. It's worth the effort to win on every front," Temple responded.

Bob Berry spoke up next. "If we have that out of the way, we need to raise more money. Mann has a war chest of some $45,000. The unions and NOW are giving her the bulk of her money. You talk about a number of races to win. The race for the dollar is another crucial one if you expect to beat a three term incumbent."

Mathews looked at Temple. "We need you to spend at least every morning calling people to give to the campaign. The big hitters, you need to meet with personally." He turned to Cordis. "It's up to you to schedule him in for the fund raising. When I worked on the Congressman's campaign, we literally forced him to sit down and call people. It's expected, and it has to be done."

Temple moved uneasily in his chair. "I have to tell you. That makes me very uncomfortable. I do not like asking people to give money to me for my own use."

Mathews responded, "Jay, that's a luxury you gave up when you entered this race. Nobody likes to ask others for money, but everyone realizes that without money there is no campaign. And everyone wants the candidate to ask them. It makes them feel important, and they will respond."

Berry laughed. "The first campaign we did with the Congressman, we had to dial the phone numbers and hand him the phone. Now he calls from his car phone so that he doesn't lose any opportunities. After the first few calls, you'll get used to the routine."

Cordis stood up to get some coffee. "We'll schedule it in. We also need to start looking for office space. I've got a couple of spots in mind, but if anyone knows someone in the district who will donate space, let me know. Local 104 is providing Mann with her space in the union hall."

Temple turned to Roth. "Kevin, as treasurer, are we going to be able to afford the grand design that Ted and Bob have laid out for office space, television, radio, newspapers, and billboards?" Cordis and Berry had submitted their ideas in writing to the advisory board for consideration.

Roth smiled. "Only if Ken and Doc Carey throw in ten thou' a piece!" Everyone laughed except for Mathews and Carey. "Seriously, we have raised about $14,000 in the last week. The good news is that this was without the candidate making phone calls. The bad news is that it isn't enough to do what we want to do."

Rick Handon had been involved in senate races before. He suggested, "How about going to Albany and asking for money from the State Republican Committee? They should want to see this district back in Republican hands. We have a good candidate. Let's get them involved."

Mosby added, "Don't forget the Republican Senate Committee. They have lots of money and have a vested interest in this race."

Temple summed up, "Let's see. I visit Martha Edwards, Tony Fitzgerald, the State Republican Committee, the Senate Republican Committee, make calls every morning to potential contributors, meet personally with big givers, campaign, hold news conferences and debate in my spare time. Sounds like a good political campaign. Let's go to it!"

Chapter VIII

April: Month Four
Polls and Politics

The following week, the road show began in earnest. Martha Edwards turned out to be a great supporter not only for the nomination but throughout the campaign. Tony Fitzgerald threw his support to Temple with the comment that he had known Mosby since college, and if Temple was "OK" with Mosby, then he was "OK" in his book as well.

Cordis and Temple made the trip to Albany for prearranged appointments with the State Republican Committee, the Senate Republican Committee and the Assembly Republican Committee. The latter was a late suggestion by Terry Levin. He had worked for the Assembly and thought it was worth a visit if for no other reason than to get their input for the campaign.

Cordis' and Temple's first call in Albany was on Reed Patelli. Patelli had been hired by the New York State Assembly Committee to Elect Republicans to the State Assembly as their strategist and public relations expert. He had spent the last six years working for the Republican National Committee in the same role.

Temple was brought into Patelli's office, given a cup of coffee, and asked to wait.

The walls of Patelli's office were covered with pictures of Patelli with Reagan, Bush, Nixon, and Rockefeller. On one wall, there was a large framed map of New York State with each Assembly District clearly marked and each district had a colored coded pin stuck into it.

As Temple was studying the map, Reed Patelli walked in. "Mr. Temple, this is a pleasure." Patelli stuck out his hand and shook Temple's with a strong grip. "Like my map?"

Temple looked once more at the map. "I'd like it better if it had more white capped pins."

Patelli laughed. "So you figured out my color code?"

Temple nodded and pointed at the map. "White, sure thing for Republicans. Red in the Democratic column, Blue could go either way."

Patelli smiled at his new acquaintance. "Right! We're here to move those blues to white and maybe even a red or two. But how can I help you?"

"Terry Levin said that there was no one with your knowledge and ability when it comes to political savvy. I'm running against a six year incumbent and could use all the help that's available."

Patelli liked being the expert. "Terry is too kind. I just happen to have been in the right places at the right times." He looked at the pictures adorning his walls. "So you are going to run against Mann? She's been a thorn in the side of the Republican-controlled Senate for what? Six years. And she is getting harder and harder to beat. You sure this is what you want to do?"

Temple didn't hesitate. "Yes."

Patelli nodded. "The plan is clear; it's the results that get blurred. You need to get the support of all the Republicans in your district, and you need the Conservative endorsement. Do that and you should win."

Temple questioned the simplicity of this answer. "Senator Ahern had the Republican and Conservative endorsements and lost to Mann. Each year since then, her margin of victory has grown. There has to be more to the equation than that."

Patelli looked at Temple in a new light. "Ahern took too much for granted in his last race. The other two couldn't appeal to a banana, even less to the public." Patelli walked over to his map. "This is Madison County. Republican voters outnumber Democrats three to one. Mann carried a majority of the vote in the last two elections. This is the City of Syracuse, the largest single voting bloc in the district. Democrats outnumber Republicans five to one there. Lose both Madison County and Syracuse and you lose the election."

Patelli could see that Temple was taking all this in. He went on, "You haven't got enough time to win the City of Syracuse. You have no track record and no name recognition. You have to concentrate on everywhere else. The City of Rome might help you. Mann plays favorites, and Syracuse with its Democratic Mayor gets more from her than Rome with its nominal Republican Mayor. Go after Rome. Go after the farmers and go after suburbia where your politics are their politics."

Temple smiled. "Terry was right. You are a pretty good strategist. If this works, I'll add my picture to your walls."

An hour later, Cordis and Temple were again in the Senate Office Building. Senator Valli was designated by Senator Manto to chair the Senate Republican Campaign Fund. No moneys went out or came in without first passing over the desk of Senator Valli.

Valli was a very busy Senator. He was a politician's politician. Everything he did was politically motivated including this time with Temple. If Temple were to pull off the miracle upset, out with the pain in the neck and in with a grateful supporter.

Valli hung up his phone and turned to Temple. "That was our damned U.S. Senator. Can you believe this. We got a hundred dead Colombians rotting on the runway in New York, and he can't get Customs to release the bodies for the flight back to Colombia. My office is jammed with calls, and I got no influence with Customs, and he talks to me about paperwork. Geez."

Temple looked at Cordis then back to the Senator. "Are you talking about the victims of that club bombing in New

York?"

Valli picked up a pencil and pointed to Temple. "Bingo. The families want their loved ones back home and paperwork ain't going to buy it with them. But you fellows didn't come here to talk about my problems. What's on your minds?"

Temple spoke up, "Money. We would like some seed money for my campaign, and I'm told the best source is the Republican Senate Campaign Committee."

Valli sat back. "We got money, but we also have everyone and their brother asking for it. Incumbents want it so that they stay incumbents and guys like you want it in the hopes that you'll become an incumbent."

Temple asked, "Who decides?"

Valli smiled, "I do. With the help of a million dollar computer system and the best brains money can buy."

Valli explained how the money would be given out and what the candidates, both incumbents and non-incumbents would have to show to the Committee. He suggested that Temple and Cordis introduce themselves to Toby Hagan, the director of NYSSRC. Temple and Cordis were given directions to the downtown Albany headquarters and sent on their way.

* * *

NYSSRC headquarters were located in a recently refurbished former union hall. Temple was amused by this as he and Cordis took the elevator to the third floor.

When the elevator door slid open, they were greeted by a pretty young receptionist named Janet. "Good afternoon, gentlemen. Can I help you?"

Temple smiled, "Yes. Senator Valli sent us over to meet Toby Hagan."

Just then Hagan came out of his office. "Jay Temple, I'm Toby Hagan. Senator Valli just called and told me that you were on the way over."

Temple and Hagan shook hands and Temple introduced

Hagan to Ted Cordis. The three men spent the next hour touring the computer complex that the Republicans had put together for the campaign. Hagan pointed out the fact that they could tell how segments of the population had voted in every election for the last fifteen years.

One monitor displayed a map of Syracuse and then identified Republicans living in the city by name and address and marked the exact location on the map. Temple thought to himself how remarkable this was and how all-pervasive the computer age had become.

After the tour, they all sat down in Hagan's office. Temple asked Hagan how he became involved with all this.

Hagan looked from Cordis to Temple. "Well, actually, I'm a Democrat who saw the light. The Democrats didn't want to waste the time or money on this system so I went to Valli and told him my idea. He liked it and sold the rest of the committee on it. A month later, I was an enrolled Republican and developing computer programs that could help win elections."

Cordis asked, "What's your track record?"

Hagan smiled, "Eight of twelve that we worked on so far have been in the victory column. The other four, we predicted losses two months before the election. This helps us put our money where it will do the most good."

Cordis leaned forward. "Can we expect financial help from you?"

Hagan turned to Temple. "Depends on what you show us. How much money you can raise on your own and what the polls look like."

Temple wondered about the polls. "Who does the polling and when?"

"We do with our own people. We use the phone bank I showed you earlier and randomly call five hundred people in your district. Our system has a margin of error of ten percent either way." Hagan was obviously quite proud of his operations and their importance.

"When will you poll our district?"

"In about a week. It will be a name recognition poll in which we will ask people if they have heard of you and several others. Probably Mann, Senator Lansing, your Congressman, County Executive, those kinds of people."

Temple stood up. "If you are going to do this in a week, I'd better get back to campaigning. Thank you for your time."

Cordis said to Hagan, "I'll be in touch with you about the poll results and funding for the campaign."

The poll was taken and showed:

Senator Mann 91%
The Congressman 71%
The County Executive 59%
Senator Lansing 59%
Jay Temple 9%

Temple, upon hearing the results, told Cordis that "with a margin of error of 10%, it is conceivable that even my own family doesn't know me."

Temple and Cordis also had paid a courtesy call on the State Republican Committee while in Albany. It was obvious to both that the SRC was not well organized and not in a position to be of any real assistance. Peter Conway, the director of SRC, had met with them and had suggested that they might help the State Committee raise funds as a show of Republican support. As Cordis had said to Temple on the way out, "right church, wrong pew."

* * *

Arnold Ophidia had worked on Republican campaigns all over the State. He knew many people and what made them "tick." As he sat waiting in Senator Valli's office he thought about his approach to Valli.

"Arnie," the Senator said as he entered his office and sat down. "How much money are you out to get from me today and for which of your candidates?"

It was well known that Ophidia had been appointed PR

manager for seven candidates, four State Senators, two Congressmen, and one Assemblyman.

"Who do you like?" was Ophidia's reply.

"Belafonte in Rochester and DiFachio in Westchester," Valli said as he lit up a cigar and began to puff on it. "What do you think?"

Arnold pulled out a cigar of his own, cut the tip off with a pocket knife he had brought for just such an occasion, and he too lit up. He puffed thoughtfully and said. "Belafonte will be close, DiFachio will make it, but I think we have a dark horse in the race up in Syracuse."

Valli looked through the smoke at Ophidia. "Temple?"

Ophidia put his cigar down. "Yes. The guy is already way ahead of the rest of my candidates with his organization, and people are coming out of the woodwork to work on his campaign. He's also got quality people with influence behind him. He just might make a race of it."

Valli said, "If I could believe that, we'd throw in the kitchen sink just to get rid of Mann. The polls only show him at 9%?"

"Yeah, but this is a guy who has never held office. 9% is pretty good considering his background."

Valli asked, "How much do you want?"

Ophidia decided to go for it. "Fifteen thousand for a TV blitz and more later if I am right about this guy."

Valli approved. "Fifteen thousand it is. When you are done, we'll take another poll and see how Mr. Temple is doing."

* * *

The phone rang in Temple's office just as Temple was taking off his coat.

"Hello, Jay Temple."

"Jay, this is Bob Berry. I have some good news for you. The State has come through with fifteen thousand toward a media blitz. I've checked and we can cover all three stations for two

87

weeks plus produce a couple of 30 second spots for about twenty thousand."

"Have you checked with Kevin to see how the treasury is holding up?" Temple always wanted the dollars and cents information before giving any green lights. He knew that all too often, in the heat of a campaign, candidates spent what they did not have and later had a hard time getting what was needed to pay off campaign debts. He did not want to be in that position come November.

"No, I haven't, but I can guarantee you will have that much and then some by the time we are billed."

"Bob, are you going to personally guarantee this?" Temple smiled as he asked the question.

"No, I mean I can't. It wouldn't be ethical."

"Call Kevin."

"If you have it, should I go ahead? You know the State may pull back on the fifteen if we don't use it." Berry wasn't used to the Temple–type candidate.

"If Kevin says we can pay the bills, I'm ready to go."

As soon as Berry hung up, Temple called Roth.

"Kevin, this is Jay."

"Hello, Senator! What can I do for you."

"I hear you actually wore a tie to work today. What's the occasion?" Temple asked.

"It's not a tie, it's a rope. I'm going to hang myself for ever agreeing to be the campaign treasurer for a certain would-be politician," Roth countered.

"Would-be is right if you don't learn to add and subtract! Listen, Berry is going to call you shortly about some PR expenses. Apparently he has found out that the State Senate Republican Committee is donating fifteen thousand to the campaign. Bob estimates twenty thousand for a TV blitz. I don't want to make any commitments if we can't pay as we go."

"Gotcha, chief!" Roth knew Temple meant it, and it was one of the reasons Roth had agreed to be the campaign treasurer. "The other good news is that you have received four checks of a thousand or more and about twenty checks ranging from five dollars to five hundred. We can handle a twenty thousand tab if the State really comes through with fifteen thousand."

"Okay. Give Berry the go-ahead when he calls."

Roth laughed, "He's on the other line!"

* * *

Donald North had known Jay Temple for many years. He had succeeded Temple on the school board, had played tennis with him, and they both attended the same church.

When North had heard that Temple was running for the Senate, he decided to give Temple a hand. He called a mutual friend, Ken Mathews, to see if Ken had any suggestions.

To North's surprise Ken not only had suggestions but had North on his list of people to call.

"Don, I'm glad that you called. Jay is really going after this Senate seat, and I think he can win it. Mann has never had an opponent that can stand up to her and debate toe to toe. Temple's got the brains to do that, and you know he's pretty good on his feet." Mathews had been active with the Republican Party in Onondaga County for some time, and he liked having a fellow businessman running for office.

"I agree," North said. "Why do you think I am calling? Mann's a tough act to beat but just maybe Jay can do it. She's 'god awful' when it comes to business, and we could use a guy like Jay who knows the score!"

"Listen Don," Mathews had been thinking about the best way to raise money quickly. "I've got an idea that I think you and I and maybe Tom Mosby can pull off. What do you say if we host a series of luncheons, invite a few key people to each, have them meet the candidate, and then hit them up for a contribution? Between the three of us we ought to be able to develop a pretty good list."

"I like it. I think I can come up with ten or twelve people who would be interested." North's mind was running

89

through lists of people who might give to Temple's campaign.

Mathews interrupted his thoughts. "Great! I'll get some dates from Temple and we'll go with it."

The next day Mathews met with Mosby, North, and Temple to discuss who would be invited to the luncheons and what they would ask from each. Temple learned that you can not be shy about the amount that you go after.

* * *

The room was well-appointed in turn of the century furniture. In the center was a long cherry dining table set for eight. The waitress was taking drink orders.

Temple had just arrived, and North was introducing him to their guests both known and unknown to Temple. After all had been served a drink, they sat down around the table.

North opened, "I think you have all met Jay Temple. Before you leave today, I hope you will get to know a side of Jay you may not have seen before. It's an important side for all of us. He's trying to accomplish something that could greatly benefit this State and the people who work and do business here.

"Some of you have asked me why I am involved with this campaign. Politics is something I have not been involved in and purposely so. But I have known Jay a long time and not only is he a good friend, he is the type of person we need in public office. I strongly believe that what we don't need is another professional politician. We have too many of those now, and they are costing us a bundle!"

Temple could see that North was getting no argument from those around the table.

North continued, "My company has been in New York State for three generations. It was founded here in Syracuse. Our family and the families of my employees have all grown up here, and we like this community. But frankly, I am thinking seriously about whether I can afford to stay in this State. Taxes are higher than anywhere else in the country, and I still have to compete to stay in business. Somehow this message has to get to Albany, and I think Jay's campaign will help do that. If enough people agree with that, Jay Temple will be our next State Senator."

North looked at Mathews. "Ken, you must feel that way too!"

Mathews leaned forward placing both his hands on the table. "Absolutely. I don't know of a single businessman who could argue with a thing that you have said."

Mathews turned toward the other businessmen sitting around the table. "We have a very unique opportunity here. One of us is interested in actually getting involved in the political process. It is hard to attract good people to the political arena today. If the press doesn't scare you away, the cost sure can. As a non-incumbent running against an incumbent who has great media coverage, Jay will have to out–spend Senator Mann two or three to one just to have a chance! But we have the right candidate, and if we do not support him, then it's our loss and in the future we'll have no one to blame but ourselves."

Mathews then introduced Temple. Temple outlined his vision for New York and its becoming, once again, the "Empire State." He talked about the role that government and business working together could play in rekindling the fires of success. He concluded with an appeal to be given the opportunity to make a difference in State government.

That first luncheon yielded twelve thousand dollars and two more workers for the campaign. The format was to be repeated on ten additional occasions with equal success. By the end of the campaign, North, Mathews, and Mosby accounted for 25% of the total revenue raised for the campaign.

Chapter IX

May: Month Five
The Media

The April rains were about over and Central New York was in full bloom. Now the campaign would get into high gear.

Bob Berry arrived at Temple's home about eight o'clock in the evening for the core committee meeting. Cordis, Mathews, Summers, Mosby, Roth, Dr. Carey, Laney Gardiner, Dave Yondle, and Temple were busy discussing office space for the campaign while Pat Temple was busy as the hostess for her husband's group of friends and supporters.

"Bob, you are just in time. We think we have found a home for the campaign and want to schedule some PR for the opening." Temple took Berry's coat as he spoke.

"Great! That means we have money?" Berry was ready to spend Temple's way to success.

"We have money as long as you don't get hold of the checkbook!" Roth liked needling Berry good-naturedly.

Berry laughed. "Hey, Jay! That interview on Channel 7 with Karen Lastri was great!"

"Thanks." Temple smiled.

"What's this all about?" Dr. Carey asked. "I've been tied up at the hospital and must have missed it."

Berry pulled up a chair at the dining room table and joined the others. "Jay was interviewed yesterday by Karen Lastri for the six o'clock news. She was impressed with his swings through the three counties and commented that every time she turns around, Temple or one of his workers is sticking a Jay

92

Temple brochure in her hands."

Temple interrupted. "We should thank Ken Mathews for that. The brochures are great. I also want to thank Kevin, Ted, Dave, and Laney. They have been out with me every day, from morning to night handing out buttons and brochures. It's a great effort, and we have some great stories to tell!"

Cordis spoke up. "Yeah, and only six more months to go!"

Dr. Carey asked, "How can I sign up for these trips? I got some time off coming, and I'd like to get in on this."

Cordis grinned. "Tomorrow at eight a.m. We'll meet here and be off to Rome for a day of hand shaking, chicken salad lunch at the Flower Club, and meeting with the Upstate Rod and Gun Club."

"I can't tomorrow, but next week I'll join you."

"Okay. I'll get you a schedule," Cordis nodded.

"We were discussing office space and seem to have concluded that of the four sites we've looked at, the corner of Thompson and Erie is best." Temple wanted to get a lot done and had to keep the group focused. "It's in a high traffic area, has good visibility, parking, and is easy to get to."

Berry asked, "Can we put signs on the building?"

Cordis had done the work on locating space. He answered, "As long as we don't put any permanent signs on the building we are okay with the landlord. The building is actually within the city lines so we don't have any sign ordinance problem with DeWitt."

"What's the cost?" Berry asked.

"Ten thousand for five months. We will get part of that back when we vacate if there's no damage and the place is clean." Cordis had done his homework. "I've checked with the phone company and the lines are in the building for about twenty-five phones. I got a lead on the phones themselves. All we need is furniture."

"Let me take care of that," Yondle said. "I know where we can get some loaners till the campaign is finished."

93

"Anyone have any other questions about the headquarters? Okay, Ted, you'll get the contracts?" Temple asked.

"Yes." Cordis said.

"Make sure that all the contracts are signed by the Election Committee, not individually," Temple cautioned. "Now, what about our PR schedule?"

Berry smiled. "Our first buy will be the last two weeks of May: radio and TV. Next week we do the camera work. I have an NBC crew coming in to film some footage that we can use throughout the campaign. I have arranged for the voice-over by a recording company in Philadelphia. It'll be great." Berry paused, looking quickly around the table. He continued, "I've talked to Arnold, and the Senate Republican Committee is going to do another poll after our media blitz. If our recognition is heading in the right direction, more help will be forthcoming."

"What do you need from us?" Temple asked.

"We need to shoot you with your family and in your place of business. Then we will shoot some man-on-the-street stuff. You need to give us the names of the people who can do the interviews. A housewife, bluecollar worker, businessman, professional woman, that type of thing," Berry suggested.

Temple thought for a moment, then spoke. "Bob, when I decided to run I had this vision of what my campaign would look like. How about doing some filming on the road to tie in my background with the campaign?"

"What do you mean?" Berry looked puzzled.

"Well, we could do a piece at a school with kids to tie in with my school board activity, a piece with kids playing basketball to pick up on my coaching days, a talk with farmers to press my concerns for their problems in the State, and some old-fashioned door-to-door stuff," Temple said.

"What about the business and family shots?" Berry pleaded.

"Sounds good to me. The family is a must," Temple

94

said. "They are the reason we are all here. We are going to make this a better place for my kids and everyone else."

In between campaign stops, lunches, and dinners, the television schedule was set up, people called to appear, and locations selected for shots of interest throughout the Senate District.

Television acting was something totally new to Temple. He had been on television a few times, being interviewed or involved in panel discussions, but had never playacted as he was being called upon to do now.

A meeting had been called of the campaign team in the board room of the County Republican headquarters. The idea was to film the meeting with Temple presiding and tie this in with the businessman-turned-political candidate.

Temple watched as Berry placed people around the conference table. Roth and Summers were positioned at one end. Mosby, Mathews, Cordis, Handon, and Carey were spread across the window side of the table with Temple to sit in the middle and the cameras were placed at the far end of the table for a long shot and then moved to the center of the wall side of the table for close ups. Laney Gardiner was left standing by the camera crew.

"That should do it," Berry said. "We're ready for you, Jay."

"I have a few suggestions for you before we do this." Temple got up from the chair he had been sitting in. "Wouldn't it be a good idea to get Laney into this? Right now, it looks like stag night at headquarters!" There were a few laughs around the room.

"We can do that, sure." Berry turned to Laney. "Would you mind?" he asked her.

Laney Gardiner had been a model for two years prior to joining Temple's campaign staff. She was very comfortable in front of cameras and did not mind adding a feminine touch to Berry's production.

"One other suggestion." Temple looked at Berry. "Does

95

it make sense to have the window behind us or would the wall side of the room be better?"

Berry wanted to retain some control over the process. "No, the window is what we want. At this time of the day it provides good light and we do not have to back light the area."

"Okay. You're the expert." Temple didn't want to push too hard in an area that wasn't really his forte.

Forty-five minutes later the filming was complete and Berry announced its success. The final version, used during the campaign, was a ten second slice that had the camera moving in for a close up of Temple from a wider angle that included Handen and Gardiner. The other participants in this early morning show never left the cutting room floor.

After the boardroom shots, Berry, Cordis, Temple, and the two camera crew men left for a day of filming at preappointed locations. The first stop was at a local elementary school. Temple had worked with the school and with its principal while he had been on the school board. They had built a playground that was state-of-the-art, had put in a museum for the local community, and begun a seniors program that allowed senior citizens to visit the school as volunteers during the school day. It had added a lot both to the lives of the students and to the lives of the seniors involved in the program. It had also brought back seniors as supporters of the school and the school budget. The whole community had benefitted.

Temple had set this up, suggesting that they film the principal and him walking out of the school and discussing the current educational needs of students. It was a great shot and worked well. This would be part of Temple's favorite television commercial and the one that garnered the most positive response.

Next, Temple and his filming group drove to the Lacey Farm. Jim Lacey was a local farmer who had sold corn to Temple over the years and who had known Temple for his school board work. The two men got along well.

"I ain't much on soap operas!" Lacey laughed.

"Jim, we're going to make you a household idol!"

96

Temple joked.

The cameras were rolling, capturing this conversation and the two men as they walked through the rows of corn toward the pasture and Lacey's herd. This too became a part of Temple's best campaign commercial.

From the Lacey Farm, they drove to eastern Onondaga County where they stopped at a local school yard and met with Temple's youth basketball team. Temple had changed into his familiar "sweats" on the way and was ready to reprise his coaching role.

Tommy Amers ran up to the campaign van as "Coach" Temple stepped out. "Hi, coach! Are we really going to be on television?"

"I hope so, Tommy. It depends on how well you shoot today." Temple smiled at his star player from last season.

"I've been practicing ever since you called my mom," Tommy answered.

"Then we'll both be on television!" Temple reassured him.

Temple turned to the camera crew and Berry. "My idea is that I'm going to go over and coach, run some drills and try to do this the way I usually do. You film whatever part, or all of this, and we will see what it looks like."

Mike, the cameraman said, "I like it. This'll be a hot ticket!"

Berry said, "Let's hope it sells."

Temple shouted back at Berry as he walked over to his team, "Think positive, Bob, think positive."

The team practiced for an hour. The kids enjoyed every minute of it and actually played above the level that they had been playing during the season. Temple noticed that a number of parents had come to watch this event and seemed to be enjoying it too.

When the practice was finished, Temple called the boys over for a final huddle. "You guys were great! Next year, we will have to televise all our games!"

Temple thanked the boys and their parents for coming and let them know when the commercials would be running. This segment also made it past the final cut.

Back inside the campaign van, Temple changed back into his street clothes as they made their way to Madison County. In the Village of Cazenovia, Temple asked Cordis to stop the van.

"What's up?" Cordis asked.

"I just had an idea. Come with me," Temple responded.

They climbed out of the campaign van just as Berry was getting out of the camera crew's van.

"What did we stop for?" Berry asked.

"I had some work done here by the local shoemaker during one of my recent campaign swings. He was kind enough to put one of my flyers in the window of his shop. I'd like to include him in our schedule." Temple was already on his way to the shoe repair shop.

Berry looked at Cordis as Cordis answered the unasked question. "He's the boss." Cordis smiled to himself. Temple was a different kind of politician.

The shoe repair shop was small and overcrowded. At least a hundred old shoes had been thrown into one corner and the shoemaker's wife had filled the remaining space with chairs that she was trying to repair and paint. A short counter by the window served as his work space and he sat on a stool behind it.

Temple greeted his new friend with a smile and a handshake.

"The Senator!" the shoemaker grinned.

"Hi, Walter. How would you like to become a movie star?" Temple asked.

"Sure. How much will it cost?"

"A little time, that's all. We're shooting some spots for my campaign commercials, and I would like to have you a part of it."

The shoemaker's wife asked, "Can I be in it too?"

"You sure can," Temple said.

Because of the tight space, the camera crew actually shot

98

the piece from outside the store through the door and window. It caught Temple, the shoemaker, and his wife in a lively conversation. The scene was so well received that it was the lead shot in the commercial.

Temple's caravan had lunch in Cazenovia and then continued to Hamilton for a town meeting style question and answer session with the candidate. About 35 people showed up for the session and both the candidate and the filming crew agreed later that this segment of the production would be best left undiscovered.

The final sequences for the day's filming were first at a landfill site, where Temple talked about his environmental concerns and then back at his office where about seventy-five of his volunteers heard Temple give what was to become his best stump speech.

Buoyed by his supporters' cheers and what he felt was a profitable day of preparing for the next phase of the campaign, a tired but exuberant candidate returned home. The next day would begin all too soon with the family shots and the still photographer.

* * *

It was the first Saturday in May. The sun was shining. Trees were freshly greened. Birds seemed to sense the coming of spring after a long winter.

Berry and Cordis appeared at the Temple doorstep with photographer in hand at exactly eight a.m.

Temple greeted them. "Hello, fellas! The rest of the clan's still getting ready. How about some coffee or tea while we wait?"

Berry answered, "Sounds good! Jay this is Frank Dento. He's going to be shooting the stills of the family this morning."

Temple extended his hand and shook Dento's. "I'm glad to meet you. Hope you can do something with some questionable material."

99

Dento asked, "Pardon?"

Temple laughed. "Me. I know my family will photograph great, but I think you have your hands full with me!"

"Oh," Dento laughed. "We'll do the best we can, but don't worry."

Cordis looked at his watch. "How long before everyone will be ready?"

Temple smiled at his campaign manager. "A true bachelor! Where wives are concerned, never ask! My guess is ten or fifteen minutes."

Dento said, "That's all right. It will take me that long to find some spots inside and out to shoot a few rolls."

Temple had ushered everyone into the kitchen. "Before we get too far afield, who wants coffee and who would like tea?"

Two of each were served.

Cordis reminded everyone that it was a full day. The campaign team was scheduled to meet in Manlius at ten a.m. for a day trip that included mall appearances in Hamilton and Canastota with stops along the way in Munnsville and Stockbridge. That evening, there was a speech to be delivered at the Valley American Legion Hall in Syracuse.

Pat Temple appeared in a yellow dress with their daughter and two sons close behind. Pat and their two older children, Amy and James, were a little embarrassed about the whole thing. It was unnatural for them to be posing for political pictures, and they were uneasy with all the preparation work that went into posing for the shots.

Tyler, the youngest of the Temple children, took it all in and was ready for anything. He and his dad went through their usual clowning around for the cameras, and as it would later prove, some of the best campaign shots came out of Tyler's performance and the natural laughter that it created with the whole family.

At 9:45 a.m., Berry and Dento were saying good-bye to the Temples while Cordis checked the campaign supplies out in the van. All was in place for a day of campaigning in Madison

County and the night's speech in the Valley.

Temple said goodbye to his family and walked out to the van. "Ready to take on the world, Ted."

"Always ready," Cordis answered as he went around the van and climbed in on the driver's side.

At the Manlius Village Hall, they picked up Laney Gardiner, Fred Childs, Mary Price, Mary Tarkings, and Patrick Fitzgerald. Spirits were high as Cordis pointed the van southeast toward Hamilton, New York.

Hamilton is a small college town anchored at one end by Colgate College and at the other by the Colgate Inn. A wide green, or commons, runs for several blocks between the two, and most of the businesses are located on one side or the other.

As the Temple campaign team arrived this sunny noontime, the commons was filled with crafts people and shoppers. Through no preplanning of their own, they had arrived at one of the busiest times of the spring in Hamilton.

"Can you believe the people?" Cordis laughed. "All of Madison County must be here."

"Hardly all, but certainly enough," Temple said. "Let's park this van and start meeting some people."

Luck is always a part of any campaign. This day in May was one of Temple's lucky days. As they drove up to the Colgate Inn, a car was pulling out of a spot right in front of the commons. It was a perfect parking space for two reasons. First, the van was positioned so that everyone could read the campaign signs on the sides and back of the van.

Second, as the van pulled into the spot, one of the local television crews from Syracuse also arrived and immediately saw a story.

Temple and his team decided how they would work the crowd. Cordis and Mary Tarkings would go to the far end of the commons and work their way back to the van, handing out literature and letting people know that the candidate was actually here. Childs and Mary Price would start at the near side and do the same thing while Temple, Fitzgerald, and Laney Gardiner

101

would follow and mingle with the crowd. Gardiner and Fitzgerald would keep the candidate moving and take notes and names as needed.

The plan worked for all of two minutes before adjustments were made.

Temple was talking to a couple of crafts people when Terry Davis came up with cameraman and crew.

"Excuse me. Are you Jay Temple?"

Temple turned to see Davis looking up at him, microphone in hand. "Yes, I am."

"I'm Terry Davis of Channel 7 News. Would you mind if I asked you a few questions?" She smiled.

"Fine. I'd be happy to answer," Temple answered.

Davis gave a few directions to the cameraman and to another assistant carrying equipment. People began to gather around Temple and Davis to see what was going on.

Davis turned back to Temple with a smile. "This is a take, Al," she said, apparently to the cameraman even though her attention was focused on Temple.

"Mr. Temple, you are running for the New York State Senate this year against Senator Laura Ann Mann?"

"Yes, I am." Temple smiled back at the attractive young reporter.

"Senator Mann has very strong support in Madison County and in particular here in the Hamilton area. Is that why you are down here for the craft show? To begin your campaign in her own backyard?"

Temple paused for a moment and then said, "There are a little over six months between now and election day. This Senate District has over 180 square miles, and it is my hope that I will have covered most of those 180 square miles before November 6th. As far as this craft show is concerned, it is purely by accident that we picked this day to be here. I felt Hamilton was an important place to visit, and I am happy that so many people felt the same way that I do on this first Saturday of the month."

Davis went on. "A lot of people think that you are a real dark horse in this race. Do you think that you can win?"

Temple smiled. "Terry, I think that the people of this Senate District and this state need someone who will represent them and speak out about the things that are important to them. Jobs, taxes, state spending, education, and crime. Those are the issues this year. I plan to talk about the issues during this campaign. If people agree with me that we need jobs, that we need to reduce taxes, reduce state spending, if they agree with me that we should prioritize the money we do spend and that our top priorities are education and a reduction in crime in this state, then I have a good chance to be successful in this race."

Davis followed, "Then you think you can win?"

Temple answered, "If the people want change, truly want a new direction in government, then yes, I can win."

"Thanks for the interview." Davis clicked off her microphone. "Is this your first campaign swing?"

Temple smiled again. "We've been out campaigning, but this is my first trip to Hamilton."

Davis handed the microphone to the equipment man. Still looking at Temple she went on. "Your opponent lived only a couple of miles from here. She really considers this part of Madison County her own. If she knew that you were here, she'd be down here in a flash!"

Just then, a man in his early forties walked over to Temple. "You the guy that is running for the Senate?"

Temple turned from Davis to the stranger. "State Senate, yes."

The man shook his head. "Senator Mann gave us a grant to help build our library."

"Well, having been a trustee for our community library, I know how important those things are," Temple responded.

The man wasn't through. "I talked to one of your assistants, and she said you are against member items. That's where the money came from. What do you have to say about that?"

103

Temple knew that a lot of people were listening to this exchange, and he wanted to be certain that he answered clearly. "Member items really are tax dollars that everyone of us have paid and then are turned over to our elected officials to spend any way they please. They don't even have to report how they spend it. I believe this is wrong.

"I believe taxpayers have a right to know where all their tax dollars are spent. If libraries are worthwhile, then we should have a budgetary item to support them. But our elected officials should set priorities and spend what money is available accordingly. Jobs, education, crime, and health issues top my list of priorities. But tell me what your priorities are?"

The man was taken aback. "I guess the same as you mentioned. But Senator Mann is the only politician who has taken an interest in us."

Temple looked the man squarely in the eyes. "I wouldn't be here if I didn't have an interest in you and in this town."

"But will you after the election?"

"Try me and see. If I don't, I hope you vote me out of office in another two years."

"We will," the man laughed.

Temple worked the Commons from the Colgate Inn to the College and back again. He talked easily with the crafts people and with the shoppers. Politics played only a minor role in his conversations. He was interested in what was being displayed and was having a good time mingling with the people.

Ted Cordis had suggested that Temple at least mention that he was running for the State Senate to everyone Temple talked to. Temple told him that if it were easily done, he would, but that otherwise, he would prefer to have the campaign staff see to it that everyone he talked with received a flyer. They did.

Channel 7's camera crew followed Temple, filming shots of different groups with the candidate. By the time Temple and his staff were back in the van, Davis had enough stock footage for the entire campaign.

The van was under way again, this time to a field day in

Munnsville.

Temple joked that having bought several things for his family in Hamilton, he would be broke by the time they left Madison County that day.

In Munnsville, they visited the few stores in town, went door-to-door, canvassing the entire community, and then worked their way to the field day celebration at the edge of the small town.

After looking at the setup for the Munnsville Field Day, they decided to work this gathering as they had the Hamilton Fair. Temple, Fitzgerald, and Gardiner had just started down a worn dirt path between two tables when Jed Hirth came up to Temple.

"Jay Temple, right?" Hirth said with a smile.

"Right," Temple extended his hand.

Taking Temple's hand in a good strong grip, Hirth said, "I'm a committeeman from this area. I heard you speak at the Madison County Convention. That was some talk you gave."

"Thanks." Temple smiled.

"You gonna speak here?"

"I'll speak anywhere, but we have nothing planned here. I just wanted to let people know that Madison County and Munnsville are as important to me as anywhere else in this district."

Hirth took Temple's arm. "We're not going to let you off the hook that easily. C'mon with me."

The field days' setup was such that there were a series of tents, shelter flaps, and tables surrounding an open field area where all the entertainment was centered. Exhibits of mostly homemade items and food were everywhere, and at this early afternoon hour there were about three hundred people in attendance.

Hirth took Temple up to a microphone set up by some tables in the field. He lifted the mike off its supporting stand and announced over the loud speaker system, "Ladies and gentlemen, boys and girls." People turned to look. "I want you to meet Jay Temple, the Republican candidate for the New York State Senate. He tells me he's here to say hello."

With that, Hirth handed the mike to Temple.

"Thanks, Jed," Temple began. "This is my first time in Munnsville but it won't be my last. Earlier today, I went door-to-door in your town and had a really warm reception. You really know how to make a person feel welcome." Temple paused then went on. "One of the things that has impressed me most as I have been running for office is how really wonderful the people in this area are. Republicans, Democrats, Conservatives, Liberals, it doesn't make any difference. People are very kind and very receptive. They listen and they offer some pretty good ideas to take to Albany. Most of those whom I have talked to think that a lot needs to be done to help the people of this state. I agree. That's why I'm running. I'd like to see more jobs and better paying jobs. I'd like to see less taxes and better use of the taxes we do pay. I'd like to see less government in our lives and more neighbor helping neighbor. Those are the things that made this country great. Those are the things that will keep this country great. I'd like to take that message to Albany for you and for everyone in this district."

People were applauding from tables, stands, and inside the field. Temple noticed Cordis and several of his aides smiling and shaking their heads.

Temple shook all three hundred plus hands before he left the Munnsville Field Days. He also received a lot of good advice, most of which centered around the economy and taxes.

In the van, Cordis asked, "Was that a prepared speech?"

Temple laughed, "That bad?"

Cordis shook his head again. "No, that good!"

* * *

Stockbridge was the next stop on this initial trip to Madison county. No one in the group had ever been there although Fitzgerald had remembered that Stockbridge Valley

106

Central Schools were usually the first to close in the winter.'

"Now, how do you know that, Patrick?" Temple asked.

"I used to get up early and listen to WSYR when I was in high school. They were always closing Stockbridge Valley Central and West Genesee was always open." Fitzgerald looked seriously hurt by this, but everyone else in the van laughed.

Cordis interrupted, "The map shows this to be the place, but all I see is that ice cream shop."

Temple said, "Well, let's get some ice cream and find out if school is out."

The ice cream parlor/restaurant had two tables and four stools at the counter. Temple's entourage filled the room. Temple looked up to the list of flavors and said, "Peach, is that homemade?"

The man behind the counter answered, "Everything in here is original. Peach ice cream is made by my wife."

Temple smiled. "Great. Two scoops please. What will everyone else have?"

As a variety of orders were made by the campaign crew, the man's wife and daughter appeared from the back room to help with the requests. The ice cream and food were homemade and tasted great. Although Temple was to learn that not only were the owner, his wife, and daughter Democrats, but the wife was the local 'Mann For State Senate' Committee head, nevertheless, the parlor was to be a regular stop for Temple in his swings through Madison County.

"You folks workin' for Temple?" the owner asked once all were served and the bill paid.

Cordis answered with a smile. "Yes, we are. Is this Stockbridge?"

"Dead center."

Fred Childs leaned over and whispered to Mary Price, "No pun intended."

Cordis asked the owner, "Any other businesses around?"

The owner glanced quickly at his wife who had a not–so–pleasant look on her face. Then he said, "A few here and there. Some of the houses have 'em. There's the repair shop and gas station. Mostly people here go up to Oneida or Canastota to shop."

The owner surveyed the group then settled on Temple. "Are you Temple?"

"Yes, I am. And that was great peach ice cream. Do you always carry it?"

"Sure do. I sell a lot of it too."

Temple nodded. "I can see why. We'll be back."

Temple got up from his chair, and as if at a signal, everyone else got up and began filing out. Temple and Cordis were the last two out.

"You got a tough race, mister," the owner's wife said.

Temple turned, looked at her, and smiled. "I know." And with that, he left.

Temple and his volunteers canvassed Stockbridge and then went on to Canastota where they handed out literature at a small shopping center on Route 5.

Back in Manlius at 6:30 p.m., Temple thanked everyone for their help and then he, along with Cordis, Gardiner, and Fitzgerald went on to the Valley American Legion Hall.

Temple was no stranger to the Legion Hall nor to the Republicans who met there. He had taken part in the Congressional debates there two years earlier.

As Temple and his staff walked into the Hall, he was greeted enthusiastically by a host of people.

"Hey! It's our next Senator!"

"Give her hell, Jay!"

"Hey, Temple. . .kick butt!"

Cordis thrust a clenched fist into the air. "Yes!" He exclaimed. "My kind of people."

Cordis, Fitzgerald, and Gardiner immediately began passing out literature and placing Temple material along the rows of tables set up in the hall.

Temple busied himself renewing acquaintances and asking for help with the campaign. By the time the room was filled and the chairman had called the meeting to order, Temple had shaken every hand in the room.

Temple found that shaking everyone's hand made him a lot less nervous about speaking, and it was a technique that he would use many times in the weeks and months ahead.

"Ladies and gentlemen, fellow Republicans, we have with us tonight the next Senator from the 48th District. Join me in welcoming Jay Temple, our candidate for the New York State Senate and a guy who tells it like it is!" John Felice ran the Valley Republican organization. He liked Italians, Irish, and Poles, disliked the wealthy 'east siders' and had a strong machine in a Democratically controlled city.

Temple waved to the applauding Republicans as he walked to the microphone. "Thank you, John," he said, looking at Felice. Nodding and turning to the assembled crowd, he raised his voice. "And thank you, Valley Republicans!"

The applause rose and then died down.

"It's a pleasure being here tonight. I feel very much at home. As you know, two years ago I was here during the Congressional debates, and you all treated me very well. I'm happy to be able to come back tonight to thank you."

Again the applause.

Temple went on, "I'm also happy to be back tonight, not as a wanna-be candidate but as your candidate for the New York State Senate."

They responded to his rising voice by louder applause.

"We have a mission, you and I. We are sending out a call to all New Yorkers who are tired of huge taxes, huge rates of unemployment, poor educational results for our children, and high crime in our cities. A call to join us in getting rid of the status quo, in getting rid of an ineffective Senator, and in getting rid of a high taxing, high spending Governor." They were on their feet now chanting "Tem-ple, Tem-ple."

Temple had been jabbing a finger at the air. Now, he raised his hands and spread them wide apart. "It's time for a change, a new direction in Albany. New priorities. New goals

109

and a new agenda. With your support and with the support of all the people of this district, we will make a difference."

They cheered and applauded. They stamped their feet, yelled, and surged forward to congratulate their newest candidate. Cameras flashed, TV cameras recorded the scene, and other politicians and candidates wondered what was happening. Temple also wasn't quite sure about all of this, but he knew it felt good, and he was energized by it.

Chapter X

The Race Is Joined

It was 10:30 p.m. when Senator Laura Ann Mann got the call.

"Laura. This is Steve at Channel 7. You might want to catch the 11 o'clock news tonight."

"What's up?" Mann had been working on some member item proposals with Tork Johns and was feeling pretty good about their decisions.

"Your opponent had a big day."

"Lansing?"

"No! Temple. I gotta go."

The phone went dead. Mann could feel the blood rising in her veins. She immediately dialed Joel Samuels. "Joel. Get over here for the eleven o'clock news on Channel 7."

Samuels was taken aback by the Senator's request and not a little unsettled by the tone in her voice. "What's wrong?"

"Temple!"

At eleven o'clock, Mann, Johns, and Samuels were watching the news as Terry Davis turned to the local stories.

Davis looked into the camera. "Well, today marked the thirty-fifth annual celebration of the Hamilton Craft Fair and the beginning of at least one candidate's run for office."

The screen first showed a sweep of the craft fair, people milling about, craftsmen showing their wares, kids playing on the commons. The camera then focused on Jay Temple talking with merchants, shaking hands and sampling offered pastries.

Davis narrated, "Jay Temple is the Republican candidate

for the New York State Senate seat held by Senator Laura Ann Mann.

"Today, Mr. Temple took advantage of the good weather and good turnout for the Fair, to shake a few hands and talk to people about their concerns with State Government."

The camera now held a close-up of Temple, and he was saying, "I think that the people of this Senate District and this state need someone who will represent them and speak out about the things that are important to them. Jobs, taxes, state spending, education, and crime."

The camera in the studio went back to Davis. "Mr. Temple also took exception to Senator Mann's use of member items."

"Jay Temple is a businessman and an attorney. He lives in Fayetteville and works in Syracuse. He said he was in Madison County today to let the people there know that they are just as important a part of the district as anywhere else." Davis turned away from the camera, "Karen."

The camera faded back to show both Davis and Karen Lastri, the evening anchor woman. Karen asked, "This is a pretty early start for politics isn't it, Terry?"

Davis nodded, "Yes, it is. I asked Temple about this and he told me that he has a lot of work to do if he's going to win this race."

The camera zoomed in on Lastri as she turned toward the camera. "I saw Temple at the grocery store in Cazenovia last weekend handing out brochures. This is going to be quite a race if he keeps this up."

Lastri went on to the next story. Mann clicked off the television. "Where does he get off criticizing my use of member items? I want to get a response out to this tomorrow."

Johns suggested, "Maybe we'd be better off ignoring this. By responding, he's dictating the game, and we are the ones who should control the direction of the race."

"What race?" Mann exploded. "This guy has done nothing. Now it's a race?"

Samuels spoke up in a level tone. "We must not overreact, but we also must not underestimate Mr. Temple. As a lawyer, he probably knows a little bit about what makes people tick."

* * *

Memorial Day brought with it warm sunny weather and parades in every community in the Tri-County area that made up the 48th Senate District.

Temple was up just after sunrise. He ate a quick breakfast and was joined by Bill Toler, a committeeman from Manlius, Ted Cordis, Laney Gardiner, and Fred Childs.

"We have two parades on tap for today." Cordis said as he looked over the Monday schedule. "Manlius at 10:00 a.m.. Bill, you are going to drive in that one, and we'll hand out flyers."

Toler grinned. "Right. What am I driving?"

Temple opened the garage door. "How are you at handling a 1952 MG?"

Toler looked appreciatively at the red convertible. "What? Is it a stick shift?"

"Four on the floor," Temple laughed.

Cordis interrupted, "Jay, did you confirm with Ed Thatcher that he'd drive in the Minoa parade at noon?"

"Yes, Ed said he'd meet us at the ball field."

Cordis continued, "It's going to be tight. We need to get out of the Manlius traffic as soon as we can. Fortunately, we are right behind the Mayor and the trustees."

Fred Childs offered, "I'll drive the rest of us to both parades. That little two–seater would be a little tight!"

Patrick Fitzgerald arrived with Mary Tarkings. "Two more for the road," Fitzgerald announced as he waved hello.

Mary Tarkings apologized to Cordis for being late. "We got tied up in the East Syracuse parade traffic. Everyone is out on the road today."

113

"Great!" Cordis looked at his watch. "Let's get the MG decorated and head out."

They put signs, flags and streamers on the MG and then drove off to the Manlius parade. Toler was also a village trustee and was well known in his community. Temple knew a lot of the people too, from his coaching days in the town recreation program. The Manlius parade was judged a success.

Toler left the group after the parade. Cordis and Temple took the MG to Minoa while Childs piled the rest of the Temple workers into his 1988 Chevrolet. When they arrived at the baseball field, Thatcher was already waiting.

"Hey, great car!" Thatcher said. "This the one I'm driving?"

Childs in his usual dry wit said, "No. It's the Chevy."

Thatcher paid no attention. Looking at Temple he said, "I've talked with the Mayor, and he has us right behind the high school band."

"Okay. Where should we put the MG?" Cordis wanted everything ready and in place.

"I'll take it over. Follow me." Thatcher climbed in behind the steering wheel and drove the MG down the length of the field, pulling into a spot next to two bass drums mounted on a cart-like apparatus. The rest of Temple's people followed on foot.

Within fifteen minutes, the entire East Syracuse–Minoa band was on hand, admiring the red convertible and talking with Temple about its particulars. Temple enjoyed the interest in the car and Cordis enjoyed handing out the literature for the band to take home.

The Manlius and Minoa parades also began the "penny candy brigade." Temple's staff had purchased bags of penny candy to hand out along the parade routes. They were constantly amazed at how much people enjoyed getting this. At one parade during the course of the summer, a Democratic candidate for a local town office criticized Temple as the Pied Piper of politics. Kids would follow Temple and his volunteers hoping for a few

114

extra treats, and they became a parade within a parade.

After Minoa, it was on to Rome for a memorial tribute at the American Legion Home. For the second time in the campaign, the two Senate candidates came face to face.

Mayor Tony Eiles had just finished his introductions of visiting dignitaries including Senator Laura Ann Mann. She smiled and then posed with the Legion color guard while cameras clicked.

Mann's expression changed ever so slightly as she saw Temple striding up to the ceremony with a group of young people around him. She turned to the color guard, thanked them, shook hands with Eiles, and then signaled Tork Johns that she wanted to leave.

Cordis caught up to Temple. "Look, she's bailing out of here." He pointed to Mann and Johns who were now joined by Annie Wilson, Mann's secretary, and all of whom were working their way clear of the crowds.

Mann glanced back to check Temple's activities and at one point eye contact was made between the two politicians.

Temple continued to move toward the ceremonies. "If it get's too hot in the kitchen, get out."

"What?" Cordis looked at Temple.

"Truman said it. Maybe Mann believes it," Temple laughed.

Congressional Medal of Honor winners were introduced from the famed 'Rainbow Division,' a New York Army Division that distinguished itself during WW II. Speeches were made remembering the past and those who "paid the highest price for our freedom."

Temple was then greeted privately by the Mayor and introduced to the dignitaries still present.

"This is Major Ikes, a winner of the Congressional Medal of Honor and resident of Rome. Major, this is Jay Temple, a candidate for the New York State Senate." Eiles introduced the two men.

Ikes was about six feet tall, kept his gray hair cut short,

115

and was fit and trim for his age. There was an immediate affinity between Temple and Ikes.

"Mr. Temple. I always admire anyone who likes a good fight, and you must like a good fight," Ikes and Temple laughed together.

"Nothing like it to get the juices flowing," Temple responded.

"You a military man?" Ikes asked.

"National Guard. Rainbow Division. 142 Armor," Temple responded.

"Were you enlisted or an officer?"

"Officer. Second Lieutenant."

"Good. Well, you get out there and make it a good fight."

"I intend to. By the way, Major, I enjoyed your talk."

"I'm looking forward to hearing yours some time."

The two men shook hands. Their paths would cross again.

Temple continued to circulate among the people still standing in front of the Legion Home. A number of people seemed interested to meet him and several offered help in the coming months. Gardiner studiously took names and phone numbers for what they all knew would be an uphill battle in the fall.

Allan Gant, the Deputy Mayor of Rome, caught up with Temple and his people just as they were about to leave. "Hey, Jay!" He smiled as he held out his hand.

"Hello, Allan." Temple shook the Deputy Mayor's hand. Temple wasn't sure whether he had the support of the Mayor and his staff, but he liked Allan Gant and was impressed that Allan had gone to Albany to lobby for the Rome Hospital in the late hours of the session.

"Hey. I'm sorry you missed the festivities at the Legion. We would have had you up on the platform if we had known that you were coming." Gant was a great politician.

"Don't worry about it. We should have made better

116

arrangements when we called," Temple said sympathetically.

"Well, I'd like to make it up to you. Three weeks from now the former County Exec. is having an Ox Roast out at Oneida Park. There'll be a huge turnout. You come and I'll introduce you around." Gant had a big smile now, and he sounded sincere.

Temple turned to Cordis. "Do you have our schedule with you?"

"Sure do. What's the date?"

Gant answered, "Thursday the twenty-first. At 3:30 p.m."

Cordis flipped through several pages of his pocket-sized calendar and then looked up. "A SALU breakfast, Citizens Foundation Luncheon, and then clear. Sounds like a perfect way to end the day."

Temple looked from Cordis to Gant. "I appreciate the invitation and the thought. We'll be there."

"Great. See you on the twenty-first." Gant moved off toward the parking lot.

"What do you think of that guy?" Cordis asked Temple.

"I think it was nice of him to make the offer."

"No. I mean do you think we can trust him?"

"I always give people the benefit of the doubt until they prove otherwise." Temple looked at Cordis for a moment, then with a half smile he said, "I always keep two lists. You never want to get on the wrong list because I never forget."

"Are you serious? You keep lists?" Cordis wasn't certain whether Temple was serious or just pulling his leg.

"I was watching a news report about the situation in Afghanistan, and I'll never forget an interview with one of the Afghan leaders. The reporter asked him how he expected to ever defeat the Russians. The Afghan said, 'You don't understand. They may kill me. They may kill my son. But my grandson will kill them.'" Temple paused, seeing Gardiner, Cordis, Fitzgerald, and Childs all staring at him with mouths half open, waiting for the rest. He went on, "Yes, I'm serious. I always

117

give people the benefit of the doubt."

Tarkings and Price came up. Price called to Temple, "Hey, Jay, your friend is coming this way." She pointed behind Temple, and as they all turned in that direction, they saw Mann, Johns, and Wilson cross the street. They were walking at a good pace and appeared to be trying to bypass Temple and his group as quickly as possible.

It was an opportunity Temple couldn't pass up. He quickly realized that they all had to go in the same direction to get to the parking lot. Without saying a word, he began walking toward the intersection at an equally good pace. He crossed the street just in time to come face to face with Mann.

"Hello, Laura," he said, looking directly into her eyes.

She returned his stare without flinching. "Hello, Jay. How do you like Rome?" She smiled.

Returning her smile, Temple said, "It's my kind of town."

"Mine, too." Johns took Mann's arm and moved her on toward their car.

Temple watched her go as Cordis and the others came up. "That was great!" Cordis said. "She knows you're not afraid of her." He paused, then went on. "When you win, all I ask is that you send me to take her Senate plates off her car. I want to see her expression when I take those plates."

Temple looked at Cordis. He was serious. In fact, Cordis would make that request of Temple several times throughout the campaign, and it was something that Temple never did understand. Temple laughed because the request did seem funny at the time.

* * *

The black Plymouth with Senate plates sped along the New York State Thruway.

"I think he purposely came over to meet me." Mann was still trying to take the measure of Jay Temple. "We need to beat

118

this guy now. Hit him hard with everything we can. He's not like those other clowns they put up against me."

Johns was driving. "Politically and publicly, the guy's a nobody. If we go after him now, it will signal everyone that we consider him a threat. A viable candidate. Even if he is, let him work his way there. Maybe he'll stumble and then we can capitalize on his mistakes. Better yet, we'll have some of our friends capitalize on his mistakes. That's how we should handle Mr. Temple."

Johns had advised Mann in every election in which she had been a candidate. He had always given her sound advice. Mann knew that even though she was ready to take on Jay Temple head-to-head, Johns was again offering the conventional wisdom. Temple was still a neophyte and there were still five months of scrutiny for him to deal with. She thought to herself, 'Yes, with five months to go, Jay will make a mistake and then I'll strike, when the timing is right.'"

Mann looked over at Johns, then at Wilson in the back seat. Both were waiting for her decision. She looked out the window at the passing farms. "Yes. We'll wait."

* * *

Eiles was leaning over his desk on the third floor of the City Hall building. Cheese from his pizza slice slid off the crust and onto his lower lip as he tried to bite through it.

"Damn it!" he shouted as the cheese burned his mouth. He grabbed a napkin to wipe off the cheese.

Gant laughed. "You need to be Italian to eat this stuff. How many times have I told you?"

Eiles looked up first with a glare, then he too laughed. "Well, too late for that now."

Gant got up and walked to the window. He stared out into the night. "What do you think of this guy, Temple?"

Eiles took another bite out of his pizza slice. As he chewed he talked. "He's all right. Nothing special. Hasn't got

119

a prayer against Laura Ann. She's the best in the business. Not bad looking either."

Gant turned from the window. "He is a Republican. He did help out with the Hospital."

Eiles looked up. "He didn't vote. He can't win. It's a waste of time and energy to work with anyone against Mann. Besides, we are a part of the Rome community; Temple's from Syracuse."

"So is Mann."

"Well, she just gave us the Museum. What has Temple given us?"

"The Hospital?" Gant asked it as a question, but he made a point.

Eiles could see that Gant was feeling badly about not giving Temple more recognition at the Legion Hall. "You still think we should have given more recognition at the Hall. Remember, Temple isn't even an office holder. Tell you what. You help Mr. Temple. It's the Republican thing to do. I'll keep the Senator happy. That's the political thing to do."

Gant smiled briefly. "Deal."

* * *

The Congressman had taken an office in Syracuse just down the hall from Republican Headquarters. His staff worked closely with headquarters' staff, and many of the Congressman's volunteers pulled double duty. The Congressman knew political power and was getting a hold on it within the party.

"June first. Nice day." The Congressman turned from the window and looked at Bob Berry. "How is Temple doing?"

"Better than we expected. His speeches go over well. He doesn't get or need any preparation. Does all the work himself and knows the issues. In fact, he's better when he adlibs than when he tries to deliver a prepared text."

The Congressman looked at his Campaign Manager and then at his PR man. Both smiled with satisfaction knowing they

120

had played a part in selecting Temple.

"What about his finances?"

Berry moved in his chair. With a half laugh he said, "You never have enough."

The Congressman waited and Berry went on. "They're up to around thirty-seven or thirty-eight thousand dollars. We've spent most of that on TV spots and radio."

"When will those begin?" the PR man asked Berry.

"Next week for two weeks. It's a low viewer, time but it will get him some exposure and the price was right." Berry looked at the Congressman. "He needs some help on posters. When the TV spots go, we need to keep his name out there."

The Congressman turned to his manager. "How are we doing?"

The Campaign Manager gave the thumbs-up sign. "We don't have much competition. I think we can spare a few bucks."

The Congressman turned to Berry again. "Price out the posters, and we'll get a check from our committee to Temple's."

Berry nodded. "Will do."

"I want Temple to kick her tail good. Scare her so that she worries about her own invincibility instead of whether or not my seat is something she'll go after next." He turned. "You guys still think that Temple has a shot?"

"A long shot but good enough that she won't have time to think about you, your race or anybody else's," the Campaign Manager said for all of them.

Berry met with Cordis, Dave Yondle, Laney Gardiner, and Dr. Richard Carey the following morning. Yondle and Gardiner were now working out of Cordis' business office in downtown Syracuse. It was centrally located and a convenient place for many of the volunteers who worked in the city to meet.

Berry was talking to the small group in Cordis' makeshift conference room. "We need to have everything ready to go with the TV commercials. We need lawn signs, more flyers, a mailer, some billboards, and a big door-to-door push. If we are going to make Temple viable, we've got to bring his name recognition up in the polls."

Dr. Carey asked the obvious, "How are we going to pay for all this?"

"Everyone's got to push for money. Jay's got to get on the phone and ask the big supporters of the party for donations. You got to hit up the doctors and other people you know. Dave's got to get some fund raisers going and start generating money that way too."

Cordis looked at the others, then at Berry. "What are you going to do to help with the fund raising? I seem to remember at one point you offered to have a fund raising coffee at your home for Jay."

Berry was ready for this question. "I just picked up a couple of thousand from the Congressman's committee. I also have his list of donors which he is willing to share with Temple." He paused to let the significance of his contribution sink in, then went on. "After I leave you people, I'm meeting with Ken Mathews to see if he'll send out a special letter request for money for Temple's benefit to the Congressman's contributors. We should get some response from that too."

The group discussed the details of what each would do to keep the financial wheels in motion.

Kevin Roth arrived late but with good news. One of the trade associations that Temple had worked with had just sent in a check for $1500. Berry was contemplating how to spend it when Roth also announced that Temple had gone to meet with a Peter Deiter, a novelty store owner who specialized in political campaign paraphernalia. Roth reported that Temple had some PR ideas of his own and was hoping Deiter could help.

* * *

The shop consisted of three rooms. A receiving area, counter, and display area opened out to the street. Behind this room was a small office where Dieter spent most of his time

122

doing paperwork and phone orders. A bathroom with a single sink and lavatory completed the one story building.

Dieter had two employees, Sally Worsal and Tommy Lansani. Tommy worked after school and evenings and Sally did a little of everything from order taking to design.

Temple arrived at noon and was greeted by Sally as he walked up to the counter.

"Good afternoon, sir. How may I help you?" Sally gave her best customer smile as she appraised the new customer in suit and tie.

"Good afternoon. I'm looking for Peter Dieter. Is he in?" Temple could see Dieter sitting in his office eating lunch.

The girl looked perplexed for a moment, then did what she had been trained to do. "One moment, I'll check. Who may I say is calling?"

"Tell him Jay Temple would like to talk to him."

Dieter heard the conversation, took one last bite out of his sandwich and came out of his office. "Thanks, Sally. I'll handle this one." The girl looked again at Temple then went back to her desk and sat down.

"Jay Temple, how are you?" Dieter was a big man at six feet and 265 pounds. He reached across the counter to shake hands with Temple. "What brings you here?"

"Hi, Peter. How are you?"

"Great! Business is good. I'm healthy and summer is here. What more can you ask for?"

"Well, I'm in the market for some posters and probably some pins for a political campaign. Do you think you can take care of that?"

Dieter gave a knowing smile. "Anyone I know?"

"Someone very close to you."

"Yeah, standing right here!" Dieter chuckled. "Glad to help you out."

Dieter and Temple had known each other through the Citizens Foundation and other groups to which each had belonged. Both were active in community organizations and each

123

enjoyed the other.

"What specifically are you looking for? Sally here is great at designing things." Dieter waved to Sally to come to the counter.

"I want to go with a red, white, and blue theme for everything. I need some yard signs, a couple of ten to twelve foot banners, some posters, and I thought some campaign buttons."

"We can do that. What do you want on them?" Dieter asked.

"I'd like to keep it simple. The idea is to develop name recognition. Maybe, 'Temple for State Senate.'"

Sally suggested, "How about your name in big bold print and State Senate in smaller print?"

"Show us what you have in mind," Dieter directed.

The girl grabbed a pad and pencil and made some quick rough drawings of her ideas. Temple liked them. "How much will it cost for a thousand buttons, four posters, two banners, and maybe a hundred yard signs?"

Dieter looked up at the ceiling and said, "Normally, design, materials, labor, taxes, around thirty-five hundred but for you twelve hundred. My cost."

"You sure?" Temple didn't want to take advantage of their friendship.

"Cut my taxes when you win and it'll be worth the investment," Dieter laughed.

"That's an important part of this race, cutting taxes." Temple was serious and so was Dieter.

"I know."

Three days later fifteen hundred buttons arrived along with a hundred yard signs. The posters and banners had to be ordered out of town and would take two weeks.

* * *

Cordis called Temple at his office that afternoon. "Jay,

124

now that June has arrived, I thought that it would be nice to have an office."

"I agree. Did you find something affordable?" Temple had asked Cordis to look for some space on the east side of Syracuse with easy access and high visibility. Several spots were available but either the costs or the restrictions on signs had prevented any deal being made.

"Yep. I think this one has it all." Cordis was excited about his new find. "You free now?"

"Sure."

"I'll pick you up in about ten minutes." Cordis hung up. He was in front of Temple's office in less than seven minutes.

"Jay, this one's great. It's perfect. Twenty thousand square feet of open space and we can do whatever we want short of destroying the place."

"Where is it?"

"Corner of Thompson and Erie. You can see it from at least six different approaches. It's on the bus line so our volunteers can get to it, and it's inside the city limits so building signs are no problem."

As Cordis turned off route 690 onto Thompson Road, he pointed to the building. "That's it. Isn't it great?"

Temple, too, was excited about the location. It was highly visible, located close to where he had hoped to set up a campaign headquarters, and would raise the profile of the campaign considerably.

Cordis and Temple did a walk-through with the owner, Jerry Issacson. When they finished, Temple pulled Cordis aside. "You sure we can afford this place?"

"Best investment we can make," Cordis answered.

"Yeah, but can we afford it?" Temple persisted.

"I've worked it out with Issacson and Roth. We can afford it."

The weekend of June 9th, Temple's campaign headquarters opened with much fanfare.

* * *

Carl Drake had been an electrical worker for twenty-seven years. He had worked his way up through the Electrical Workers Union to become its local president in 1987. Carl Drake was also a staunch Democrat as were his father and his grandfather. All three had been Democratic committeemen in the City of Syracuse and the elder Drake had once been a City Councilor.

Drake put in a call to Albany. "Let me talk to Laura Ann. This is Carl Drake in Syracuse." He wasn't big on titles and liked the idea that he could call the Senator by her first name.

"Hello, Carl. Nice to hear from you." Laura Ann Mann knew that Carl was an important part of her power base in the City of Syracuse and was always available for his calls.

"You might not think so. A couple of the boys have been wiring a building down the street for your opponent, that Temple guy," Drake reported.

Mann hadn't thought about this. "Where?" she asked.

"Corner of Erie and Thompson. It's a big spot. Nearly twenty thousand square feet. He's hookin' up a bank of phones. Got fifteen or twenty desks, conference table, the works. The guy means business." Drake was impressed by all this activity from a nobody. He didn't care for Republicans and never had. But he knew politics and this was a heck of a start for someone coming out of the woodwork.

"I didn't think about this," Mann said over the phone.

"Hey, Laura Ann. How about using our hall as your headquarters? We are right up the street, and we can go face to face with that monkey!"

Mann laughed at Drake's description. "You guys don't have a problem with that?"

"We'd love it. It'll be our contribution to your campaign. No charge and we can even do some calling from here for you." Drake was already counting the points he'd earn on this offer.

"You're on." Mann liked the idea of finally going head-to-head with Temple. She was a competitor and now she could get to doing what she did best: be a politician.

As the telephone people were finishing with the hookups, about thirty-five volunteers arrived to help set up for the opening of Temple's Campaign Headquarters.

Cordis coordinated the activity. Couches, lounging chairs, end tables, and a coffee table were set up in the front of the building. Partitions were erected to break up the vastness of what was once a showroom. Signs were being painted with the 'Temple For State Senate' logo in eight foot high letters using the red, white, and blue theme developed by Temple.

"Look what I got," a smiling Patrick Fitzgerald shouted as he came through the side door carrying a huge cardboard elephant. Cordis and Tarkings looked up and laughed.

"Where did you get that?" Cordis asked.

"A friend of mine is an avid Republican and collects elephants. I told her I was working on Jay's campaign, and she let me borrow it."

"It needs a place of honor," Tarkings said with a smile. "Let's put it in the front window next to Jay's poster."

"Good idea." Cordis picked up one end of the elephant and helped Fitzgerald carry it to the front window. Tarkings supervised the placement.

"Looks good." Fred Childs had just arrived with Don Meeker, another volunteer. "Now, we ought to get an ass to put in Mann's headquarters' window!"

"A little partisan, aren't we?" Cordis looked at Childs.

"Why not? This is a question of winning or losing. . .and I just hope the ass loses this one."

Ira Sterling now joined the group. "Nice elephant. Say, where is the candidate? I thought he'd be here."

Cordis answered. "Jay's giving a speech in Utica. Big Republican meeting there. Yondle and Gardiner went with him to hand out our new buttons, and Larry Malcolm is driving the

127

van."

     "They coming back here afterward?" Tarkings asked.

     "I think so," Cordis answered.

     "Then let's get this place fixed up and surprise our next State Senator." Tarkings was off to the back of the showroom with the others following.

Chapter XI

June: Month Six
Republican Politics

The Twin Valley Club was located on a hill overlooking Route 5 as it entered the city limits of Utica. Temple imagined that once this was a pastoral view of the valley leading into downtown Utica. The Erie Canal had been a major transportation route north of the Genesee Turnpike and this too had probably been open to view from the club site.

Now, trees blocked some of the view but most of what was left to be seen were commercial buildings, parking lots, a shopping center, and fast food and gas station outlets. The city had sprawled out into the countryside with not–all–that–pleasant results.

Malcolm parked the van in an already crowded lot, and the foursome made their way into the clubhouse.

Calvin Wendt met them at the door and explained the schedule of activities for the evening. "There is a photo session in ten minutes in the grill room with a news conference to follow. About four newspapers, three radio stations, and a TV crew from Syracuse, and one from Utica. D'Amato is already in there with Congressman Bulin, a couple of assemblymen, and Senator Bears."

Yondle asked, "Where can we go to hand out our pamphlets and buttons?"

"There is a table set up inside the dining room door for that stuff. Just put it there for people to pick up as they come in or leave." Wendt pointed toward the dining room door.

Turning then to Jay, he said, "C'mon, I'll introduce you to D'Amato and the rest."

Temple turned to Yondle and said, "You, Laney, and Larry take the campaign literature and buttons inside and pass them out. I'd rather hand them to everyone than expect everyone to pick them up."

"You got it, chief!" Yondle smiled. He, Gardiner and Malcolm left immediately for the dining room.

Wendt showed Temple to the grill and introduced him to everyone present.

After being introduced, D'Amato said, "So you're the young man I have been hearing about." He looked appraisingly at Temple. "Heard some good things about you. Heard you can speak pretty damn effectively."

"Thanks. I just say what I believe." Temple was always embarrassed when people complimented him.

"Tell it like it is! That's what mamma always says. Tell it like it is!" D'Amato made the second pronouncement to the entire group.

The photographer lined up the candidates in the grill for a group picture. Temple remembered John Lindsay saying that "in any political setting, always work your way to the middle. That way if they cut, you have a better chance of making the end result." Temple thought 'Good advice, not just for photographs.'

Temple ended up standing next to D'Amato who also ascribed to Lindsay's philosophy.

Cameras snapped and whirred. Lights flashed and glowed as newspaper photographers and television cameramen did their job. For the first time, Temple felt the heat of the camera lights and the press of competition. He was competing with candidates of his own party, not for votes but for media coverage. It had not occurred to him until this June evening in Utica, New York that there were races within races and that he was among some of the best when it came to stealing the spotlight.

United States Senator Alfonse D'Amato had seen it all.

130

One on one, he was a dynamo. He easily won people over to him with his personal interest in them and his memory for names.

Assemblyman Richard Ryan was the leader of the Republican caucus in the Assembly. His deep, gravelly voice and his jovial manner hid deeper thoughts and commanded attention when he spoke.

State Senator Bears had been in the Assembly and when the district's State Senator died, he stepped in in a special election and captured the vacant Senate seat. Bears never missed an opportunity to shake a hand or kiss a lady, and he could go several rounds with the best of them. He, too, had a female opponent but was expected to win handily.

Congressman Bulin was a popular vote getter. Some staunch Republicans were not particularly happy with his more liberal voting record, but then they didn't have the support of the bluecollar workers. Bulin did.

The questions began.

"Senator D'Amato. There is a story going around that your brother received special contract consideration because of your position in the Senate. Do you care to comment?" a young woman in a pink pantsuit asked, stone faced.

"That's a lot of baloney. It's not worth answering. I represent all the people of New York and anything I do or have ever done has been for the benefit of all the people of New York! End of sentence. Period!"

Everyone laughed, more at the way the question was answered by the Senator than at the content. Everyone, that is, except the woman in the pink pantsuit.

"Senator D'Amato. Do you think that the Republicans can beat the Governor this year?" another reporter asked in a quick follow-up question.

"At what?" D'Amato chuckled, his shoulders rising and falling as he laughed. "If the people of this state are as sick as I am with the high New York State taxes, either Cuomo has to go or they do. I think the Republicans have a shot. A good shot. But you have to remember, Governor Cuomo's been around, and he is great out there on the stump. He's also got some shekels stored away for this race. It's going to take some dough to beat him."

"What about the Conservatives?"

"What about them? They should be supporting us. They can't win on their own, and all they do is take votes from us and hand them over to the Democrats on a plate. Does that make any sense to you people?"

"Senator. Do you think that there will be any further cuts at the Rome Air Base?"

"My advice is to never let your guard down. My mamma used to say, 'Alfonse, always keep your dukes up in a fight or someone is going to give you a bloody nose.' Griffiss is in a fight. There will be cutbacks somewhere, and everyone is fair game. If you don't want a bloody nose, then you'd better pull out all the stops and lobby the hell out of Washington."

Allan Gant appeared at the back of the room to announce that dinner was about to be served and that the candidates needed to line up for their entry into the hall.

The assembled press corps began filing out while the candidates posed for a few more group pictures. Finally a young woman in a yellow suit came in and organized the procession into the main dining room. Temple was placed next to D'Amato, both for the march in and for the dinner table. He thought to himself that again fate was playing a hand. Most of the attention would be focused on the United States Senator and perhaps some of the limelight would be shared by the newcomer to politics.

The main dining room was filled to capacity. Campaign workers had to stand around the outside walls of the room and several people remained in the entryway, listening but not seeing.

As the line of Republican candidates entered the room, almost on cue, everyone rose from their chairs and began clapping. The applause continued until all the candidates had made their way around the tables and were standing behind their

132

chairs at the head table. Several times during the procession to the head table, loyal party members and friends reached out to shake the hands of different candidates. D'Amato was by far the most popular and most sought-after for this ritual.

Once at the head table, Joe Pummer, the former Oneida County Executive and still popular Republican, stepped to the microphone. With a smile and a nod, he said, "Ladies and gentlemen, good Republicans and Conservatives all, thank you for your very warm welcome to our dynamic winning team."

The applause thundered through the room along with shouts and whistles.

Pummer continued. "Tonight we begin our six-month victory celebration which will conclude on November 6th with a sweeping Republican victory for all our candidates!"

Again the thunderous applause.

Pummer held his hands up after giving his audience a chance to unwind and vent a little of the excitement that accompanies large gatherings of politically minded people.

"Before we begin tonight's activities, let me call on Father James O'Dowd for the invocation. Father O'Dowd."

Father O'Dowd was a Catholic priest from Saint Matthew's Church and a good Republican.

"Ladies and gentlemen. It's not without interest to me that I note tonight as being the twenty-seventh invocation I have given on this occasion and that this is the twenty-eighth annual candidates night.

"It is obvious that the results of that very first invocation were less than to be desired and that Joe Pummer saw the need to turn to his own parish priest for a little extra help! Twenty-eight years ago in November, we lost all but four races. Twenty-seven years ago in November, we won all but four races and we've been on the winning side ever since!"

"Let us put our faith in the Lord. Dear God, we ask that you help our good Republican candidates to run successful campaigns. You know that our State of New York is in grave financial trouble. Help our candidates find solutions that will

133

benefit all our people. Give our Republican candidates mighty armies of volunteers to do political battle with their adversaries. Let our candidates' messages be heard throughout their districts. And bring home the victory to which we all aspire. Amen."

Pummer shook Father O'Dowd's hand, said a few words which only the two heard, and returned to the microphone.

"Ladies and gentlemen, enjoy your meal."

Waiters and waitresses appeared everywhere. Pummer had given the signal that dinner was to be served and the well–organized program continued on schedule.

"So, Mr. Temple, you want to be a State Senator. That's good. What experience have you had?" D'Amato had already begun eating his dinner as he leaned toward Temple to make conversation.

"Experience helping my dad on several campaigns, some work for Mayor John Lindsay in New York City, some local campaigns in Onondaga County, Assemblyman Duryea's campaign for Governor, and a race for our local school board."

"You ran for the school board?"

"Yes. Jamesville–DeWitt. I served for six years."

D'Amato finished a mouthful of food, looked at Temple and said, "I always wanted to know why anyone would run for the school board. There is no pay, lots of headaches, parents hate you, teachers hate you, and the only news is bad news."

Temple looked directly at the United States Senator. "That's the positive side!"

D'Amato paused a moment then laughed in a high–pitched voice. "You crack me up. The positive side." Again he laughed.

Temple smiled. "Seriously, there are great benefits to serving on a school board. Contrary to popular belief, your constituents are the children. Your job is to offer them the best education possible and as many opportunities as you can. With no pay, there are no obligations to anyone other than the kids. And you know what I found out in the six years on the board?"

D'Amato shook his head.

134

"I found out that the children really do appreciate what you sincerely do for them. So do the parents, the teachers, and the administrators. That's what makes that job so special. I'm hoping to get an equal amount of satisfaction out of being a State Senator."

D'Amato looked at Temple as if he were suddenly seeing the man that he had been talking to. Finally, D'Amato said, "I hope you do."

As dessert was being served, Pummer stepped to the microphone.

"Ladies and gentlemen." He paused to let the crowd quiet down and began again. "Ladies and gentlemen. . .tonight, we are honored to have all of our candidates for public office here before you." Pummer spread his arms indicating the two rows of tables which made up the head tables. There was much applause as the audience warmed to the occasion.

"Let me introduce our winning team to you." Pummer then proceeded to introduce some fifty candidates for local, state, and national office. He concluded by saying, "I was going to have each candidate say a few words but realized that if I did that we'd be here until after election day!" The crowd laughed and cheered. "No, we need to get out and work. So tonight, we are going to hear from four of our candidates. First the honorable Alphonse D'Amato, United States Senator."

Pummer paused for the applause.

"Then we will have a few words from our own Minority Leader in the Assembly, Richard Ryan."

More applause filled the room.

"Finally, our two State Senate candidates, Tommy Bears and Jay Temple, will say hello. These two guys are going to do a great job for us. Tommy is running to fill the vacancy created by the death of Senator Fullsome and Jay Temple is going to give Laura Mann the race of her life."

Again applause.

"Ladies and gentlemen, a man who needs no introduction: our United States Senator from New York, the

135

honorable Alphonse 'Al' D'Amato."

Everyone came to their feet as if on cue. They applauded their embattled United States Senator. D'Amato smiled quickly, waved, and leaned into the microphone. "Thank you, thank you very much."

He waited while everyone sat down.

"It's nice to be somewhere where the words 'honorable' and 'Al D'Amato' are used in the same sentence!" D'Amato chuckled. "My friends in the press are not always so kind of late. Momma says its their upbringing."

The United States Senator talked briefly about his troubles in Washington, then about the role the Bush Administration was playing in the changes taking place in the Soviet Union. He noted that he had consulted with the President on these and other matters and that he was impressed with the total grasp which the President had on the thorny issues dominating world politics.

D'Amato concluded, "These are difficult times, but you can be assured that while it's my watch in the Senate, I'll be guarding your best interests and with the help of God, our country will survive and prosper."

The crowd again jumped to its feet, shouting and waving D'Amato signs in the air.

Assemblyman Richard Ryan was next. His deep, gravelly voice rolled over the crowd extolling the virtues of a Republican sweep in November and the need for the Republican Party to take back the Assembly from Democrat control.

"For too long our hard earned dollars have flowed into the bottomless pockets of a handful of New York City Democrats. It's time for us to throw the rascals out and bring state spending under control. We, in upstate New York, are not the bankers for the City and should not be expected to bail the City out every time it goes into hock. We need to put Republicans in the Assembly, we need to put Republicans in the Senate, and we need to put a Republican in the Governor's Mansion!"

136

Tommy Bears had been an assemblyman for fifteen years. He had paid his dues as a loyal member of the Republican Party and now was being rewarded by being nominated to run in a strong Republican District that had never had a Democrat elected to the State Senate. Tommy was a little nervous as he acknowledged his introduction.

"Thank you a-Joe-a-Pummer for your kind introduction. I want you to know," Bears was looking at Pummer then turned to the audience, grabbed hold of the podium, shifted his weight from one foot to the other and leaning a little to the left, spoke into the microphone.

"I want you all to know that I appreciate receiving your designation to run for the Senate. The 47th District has a four to one Republican enrollment. I plan to keep it that way and win in November."

Bears shot both arms up over his head and waved, signaling the end of his speech.

The Republicans again applauded their candidate amidst conversations, drinks, and laughter.

Pummer stood for the fourth time to introduce the final candidate for the evening.

"And now it is my pleasure to introduce a new face on the political scene for many of you, but someone who I know we are all going to be hearing a lot more about. Fellow Republicans, let's welcome our next Republican State Senator from the 48th Senate District, Jay Temple."

The applause was polite, but Jay noticed that people were turning from their conversations, drinks, and laughter to take a look at this guy who came out of nowhere to run against the entrenched Laura Ann Mann.

Temple looked out at the room, filled to capacity with the heart of the Republican Party for Oneida County.

"Ladies and gentlemen, I'm truly impressed with all of you. You are to be congratulated. This is a great turnout tonight. Your chairman, Joe Pummer, promised that if all the candidates were here tonight, he would guarantee a capacity

137

crowd, and you've made believers out of all of us. I'd like to thank Joe and thank each one of you for being here and for your commitment to the principles for which the Republican Party stands."

There was some applause as the audience continued to assess this new face.

"Let's get down to business. People ask me 'why are you running for the State Senate?' The answer is simple. New York State is in a financial crisis. Last year's state budget was $46.9 billion. We had a $3.5 billion deficit. This year's budget is proposed at $51.3 billion. It has a built-in deficit of $4.4 billion along with $7.9 billion in new taxes. We don't need new taxes. We all know that what we really need is tax relief!"

Cheers and applause began to rise throughout the room. These were Republican battle cries.

"New York State has been labeled as one of the ten worst run states in the country. The rating agencies have given New York the worst credit risk of any state in the country. That means that when we have deficits and have to go out and borrow money to pay our debts, we pay the highest, the very highest rates to borrow that money. Who ends up paying those exorbitant rates, you, me and every taxpayer in New York State.

"How can our state government be surprised when 230,000 jobs left this state over the last eight years? Business wants to go where there are less taxes and less government spending programs.

"Do you know that during that same period of time New York spent over $80 billion on member items? These are expenditures that are never voted on but for which you paid $80 billion in taxes to support.

"Governor Cuomo has proposed for this year, that corporate taxes be' raised 20%; that 150 new commissions be formed by the state; and that to help make ends meet, the state borrow money from the State Teachers' Retirement Fund. These are not solutions, these are examples of mismanagement.

"I'm running because I think we need a new direction in

state government. I think we need someone in the 48th Senate District who will speak out on these important issues. Someone who will provide leadership and offer a plan to bring New York State back from the edge of disaster.

"We need change. We need focus. We need to set our priorities."

They came up en masse. Everyone on the floor and at the head table stood in response to the challenges that Temple was laying before them. "Yes! Yes!," they shouted as they applauded their newest champion.

Temple concluded, "Let's send a message to Albany. Don't spend more than you earn. Bring jobs back to New York. And deal first with the important issues of the day that are the lifeblood of this great state."

Temple waved as they cheered. He shook hands first with Pummer then D'Amato and then with a host of others who worked their way over to him.

The campaign was gaining momentum.

* * *

At six a.m. on June 5th, Temple was on the move again. Ted Cordis had dropped him off at two a.m. and was now waiting for the candidate in the mobile headquarters parked in Temple's driveway.

Temple sprung the door open on the van as Cordis jumped out of a quick doze.

"Jesus!" Cordis yelled.

"Catching up on some lost hours?" Temple laughed.

"I didn't hear you coming."

"So I noticed. You're the one who volunteered for this job."

Temple really appreciated the commitment Cordis had made to the campaign. Already, Cordis was emerging as Temple's most dedicated worker and friend. He traveled with Temple to most of the speaking engagements, was overseeing the finances with Yondle, was running the campaign office after having negotiated the lease space, and had recruited a number of Young Republicans to work on the campaign.

"You want me to drive this morning so that you can get some rest?" Temple was sensitive to not asking too much from anyone, especially a person like Cordis who was already giving above and beyond anything that Temple had expected.

"Hey, you didn't get much more sleep than I did and you're the one performing today. I'll drive."

Twenty minutes later they were at the Onondaga County Republican Headquarters.

As Temple and Cordis entered the second floor suite of offices, they were greeted by Laney Gardiner and Nancy Sandlin. Nancy, wife of the senior member of the County Legislature, acted as the office manager for the County Republican Committee. She was always very helpful to all the candidates and had been especially supportive of Temple's candidacy.

Gardiner and Sandlin had already gotten the coffee pot going, doughnuts on the table, and were placing the morning agenda at each of the places around the large oval conference table.

"Good morning, Senator!" Sandlin smiled at Temple.

"Good morning, Nancy. Hi, Laney. You two must have spent the night here."

"No, just half of it," Laney smiled.

At that moment, Tom Mosby, Arthur Gaines, Bob Berry, and Ken Mathews walked in followed by Jim Summers, Kevin Roth, and Dave Yondle.

"The bus must've arrived," Cordis offered.

"Hey, good to see you too," Gaines responded. You could never have the last comment with the party leader in attendance.

After everyone had shaken hands and said hello, Temple took his place at the center of the table.

"Help yourselves to coffee and doughnuts. We're going

140

to get started because we have a lot to cover in a very short period of time. Bob wants to run some survey information by us on issues and the race.

"I appreciate your coming this morning and hope you'll all feel free to offer any suggestions or comments that you might have. Bob, why don't you start."

"Thanks, Jay. Arnold Ophidia and I have worked with the State Committee and done a survey on voter thinking and trends in New York State and in the Senate District. The results are interesting. I'm handing out a printout of the results and would just like to point out a couple of responses.

"If you look at the CNY Data Sheet, the first question: 'Direction of NYS,' 48% of those surveyed thought New York was going in the wrong direction, opposed to 39% who felt New York was going in the right direction. 13% were undecided.

"On most important local issues, they identified the environment, taxes, economy, drug, and education as major concerns, in that order.

"On the job that the State Legislature is doing: 49% disapproved, 31% approved, and 20% were undecided.

"Based on these factors, Jay's direction is right on target. Every time he speaks to a group he should remind them that the Senate recently approved $80 million worth of hometown pork barrel projects in member items. This is a vote buying gimmick used to ensure the reelection of incumbents. It comes right out of the taxpayers' pockets. It has no relationship to government.

"Mann is as guilty as any senator for these expenditures.

"We also looked at Mann's last three races.

"She beat Ahern 51% to 49%, Bonney 58% to 42%, and Reston 63% to 37%.

"We've broken down the areas where she was strong in each of these races and also have a voter profile of those groups that supported her.

"We have to attack her every time we have the opportunity or she's going to roll up the numbers in this race. She has worked the district well and has increased her margin of victory in every race.

"She is strong in farm areas in Madison County, strong in the City of Syracuse with great support among minorities, has good response from a variety of ethnic groups, and is well-liked by bluecollar workers and women activists.

"Her financial strength comes from women's rights groups, unions, and surprisingly, newspaper and other media personalities.

"We expect that she'll raise between $165,000 and $225,000 for this campaign. She expects to be able to divert some of that money to other Democratic candidates. She expects this race to be another race like the Reston race.

"To win, we need to raise about $250,000. And we need to start spending it now. The key between now and Labor Day is to at least get Jay's name recognition up to around 55% to 60%. We want to be around 80% by Election Day."

Temple leaned forward in his chair. "I was hoping it would be more like 100% by Election Day!"

Mathews looked at Berry and asked, "Why not closer to 100%?"

"You've got to understand, that other than the President of the United States, no one achieves a 100% rating. 80% would be outstanding.

"Mann's own polls show her at around 83%. In the Ahern race she was at 48%. In the Bonney race, she was at 60% and in the Reston race, she was at 72%."

Mathews again asked, "How does that relate to the vote results?"

"Name recognition has no bearing on the outcome of the election other than the higher the recognition the better chance you'll have of winning. The recognition has to be positive and you have to get those that like you out to vote for you. It's a big task with only five months left to election day!"

Gaines put his coffee cup on the table. "Don't you worry about getting out the positive vote for Jay. Our people like Jay and will turn out the vote for this guy."

Mosby had worked on the three previous races against Mann. He spoke next. "Art, you have to remember that three other Republicans ran against Mann over the last six years and despite the positive Republican to Democrat enrollment in this Senate District, Mann won each time and each time by a larger vote."

Berry added, "You can't count on Republicans voting Republican in this race. Madison County went big for Mann and with the registration there, that means Republicans crossed over in large numbers."

Cordis looked at Temple and then to the group. "We've done some checking and there is one group that really is crucial in this race. The NE's. Non enrolled voters comprise almost 25% of the total registration, and they do get out and vote. We think that we have to have a message that appeals to the Republicans, Conservatives and the NE's. That's where Mann has gone and that's why she has beaten us for the last six years."

Jim Summers had practiced law with Temple and knew him well. "I'm not a seasoned politician, but I believe Jay has the appeal for that group of people. I've known Jay for about fifteen years, and he is honest and straightforward. He stands for what is right for Central New York.

"Look at this survey." Summers held up the Berry-Ophidia handout. "Environmental issues. Jay wrote a series of articles for the papers in the seventies promoting a cleanup of the environment and protection of our resources.

"Taxes. Jay can cite line and verse on the budget and taxes and who is going to argue with that?

"Economy. Since he left Law for the business world, he's seen first hand the disastrous condition this state is in with the loss of industry, jobs, and business.

"Education. As a past Vice President of a school board and a college professor, Jay knows the educational issues.

"Drugs. I don't know how much he knows in this area but I do know that he'd be tough on any criminal involvement with drugs and he is creative enough that he may just come up

143

with some new ideas on this that could help with the problems surrounding drug use in this state.

"I have to agree with Berry. We have the right candidate. Now, we need to get his name out there and get people to know him the way we do. If we can have people see him the way we do, he'll win even against Mann."

"Maybe I ought to have Jim do my commercials!" Temple smiled. "I appreciate the kind words."

Roth had known Temple as long as anyone in the room. "Jim is right. If we can get the public to see Jay as he really is, I can't believe that he couldn't win and win big."

"Well guys, all it takes is money." Berry was considering the costs associated with the advertising to get the recognition that they would need.

Yondle was running the finances at headquarters for Temple's campaign. "Ken Mathews has given me a list of donors to several other recent campaigns. We are beginning to get the list computerized so that we can get mailings and solicitations out. We also have a number of fund raisers scheduled over the next several weeks. I'm hopeful we will start seeing some good money flowing into the campaign."

For the next hour the group reviewed fund raising strategies and how to get the candidate intimately involved in the 'ask-for' contributions. It became apparent to Temple that half his time between now and election day would be spent in fund raising. It was an essential part of the campaign but not his favorite. He thought to himself that this was an aspect of a candidate's life that he had never paid much attention to, but was really at the heart of a successful career as a politician. He was still learning.

* * *

Berry met with Major Germain the following morning. The Major was the OIC (officer in charge) of a special army intelligence unit assigned the responsibility of drug interdiction

144

in Central and Western New York.

Berry looked across the Major's desk at the very fit commander, with close cropped hair and direct eyes. "Jay Temple is someone you may want to cultivate."

"You think he has a chance of winning?"

"If not this time definitely the next."

"Why not this time?"

"Not enough money and time."

"Will he run again?"

"He's got the bug. He wants to serve, and he wants to serve for all the right reasons. He's an issues guy."

"Is he tough enough to confront all that we are dealing with with these drug lords and pushers?"

"I think so. At least he's a big John Wayne fan." Berry's attempt at humor didn't get quite the response he had intended so he went on.

"He has some military experience. Was an officer in the Reserves. Armor, I think."

"Good. We'll check his records. If that pans out, we'll keep an eye on the race and see what develops."

"Have you had any luck with the Syracuse Police?"

"No. They really don't want to work with an outside agency. I'm not sure they buy our information on the Angels and the Jamaicans."

"Geez. What do they want? A street war?"

"We'll see to it that it doesn't get that far." Germain made the statement with an air of confidence that stopped Berry from asking any more questions.

Chapter XII

Commitments

Temple had been campaigning hard for weeks. He had been living on Coke, black tea, and chocolate to help offset the lack of sleep. The caffeine had become so high in his system, that unknown to him, his blood vessels were beginning to react. On June 5th, it hit home.

Temple had just finished a speech to a local service club and was walking out to the van with Cordis. "Ted, I'm not feeling too well."

Cordis looked at Temple quickly. He had never heard the candidate complain about anything. "What's the matter."

"I don't know, but I'm getting dizzy, and I've got a splitting headache."

"Get in the van, and I'll take you home. You don't have anything more today anyway."

By the time they arrived at Temple's home, he was not looking well. His color was gone, his eyes were tearing from the pain, and he was struggling for composure.

Pat Temple took one look at her husband and called the hospital. She also called Dan Seward, a personal friend and prominent neurosurgeon. Dan told her to get Jay to the hospital, and he would meet them there.

Cordis drove while Pat comforted her husband. When they arrived at the emergency room, Seward was waiting with a stretcher. He took one look at his friend and knew that this was no time for small talk.

Seward was highly respected by the hospital staff. When

146

he came down the hallway, personally wheeling Temple's stretcher and ordering IVs and a setup for a CAT scan, no one hesitated or questioned the directives.

Once in the emergency room, Seward asked Temple a few questions.

"Jay, can you hear me?"

Temple was almost audibly crying from the pain in his head and neck. He never had known such pain before in his life. He heard Seward and nodded 'yes.'

"Jay, where does it hurt?"

"Head and neck."

"Can you squeeze my hand?" Seward took Temple's hand and placed two fingers in it. Temple squeezed.

The nurse and another intern came in with the IV. They inserted two needles in Temple's left arm. Temple felt the pin pricks. They were nothing compared to the pain in his head. He could feel the liquid go into his arm. He tried to open his eyes but the light hurt.

"Jay, I'm sending you for a full CAT scan, as a safety precaution. The medicine we just gave you should help the pain. I will be right outside when you come out of the scan. Don't worry. You'll be all right."

Temple didn't remember a whole lot after that. He remembered being encased in a machine and the table moving. Then he remembered that everything seemed totally white.

By the time they had him back in the recovery room, he was beginning to feel some relief from the pain. They had also done a spinal tap and now he was beginning to feel an ache in the small of his back.

Seward was there looking concerned but also relieved.

"How's the State Senator?"

"Better, thanks to my doctor."

"You gave us quite a scare."

"Gave you a scare? You should have been on this side of the table." Temple smiled weakly.

Pat Temple came closer to the bed. "Is he going to be

ok?"

"He should be, in a week or so."

"A week?" Temple looked up. "I've got a heavy schedule this week. I'm supposed to go to New York tomorrow night."

"Jay, you're a lucky guy. I thought you were having a stroke when you came in here. Your blood vessels were all dilated and the head and neck pain didn't look good. Very fortunately it was more an allergic condition. Caffeine. How much soda, coffee, tea, or even chocolate have you had?"

Temple thought. "A lot. I've been living on it for a boost and energy."

"Well you almost boosted yourself right out of here. The medicine we have given you will take care of the allergic reaction but the spinal tap we did will have a little longer lasting effect."

"What kind of an effect?"

"You'll find that you get dizzy when you stand up until the fluid we took out is replenished. It may be a few days or it may be a week."

"If I feel all right can I do whatever I'm up to?"

"Yes, but I think you will find that for a few days that isn't going to be much."

Temple had other ideas until he tried to sit up to thank Seward. It was like being hit in the back of the head. He lay back down on the bed, dizzy and a little nauseous.

"Thanks, Dan."

"Win one for the gipper," Seward smiled, said goodbye to Pat, and left the room.

"I've got to go to New York tomorrow."

"If you can."

It was four in the morning on June 6th before Temple could muster enough strength to leave the hospital. His head still had a pounding in it, but this was from the spinal tap, not the caffeine.

It only bothered him when he sat upright.

"I've got to make that plane trip to New York this afternoon."

His wife looked over at him in disbelief. "You can't possibly go to New York today. You're having trouble just sitting up. How do you expect to fly to New York, much less get around once you are there."

Temple thought about the reception some of his friends within the industry had planned for him that evening. It was his first large fund raiser and the campaign needed the infusion of cash.

"I'm going to call Tom Mosby to see if he'll fly down with me. He wanted an opportunity to meet some of the people that will be at the reception tonight, and if I have a problem, he'll be able to help out."

"I think you're crazy." Pat knew her husband well enough to know that if he planned to go, nothing she could say would really stop him. He'd have to learn the hard way.

Temple was dizzy as he walked from the car to their house. He didn't even bother taking his clothes off before going to bed. He just kicked off his shoes and went to sleep.

He woke about eleven a.m. and had Pat place a call to Tom Mosby. After giving Tom the details of the day before, Mosby agreed to fly down to New York with Temple. He picked Temple up at three-thirty that afternoon and by four-fifteen, they were on a USAir flight to New York City.

Temple was still having an equilibrium problem. Fortunately, the plane was almost empty so Temple took a row in the rear of the plane and lay down across the seats. This brought immediate relief. He wondered how he'd manage the reception. Mosby was wondering the same thing.

The location was spectacular. Overlooking Central Park from the fifty-second floor of the corporation's headquarters, New York seemed pristine and sterile. The room itself covered three-quarters of the floor with wrap-around floor to ceiling windows.

There was a raised platform area in the center of the

149

room that had been set with an ice sculpture of New York State and a variety of hors d'oeuvres. Near the windows, a portable bar had been set up and two bar tenders and two waitresses were busy getting ready for the evening's reception.

Mosby and Temple were greeted by Anson Harill, president of the company hosting the event, and Peter Flannery, president of the trade association.

"Jay, welcome. We're really happy to be able to welcome you to New York City. I hope we generate a lot of support for you this evening." Harill shook Temple's hand.

"Thanks, Anson. It's nice of you to go to all this effort. Peter, it's good to see you. I'd like both of you to meet Tom Mosby, a friend and attorney from Syracuse. Tom, this is Anson Harill and Peter Flannery."

As the men shook hands, a tall, slender, blonde woman walked into the room. "Am I early?" She smiled as she walked over to Temple. "How is our next State Senator?" she asked as she extended her hand to Temple.

"Much better, now that you're here." Temple shook her hand. "Tom, I'd like you to meet Carin Clarke. Carin is a lobbyist for one of our bigger companies and a co-hostess of tonight's reception."

Mosby recognized Clarke from his dealings in Albany. "It's nice to meet you, Carin. I think I've seen you in Albany."

"I've been known to spend some time there. As a matter of fact, I believe we've met before. Aren't you a friend of Senator Harrison?"

"As a matter of fact, I am."

"Yes. We met at a fund raiser for the Senator at the Desmond a year ago."

"You're right. I think I remember that. You were with Senator Bemann."

"I think I was." Clarke turned to the other men. "Hello, Peter, Anson."

Temple excused himself and went to the rest room. His head was spinning, and he felt very warm. He ran cold water

150

over his wrists while he bent over the sink. Then he splashed cold water over his face and took a towel soaked in cold water and rubbed the back of his neck. All this seemed to give him some temporary relief.

He dried his face and hands just as Mosby walked in.

"How are you doing?"

"I'll live," Temple responded, not quite sure.

"A lot of people just came in. Are you going to be able to get around?"

"No choice. I think I'll be all right for a while. But if I give you the high sign, we will have to leave quickly."

"Right. Anything else I can do?"

"No. But I do want you to know how much I appreciate your coming down here with me. It's above and beyond the call of duty."

"Hey, that's what friends are for. I'm glad I could do it."

Temple went back to the reception and for the next hour and a half mingled with the heads of a number of companies and their legislative people.

At eight that evening, Temple thanked everyone for their support and left the reception for the hotel. His head was pounding, and he was dizzy again from the loss of the spinal fluid, but he had kept his appointment.

The reception brought in twenty-one thousand dollars and was one of the biggest fund raisers of the campaign.

* * *

The next morning, Temple awoke with a start to the sound of the hotel telephone. He rolled over in bed, feeling as though he had a hangover from the night before, and picked up the phone.

"Good morning. It's 7:30, the temperature is eighty-one degrees and the forecast is for sunny skies with temperatures in the upper eighties. Have a nice day."

151

Temple put the phone back on the receiver. He dreaded the next step. To sit up and determine whether the dizziness and pounding would return to his head.

Slowly, he raised himself up and swung his legs out of the bed. A moment's light-headedness passed quickly. Okay so far.

He showered, dressed, and made his way down to the trade association meeting with only slight discomfort. He looked forward to just sitting and listening to others talk for a change.

The trade association met quarterly to discuss legislative issues of importance to the industry. The meeting was followed by a reception, luncheon, and guest speaker. Today, Mayor David Dinkins was the scheduled speaker.

Temple was greeted by a half dozen or so people who had been at his fund raiser the previous evening. They all wished him well in his bid for the New York State Senate.

Peter Flannery walked over and put his arm around Temple's shoulder. "How's our next State Senator?"

"Great! I really appreciate all the work and effort that you put into last night's reception. It was very nice."

Flannery smiled. "I'm glad to hear you say that because I need some help from you today."

"Sure."

"We've been informed that Mayor Dinkins is tied up today with police negotiations and cannot make the luncheon. I thought this would give you an opportunity to be our guest speaker and maybe pull in a few more pledges for your campaign. What do you say?"

"How can I say no? Be glad to help out, Peter."

Temple hardly heard any of the reports during the meeting. He was busy mapping out his own comments for the luncheon. They had to tie into both the campaign and the industry. He kept hearing a favorite saying of an assemblyman from his district. "You have to learn to work out of your bag." He now understood better what that meant. He also knew that some of his best talks were ad lib.

Flannery stepped to the podium. "Well, we've had a fine meal, and now we are going to be treated to what I think will be the highlight of the day.

"As you know, Mayor Dinkins was supposed to be our speaker today. Police negotiations have prevented the Mayor from being with us so I've asked Mr. Jay Temple to fill in for the Mayor.

"Jay, as most of you know, is running for the State Senate seat now held by that tough incumbent, Laura Ann Mann. From what I have been hearing in Albany, he's running a pretty tough campaign and has a good chance of winning that race.

"Jay could use our help, and I am sure after you have heard him speak, you'll welcome the opportunity to support him.

"Ladies and gentlemen, Jay Temple, the next Senator from the 48th Senate District."

Temple walked up to the podium, shaking Flannery's hand as they passed each other.

"Peter, thank you for that generous introduction and the opportunity to speak today.

"I talked to the Mayor this morning and told him that I'd be happy to handle the police negotiations if he preferred to come here and speak. He said given the choice between the New York City Police and a room full of lawyers and insurance executives, he'd rather take the easy group. . .and he did."

The some one-hundred and fifty people in the room laughed and then paid closer attention to the day's speaker.

"This is a challenging time for all of us. I don't have to tell you the problems business in New York State is facing. We all know what overregulation is. The insurance industry is one of the highest regulated industries in the state.

"I also don't have to tell you what high taxes are all about. As a state, we have the highest taxes in the country, and as an industry, we pay the highest corporate taxes in the state.

"On the expense side, New York has consistently shown over the last several years that it doesn't know how to budget and doesn't know how to live within the budget that it prepares.

153

"The cost to the state for its financial mismanagement is in the billions of dollars. Our rating as a state is the lowest of any state in the country. Every time the state borrows money, which is often, it costs us more to borrow because of the risk involved as demonstrated by our ratings.

"All of this means higher taxes for business and higher taxes for the people of the state.

"We need to establish priorities for state spending, we need to eliminate unnecessary expenditures, and we need to bring to this state a balanced budget.

"If you or I spent more than we earned, we'd be put in jail. If our companies were unable to meet their financial obligations, we'd be put out of business. But if New York State does that, they simply go back to the taxpayers and raise taxes.

"That's why industry and people are leaving this state.

"We have a lot to offer in New York. We have an educated work force, a wealth of natural resources, good transportation, and we are at the heart of the world's commerce system. We can not afford to lose these advantages because of mismanagement of our State Government.

"People ask me if I truly believe that one man can make a difference. I believe that that's where it starts. One voice in the wilderness but one voice supported by the voters of this state, the voters in my district. If the people of this state believe as I do, then change will occur. Realistically, we have no choice.

"I decided several months ago that I wanted to try do something about these problems and many others. We need to deal with the problems of the environment, education, drugs, crime and even the dignity of our workers. I've got some thoughts on these matters too. But that's for another time.

"I hope to send a clear message to Albany that New York State is not in a very healthy condition and that the people don't want to hear the same rhetoric that they have been hearing over the past several years.

"The winds of change are blowing toward Albany, and I want to be a part of that.

"I'd be happy to answer any questions that you might have."

* * *

Mosby had some business to take care of while in New York City. He arranged to meet Temple at LaGuardia Airport for the afternoon flight back to Syracuse.

Mosby arrived at the USAir counter to find Temple checking in. Temple was a little flushed in color, but his spirits were high.

"How'd the meeting go?"

"Fine. How are you feeling?"

"A little wobbly but I'm holding my own. Had to pinch hit for the Mayor at lunch."

"What?"

"Mayor Dinkins didn't show up so they asked me to fill in as the luncheon speaker."

"Boy! You needed that like you need another spinal."

"Please."

"Well, how did you do?"

"I'm prejudiced, of course, but I'd say all right. In any event, one of the CEO's wrote me a personal check for five hundred dollars after I finished with the questions and answers."

Great. Does he have any friends that would care to join him?"

"I forgot to ask."

"Ken Mathews won't like that."

The two men made their way down the jetport. The plane was full this time, which meant no room for the candidate to stretch out. Temple suffered through the flight back and the car ride home.

As he was getting out of Mosby's car he turned to his friend, "Tom, I really appreciate your help yesterday and today. I'm not sure I could've managed otherwise."

"My pleasure. You better get some rest. We have a lot

155

of work to do between now and election day. We need a healthy candidate."

It would be two weeks before Temple would be back to full strength. Each day showed some signs of improvement, but it was slower than it might otherwise have been were it not for his schedule.

On June 7th, Temple was at a campaign meeting at 7:30 in the morning, then off to a 9:00 a.m. business meeting, followed by a talk to the Syracuse Rotary Club at noon.

At 2:00 p.m., Berry had him scheduled for a news conference on the environment. The site was a landfill in the town of DeWitt.

As Cordis pulled the van into the Erie Canal Park next to the landfill, Berry reviewed the topics that they had planned on having Temple talk about.

Laney Gardiner and Larry Malcolm also had come along to help set up the site before the press arrived. Their responsibility was to pick a location that would provide a meaningful backdrop.

The landfill was on the far side of the canal. A truss bridge dating back to the mid–1800s connected the park to the landfill. Once below the level of the canal, the landfill site was now fifty to sixty feet above the canal and covered several hundred acres.

The site was used for raw garbage and was covered daily with a thin layer of topsoil. Once a year, the town would go through the landfill and using a "flame-thrower" device, burn any exposed garbage not covered by dirt. On this June day, the town had not yet brought in the "flame-thrower."

Gardiner and Malcolm had first thought of putting the portable podium at the base of the hill, but then, at Gardiner's suggestion, they moved the podium to the top of the hill. This view showed a much more far-reaching problem than would be visualized at the base.

They had just finished setup when the first TV crew arrived from Channel 7.

156

Cordis looked back in the van at Berry and Temple. "Terry Davis is here with a camera crew."

Berry and Temple looked out the window.

"You ready to go?" Berry asked.

"All set."

Temple climbed out of the van followed by Berry and then Cordis.

"Hello, Mr. Temple." Davis was a highly thought of reporter for Channel 7. She stood about five feet four inches, had short brown hair, green eyes, and a trim figure. She always wore a tailored business suit, and today was no exception.

Black was her favorite color. It accentuated her slim outline and always captured the attention that she desired. Dark nylons and black stacked heels finished her rather attractive features, all of which did not go unnoticed by the men present.

"Are we going to interview you here or are you intent on making me climb up there?" she pointed to where Gardiner and Malcolm were standing.

Berry interceded on behalf of the candidate. "Do you want a small story or do you want the big picture?"

There was a moment's pause, and then Davis laughed. "Always look at the big picture. That's what they told us in Journalism 101. Right, Bob? I guess we climb to the top." She was already on her way.

Temple walked up the hill with her as two radio station trucks pulled into the parking lot.

"Sorry for the inconvenience. The view should be worth the effort." Temple smiled.

Davis looked at the candidate and then out over the canal. "It already is."

Her cameraman was half-stumbling up the hill behind them, puffing under the weight of the camera, batteries, and microphones. He also was checking out the view for the best angle and lighting. It was his job to make Davis look good. Not a hard job but not an easy one either, he was thinking as he looked at her from behind.

157

At the top of the hill, the cameraman set up his equipment about fifteen feet from the podium with the sun directly behind him. Next he ran mike lines from the batteries to the podium and checked the sound system. Finally, he asked Davis to stand by the podium and say something. Channel 7 was ready.

Two radio reporters had now climbed the hill and had also placed their microphones on the podium. The last reporter to arrive was from the Suburban Press. Pad and pen in hand, he asked Temple when the news conference would begin.

Looking at his watch, Temple said, "It's two fifteen, let's get started."

Cameras whirred, recorders taped, and reporters began their critical analysis of the Republican politician.

"First, I'd like to thank all of you for covering this news conference. The environment is an important issue today, and I haven't heard my opponent or for that matter, many other candidates for public office address the issue.

"Today, we are standing on a landfill that not so long ago was a marshy area next to the old Erie Canal. It was thought that using this site for garbage disposal accomplished two goals. One, land reclamation and two, an inexpensive way to take care of the garbage problem.

"The cost to the environment was steep. It has been discovered that landfill sites, and this one in particular, give off dangerous amounts of methane gas. Because of this, nothing can be built on the site, and therefore, the idea of land reclamation loses some of its significance.

"Because there is little supervision as to the type of garbage that is dumped in a site such as this, certain contaminants have been leaching into the water, causing pollution and making the fish inedible for human consumption and the water unfit to drink.

"These same contaminants are leaching into the surrounding soil and are now under federal investigation for their toxicity.

158

"We need closer monitoring and well–defined standards state-wide for all future landfills.

"The Governor is talking about a nuclear waste disposal site now, in Cortland and up in the Adirondacks. Where are the studies and reports, where are the standards by which the Governor judges what is a good location for such a site? I'm told that cost and availability of land are the yardsticks being used. Where is our State Senator, and why isn't she involved in this issue?

"Members of my own party are talking about dissolving the Adirondack Park. This would be the single biggest mistake this state could make.

"The Adirondack Park is the largest State Park in the United States. Not many people realize this. It is in some respects the last frontier. Some very wise people created the Park to protect its beauty and resources for future generations. Now, some politicians want to remove that protection and open the Park to development by land speculators. Where is our State Senator's involvement in this issue?

"What about the bottle and can return deposit law? A simple method to help keep bottles and cans from becoming discarded junk on our roads, highways, forests, and parks. How did our State Senator vote on this bill and why?

"As a young boy, I enjoyed the Adirondacks, camping, fishing, hiking, and canoeing. I'd like to think that my children and my grandchildren would be able to enjoy those same experiences. But they won't! They won't be able to if the state sells off park land to help balance the state budget.

"And where does our State Senator stand on this issue?

"We need a leader on environmental issues. Not a follower, or worse yet, someone who stays out of the fight.

"One of my highest priorities is to protect the environment, and in particular, the Adirondack Park. We need to develop a well thought out plan that will manage the Park into the twenty-first century. We need interstate compacts that will eliminate the acid rain problem. We need a senator who will

159

represent our interests and those of future generations.

"I'd be happy to answer any questions."

Terry Davis lifted a microphone to the candidate. "Where does Senator Mann stand on these issues?"

"That's my point. We should know. But in reviewing her voting record, the only vote she is on record with is one against the container deposit law. She argued on the floor of the Senate against the bill requiring return deposits."

"Are you saying that Senator Mann is an anti-environmentalist?"

"I'm indicating to you that she certainly is not in the forefront of any of the issues that would positively impact our environment, and she should be. I plan on being an advocate for landfill standards, clean air and water, and preservation of the Adirondack Park."

Tommy Henson of the Suburban Press commented, "You don't sound much like a Republican."

Temple responded, "The environment isn't a Republican or Democratic issue. It's a people issue. It's an issue everyone needs to be concerned with. It's our future."

Louise Ferara of radio station WKPO asked, "You seem to indicate that you take issue with the Governor's proposed sites in Cortland and the Adirondacks for the disposal of nuclear waste. Where would you recommend we put it?"

"Good question. There are states, South Carolina being one, that have set up sites for nuclear waste disposal, and they are actively selling their sites for use by other states.

"Why would New York want to set up a site in our own state when we have that option. Cost, I suspect, would be the Governor's answer, but I would argue that the long term costs to the state for containment of the nuclear waste will far exceed the cost for disposal in South Carolina.

"We also have no idea at this point in time what the effect of nuclear waste disposal will be on our environment. Why create a multitude of locations to have to deal with and why create one in New York if we have other options?"

Terry Davis turned to the cameraman. "Get a long–range shot of the landfill and a few close ups on the exposed garbage."

Temple answered a few more questions and concluded the news conference by personally thanking each of the reporters and the cameraman for coming.

On the way back to the studio, the cameraman asked Davis what she thought of Temple.

"Actually, he's not a bad candidate. Nobody knows him, but he is pretty good on his feet."

"Do you think he can beat Laura Ann Mann?"

"No one has yet. But he will give her a run for her money."

Davis was thinking about the news conference. She picked up the cellular phone and called the station.

"Hi. This is Terry. Do we know if Senator Mann is in town today?"

The receptionist said, "Let me check." There was a pause and then, "Yes, she will be attending a dinner at the Jewish Community Center at five o'clock tonight."

"Tell Bob I want to hold the Temple piece until after I do a quick take with Mann."

Davis clicked off the phone and sat looking out the window. "John, I want to talk to Mann about that container deposit bill."

* * *

Mann and her aide, Tork Johns, walked into the Jewish Community Center at five-thirty. She made it a point to always arrive late, after everyone else had arrived, in order to maximize the focus of attention she received.

Ira Slanasky, the director of the Center, met her at the door. "Senator. It's so nice to have you join us. We've been looking forward to this for some time." He looked at Johns after kissing Mann on the cheek. "Mr. Johns, it's good to see you

161

again."

Johns nodded as the Senator spoke. "Is that Terry Davis?"

"Yes. We didn't invite the press, but she showed up here fifteen minutes ago. Do you want me to ask her to leave?"

"No, no Ira. I don't mind. I'll talk to her before dinner. I'm sure she'll leave before we get to the program."

Mann walked across the room. Davis saw her coming and had the cameraman get his equipment ready to record.

"Good evening, Terry," Mann said to the reporter.

"Hello, Senator. How are things in Albany?"

"The same. Closed door meetings, back room deals, and no access for the public. You ought to come to Albany sometime and see how we women are treated by the men running the state."

"I may take you up on that some day. Can I ask you a few questions on the record?"

"Sure." Mann sounded a lot more comfortable with this than she really was. She did not like spur of the moment interviews, and she liked to know what the topics were before they were brought up.

"Jay Temple. . .."

Mann immediately felt her stomach tighten. This really wasn't on her agenda for discussion today.

Davis continued, ". . .your Republican opponent, said today that you are weak on environmental issues. That you have not been a leader in the Senate on environmental concerns and that in fact you voted against the bottle deposit bill which is considered an environmental cleanup bill. Do you have a response to these comments?"

Davis had been a reporter long enough to know she had hit a nerve with the Senator. This surprised her because Mann was known as a fighter and usually made short work of her opponents.

Mann forced a smile. "My opponent needs to get his facts straight. The container deposit bill was not an

162

environmental bill. It was an anti-business bill. It had the potential for costing jobs right here in my own district. I opposed it because it costs consumers more money, they pay the extra cost, it costs grocery stores more money in handling, and it costs container manufacturers more money to have to recycle the used material. With the economy the way it is, we hardly need more expenses."

Davis followed with another question. "When you say that container manufacturers have to recycle the used material, isn't the recycling considered an environmental action?"

"Recycling dramatically reduces the profits of container manufacturers. Again, it becomes a jobs issue. The environmental benefits of a container deposit bill have not been proven. The costs to business have."

Mann turned to Johns. He stepped forward on cue and said, "Senator, you need to get to the dinner. We are already running late."

Davis also knew the routine. "Thank you, Senator. Have an enjoyable evening."

Mann thought 'Bitch!' but said, "You too, Terry. Good to see you again." She and Johns followed Ira Slanasky into the dining room.

The cameraman laughed as he folded his equipment and stored the wires in their case. "If looks could kill!" he said.

"John, you'll be taking my job with all your insight," Davis laughed. "I think we have a story."

Back in their car, Davis looked up Bob Berry's phone number and called. Berry answered on the third ring.

"Ophidia and Berry. Bob Berry speaking."

"Bob. This is Terry Davis."

"Hi, Terry. How'd we do today?"

"That's why I'm calling. I'm putting this story together and am following a hunch I have."

"What's that?"

"On that container deposit bill that Mann voted against. You wouldn't have access to her contributors list would you?"

163

Berry smiled to himself. Ophidia sure knew his players. "As a matter of fact I do. And your hunch is right on target. Hanover Container's Danforth Steele has been a major contributor to Mann's campaigns. I'd prefer though, that you not attribute that information to me."

"Can you fax me the list?"

"Be happy to. What's the fax number?"

By the time Davis reached the station, the fax was on her desk. It confirmed that Danforth Steele, President of The Hanover Container Company had given very generously to the Mann Campaign. Further checking showed that the timing of the contribution and the container deposit bill vote were, coincidentally, within days of each other.

Davis thought to herself as she put the story together for the eleven o'clock news, 'So much for my invitation to visit Albany with Senator Mann.'

* * *

Within an hour of leaving the landfill, WPKO and WPTT were on the air with Temple's comments on the environment and particularly the nuclear waste site issue.

Berry had sent out over 150 news releases covering Temple's positions on environmental issues. Stations that had not attended the conference began reporting on the conference using the releases. Temple laughed at this because to the unknowing listener, it sounded as though the commentators were at the landfill reporting live.

By eight o'clock that Friday evening, Temple's campaign headquarters were receiving phone calls supporting the Senate candidate's stand and offering to help get the candidate elected in the fall.

Some calls were from the media, asking for additional information or for clarification of some details. By 10:30 that evening, Cordis concluded that on the environment, Temple was a clear winner.

Temple arrived at campaign headquarters at 10:50 along with Ken Mathews, Kevin Roth, and Dave Yondle. They had been at a fund raiser that had netted a little over three thousand dollars.

Berry, Cordis, and Gardiner were sitting in front of a television that had suddenly surfaced while Temple had been out raising money.

Berry was the first one up as Temple came through the front door. "Congratulations! We've had our first PR coup! Terry Davis has a spot coming up on the eleven o'clock news that will have Laura Mann spitting nails."

Temple asked, "How do you know?"

"That's what I'm paid for. To know these things. Ted got us a TV. Come on. We'll miss the news."

Karen Lastri finished the national news and then turning to Terry Davis said, "Now, for local news. Terry Davis has been working the political beat, and today Terry talked with the two candidates for the New York State Senate's 48th District. Terry."

"Thank you, Karen. Jay Temple, the Republican candidate for the New York State Senate, held a news conference at the landfill site in DeWitt."

As the television screen showed first a long shot of the landfill, and then a close up of some discarded beer and soda cans, Davis continued the voice over.

"Mr. Temple indicated that we need more regulation of landfill sites along with stronger clean air and water legislation. He said he opposes nuclear waste sites in New York State."

The screen panned from a view of the canal up the landfill slope to the podium where Temple was standing. The sound cut into Temple's comments. "There are states, South Carolina being one, that have set up sites for nuclear waste disposal and they are actively selling their sites for use by other states."

The screen came back to Terry Davis and the live newscast.

"Mr. Temple said he doesn't think that it is a wise decision to open new nuclear waste sites when there are already other options.

"He then took aim at Senator Mann. He pointed to her vote in the Senate opposing the container deposit bill as an anti-environmental vote and challenged her lack of leadership on environmental issues.

"I caught up with Senator Mann tonight, at a dinner at the Jewish Community Center. This was her response."

The screen showed a somewhat agitated Laura Ann Mann.

"The container deposit bill was not an environmental bill. It was an anti-business bill."

Again, the screen went back to the live news cast and Terry Davis.

"Senator Mann said that she voted against the deposit bill because of the cost to the consumer, the merchant, and to the manufacturer. She said that recycling costs outweigh the benefits of the law."

The camera widened to show both Lastri and Davis. Lastri commented, "This is something new isn't it, Terry? The Republican arguing for the environmental legislation and the Democrat arguing for business?"

"Temple said that the environment isn't a Republican or Democratic issue. He said it's everybody's issue.

"One point should be made and that is that the container industry has contributed generously to Senator Mann's campaigns in the past.

"I suspect that if they have not already, the environmentalists will be offering support to Mr. Temple."

"Thanks, Terry. Well, it looks like this year's electioneering is off to an early start with some interesting twists. We'll follow this and other stories as they develop."

166

Chapter XIII

Strategy

Mann flipped off the switch to the television in her local Senate office. She turned to Johns.

"What kind of crap is that? Who gave them the right to speculate on why I voted the way I did on any bill?"

Johns had seen the Senator blow up before but never over an opponent's news conference. He knew that his role was to sit and listen until the Senator had fully vented.

"I help get them their ratings. I give them stories that they never would have access to and then the first chance they get, they stab me in the back." Mann was pacing now. Her face was red with anger and more than once, she pounded her desk with a closed fist.

"That little bitch, Davis. . .it'll be a cold day in hell before I give her a story. Damn. If Danny Steele sees that he'll be shitting bricks!"

Mann flopped down on her couch next to Johns. "What do we do now?" she asked as she stared across the room.

"Who gave Davis the story?" Johns asked.

Mann sat up and looked at Johns with renewed admiration. She had picked him as her right-hand-man for moments just like this, and he had not let her down.

"You're right. Davis got the story from Temple, and he must've gotten his information from Albany. Those good old boys are after my scalp again."

Johns nodded. "You know they want you out of there for just the reason you said. You let the outside world know the games they play. The media wouldn't know half of what goes on in private in Albany if you didn't leak the stories in the first place. You need to concentrate on striking back through the same channels they are using. First, through the Davises of the world, then through Temple, and finally through the good old boys themselves."

Mann smiled. "You are right, of course." She stood up, stretched her arms over her head and turned to face Johns. She knew, as most attractive women know, that Johns was watching her with more than passing interest. She leaned over, her brown hair falling to both sides of her face, and placed her hands on his shoulders. "Tork, I don't know what I would do without you."

A moment of silence passed as they looked directly at each other, then she stood up and walked purposefully back to her desk.

"We have some work to do."

Mann wasted no time in getting down to business. While Temple was preparing a speech for his son James's Eagle Scout Award dinner, Mann was meeting with her campaign staff to map out a course of action.

It was a warm June morning. As usual, the air-conditioner in Mann's State Tower Building office in Syracuse was not operating properly, so fans had been brought in to move the air around.

In addition to Mann, Tork Johns, Annie Wilson, her secretary; Joel Samuels, her campaign manager; Ed Labsby, a carpenter's union leader from Rome; and Patsey McCarthy, a Syracuse city ward leader, were present to discuss strategy.

Mann opened the meeting.

"You all heard the reports on my container bill vote and Temple's labeling me as an anti-environmentalist. I need to come away from here today with a plan of attack that will carry me through to election day. I'd like to spend an hour or so brainstorming ideas and then have us zero in on a specific plan. No idea is too bizarre so let your imaginations go for a while."

They all laughed.

168

"What's Temple's weakness?" McCarthy asked.

"We haven't spent a lot of time on that because we really don't think he'll be much of a match." Johns said.

"I'd re-think that." McCarthy smiled. "This guy hasn't done much in politics, but he's been around, and he's well known. You should always know your opponent and never underestimate him."

"I agree. Let's get as much on Temple as we can," Mann directed.

"Unions don't know him. But he looks like another up-tight asshole to me," Labsby laughed. "Sucker him into a debate in a union hall, get the press out, and finish him off."

"What about women's issues. Abortion. Where does he stand on abortion? That could be his weakness. If it is, get Alice Kennedy at the League to set up a debate and do your usual number on him there." McCarthy looked at Samuels. "What do you think?"

Samuels leaned back in his chair. "It all sounds good to me, but I think we should do a two step approach. First, get our Senator out in the public in every way possible without any acknowledgement of Mr. Temple's existence. Just as we have been doing. If he starts to make a credible run then we debate and knock him off.

"Right now he doesn't have a pot to piss in. His ad money will be gone by the end of the month, and he'll struggle just like the last two did to get any press.

"Phase two is to have everything in place to blow him out of the water if he does make a run. Quick and decisive! Four debates, each in our strongholds and he's history." Samuels made it sound easy.

"What if he doesn't accept our debate locations?" Johns wasn't sure about this strategy.

"What choice will he have. Laura Ann is the Senator. He's got to come to her if he wants to be in the game."

Three hours later, the group had hammered out a plan that they hoped would take them to an election victory in the fall.

* * *

June 11th was a big day at the Temple home. Temple had put the campaign on hold for a day while the family gathered for James Temple's Eagle Scout Dinner that evening.

Temple drove to the airport in the morning to pick up his mother and father. They had flown in to see their grandson receive his award.

Less than one percent of all scouts receive the Eagle Award and grandpa was particularly proud to have a grandson follow in his own footsteps to receive this honor. He had brought a special gift for his grandson on this occasion, his own Eagle Scout Badge which he had earned fifty-six years earlier.

Pat Temple had planned a big party for relatives and friends. Her specialty was dessert, and for this occasion she had baked a sheet cake with a camping scene and the Eagle Badge inset with frosting. Jay was to be the featured speaker at the ceremony.

At six-thirty that evening, John Hauley, the Scoutmaster of Troop 56, called the meeting to order. Following the presentation of the colors, scout oath, and pledge, he introduced Temple to the scouts, scout committee, and parents in the room.

"Tonight we have two honors. First and foremost, the presentation of an Eagle Scout Award to James Temple, a young man who has earned his award at a very young age with a lot of hard work.

"The second honor is having his dad as our speaker for the evening. In addition to having been a scout and serving on our troop committee, Jay Temple is currently running for the New York State Senate. Jay told me that he has taken the night off from politics to enjoy his son's ceremony, but I thought I'd throw in the plug anyway."

The audience gave a polite laugh.

"So, without further ado, Jay Temple."

There was mild applause as Jay stepped up onto the stage and looked out, first at the parents and committee people, then

170

at the scouts sitting in the front of the room, and then at his own son.

"There is no experience that I know of that prepares a boy for life better than being a boy scout. Tonight, we are here to recognize a great achievement by a young man who is very special to me. But we are also here tonight to recognize all scouts and those who work with them in their scouting activities.

"I'd like to say a special thank you to John Hauley. John spends countless hours working with our sons and giving them the opportunity to have a great scouting experience."

There was a good round of applause as the Scoutmaster acknowledged the tribute.

"Fifty-six years ago at the age of fourteen, James' grandfather earned the Eagle Scout Award. Tonight, he is here to share in this very proud moment with my son. My mother, my wife, Pat, and James's sister, Amy, and his brother, Tyler, are also here tonight for this important occasion.

"To become an Eagle Scout, James had to sacrifice time with his own friends. I am sure there were times when he would rather have been out playing ball or going to a movie, but he didn't. He worked hard, learned many new things and met many different people as he earned twenty-two merit badges and completed his scout project.

"I asked him the other night what badge he felt that he got the most out of? He said it wasn't the badges, it was the people he had met that meant the most to him. Pretty good observation from a fifteen year old young man.

"For his Eagle project, James decided that he would conduct a clothing drive for a poor parish on the south side of Syracuse. He organized the drive at his school, collected two truck loads of clothing with the help of classmates, and delivered the clothing to the parish. Last week, the parish priest called on James to thank him for the effort and to tell him how much the parish appreciated his efforts.

"This is scouting at its finest. Helping others and providing community service. I think you'll find throughout life

171

that you'll be happier and feel more satisfied with yourself if you give to others.

"Scouting also provides many opportunities for you beyond your days as a boy scout. When I was in the army, at the end of our first week of basic training, the company commander lined up all two hundred and fifty trainees outside our barracks.

"He said 'All trainees who have been boy scouts take one step forward.' About seventy soldiers stepped forward. He then said 'All who achieved the rank of First Class or higher take another step forward.' This time about fifteen men stepped forward.

"The company commander repeated this procedure for Star, Life, and Eagle. There was one Eagle Scout. The Eagle Scout became the company commander for the trainees, the Life and Star scouts became the platoon leaders for the trainees. It was an experience I will never forget. It shows the importance people place on the things that you learn as a scout.

"A friend of mine is in the admissions office at NYU. He told me once that if they see that an applicant for admission to NYU has his Eagle Award, they will automatically accept his application. I asked why, and he said that it shows that the applicant has 'stick-to-it-ivness!' That the individual is willing to put in that extra effort to succeed. And that's what they are looking for in their students."

Looking at the boy scouts seated in front of him, Temple went on.

"So, boys, stay in scouting. Follow the trail of the Eagle and enjoy the great experiences that scouting has to offer to you.

"I want to thank Mr. Hauley for inviting me to say a few words tonight. I also want to be the first person to congratulate my son on his becoming an Eagle Scout. Great going, James!"

The applause was heartfelt as everyone could appreciate what Temple had to say and what he was feeling at this moment.

James T. Temple received his Eagle Badge from his mother and father during the official ceremony and then was given a second badge by his grandfather. He would take both badges home and frame them side by side. June 11th had been a proud day for him.

* * *

On June 12th, the polls by the NYSSRC were completed. The results surprised everyone, not the least of whom, was Senator Gabe Valli. His Rochester Senate candidate was struggling and his Westchester Senate candidate was barely ahead of the Democratic opponent. But the biggest surprise was the jump in the polls by Temple. Barely at 9% in an earlier poll, Temple was now at 28% and that number appeared to be holding.

Valli called Toby Hagan, his computer whiz and pollster, into his Senate office.

"What the hell is going on out there?" Valli held up the poll results.

"Belafonte was given twenty-five thousand and blew it all. For what? To run even with some bean counter just out of school? And DiFachio! The Great White Hope! Thirty-thousand for him and he still can't pull away from Miss Goody-two-shoes.

"I give fifteen thousand to a nobody lawyer in Syracuse who is running against the toughest broad in the state and in one month he has jumped nineteen percentage points. Who'd believe this?" Valli looked at Hagan for an answer.

"I know, boss. But it's accurate. We ran the program twice and got the same answers. In Temple's case, we actually did two separate polls. One thousand phone contacts. Twenty-eight percent is correct." Hagan was nervous. He knew Valli would hang him out to dry if he screwed up.

Valli looked at Hagan long and hard. "Okay. I want you to go to Syracuse and meet with Temple and his staff. Ask around and find out first hand what gives. Then come back and let me know.

"I'm going to get Ophidia in here and ask him to beef up Belafonte and DiFachio."

Hagan returned to his office and called Cordis.

"Ted, this is Toby Hagan."

"Hello. How are things in Albany?"

"Better than you know."

"The polls are finally in?"

"Yes. Jay Temple is in play." Hagan smiled to himself at his knowledge of political metaphors.

"In play?" Cordis asked.

"Yes. He came in at twenty-eight per cent. A nineteen point jump in one month."

"Great! He's working the district."

"Yeah. It shows. I've been asked by Senator Valli to go to Syracuse to get a sense of your plans from here on out. If it looks good, I think you can count on some more money from the NYSSRC."

"Well, we can always use more money. When do you want to come in?"

"Tomorrow."

"Tomorrow! That's pretty short notice."

"I'm only going to observe and report. You don't need to change any plans or schedules."

"No, that's all right. We can meet with you right after our staff meeting."

"What time is your staff meeting?"

"Eight o'clock in the morning."

"I'll be there."

"At eight?"

"Yes. This is the type of thing I need to see if we are going to invest in Temple's campaign."

As soon as Cordis finished his call from Hagan he called Berry. The two men quickly developed a game plan for Hagan's visit and began calling other members of the campaign team to insure their presence at the eight o'clock meeting.

Cordis caught up to Temple at a Garden Club luncheon

174

in downtown Syracuse. He gave Temple the news on the poll and filled him in on the plans for tomorrow's meeting with Hagan.

Temple began to appreciate Cordis's ability to run the office side of the campaign. It sounded like quite a show was being planned for Hagan.

Toby Hagan arrived at Hancock Airport at 7:20 in the morning. The airport was busy with the rush of morning travelers, and as he went through the turnstile he heard someone call out his name.

Hagan turned to see Ted Cordis and Mary Tarkings coming toward him.

"Hi, Toby. Welcome to Temple country!" Cordis laughed. "This is Mary Tarkings. Mary this is Toby Hagan."

Tarkings and Hagan shook hands as Hagan asked, "Are you part of the campaign?"

"Yes. I am the volunteer coordinator for Onondaga County."

"Great! How are the volunteer efforts going?"

"Our biggest problem right now is keeping everyone busy. We have over 350 volunteers."

"Really?"

"Yes. A lot of young people are just getting interested in politics because of Temple. We also have a lot of his personal friends volunteering. Are you going to be here for the day?"

"Yeah. My flight back is at eight–thirty tonight."

Mary smiled. "You'll see some of our activities at headquarters later on then."

Mary Tarkings was a smart, good–looking brunette. She had worked with Cordis both in business and with the Young Republicans. Cordis had filled her in on the importance of impressing Toby Hagan during their drive to the airport. Cordis figured that if anyone could impress Hagan, Mary could. He was right.

Cordis interrupted Hagan's appraisal of Tarkings. "Do you have any baggage?"

175

"No, just my briefcase."

"Okay. My car is just outside the terminal. We'll have to move along in order to get to the meeting on time."

On the ride from the airport to Temple's headquarters, Cordis and Tarkings filled Hagan in on the day's events and the schedule that they had worked out for him. Hagan was impressed.

Cordis pulled his 1989 black Caprice up in front of the campaign headquarters. He always enjoyed the impression that the headquarters made on first-time visitors.

Hagan climbed out of the car and stood staring at the building. "This whole building yours?" he asked.

"Yes, sir!" Cordis smiled. "C'mon in and I'll give you a quick tour. We have five minutes before the staff meeting."

As they entered the building, Laney Gardiner and Dave Yondle came over to them to say hello. Cordis handled the introductions.

"Toby, this is Laney Gardiner, our campaign office manager, and Dave Yondle, our fund raising manager. Laney, Dave, this is Toby Hagan. Toby is with the State Senate Republican Campaign Committee."

"I'm pleased to meet both of you. One of the requirements for working on Temple's campaign must be good looks!" Hagan laughed.

Cordis showed Hagan the setup for the headquarters. As they went through the front of the building, there was a set that resembled a living room complete with couch, coffee table, leisure chairs, and end tables and lamps. Cordis explained that this was where Temple met with the press to have informal news conferences.

Further back in the building, twelve foot long tables were set up with folding chairs for doing assembly work on mailers and door-to-door packages.

Toward the back of the finished space were fifteen desks and phones. These were used for phone banks and for the staff when they were working at headquarters.

176

Behind a side wall were three partitioned rooms. Cordis had his office in the back corner of the building. Temple's office was next to Cordis' and opened into a conference room, where staff meetings were held. Hagan noticed that all rooms were well furnished and functional.

Cordis took Hagan through a set of double doors in the rear of the finished area and into a huge warehouse area. As planned, Larry Malcolm, Patrick Fitzgerald, Mary Price, Kerry Heathrow, and Ira Sterling were all painting billboards for use in the campaign.

Cordis introduced each of the campaign team to Hagan and then led him back to the conference room where the staff meeting was about to take place.

The meeting lasted about two hours and covered, in detail, the different aspects of the campaign, where they had been and where they needed to go.

Kevin Roth reviewed the finances indicating that there was on hand seventeen thousand dollars after all bills incurred to date had been paid.

Dr. Carey reported that the Onondaga Medical Society would be making a five thousand dollar contribution to the campaign and that Dr. Merano had agreed to host a medical fund raiser at his home in Cazenovia.

Ken Mathews reported that PAC contributions were about to be solicited, and Bob Berry passed out the solicitation kit that he proposed be used for that purpose.

Tarkings gave a report on volunteer assignments, Gardiner reported on the candidate's upcoming schedule, and Rick Handon reported on the county committee's work on the campaign.

Cordis then turned to Hagan. "Toby, you have been very patient with us. Do you have any questions?"

"Yeah, one. Where do I sign up?"

Following the staff meeting, Hagan met with Mathews, Berry, and Cordis to discuss the financial needs of the campaign.

"I need to know what you think you'll need from now

177

until November," Hagan said.

Mathews took the lead. "I think it is important that you first understand that we have a winner here. Jay Temple can beat Laura Ann Mann!"

Hagan saw in Mathews' eyes, that this was more than just a pitch. Mathews believed in what he was saying.

Mathews went on. "I've worked on a number of campaigns. Most recently, the County Executive's race, and before that, the Congressional race. This race is different. There is a purpose here that people are responding to.

"The guy is sincere and he comes across that way. We just need the dollars to get his message out there."

Hagan shifted uncomfortably. "What is his purpose?"

"Change. A more responsive government. A less expensive government."

"You think the State Senate needs to be more responsive and less expensive?"

"Jay Temple thinks so. And I and a lot of other business people agree with him. The State Senate can be in the lead in making these changes happen. That's why we are all working so hard for Temple.

"Republicans have an opportunity here to make a statement. We should be the party of lower taxes, less government spending, and for creating a strong business economy. That's Temple's message and that should be the party's message too."

Hagan listened to Mathews and wondered how Valli and the others would react to all this. 'Pretty idealist stuff,' he thought to himself. It would be different.

"What's the cost?" Hagan went back to his original question.

Berry answered, "One hundred thousand. That'll buy the air time we need, radio spots, and limited newspaper advertising."

"A hundred thousand! Some of our veteran Senators won't raise that much."

178

"They're not running against Laura Ann Mann," Berry smiled. "You know as well as I do that she'd chew up most of your senators if they had to run against her.

"I heard that Senator Lansing and Senator Fuller made a special effort in the redistricting to keep her out of their districts. Lansing is supposed to be unbeatable and yet he doesn't want any part of Mann."

Hagan knew that Berry was right. "That brings up a good point. You should solicit all the Republican incumbent Senators for contributions from their war chests to help Temple. As you have said, Lansing and Fuller at least have a vested interest in her losing."

Cordis said, "It's as good as done."

Mathews asked, "What can we expect from NYSSRC?"

"I think you will get help. A hundred thousand? Not yet. They'll want to see what you can raise on your own. I can tell you this. You keep doing well in the polls and the money will continue to flow from Albany. Your boy has moved into play. That means we're watching him, and that is good news for you."

Berry took the opportunity to put in for his next round of TV spots. "Toby, we can make a big buy in July and August in the local market for a really low price. Prime time is cheap because of low viewership during vacation time. This would be a smart move."

"How much?"

"Twenty-seven thousand."

"How much do you have toward this?"

"A couple thousand."

"I'll see what I can do. Can you put a hold on the time?"

"I already have," Berry laughed. He always put holds on when he knew that the money would be found one way or another. He knew Temple was going to be a lucrative candidate for his agency.

Tarkings came into the room. "I hate to break this up,

but if Mr. Hagan is going to catch up with Jay, I've got to take him now."

"Thank you, Mary. Five more minutes with these guys and the NYSSRC will be broke." Hagan shook hands with everyone and left with Tarkings.

Tarkings and Hagan left the Headquarters in her Celebrity.

"Everyone in this campaign drive Chevys?" Hagan asked.

"No. Jay has an MG and a Dodge Van."

"I was just kidding, Mary. Tell me. What makes you think that Jay can win this race?"

Tarkings smiled. "He's for real."

"For real?"

"Absolutely. You haven't seen him out there. With the people. He really wants to do something for them. He's a good guy. We need a hundred more like him in government, but at least he's a start."

Hagan was impressed. "What do you do when you are not working on a Senate campaign?"

"I'm a CPA. Used to work at C & L. Now, I work for Ted Cordis."

"Are you part of the Young Republican group that Cordis brought to this campaign?"

"Vice President!" Tarkings beamed.

"How many others are working on this campaign?"

"All of us. Twenty-seven in all."

"Is this a project for all of you?"

"Well, to be honest it started out as sort of a project. We felt that working on one campaign would give us more of an impact. But as we got to know Jay, it's become more than that."

"Yeah, you told me. He's a good guy. But can he win? If not, all your work is for nothing."

Tarkings almost drove off the road. "For nothing? You don't get it, do you?

"Jay is going to win. But even if he doesn't win this

time, he will the next time. In the meantime, we are getting the message out. We are making a difference. Someday the voters in this state will wake up to the fact that our biggest problem is big government. And do you know why they will wake up? Because people like us are out there working for change. No, Mr. Hagan. All our work won't be for nothing!"

Hagan liked Mary Tarkings and didn't mean to come across the way that he had. "I'm sorry. I'm afraid I didn't say that well. I just meant that it is tough to win your first race, especially against a politician like Mann. I'd hate to see all of you disillusioned with the system. We do need young people."

Tarkings glanced at Hagan. She sensed this was his peace offering, and she accepted it. "We'll be okay. Besides, Jay will beat Mann, and when he does, politicians will take notice."

"We agree on that. If he beats Mann, he has a clear road to the Governor's mansion."

"Don't think he won't take it!"

This time it was Hagan who glanced over at Tarkings.

Tarkings and Hagan caught up with Temple at a day care center on the south side of the City of Syracuse. It was a mixed population of preschoolers. Some two hundred children with ten teachers, six aides, and one administrator crammed into a former single family residence.

The children were scantily clothed with well worn T-shirts, shorts, and sneakers. Some were barefoot. They stared at the strangers with a mixture of fear and curiosity.

Temple sensed the children's thoughts. As he talked with the school's administrator he took off his tie and jacket, laid it over a chair, rolled up his sleeves, and began his tour of the facility. Hagan and Tarkings watched from a distance.

A group of five–year–old girls sat in a small circle, watching Temple approach them. He sat down next to one of the girls who was clutching a well–patched Raggedy Ann.

"Hi."

The little girl hugged the doll more tightly.

"Who is this?" Temple asked.

"My baby."

"Does she have a name?"

"Yes, but she's sad."

"Why?"

"She has no daddy." The little girl sighed. "Only a mommy."

"Well, she's lucky she has a mommy. I'll bet her mommy really loves her."

The little girl suddenly looked up at Temple. "Why?"

"Because she takes care of her all by herself," Temple smiled.

The little girl thought about this for a moment then smiled at Temple. "She does love me."

Temple patted the little girl on the head and then moved on.

When the tour of the facility was completed, Temple walked over to Hagan and Tarkings. They had been talking with some of the teachers.

One of the teachers looked up at Temple and said, "Mr. Temple, you are a nice man."

"Thanks, but you're the one that deserves the praise. You and everyone else working here. These children have a lot of needs beyond the obvious physical needs. You are doing a great job in meeting those needs. I hope that I'll be able to help you."

The teacher smiled. "God willing, you will."

Hagan said to Temple on the way out of the school. "What would you do for that little girl?"

Temple knew who he meant. "Find the father and get him a job."

"I don't understand."

"I asked her teacher about her. Her mother works in a laundry. She qualifies for welfare as long as there is no father around. The father has no job so he makes himself scarce. He collects unemployment. The system encourages all this, and it's wrong."

As they walked out to the cars, Tarkings poked Hagan's arm. "Good guy."

"Where to now, Jay?" Hagan asked.

"Rotary meeting at Drumlins. You'll be my guest."

"A free lunch!"

"Toby, you know there is no such thing as a free lunch," Temple laughed along with the other two.

Tarkings drove back to campaign headquarters while Hagan and Temple went on to Drumlins.

Drumlins was a country club owned and operated by Syracuse University. It boasted two eighteen hole golf courses, an Olympic sized swimming pool, a driving range, indoor and outdoor tennis courts, several meeting rooms, and two ballrooms.

A number of service clubs held their meetings at Drumlins, including Rotary.

As a former club president and a former district governor of Rotary, Jay Temple was well known in Rotary circles. He had been both the youngest club president and the youngest district governor to serve in either capacity.

"Jay, welcome to Syracuse Rotary." Rotary Clubs always had a greeter at the door and Sam Tyler was this week's official welcome person.

"Hi, Sam. I'd like you to meet my guest Toby Hagan. Toby, this is Sam Tyler."

Hagan and Tyler shook hands while Temple signed the guest book.

Once inside the meeting room, there was a constant stream of well wishers coming over to Temple with words of encouragement for his campaign.

The meeting was called to order, and following the pledge of allegiance and prayer, the club president called on Sam Tyler to read the list of visitors and guests.

"We have visiting with us today our good friend, fellow Rotarian, and past district governor, Jay Temple. As a Democrat, I think I can take some liberties and also mention that

Jay is a candidate for a certain political office in New York State. Good luck, Jay."

Temple stood to acknowledge the introduction and thank Tyler for his good wishes.

Hagan asked Temple why Tyler didn't just introduce him as the Republican candidate for the New York State Senate.

"Rotary is a nonpartisan organization. It doesn't get involved as an organization in political campaigns."

"Does that mean none of these people will be working on your campaign?"

"Not at all. In fact many of these people have already given me financial support and several are actively working as volunteers."

Hagan noted the enthusiastic applause Temple received after his introduction. Throughout the meeting, people continued to come over to Temple's table offering help and wishing him good luck.

After the meeting, Temple and Hagan spent about an hour reviewing what each expected of the other. It was clear that Senator Valli would be calling the shots on any and all financial help from the NYSSRC. It was also clear that the Belafonte and DiFachio races had higher priority than Temple's at this point in mid–June. Temple took some solace in the fact that Hagan appeared to like what he saw and promised to be an advocate for support of Temple's campaign.

"If you ever beat Mann," Hagan paused as he thought about the possibility, "that would be unbelievable! You know, they don't really think that it can be done. It's not you; it's her. She intimidates all of them. She doesn't play the game. She's a loose cannon even in her own party."

"I've heard that. I have been invited to an end–of–session party in Albany next week. I'm told she has been invited every year for the last six years and has yet to make an appearance."

"That's true. How did you get invited to that?"

"The minority leader in the Senate went to law school

184

with me. He and our host thought it would be a great gag to have the 48th District represented by someone other than Senator Mann. I thought it would be a nice occasion to meet my future associates."

"Politics takes some strange twists and turns," Hagan said as he thought about this Republican candidate having the blessing of the Democratic leader for an invitation to the end-of-session party.

Hagan had an appointment with Senator Lansing and his staff at 4:00 p.m. Patrick Fitzgerald was assigned to act as Hagan's driver and drove Hagan to Lansing's office at the appointed hour.

"Hi, Toby. How has your day gone?" Lansing smiled as he shook hands with Hagan.

"Great. I don't know how you politicians keep up the schedules you do. I am already done in and Temple's back on the road again in Madison County."

"What's he doing there?"

"He has a meeting with some potential volunteers. I guess he's trying to build separate volunteer centers in each of the three counties that he is running in."

"Thank God I only have Onondaga County!"

"Yeah. There are some benefits to having seniority. Gabe wants to know what your thoughts are about Temple's campaign."

Lansing thought for a moment and then said, "Temple's a nice enough guy, but Mann's too tough for him to win. He's new at the game, and she's a seasoned veteran. The Democratic machine in the 17th Ward in Syracuse and the farmers in Madison County will put her over the top again as they have in every other race."

"Gabe wants to know if money would make a difference."

"May shave a few points but not enough to count for anything. He might better spend it elsewhere where we have a chance to win."

185

"Our polls show a big jump to Temple."

"Yeah. I've seen the polls. But he's out there hustling, and she hasn't even begun yet. Labor Day is the real kick off. Temple may burn out by then. In any event, she'll pour it on after Labor Day and leave Temple far behind."

"Last question. Will you be giving to Temple's campaign? It would look good if nothing else."

"Hey, I have a campaign too. Even if I'm unopposed, I need to let people in my district know that I'm out there working for them. In this business if you slack off, first thing you know a young 'Mann' comes along and you're history."

"Well, thank you. Senator. I'll let Gabe know your thoughts when I get back to Albany."

"Fine. Tell him I'd be happy to sit down with him anytime and give him the benefits of my thinking personally."

"I will."

Hagan and Fitzgerald returned to Temple's headquarters just as Gerald Blakesley walked in. Blakesley was a reporter for the Syracuse Gazette and spent most of his time in Albany. He knew Hagan and had a good idea why the Albany pollster was at Temple headquarters.

"Good afternoon, Mr. Hagan," Blakesley said as he pulled out an old pad and pencil. "What brings the king maker to Syracuse?"

Hagan smiled at Blakesley even though this meeting was not what he would have wanted right now. "Just delivering some good news."

"What might that be?" Blakesley inquired as he jotted down some notes.

"Jay Temple has jumped nineteen percent in our recent polls. That's a major move in one month's time."

"Yes, it is. Does that mean that the State Senate Republican Campaign Committee is going to help Mr. Temple in his race against Senator Mann?" Blakesley studied Hagan for his body language as well for what he was about to say.

Hagan shifted nervously, "We help all our Republican

186

candidates, incumbents, and first–timers. You know that, Gerry."

"Does that mean financial help?"

"I don't make those decisions."

"Who does?"

"A committee reviews all the races and then determines what kind of help will be given."

"Is it fair to say that Mr. Temple is being considered for some assistance because of the recent poll results?"

"Yeah. I think it's fair to say that."

"Thank you, Mr. Hagan." Blakesley folded his pad and carefully put both pad and pencil back into his coat pocket. He nodded at Fitzgerald and then turned and walked slowly out of the campaign headquarters.

Hagan turned to Fitzgerald. "Do you read his column?"

"Yes, I do."

"Get me a copy of the next one, will you?"

"Sure."

Cordis and Temple arrived a short time later. They were excited about the meeting with volunteers in Madison County and shared the good news with their headquarter's staff.

Laney Gardiner took the list of names and addresses and began the task of getting follow–up letters out from Temple.

Dave Yondle had been talking with Hagan and Fitzgerald. He, too, had some well–timed good news. Three more fund raising parties had been set up with friends of Temple. Two would be in private homes and one at a local restaurant.

Temple suggested that they go next door to the diner for a quick bite to eat before Hagan headed back to the airport.

Accompanied by Tarkings, Gardiner, Cordis, Fitzgerald, and Yondle, Hagan and Temple walked next door to the Erie Diner. Kevin Roth drove up just in time to join the group along with Dr. Carey. It was an enthusiastic gathering for midway in an uphill political campaign.

Nellie Blyth, the hostess at the diner saw Temple and his

entourage enter and joked with the candidate that 'he was buying votes again.'

"Best way to a voters' heart is through his stomach," Temple responded.

"Yeah, but not at this greasy spoon!" Cordis added.

"No food for you tonight, Mr. Cordis!" Nellie shot back as she led them to a special table in the corner of the restaurant.

The food was plentiful and good. Hagan enjoyed himself. He knew that tomorrow's report would be positive and he half-believed that this newcomer to State politics could pull off the BIG win. If he did, he'd be a bright star on the horizon. Hagan thought that he wouldn't mind being a part of that.

Hagan was winging his way back to Albany as Temple sat back in his office chair and stared at the sunset through the campaign headquarter's window.

Cordis walked in and sat down in a side chair next to Temple's desk.

"Nice job today, Ted. I think you got Hagan on our side."

"Thanks. I hope so. I don't feel comfortable with the Albany crowd. For the most part, they're two-faced hacks who'll stab you in the back just as quickly as they can."

"Hey, hey! You are talking about my counterparts," Temple chided.

"You may become a State Senator, but you'll never be a part of that crew."

"Is that a compliment?"

"You better believe it."

Temple looked out the window again. A golden red glow filled the sky. Traffic on the highway was still heavy.

"Four and a half months to go. We still have a lot to do."

"I know. You regretting that you got into this?"

"No. I just wish there was more time. November isn't that far away, and there are so many people I haven't reached."

"You'll never get to them all. That's impossible."

"Right. But the trick is to get to enough. Just a plurality. That's what I am after."

"Well, we can't count on Lansing."

Temple turned to Cordis. "Why not?"

"Patrick talked with Hagan after his meeting with the Senator and got the impression that Hagan didn't get a very positive reaction from him."

"What did he say?"

"Patrick said it was more in what he didn't say. Hagan told him that he would have expected more from Lansing."

"It may be hard for him to share the Senate spotlight or even the thought of it."

"Could be. He is the State Senator for most people around here. Certainly on the Republican side. With Senator Hayes out of here and Senator Ahern beaten, Senator Lansing has been the top dog."

"What else did Patrick say?"

"He thinks Hagan is for you. They talked about what would happen if you win. Hagan seems to think that if you pull this off you could end up Governor."

"Then let's pull it off!" Temple laughed as the sun was setting.

Chapter XIV

Grass Roots

The Syracuse Gazette ran Blakesley's story under the caption:
'Mann To Face Senate Republican Machine.'
The story read:
The Senate Republican leader is again taking aim at Senator Laura Ann Mann, the Democratic incumbent in the 48th Senate District. Senator Mann beat Senator Marcus Ahern six years ago in a tireless door–to–door effort and has successfully defended her Senate seat in two successive races, marked by name calling and mud slinging by her Republican opponents. This time, the Republicans intend to buy the election by running wealthy business executive, Jay Temple, against the embattled Senator. Mr. Toby Hagan, director of the State Senate, was in Syracuse yesterday to meet with Temple's campaign committee. Hagan said, 'The NYSSRC is here to help our candidate.'
Mrs. Dahlia Thomas, director of the Democratic Fund for Senate Candidates said that the NYSSRC could throw as much as one hundred and fifty thousand dollars into the Mann - Temple race. When contacted by this reporter, Senator Mann said, 'The people in the 48th Senate District won't be bought by the NYSSRC.' Let's hope that she is right.

* * *

Temple found Cordis at Headquarters bright and early Saturday morning.

Waving the Syracuse Gazette in his hand, Cordis shouted, "Did you read this shit Blakesley wrote!"

Temple walked back to his office as Cordis followed. He walked around his desk and turned to Cordis. "I read it. The real question is what do we do about it?"

"Sue the damn paper."

"For what?"

"Misrepresentation, libel, slander, defamation, who cares. This is the most biased story I've ever read."

"You must not read the Gazette too often," Temple joked. "I went through all the same reactions that you did and concluded that going after the paper is just what someone wants us to do. No. We need to control the direction of the campaign. We don't want the Gazette, Blakesley, or anyone else dictating the direction we take."

"Yeah, you're right. But I'd like to stuff this paper right down Blakesley's throat."

"You'd have to stand in line." Temple felt the same way about the story but he had learned long ago that the most successful campaigns are the ones that stay focused. He knew that if he stood any chance at all of winning this race, he had to control the issues and the pace.

Temple looked out the window at the traffic on the highway. "All those people out there know where they are going. They'll get there too, unless something interferes with their travel. The trick is not to let anything interfere. No roadblocks, detours, or accidents." He looked back at Cordis, "Understand?"

"Yeah, no detours."

"Right. We need to get back in the news with something positive. Get Bob Berry on the phone. Tell him we'll get together this afternoon when we get back from Rome. Ask him

191

to think about a positive way to get back out front in the press.

"Also give Kevin and Doc Carey a call. See if they can join us for a little brainstorming session."

"Okay."

As Cordis walked out of his office, Yondle, Gardiner, Fitzgerald, and Mary Price walked in. They were laughing and ready to go with Temple to Rome for the day's campaigning.

"Hi, Senator! How's the 'people's candidate' doing today?"

"Better, now that you're all here. Guess none of you read the paper?"

Mary Price perked up. "I did."

"Did you read Blakesley's column?"

"Sure did. You must really have old Annie Mannie on the offense."

"I must be a little slow this morning. I don't understand."

"Hey, she owns the media. The newspapers and Blakesley love her. If they weren't worried about you, you wouldn't see the light of day in that paper. Annie's running scared."

"Well, that's a different way to look at it."

Yondle laughed. "I read it and I have to tell you, I like working for a wealthy business executive!"

Temple didn't know if they were putting him on or really reacting honestly to the article. He decided whichever it was, it was better to go out on the road in a good frame of mind than in a sour one, so he joined the group and they left for Rome.

Rome, New York, was a key city in the Temple campaign strategy. It was the largest populated center in Oneida County, one of three counties included in the 48th Senate District. It also represented almost sixteen percent of the total vote cast within the District. Temple knew that if he were going to offset the big vote that Mann had been getting in the City of Syracuse, he'd have to carry Rome big! Mann had carried Rome in the last two races.

Yondle was driving the van. "First stop, the Rome Police station. We are in trouble already."

Mary Price was coordinating the Rome effort. She had spent the past week there, meeting local Republicans and arranging for a day of meetings and campaigning for Temple.

Price turned to Temple as they pulled into the police station parking lot. "You and I are going to see Commissioner Frank Catallana. His wife heard your speech at the Oneida County Committee meeting and has volunteered to be your local contact."

"What's her name?"

"It's a toughie! Mary!"

"That makes three. Hope this one is better than the first two!"

Yondle groaned, "We better get out of this van. Those are fighting words!"

Yondle, Gardiner, and Fitzgerald were going to spend the morning handing out Temple brochures in downtown Rome while Mary Price and Temple met with the Commissioner and were taken around town for various meetings. They planned to meet at one o'clock at City Hall for a news conference.

Rome's Police Commissioner had one of the most unique offices Temple had ever seen. The police station itself was the standard brick two-story construction that is common in many communities. But that was not where the Commissioner was stationed.

In a corner of the parking lot, there was what appeared to be a concrete shed with a combination lock door. This shed actually enclosed a steel staircase that descended some thirty steps to an underground passageway. The passageway led to another steel door that opened into an underground bunker. Overhead cameras followed the progress of Temple, Price, and Officer Samuelson as the police officer led them to Commissioner Catallana's office.

Price summed up Temple's thoughts as they entered the bunker, "This is wild."

193

"It sure is."

A tall, heavily bearded man in a business suit stood up as they entered. "Jay Temple, our next Senator. I'm Frank Catallana, Commissioner of Safety, glad to have you here."

Catallana walked around a table littered with maps and reports to shake Temple's hand. "My wife thinks you're a cross between Sean Connery and Jack Kennedy."

"Are they both Republicans?" Everyone laughed.

Catallana looked at Price. "You must be Mary Price. My wife, Mary says you are a great lady."

Price, flustered, thanked the Commissioner.

Temple asked, "Why Commissioner of Safety?"

Catallana smiled through his beard. "Besides being Police Commissioner, I'm Commissioner of the Fire Department and the Water Department. As a matter of fact, we have a water main break on the north side that I have to visit before our first meeting. You ready to go?"

"Point the way."

Ten minutes later, they were at a huge hole in the center of an intersection. Catallana got out and immediately the work crew of twenty men looked up.

"How's it going, Harry?" Catallana said to one of the men who appeared to be supervising the work.

"It keeps caving in. I think we are going to need more wood."

"Get it," Catallana replied. He looked down into the fifteen foot deep hole at the five men working on a ruptured pipe. "What do you got?"

"One hell of an old pipe," Someone shouted.

Catallana nodded. He walked back to where Temple and Price were standing. "These guys have been working all night. I left them around two this morning. They thought they had it licked then, but it keeps giving way. The pipes are old. It's dangerous work."

They climbed back into the police car and headed to 'Tommy D's,' a restaurant and sports bar.

194

"I told my wife I was taking you to Tommy D's, and she thinks I'm nuts. Tommy is a Democratic Councilman. But he hates Mann. With Mary here I won't tell you what he calls her, but it's not very complimentary.

"Tommy controls a big union vote in Rome. He could be a good guy to have on your side. If he likes you."

"Should I wait in the car?" Mary asked.

"Nah. The boys appreciate an attractive young lady. This isn't a 'guys only' place anyway. I think you'll like it."

Tommy D's was located opposite a huge china factory and next to a railroad track. It was a long narrow building with a bar room in the front and meeting room in the back. Tommy D. was presiding over the bar as they entered.

"Nix it, guys, it's the cops!" he yelled out as Catallana, Temple and Price walked in.

"Hey. Hey, I bring in some paying customers and you treat me like this? We can take our business to good joint." Catallana waved a hand at Tommy and led Temple and Price to a table in the center of the bar room.

Someone at the next table yelled over, "Hey, Frank, who you like at Belmont today?"

Catallana yelled back without looking, "The Wild Irishman looks good if the track is dry."

"Eh, your wife's got you riding that one."

Catallana shrugged. Tommy came over to the table. "Who you got here?"

"Tommy, this is Jay Temple and Mary Price. This is Tommy D."

Temple stood to shake his hand while Mary said 'hello.'

"Good handshake. Teach Frank. What'll you have?"

"Coffee for me," Mary said.

"Same," Temple followed.

"Make it three and add a muffin to mine," Catallana finished.

Less than two minutes later, Tommy was back with the order and having placed it on the table, he sat down.

195

"So you're the guy that's running against Ms. Mann?"

"I'm the one."

"Hear you gave a pretty good speech to all those right-wing Republicans the other night. What do you say to us Democrats?"

"I say that you need jobs as much as any other New Yorker. I say that your kids need a good education too. I say that crime probably hits you as much as it does Republicans and probably more so because there are more Democrats in the cities than there are Republicans. And I say the 'Tommy D' has probably seen its taxes sky rocket in the last six years no thanks to our current State Senator." Temple took a drink from his coffee cup. "Not bad."

Tommy D laughed. "I was going to say the same thing. How can I help?"

Tommy D was to give Temple a lot of help. On Election Day, the union vote in Rome split. Fifty-one percent for Mann, forty-nine percent for Temple. It was the largest union vote for a Republican in Rome since Eisenhower ran in the Fifties.

Temple spent another hour with Tommy D and his Saturday regulars. Temple shared a passion with them called S.U. sports. A big fan himself, Temple found that Rome was a real Syracuse University sports city. They talked about the upcoming season and S.U.'s chances for the triple crown, Football, Basketball, and Lacrosse National Championships.

"It's do-able," Temple concluded for the group.

The patrol car turned up Black River Road and headed North.

"We're going to meet my wife and Sam Laguzzi at MacDonald's," Catallana said as he maneuvered in and out of traffic. "Sam knows everybody in Rome. He's our process server."

"Process server!" Temple said with surprise. "You think it makes sense for someone running for office to be campaigning with a process server?"

"Probably not, normally," Catallana laughed. "But

196

Sam's different. Everybody in Rome likes him. Besides, he's related to half of Rome."

"How so?" Temple asked.

"You'll find that a lot of the families in Rome go way back. Few of us ever leave. So over time, you develop a lot of aunts, uncles, and cousins."

As Price, Temple, and Catallana entered MacDonald's, an attractive redhead came over with a little man who could have been anyone's kindly old grandfather.

The redhead spoke first. "Hi, Mary. I see you've brought our next State Senator with you."

Price turned to Temple. "Jay, this is Mary Catallana. Mary, this is Jay Temple."

"I'm pleased to meet you," Temple said, taking her outstretched hand. "Mary tells me that you are going to give us a hand organizing Rome."

"Yeah, I'm looking forward to working with you. As a matter of fact, I've already recruited a co-chairman for Rome. Mr. Temple, I'd like to introduce Sam Laguzzi."

Temple walked around Mary Catallana to the kindly old man. "Mr. Laguzzi, I appreciate your volunteering to help out."

"Mr. Temple, the pleasure is mine. My wife is in St. Mary's hospital. If it weren't for you, she might not be alive. I know what you did to keep it open, and I want to help you as you have helped me."

"Anyone would have done the same thing given the opportunity."

"No. Excuse me but you're wrong. Nobody in Albany was going to help Rome. It was all politics. But you came as a stranger to our city and you helped. Now we should help you."

Frank Catallana interrupted. "Let's sit down and get a quick burger while we talk. I gotta get Jay back to City Hall by quarter to one."

Over lunch Temple gained a lasting respect for Sam LaGuzzi. At eighty years old, he was still full of life. His

197

enthusiasm was contagious, and he seemed really committed to Temple and his efforts to become the next State Senator for Rome.

As Temple and his small group got up to leave, LaGuzzi stepped in front of Temple. With a tilt of his head that became very familiar as the campaign went on, he looked Temple directly in the eye and said, "Mr. Temple, I promise you that Rome will support you."

There was something in his look and his composure that told Temple that Sam LaGuzzi believed this.

"Well, Sam, if I have ten more people like you, the entire state would be mine! Thanks."

The two men shook hands, and it was off to City Hall.

Back at the police station, Catallana said goodbye to Temple and Price. He had to get back to the watermain break. His parting advice was to spend as much time in Rome as possible. Temple wished he had begun this campaign a year earlier.

Yondle, Gardiner, and Fitzgerald caught up with Price and Temple at City Hall. Bob Berry and Ted Cordis had arrived earlier to set up the podium, check the microphones, and direct the media to the appropriate location.

Some local residents had gathered to watch all the activity and the Mayor and his assistant Allan Gant were on hand as well.

Temple walked over to Berry. "Are we all set for this afternoon?"

Berry was bursting at the seams. "Better than that! You wanted some positive spin?" He looked past Jay toward the parking lot of City Hall. "Look over there."

Temple turned to see Terry Davis getting out of Channel 7's news van.

Berry went on, "Channel 4 said they'd be here, and we already have four radio stations – one from Rome, one from Oneida, one from Utica, and one from Syracuse. You should get some positive media today with this coverage."

"Nice job, Bob. I think we should still meet after this is over. Did you drive over with Ted?"

"Yeah but in my car."

"Any objections to having Dave take your car back to Syracuse and you and Ted going back in the van? We can talk then."

"Sounds okay to me. Ted said that you have Kevin and a couple of others coming later on?"

"Yes, I do. But we need to do some planning, and this will give us some added time."

"Fine."

Tony Eiles saw all the media people, whispered something to Allan Gant, and walked over to Temple.

"Hi, Jay!"

"Hello, Tony. I'm glad you could be here."

"Well, that's why I wanted to talk to you. I'm here to help you all the way, but I've got to pick up my mother-in-law at the airport in Syracuse, so I can't stay for the news conference. But I did want to wish you luck. Allan is going to stay, so he can fill me in."

Temple suspected from all that he heard that Tony Eiles didn't want to be too closely associated with Temple's race against Mann. Rumors abound in politics and one was that Eiles and Mann were close friends. In any event, Eiles was a politician and wanted to be on good terms with the winning side.

"That's too bad that you can't stay," Temple said, then as an afterthought, for his own amusement Temple added, "I was going to include you in the news conference."

Eiles flinched. "No, no. This is your party. I wouldn't want to take anything away from it." He smiled a quick smile, wished Temple good luck and left the City Hall Promenade.

Cordis came up to Temple. "Where's the Mayor going?"

Temple gave a last look at the retreating Mayor and said, "It got too hot in the kitchen so the Mayor decided to get out!"

"Truman?" Cordis asked.

"There's hope for you, Mr. Cordis." Temple clapped Cordis on the back and they walked over to the small gathering of press.

Temple began, "Cities across this country, across this state, and right here in Central New York have great needs. But cities are people. So when we talk about needs we are really talking about people's needs.

"This morning, I had an opportunity to tour Rome, talk to some of the people here, and hear first hand what they were thinking about. Jobs and taxes are at the top of the list.

"Those without jobs want to work. Those with jobs are in fear of losing them. Both agree that the business climate in New York is the main reason for their concerns. Everyone I talk with agrees that taxes are too high.

"Next on the list of needs is education. Parents want their kids to get a good education. For Rome that means a new high school to alleviate the overcrowded conditions.

"Crime in the streets is another major concern. More police, better street lighting and tougher courts are some of the suggested solutions.

"Finally, the city's infrastructure. This morning I saw men working in a fifteen foot deep hole with water up to their knees and the earthen walls caving in as they dug. These men were risking their lives to repair an old watermain whose pipes couldn't hold the seal they were putting on it. Cities need to develop a plan along with state and federal help to begin to rebuild the infrastructure that services the people in our communities.

"You'll raise the question, how can you talk about reducing taxes and spending while at the same time pointing to so many needs? A good question. The answer lies in prioritizing needs and matching those needs with available revenue.

"You do it in your homes, we do it in business, but for some reason government fails to do this.

"The philosophy of government is to spend and then find

200

the money. I don't think we can afford that kind of mentality in government. I think that there are a lot of people out there who will agree with me."

Temple gave the media what they wanted, a lot of out-takes and something different to report. Channel 7 gave a complete list of the concerns Temple had pointed to for cities in the district and picked up with his statements on prioritizing in the home and business but not in government. A lot of viewers nodded in agreement as they watched the evening news.

Cordis was behind the wheel of the van as they left City Hall. Gardiner and Berry were in the back with Temple. Price and Fitzgerald had taken Berry's car with Yondle.

Temple looked up at Cordis in the front and said, "We need to take a quick trip to the hospital."

Cordis glanced in the rear view mirror. "You sick?"

"No. I want to visit Sam LaGuzzi's wife."

"Who is Sam LaGuzzi?" Cordis asked.

"He's my secret weapon in Rome. A real nice old man, but I think his wife is not doing too well."

Cordis found the hospital and waited outside while Temple went in. The receptionist recognized Temple. "Mr. Temple. This is a surprise. I'd like to say thank you for all the help you gave to the hospital."

"My pleasure. It's needed here in Rome. Could you tell me what room Mrs. Sam LaGuzzi is in?"

"Sure. Room 212. Take the elevator to the second floor, and it's half way down the hall on the right."

"Thanks." Temple was amazed that the receptionist knew the room without looking at any charts. As he thought about this he laughed to himself and concluded that she must be a 'cousin.'

When Temple arrived at Room 212, he found Sam, a woman who turned out to be Sam's daughter and a nurse with Mrs. LaGuzzi.

"I hope I'm not intruding," Temple said as he walked into the room.

LaGuzzi was on his feet with a big smile. "Mr. Temple, you didn't have to do this. This is an honor."

"I wanted to meet the woman behind Mr. Energy!" Temple walked over to Mrs. LaGuzzi's bedside. Sam's wife was an attractive elderly woman in her mid-seventies. Temple noticed her hair was perfectly done and her makeup had also been expertly applied. Only her eyes gave any indication that she was in pain.

Sam walked to the other side of his wife's bed and leaned over putting a gentle hand on her shoulder. His wife lifted a weak hand to cover his.

"Honey, this is Mr. Temple, the fellow I was telling you about." He looked up with his head cocked to one side. "Mr. Temple this is my wife, Maria LaGuzzi."

"Hi, Maria. I kind of expected to find a pretty woman in this bed. I thought Sam had great taste, and I was right."

Maria LaGuzzi blushed. "Thank you for the nice words but I'm afraid I don't look very good like this."

Sam and Temple both said at the same time, "You look great!"

Turning to his daughter, Sam walked over and took her hand and guided her around the bed to where Temple was standing. "This is my little girl, Elaina."

Elaina was in her early fifties and a younger version of her mother. She had dark hair, dark brown eyes, and a quick smile that would win any father's heart. "Dad thinks you're great, Mr. Temple."

"Well, I think he is too. It's nice to see the people that keep your Dad so full of life. I can see there is a lot of love in your family. That's something that can't be replaced. Take good care of each other."

Temple smiled at the LaGuzzis and left the room. Maria looked at Sam and said, "I'm glad you are going to help that nice man."

As the van pulled out of the hospital parking lot, Temple looked out the window and said, "This is what politics is really all about. It feels good to know you've had even a small part to play in taking care of people with needs."

Berry looked at the hospital. "Well, Mrs. LaGuzzi and all the other patients in there might have had to go to Syracuse or Utica for their care if you hadn't made the deal with Senator Manto. You should feel good about this." Berry paused, then said, "Geez, where is a camera when I need one. We should have gotten some photos with you and the LaGuzzi's. That'd be great stuff for the press."

Temple looked at Berry. "That's not why I went there."

"I know, but why not take advantage of those opportunities? Everyone else does."

"Maybe, but I'd like to think that I'm not like everyone else."

"I guess that means there is no going back there."

"You guess right. The LaGuzzi's need their privacy."

Allan Gant called Temple early Sunday morning.

"Jay, this is Allan Gant in Rome."

"Hi, Allan."

"Hello. I wanted to tell you what a great job you did yesterday."

"Thanks."

"You got pretty good coverage in the Rome papers today, and all I've heard on the radio is your quotes on jobs, education and crime."

"Well, let's hope when this is all over, we can get to work on making an impact in those areas."

Gant nodded to himself. "Listen, Joe Pummer asked me to remind you about the Ox Roast this Thursday. A lot of Rome people will be there, as well as half of Oneida County. Pummer and I think this would be good exposure for you."

"We've got it on the calendar."

"Good. It'll be held at the Oneida County Park, and the time is 3:30 until whenever. I'll send you directions."

"Great. Thank Joe for including me."

"Okay. Say, you're welcome to bring some volunteers

203

with you. This is not a Republican Party function, but you could hand out brochures."

"We'll take you up on that. Would three others be too many?"

"Nope. That'll be fine."

"Thanks, Allan. We'll see you Thursday."

"Take care, Senator."

Temple wrote the date in his appointment book. He thought to himself, 'This is going to be another busy week.' He looked down the list of activities: Lions Club meeting in Syracuse, Monday; Oneida Flower Club, Tuesday; Salvation Army luncheon, Wednesday; Citizens Foundation luncheon, Thursday along with Pummer's Ox Roast; and Friday, his daughter's graduation from high school.

Temple said half out loud, "Hard to find time to work!"

The week flew by as Temple had known that it would. He was finding that juggling his business needs with his political demands was not an easy thing to do.

He had told Jack Whittaker, his company's president, that he would put in enough time at the office to keep up the company's legal work while he was running for the Senate. Temple's plan was to work overtime on those days when the campaign called for him to leave early or arrive late. His four weeks of vacation were being held in abeyance for the final drive in October.

Cordis had been a real find. He was there with the van to pick Temple up at his office and drive him to events. He planned their travels well and always got Temple to speaking engagements with a minimal amount of wasted time.

Cordis was becoming a second brother to Temple as the days went by. Temple found that he could rely on Cordis and that he was totally dedicated to the campaign.

Temple was just wrapping up some work in his office before Cordis was to arrive for the trip to the Citizen's Foundation meeting when Whittaker walked in.

"How's the campaign going, Jay?"

"Hard to judge. I know I'm busy, but I'm not sure whether we are moving ahead fast enough."

"What do you think your chances of winning are now?"

"Forty - Sixty."

"Really? I read the papers and saw you on television. Looked to me that you should be improving your odds."

"I hope you're right."

"Is it that bad working here?" Whittaker seemed concerned.

"No. I didn't mean it that way. I just don't like to lose, so when I get in a race like this, I'm in it to win."

"That's why you're our attorney," Whittaker smiled.

Cordis walked in at that moment. "Oh excuse me, I didn't mean to interrupt."

Temple said, "It's okay, Ted. I want you to meet Jack Whittaker, our company President. Jack, this is Ted Cordis, my Campaign Manager."

Whittaker shook hands with Cordis. "What do you do when you are not running Jay's campaign?"

"Praying that he wins! No, actually I am a CPA and have several businesses that I manage."

"How are they doing with all your campaign activities?"

"Fine. I have some good people."

In the van, on the way to the luncheon, Temple asked Cordis, "How are you doing with your business, Ted?"

Temple had been concerned with the huge amount of time Cordis had been spending on the campaign. He didn't want Cordis to lose business because of his efforts for Temple, and the campaign didn't have the wherewithal to pay Cordis a salary.

"Don't worry about me. Business is fine. You concentrate on the campaign. I want to see you in Albany. You have what we need in government, and all I want out of this is the satisfaction of getting you elected."

"Well, thanks, but if you ever need time off to take care of the shop, be sure you take it. You've already given your full share of time to this race."

205

"Thanks, Jay. The only thing I ask is that when you are elected, you let me go over to Mann's house and take her Senate plates off of her car."

"You are sick!" Temple laughed.

The Foundation speech was a success, and after the luncheon, Cordis and Temple drove to their headquarters to pick up Gardiner and Tarkings. From there they went on to the Oneida County Park and Joe Pummer's Ox Roast.

Oneida County Park was a huge municipal park with an enormous parking lot and several large pavilions clustered around a dining hall. As the campaign team pulled up, they could smell the sausage aroma in the air.

It was four in the afternoon and already the parking lot was full, and cars and trucks were being directed onto a baseball field.

Temple's van had campaign banners on both sides and so they were given the go-ahead for a spot near the pavilions.

Gant was right there when the van came to a stop.

"Hey, Jay. Glad you and your people could join us."

Temple introduced Tarkings and Gardiner to Gant. He could see that Gant was immediately taken with Gardiner. Gardiner had been a model and was very striking. Temple could see why Gant was stumbling through his conversation with her. Gardiner on the other hand, was used to this kind of attention and handled it well with a minimum amount of embarrassment for the gentlemen.

Gant finally regained his composure long enough to give each of them their tickets, and they all set off for the 'Roast.'

Temple had barely made it to the first pavilion when he heard a woman's voice say, "Mr. Temple, this is a surprise."

Temple turned to see Madeline Reynolds, the co-owner of the Observer Dispatch.

"Mrs. Reynolds, this is a pleasure. How is Captain Reynolds?"

"Just fine, Mr. Temple," the Captain said as he came over and joined his wife.

206

"It's nice to see you too," Temple shook hands with the Captain.

"You've been putting your time in Rome to good use, Mr. Temple," Mrs. Reynolds went on.

"How so?" Temple was interested in what Madeline Reynolds had to say. He suspected that very little happened in Rome that she didn't know about.

"Well, our friend, Sam LaGuzzi thinks that you're a combination of Superman and St. Peter."

"Sam exaggerates!"

"Of course he does, but you may be interested in knowing that Sam has never worked for a losing candidate in Rome." She studied Temple as she spoke.

"Well I hope I don't spoil his record. He's a nice guy."

"You couldn't have lined up a better person in Rome," the Captain added. "Sam knows everybody."

"I can see why he would. He seems very kind and has a nice family."

"Yes. He told us how you visited with his wife in the hospital. That would have been a great picture for the papers." Madeline continued to study Temple for answers beneath the answers.

"That was suggested once before. I don't do things like that for political reasons."

Joe Pummer walked up. "Hi, Madeline, Captain. I see you know Jay Temple. Jay, I am glad you came."

"I've never been to an Ox Roast. Do you really roast an ox?"

"We used to. These days it's a side of beef."

"I'm partial to beef."

"Good. Let me tear you away from the Reynolds and get you something to eat."

Temple excused himself from the Reynolds and as they walked over to the roasting pits Pummer said, "You know Madeline is in tight with the Governor?"

"Yes. Actually Calvin Wendt told me that."

207

"Thank goodness. I was worried when I saw her grilling you."

"It was a very polite grilling. But she sure studies her subjects."

"Yeah. She used to give me fits when I was County Executive. She's a smart woman. Too bad she's a Democrat."

The Roast was a big success. Temple met a lot of people and Cordis, Gardiner, and Tarkings emptied three boxes of brochures, six hundred handouts in all.

* * *

The Governor was accompanied to Rome the following day by Senator Mann. Mann had given member item funds to the Rome Grange to build a model of a dairy farm operation inside a downtown warehouse. The Governor, Mayor Eiles, and Senator Mann were on hand for the dedication.

The Senator followed the Governor in addressing the crowd of some eighty people who had gathered for the mid-day dedication.

Mann concluded her remarks by saying, "The dairy industry in New York State is second to none. This model in Rome will be a source of education for our future farmers both locally and throughout the Northeast.

"As people have come to Rome to visit the Canal Museum and the Fort, so too will they visit this latest addition to your tourist attractions. Rome is rebuilding, and I'm proud to be a part of that effort."

Mayor Eiles thanked the Governor for being on hand for the dedication and thanked the Senator for the funds that made the project possible. He announced that a reception would follow at the Museum next door.

At the reception, Madeline Reynolds cornered Laura Mann.

"Hello, Senator. How are you?"

"You tell me. Will I get a good spot in tomorrow's

Dispatch?"

"Yes." Madeline paused, then continued. "We are running a story on your race."

"My race?"

"Yes. Mr. Temple has been doing a lot of work here in Rome on his campaign. But you probably know that." Now Madeline was studying Mann.

"I knew he'd been here." Mann was furious that no one had told her about whatever it was that Temple had been doing.

"More than just been here, my dear," Madeline smiled. She could see that this was all news to the Senator. "Mr. Temple has started his own organization in town and attended the Ox Roast yesterday at the county park. There was a good crowd. Maybe six to seven hundred, and he worked it pretty well."

Mann had skipped the Roast, because she and Joe Pummer had clashed many times when he was the County Executive. He wanted things done his way and never gave her any room to do her thing. She wasn't about to attend any Joe Pummer function.

"Madeline, I thought you were a solid Democrat. Why would you give any space to a guy from Onondaga County that didn't even know Rome was on the map till he threw his hat in the ring for the Senate?"

"My dear, I am a Democrat, but I also have a newspaper to run with my husband. As you know, the Captain is a Republican, and we kind of like our paper to be down the middle on politics."

Mann didn't like being referred to as 'my dear' but knew there was a time to be proud and a time to be quiet. With Madeline Reynolds, it was a time to be quiet.

"Did I hear you say 'down the middle' on politics?" the Governor had just worked his way over to Senator Mann and Madeline Reynolds.

"Editorially, yes," Madeline responded.

"Well, editorially speaking, I think the Senator has given

209

Rome another attraction that this city can be proud of. Not being a farmer, I enjoyed seeing that working model of farm life. Gives one a renewed sense of appreciation for our friends in the dairy industry." The Governor looked at Madeline and winked. "You can quote me on that."

Mayor Eiles walked over. "I can use some quotes too. You can let your readers know that as Mayor of Rome, I appreciate the work that Senator Mann did to help our Grange and that it was an honor for our city that the Governor would come to the dedication ceremony."

Madeline smiled politely. "I think it is safe to say that this story will be well covered."

Later on that day, Madeline recounted the entire conversation to her husband. He sat back amused, not so much by the conversation, as his wife's reaction to it. He thought to himself: 'This fellow Temple might make a Republican out of her yet. No. That would be too much to hope for.'

Photos were assembled, copy prepared, and Madeline and the Captain both gave it their special attention.

The final run pictured the Governor and the Senator at the dedication with an inset closeup of the Senator on one side of the page and a picture of Temple at the Ox Roast talking with a group of people with an inset closeup of Temple on the other side of the page.

The caption read, 'Race To Watch This Fall.'

True to her word, Madeline had all the quotes requested in the article. The article also featured comments from such notables as Mr. Sam LaGuzzi and Mrs. Mary Catallana. The battle was joined.

Mann knew what the Observer Dispatch confirmed, her race against Temple was going to be different from the others. Temple might be a novice at politics, but he seemed to have good political judgment and he wasn't the good old boy that a lot of people had thought he was.

Mann, for the first time in her political career, heard a little voice telling her that this race was not hers for the taking.

This was going to go to the wire.

The Senator called for a meeting of her staff and key advisers that Friday evening. The discussion was centered on planning a complete campaign, pulling out all the stops. Fund raising, advertising, appearances, and even face–to–face debates were discussed and appropriate timing planned.

She was not going to sit back and watch Jay Temple climb in the polls. This would be Senator Laura Ann Mann at her best.

* * *

That same evening, Temple took a break from his campaigning to attend his daughter, Amy's, graduation.

"It's hard to believe that she's graduating from high school and on her way to college," Temple confided to Pat.

"I know. It seems like it was just yesterday when we brought her home from the hospital. Remember how tiny she was?"

"Yeah, I could hold her whole body on my arm and had her head in my hand. Now she's full grown and graduating."

Amy walked across the stage when they called her name and received both her diploma and her honors scholarship from the school principal. She immediately looked down at her father and mother and with a big smile, winked at them.

Temple's brother and his wife, and his father and mother also joined them in the graduation celebration. A party followed at the Temple household with close friends and relatives.

Temple was glad for the break. It gave him perspective.

Chapter XV

July: Month Seven
Independence

The last two weeks of June flew by for both candidates. Mann began pulling a campaign team together. Her contacts in the City of Syracuse provided most of the manpower and what she lacked elsewhere she made up for through her contacts in the media.

Joel Samuels outlined a methodical media event schedule from July first through to November 6th. Tork Johns reviewed issues where the Senator shone and began working on ways to exploit these.

Annie Wilson worked with Mann on a series of constituent letters, courtesy of the Senate, that would highlight the Senator's work for her district. The first would be out just after the 4th of July and the remaining three would be mailed between Labor Day and Election Day.

It was decided that a central theme for Mann would be election reform, with emphasis on ousting the 'good old boys' who were the cause of all the state's ills. There would also be a push to get their friends in the media to tag Temple as just another good old boy, wealthy, pro-business, anti-social legislation and with little or no experience to qualify him for the New York State Senate.

Mann was convinced that Temple would not fade. Samuels counseled Mann to bide her time and watch for a chink in the armor. "Eventually, he'll self destruct. He's a novice and his people are too. There's not a professional politician in the bunch. Yes, they'll make the BIG MISTAKE that will cost them the election."

"What makes you so sure of that, Joel?" the Senator asked.

"Just look at your past opponents. They get desperate and go off the deep end, or you push the right button and bingo, same result. You'll be back next session. Count on it."

Mann felt better. Samuels had been around a long time and knew the ropes. He had guided her through every campaign since she first ran for the New York Senate. Together they had beaten the establishment. He had taken her out of a small pond in the City of Syracuse and dropped her in the big time of New York State politics. She had become a player. There was talk of Lieutenant Governor or a Congressional seat in her future. If Joel Samuels said don't worry, that was like money in the bank. Still, she shouldn't forget that this was a race to be run and won.

Temple spent the last two weeks of June campaigning in malls, grocery store parking lots, shopping centers, and virtually anywhere that he could find a crowd.

Mornings found Temple at factory gates shaking hands with workers or working the countryside as farmers prepared for the day's chores.

On Saturday, June 30th, Laura O'Neil was preparing for her morning appointment with State Senate candidate, Jay Temple. O'Neil was a television reporter for Channel 10. She had covered many political campaigns over the twenty years that she had worked as a reporter. She had seen candidates and campaigns come and go and had developed a sixth sense for the ones who would rise above the rest by election day.

O'Neil was convinced that Senator Laura Ann Mann was the toughest politician in office to beat from the Central New York area. She knew from other interviews that Mann was being touted for the Lieutenant Governor's job or a possible run against her friend the Congressman. O'Neil had no doubt that given the opportunity, Senator Mann would take either position and be a formidable candidate. But she also had this sixth sense

213

that first, Mann had to get by this newcomer, Jay Temple.

In preparation for the interview with Temple, O'Neil had done her homework. What she found surprised her. Temple had in place a well–organized, financially sound organization with real people involved at every level.

O'Neil had talked to campaign workers and had come away with a very strong impression that there was a real sense of commitment and dedication to getting this guy elected.

She had seen Temple in other circumstances, mostly associated with his community activities, but she had also been surprised at the number of organizations that he had either been a part of, or had been president of. Clearly, Temple's contacts with people had gone deeper than she had imagined.

Her phone rang, and the receptionist at Channel 10 informed her that "Mr. Jay Temple is here to see you."

Laura O'Neil was a tall, slender woman. She judged others by her own standards. As she walked up to Temple, her first thoughts were that here was a man, a little over six feet tall, and in good shape. She knew that Laura Ann Mann was about her height and that for the first time in Senator Mann's political career, she would be looking up at her opponent. She thought 'irrelevant but interesting.'

"Mr. Temple, thank you for coming to the studio."

"It's my pleasure, Laura." He had always liked Laura O'Neil and was familiar with her background. She had been a reporter for eight years and then went to work for the Democratic Mayor of Syracuse. While with the Mayor, she had a difference of opinion with him, and left the position on principle. Temple always liked principled people.

"I thought we might do the interview right here if that's all right with you?" she asked.

"Fine."

"With the couch and plants, this is a more informal atmosphere. We get tired of the studio day in and day out."

O'Neil sat down on the couch and Temple sat down next to her. A cameraman and a sound man materialized from behind

214

the reception area wall and began setting up for the interview. A cordless mike was placed on Temple's lapel and another on O'Neil's blouse collar.

"Please say a few words, Mr. Temple," the sound man requested.

"Laura O'Neil is a great reporter for Channel 10."

The sound man laughed, "That should conclude the interview."

O'Neil blushed, "I'm not letting you off that easy."

"Sound is okay," from the sound man.

"Camera's ready," from the cameraman.

O'Neil looked directly at Temple. "I'm going to ask you a series of questions and you just have to answer them. If we make a mistake or you want to go back, just let me know. The interview will be cut later, and only a small part will probably air tonight. We may use other parts later on. Any questions?"

"No. It sounds fine to me."

"Good. Then here we go." She looked at the camera and then back at Temple. "Mr. Temple, you are running against a female, Democratic, State Senator, who by most accounts will be tough to beat if not impossible. Why politics and why this race?"

"Why politics, a good question. People are always critical of politicians. Yet politics is what ensures democracy. If people like me see things that need changing in government and do not do something about it, then soon the democratic government that we all support will fail.

"Why this race? Because I see a need for change in this state and in this district. Too many policies have either failed or are not meeting the expectations of the people of this state. Spending is out of control, our taxes are among the highest paid of any state in the country, our education system only ranks in the median level compared to other states, and yet we spend more per child than any other state, and the loss of jobs and businesses has escalated over the last ten years at an alarming pace. I'm in this race to try to change all this."

"Your opponent would argue that she is for change but that it has been the Republican majority in the Senate that is responsible for the problems you have just mentioned. How would you respond to that?"

Temple didn't hesitate. "Look only to my opponent's voting record. Over the last six years, she has voted with the majority 97% of the time. She tells voters that she is a maverick pushing for change and yet her voting record doesn't suggest that."

"You seem to indicate that you would have voted differently but then wouldn't you in effect be voting against the Republican majority?"

Again no hesitancy. "Yes. But if change is what is needed and if I believe that our current policies were the cause of our state's bankrupt condition, then a 97% voting record, and those include spending bills, is unconscionable."

"Bankrupt is a strong statement. Do you think that the state is bankrupt?"

"If I ran a business the way this state is run, yes; 'bankrupt' is the adjective that best describes where we are. New York State has to borrow money to meet its payroll and pay its obligations.

"Because of poor management, New York has the lowest ratings given by rating services. The net result is that we pay the highest interest rates for the money that we do borrow. In the end, it is you, me, and every other taxpayer in New York who bears the burden of our state's mismanagement.

"If it takes a voice in the wilderness to say no and vote no, then I will be that voice."

O'Neil was speechless for a moment. This guy was sincere, knowledgeable and had thrown out facts, the 97% voting record, that she had not heard before.

"Mr. Temple, if what you say is true, given all that, incumbents win reelection over 90% of the time. Senator Mann has, in the past, shown her popularity with the voters. How are you going to win?"

"Hard work and the right message. I think I know what the people in this district and in this state want from Albany. I offer them the opportunity to take it."

O'Neil reached down into her handbag and produced a 'Temple for State Senate' campaign button. Holding it up she said, "Well, you have the buttons, I've seen your brochures, will you have the financial means to carry this campaign on to election day?"

Temple smiled. "I have some great people working on that. Our finance committee has already raised in excess of fifty thousand dollars, and we plan to continue to raise the money needed to get our message out to the people of the district."

"Is business supporting you?"

"Businesses in this district have been very supportive but the thing that has amazed me is the support I am getting from people of all different kinds of backgrounds. Farmers, union workers, small business owners, even college students, have contributed anywhere from one dollar to one thousand dollars.

"There are really two races in any political campaign. One is for the political office and the other is for the means to get there. I hope to finish first in both races."

"Well, good luck, Mr. Temple."

Back in her office with the camera and sound men, O'Neil kicked off her shoes and said, "That guy is impressive."

The two men agreed.

One thing that Jay Temple was to learn many times throughout the campaign was that campaigns take on a life of their own.

July 1st came, and as planned, Temple took his oldest son to the Adirondack Scout Reservation for the beginning of his son's two-week camping program. But, even though the candidate was taking the day off, that did not mean that the campaign was on hold.

Kerry Heathrow, one of the Young Republicans from Manlius, had pulled together about twenty other YRs, and they were busy building the 'Temple For Senate' float to be used in

217

the July 4th parade in Manlius.

Ophidia and Bob Berry were meeting in their downtown Syracuse office to go over advertising planned for the Temple campaign and costs to be charged for the television spots coming up during the next few weeks.

Kevin Roth sat in his office in his home in the Sedgwick section of Syracuse adding up the income and expense columns for the State report on campaign spending.

Frank Catallana met with Mr. Vincent Salanza of Rome. He told Mr. Salanza all that he had been able to find out about Jay Temple.

And Army Specialist Steve Scarason told his Commanding Officer that Jay Temple was just the kind of guy that they had been looking for.

On the other side of the race, Mann was livid over Laura O'Neil's coverage of Temple during the Saturday evening news. She was especially taken aback on the comments about her voting record.

On July 1st, Mann went on the defensive. In an interview arranged with Terry Davis, Mann accused Temple of dirty politics and false statements. She said that she was the only true reformer in the Senate and that to give the impression that she always voted with the Republicans was ridiculous.

Davis asked, "Are you saying that you did not vote yes on bills before the Senate 97% of the time?"

"I'm saying that Jay Temple is throwing mud by accusing me of always siding with the establishment in passing legislation. The Republicans in the Senate would love to see me leave the Senate."

The ride back from Sabatis gave Temple the time he needed to reflect on his life, his children and the campaign. Between his working life and his many community activities, he had not spent the time with his children that he now wished that he had.

His daughter was practically a grown woman. She would be off to college this fall and that meant the beginning of a life of her own. The little girl that he had watched play in the sandbox, push a doll carriage, bake her first cake for her dad, and which he had managed to choke down, would be leaving home. Temple thought about the pretty little girl with her Cabbage Patch doll, curled up in his lap. Then he pictured the beautiful teenager with the bright smile. Those years go by too quickly.

Then there was his oldest son. There were a few more years of high school left but he knew how fast that time would go. James was a very special person. Kind–hearted by nature, he was easygoing with a quiet sense of humor and had a mature appreciation of life. Temple had spent time with this young man: first, coaching his basketball and soccer teams, then watching him play on high school teams. There had been the scouting years. Temple had worked with James as he progressed through the ranks from a Tiger Cub all the way to Eagle Scout. But still it wasn't enough time. Maybe there never was enough.

Now, he had young Tyler. At the age of six, Tyler was already showing signs of being way ahead of himself in terms of knowledge and understanding. Temple referred to him as "my little man."

Tyler was quick to laugh and enjoyed making others laugh. Given the opportunity, he would perform for hours for his parents, sister, and brother. He loved animals and read or listened to anything that had to do with them. Absorbing everything that he was exposed to, he was the resident authority on wildlife for all his friends. Temple chuckled to himself, thinking about Tyler teaching his pre-school class about the spotted leopard. Tyler's teacher had described the event in great detail to Temple and had indicated that even she learned things about the leopard that she had never known.

Temple again smiled to himself and affectionately thought, 'funny little guy.'

As he was passing through Boonville, he saw a 'Keep Mann In The Senate' bumper sticker. He wondered what her family life had been like. If his time had been limited with his

219

family, what had her life been like?

If he were elected, how much time would he be giving up with his family and with Tyler, his youngest son. He'd be sacrificing those basketball and soccer games, the scouting activities, and most especially, those quiet little moments when a child turns to you and says "I love you."

Temple's sadness shifted to thoughts of the other politicians that he knew or had known.

'I wonder if people ever appreciate the sacrifice that public officials make in their efforts to work for the people they represent.'

As Temple turned onto the New York State Thruway, the toll taker greeted him. "Hello, Mr. Temple."

Surprised at the recognition, Temple answered, "Hi. How are you?"

"Great. How's the campaign going?"

"Busy. But we'll make it."

"Good luck, my family is voting for you."

"Thanks, I appreciate that. I'll try not to let you down."

As Temple continued on, he felt good about this encounter. There were people out there who were responding to his message of hope, of change. He realized that he was in this race for the long haul and that even at times when he knew the sacrifices that he and his family would be making, he felt the need to do something larger for society.

Many other thoughts passed through his mind before he arrived home. The last thought as he turned into his driveway was that he had a new appreciation for anyone who runs for political office. He had 'walked a mile in their shoes' and he thought they deserved his respect whether they were Democrats, Republicans, Conservatives, or Liberals.

* * *

July 4th is always a big day for public officials and would-be public officials. Parades and political speeches are as much a part of this American celebration as are the fireworks, barbecues, and family gatherings. Americans love parades and politicians love Americans.

Cordis had arranged for Temple to appear in three parades and to speak at one. Manlius was the first, and it was here that Kerry Heathrow and the Young Republicans had gone all out.

Temple was greeted by a twenty-four foot float, nine and a half feet high with an American Flag and mockup of his campaign pin made out of crepe paper and wire mesh. A four-piece Dixieland band was blasting out 'When The Saints Come Marching In,' and a loudspeaker called to voters to vote in November for Jay Temple, New York State Senate.

Temple had to admit that this was an unbelievable effort and end result.

"Kerry, this is terrific!"

"Hey, nothing is too good for our next State Senator."

"You must have been working on this for weeks!"

"Well, a week anyway, but we had lots of help. Everyone here pitched in. Would you like to say a few words before we get underway?"

"Sure."

Heathrow climbed up on the float to get the YR's attention. There were about twenty Young Republicans at the float and another six or seven staff workers who had arrived to help hand out candy along the parade route.

Heathrow took the loudspeaker and said, "People, people. Before we get out into the parade, our candidate for the New York State Senate would like to say a few words. Jay Temple."

Everyone clapped and cheered.

"I just want to say 'thank you' for the great job that you did on this float. It's incredible! When Kerry told me that you were going to put something on a flatbed, I had no idea that it was going to be something that could compete in the Tournament of Roses Parade. It will be a long time before people in Manlius see something this spectacular again. Thank you again for all your help."

The parade marshal came up and signaled for the Temple people to get lined up.

As with a lot of things in a campaign, timing and opportunity are everything. With all the excitement, the driver of the flatbed had left the ignition on and the battery had gone dead.

Heathrow panicked. Cordis immediately got the staff to take off one of the banners on the bumper of the truck and with the marshals ushering, the decision was made that everyone would walk the parade route.

Temple told Kerry not to be upset, that it was a great effort and one that he would never forget.

Cordis took Temple's arm and hurried him off to the parade route.

As the parade swept out onto Route 92, the main road through Manlius, Temple heard the roar of the crowd and then the 'Saints' began to play. He turned, and not less than one hundred yards behind him he saw the flatbed truck being pulled by a pickup truck out into the rear of the parade.

Heathrow came running up all smiles. "Couldn't let you down! If you don't mind bringing up the rear, we have your float on the road."

Temple laughed. "Looks better than ever."

Heathrow raised an eyebrow. "This guy came along and asked if we worked for you. We said we did, and he swung up in front of our float and hooked on. Said he had nothing better to do."

"Volunteers are great!" Temple said with meaning.

Temple's group reformed around the tandem float exhibition and with new fervor marched along, singing with the band, waving to the crowd, and handing out brochures and candy to the adults and children along the parade route.

Temple thought, 'Norman Rockwell couldn't have painted it better.'

Laura Ann Mann was very much at home with the people of south Madison County. Her grandparents had had a farm in Brookfield and she had returned often to Hamilton, where she had strong ties with the local League of Women Voters.

The July 4th parade in Hamilton was a big draw and Mann made sure that she renewed old acquaintances and showed the colors of her campaign where it would gather the most support.

Joel Samuels, the ever–present campaign manager, arranged for a Chevy Impala convertible, white and in mint condition, to showcase Mann in the parade.

For her part, Mann purchased a white, off–the–shoulder yellow flowered print dress with a wide skirt, topped by a wide–brimmed straw hat with matching flowers. Annie Wilson, her secretary, helped arrange the Senator on the trunk of the Impala. Samuels gave the final stamp of approval, and Tork Johns drove off to the lead position in the parade.

As the parade wound around the Commons and on through the town, Mann waved to the crowd, smiled her now famous toothy grin, and flashed her dark eyes at admirers near the curb. The people loved the sight of their home–grown celebrity, and she felt the electricity and knew that she was where she belonged.

At the reviewing stand, she was helped down from the Impala by the parade marshal and escorted to the stand. Flowers were presented to her by a representative of the local Girl Scout Troop, and she was asked to say a few words to the crowd in front of the stand.

"It is a pleasure to be here in the heart of the county where my grandparents raised dairy cows, corn, and my father."

The crowd applauded with approval

"As you know, this is an election year and I am once again seeking your support for my race in the New York State Senate.

"It's not easy for a country girl to fight the big city machines and Republican power brokers in the Senate. They'd like to get rid of me so that the only voice they hear is that of the fat cats who support their pocketbooks in return for their back room wheeling and dealing.

"They don't want me there exposing their games and their deals. They don't want you to be represented by someone who speaks your language. They want you to be represented by someone who speaks their language.

"But, I think you are smarter than those fat cats. You know a phony when you see one, and you know the people who are on your side. I hope that I've proved to you that I'm on your side.

"If you vote for me this fall, I promise to continue to fight the back room politicians and to continue to try to improve the living conditions for the people in Madison County. Please help me with your support."

Mann waved to the crowd. One man in the back of the crowd yelled "We're with you, Annie!" Everyone cheered the Senator as she shook hands and kissed old friends.

Samuels smiled from the far side of the road. She had a lock on Hamilton.

Following the parades in Manlius and Hamilton, both candidates headed toward Cazenovia.

Cazenovia lay halfway between the two villages and was one of the more affluent centers in Madison County. Its residents were active, community minded citizens. They would commit both time and money to politics and both candidates realized this.

As Johns drove Mann north to the parade site, Cordis drove Temple south to the same place. Both candidates wondered if they would see the other in Cazenovia. That question was answered as soon as Cordis arrived at the parade site.

As Cordis was climbing out of the van, he looked up at a commotion in the street. There was the white Impala with the

Senator, once again sitting on the trunk with broad brimmed hat and flattering dress.

"Geez! Look at this. She looks like a southern belle dressed for the ball!" Cordis was not a big fan of Senator Mann.

Temple looked in the direction that Cordis was pointing. At that moment, Tork Johns had just told the Senator that he had spotted Temple. She, too, looked in the direction that Johns was indicating. The two politicians caught sight of each other at the same time. After a moment's hesitation, Temple mouthed a hello to Mann. She gave a quick smile and returned his greeting. Johns drove on by.

"What a get-up!" Cordis hooted. "She's the biggest phony I've ever seen."

"Maybe, but the people here will remember that she was here too and that outfit certainly will catch the eye of every man on the street."

"Yeah, but the women won't go for it."

Temple thought about that, then concluded that he had his own work to do at this parade. He gathered up an arm-full of brochures and began working his way along the parade ready route, talking to others lined up for the parade and distributing literature and buttons.

By parade time, a good number of parade marchers either had his buttons, or were wearing them. If nothing else, it sure looked good, and others would notice and remember that he had been there too.

As it turned out, Mann noticed the buttons and was upset with her staff that her campaign hadn't been able to match Temple's display of political propaganda. Samuels explained to her that it was too early for that. She wasn't convinced.

Temple's parade style changed considerably during the campaign.

Typically, politicians ride in convertibles waving to the bystanders as they travel along the parade route. In Temple's first parade, he had ridden in a red convertible with his 'Temple for State Senate' signs on the front and back. He had felt out of touch with the people as he rode and somewhat pretentious, being new to politics.

In his second parade, his jacket came off and halfway along the parade route, he climbed out of the convertible and walked the parade route waving to the people along the side of the road.

By the third parade, the car was used to carry candy, campaign buttons, and brochures. A banner had been created with the now familiar, red, white, and blue 'Temple for State Senate' logo on it, and two campaign workers would carry the banner followed by Temple.

Temple, tie undone and shirt sleeves rolled up, would walk along, first one side of the road, then the other, shaking hands and talking with the rows of people along the parade route. Other campaign workers would follow, handing out buttons and brochures to all who would take them. Other volunteers would give candy to the children along the route. Parades became quite a production for the Temple campaign team, and they were having fun. The mood was contagious. People responded.

Temple was convinced that his instincts were right. He enjoyed people, and he felt they enjoyed the directness of someone walking up to them and saying, "Hi! I'm Jay Temple. Nice to see you today." That was all there was to it. Simple, direct, and yet effective. Those he met would tell others, and as the campaign sped toward election day, his name recognition increased weekly.

Chapter XVI

War And Politics

Name recognition was the key, not only to winning elections, but also to raising money for the campaign. Big donors give to winners and perceived winners. Unknowns never get in on the really big money in political campaigns.

Temple believed that hard work accounted for a lot, but he also recognized the part that timing plays in campaigns. Temple's people had raised enough money to pay for a four week media blitz during the last two weeks of July and first two weeks of August.

This was the lowest viewer time available during the year and as a result the least expensive air time that can be purchased. Temple had purchased all newscast time on two out of three commercial networks. Temple purchased only a third of the time on the third network. His coverage on that network had been minimal and decidedly one–sided in favor of Mann.

When his ads started, so too did a war in the Middle East. At a time of traditionally low viewership, network ratings went through the ceiling. People had their televisions on constantly, following developments in the war. They also saw Temple's political commercials during every newscast. Timing plays a critical factor in a campaign, as does luck.

In late August, a name recognition poll was conducted. Temple, for the first time, broke into the viable candidate level with sixty-eight percent name recognition. More importantly, fifty-four percent knew who he was and for what office he was running. It was at this point that his financial campaign swung into high gear. Contributors began sending in unsolicited contributions with letters and notes of good wishes and support. Temple's team was ready to maximize the opportunities that this presented.

On the third day of the television blitz by Temple, Mann called an urgent meeting with her staff and campaign team. She had been around long enough to understand what was taking place and the potential it offered in terms of Temple's visibility.

"Joel, how did we get upstaged so badly on this one?" Mann's voice gave hint to her agitation.

"We were not upstaged, Annie. Normally, July and August are the worst months of the year for television viewership. Everyone is on vacation, the weather is nice and they are outside. For a hundred good reasons, television is at a low ebb. It's just not the time to run political commercials unless you can't afford the more expensive air time."

"Why didn't we know about this buy?"

Samuels smiled. "We did know. Temple was doing what he could afford. He didn't know and neither did we that war would break out in the Middle East. My people told me about the buy and even asked if we wanted to buy some offsetting time. We turned them down."

Mann heard and understood but didn't like it. "Well, now we do have a war. Everyone is watching the news. And every time I watch the news, I see my opponent at day care centers, at shopping malls, coaching youth basketball and talking with farmers and business people, all of whom end the commercial by endorsing him. I'm not happy!"

Johns spoke up, "Shouldn't we buy some time now?"

Samuels answered, "First, we haven't produced any commercials yet. Second, we are not bringing in the kind of money we need to start our media campaign this early in the race. And third, I still think it's too soon. Temple will peak and when he does, we will bury him."

Mann looked at Samuels. "What about using our old rhythm and blues commercial? It's in the can, and we can bring it back."

Samuels could tell that his protégée was on edge. He didn't want her to react every time Temple did something that she hadn't counted on. "Look, Annie. I'm on your side. You know that. I have taken you through many campaigns and won them. You'll win this one, but Temple is a different breed of cat than we are used to. He's not a professional politician. He's somewhat unorthodox so we can't anticipate him like we have the others. But he or his people will blow it. There is too much time left before Election Day. Just keep on being a Senator and don't get into a political battle."

"I hope you are right. But I'd still feel better with getting something going on TV."

* * *

Alden Young was the president of Rome Cable Construction Company. RCC had been founded by Thomas Young, Alden's great-grandfather and had been a major employer in the Rome area for many years. The Company was both progressive and paternal and had the loyalty of its workers. Not only was the management fourth generation but so too were many of the people who worked on the line.

Alden avoided politics as a matter of business. Although a registered Republican, he knew and respected the fact that most of his employees were Democrats. There was nothing to gain by bringing politics into the work place.

Alden's younger brother, Jeffrey on the other hand, liked politics and felt that too much government would be the ruin of business. He only had to point to the recent increase in workmen's compensation for employers to drive the point home. He and Alden agreed that the recent change in the law would account for a thirty percent increase in their already hefty premium to the state.

Jeff had met Jay Temple through Calvin Wendt. They had lunch together during one of Temple's swings through Rome

229

at the Delta Lake Country Club. There Jay had talked about the burden of doing business in New York State and about the loss of companies and jobs to more competitive states in the South. Jeff was impressed.

Jeff gave a minute-by-minute rendition of the luncheon conversation to Alden and by three o'clock that afternoon had Alden on the phone to Temple inviting him to a cocktail party at Alden's home.

As Jay and Pat Temple drove to Delta Lake for the Young party, neither knew quite what to expect.

"Did you ever meet Alden Young before?" Pat asked.

"Wouldn't know him if I fell over him. But I guess that's what makes politics so interesting." Jay laughed.

He knew that his wife was really uneasy about going to someone's house without knowing anyone who would be there. He continued his thoughts aloud:

"You know how boring it gets talking to the same people at every party about the same things? Well, this gives us an opportunity to learn about people we don't know and talk about something other than the latest golf scores or good restaurants."

Pat laughed, "You hope! You may find that the people at Delta Lake talk about the same things that our friends do."

"Maybe, but I'll bet we get into politics and policies and government before the first drink is served."

"You're on, Mr. Senator." Pat looked at her husband. He loved politics and seemed more alive now than he had in years. He was looking forward to a cocktail party which was also something he hadn't done in years. As much as she was uncomfortable with all this, she loved it for what it did for her husband. This was the Jay Temple she had met in college. This was the Jay Temple she had fallen in love with. 'What would he do if he lost the election?' That was a question that would haunt her daily over the next four months. But they were into the race now, and she was determined that she would support her husband in any way that she could, including walking into a stranger's home for an evening of conversation and drinks.

"What do you suppose the Youngs are thinking about right now?"

Temple looked quickly at his wife and then back at the road. He thought for a moment and said, "They're probably wondering how they ever got into this and what they are going to talk to us about for an entire evening!"

They both laughed as Temple turned his car onto Delta Lake Road and drove up to a large home overlooking the lake.

* * *

It was eight o'clock on the morning of July 9th when Alden Young asked his brother Jeffrey to join him in his office. As Jeffrey entered, Alden was pouring a cup of coffee.

"Want a cup?"

"Yeah. What's up?"

"Saturday night's party. I was impressed with Temple." Alden poured his brother a cup of coffee, and they both sat down at a table near the office window.

"Temple's a great guy. What did Nancy think? Tammy said she was uptight about the whole idea of having a party for your friends and inviting a politician to join you."

"The great thing about my wife is that she adjusts. She actually struck up quite a friendship with Temple's wife, Pat. They had a lot in common. Nancy also said that Jay Temple could have been any one of our friends who just decided to run for office. That about sums it up for me too."

"What do you mean?" Jeff was amused that his brother would call him in during business hours to talk about a politician. He knew his brother's thoughts about politics and business.

"If Joe Carter or Harvey Gehrig were going to run for office, I'd help them out. Why? Because they are friends and I know them. Well, I feel as if Jay Temple fits in that category too. Actually, I think I'm losing it! I meet this guy and his wife for one night and it's as if we have known each other for years."

"That's the way he is. I had that same feeling after Carl

231

Wendt's luncheon." Jeff sat forward.

"Well, that brings me to why I want to talk to you. I'm going to send Temple a thousand dollars, and I'm going to ask the Association for five thousand."

Jeff Young almost came off his chair. "Geez. Whatever happened to separation of Church and State?" he smiled.

"I know what I've preached, but this guy is different. I'm also thinking of inviting him to speak to our employees. You are a part of this, so before I do, I want your approval."

Jeff put his hand on Alden's shoulder. "Brother, I sent a check for five hundred dollars to Temple on Friday. You both have my vote!"

* * *

Cordis met Temple at campaign headquarters. It was a hot July day, even at eight-thirty in the morning.

"You ready for today?" Cordis asked Temple.

Temple noticed Cordis' concerned look. They had put together a lot of mileage in this campaign and there were still four months to go. Cordis had become a surrogate brother and his concern was appreciated but often unfounded. Temple had a reserve deep inside that he could draw upon to handle even the most difficult of times.

"I'm as ready as I can be. Delta Lake this past Saturday and the Southside this morning. It seems right." Temple nodded to himself.

The Southside was a section of Syracuse often passed by by politicians. It was a very poor black section of the City of Syracuse with a very high drug use and crime rate. It received little attention, except for police calls, and was generally not a place for outsiders.

But on this hot July day, Temple had been invited by the Reverend Thomas Owens to go door-to-door with him to meet the people of the Southside and learn about some of his constituents who desperately needed his help. As Temple told

232

Cordis, "It was an offer I couldn't refuse."

Cordis and Temple climbed into the campaign van and headed out to their designated meeting spot with Reverend Owens.

At the same time that Temple was leaving his campaign headquarters, Reverend Owens was calling Steve Adamson, a local political reporter for Channel 4.

"Steve Adamson here," Adamson said into the receiver as he scanned the days news assignments.

"Mr. Adamson. This is Reverend Owens of the First Church of the Saints."

Owens and Adamson had worked together on community issues of common interest and knew each other well.

Adamson immediately pulled the pencil out from behind his ear and grabbed a pad to write on. "Yes, Reverend, what's happening?"

"I have the honor of taking one Jay Temple on a tour of our little section of the city this mornin'. Thought you might find a story there."

"You are right on target. What's the itinerary?"

Owens gave Adamson the schedule with the understanding that Adamson would be there within the hour.

Cordis drove the van down Geddes Street and turned left onto Bellevue Avenue. Homes built in the late 1800s lined both sides of the street. In their day, they were stately mansions housing some of the wealthier families of Syracuse. Now, they were run down multi-family houses with broken windows, and in some cases, missing doors. At Hudson Street, Cordis took a left and pulled the van alongside the curb. Reverend Owens was standing on the sidewalk dressed in a gray suit, gray shirt, and black tie.

Temple climbed out of the van into the hot sun. It was nine o'clock in the morning and already the streets of Syracuse were suffocating for lack of any breeze.

"Hi, Thomas. I'm going to get rid of this jacket right now." Temple took off his sports coat and threw it back into the

233

van. "You want to put yours in the van?"

Owens shook his head, "No. I got to look good for the cameras."

"Cameras?" Temple looked at the minister who now had beads of perspiration forming at his temples.

"Yes, sir. I think that the TV boys may want to join us for our walk around."

Cordis had joined the two men on the sidewalk. He was still wearing his jacket too. "Did you get Adamson?"

"Yes, sir. I did. He was very interested. He'll be here." Owens smiled.

Temple looked at Cordis. "Something you dreamed up, no doubt?"

"Well, media coverage is media coverage. And that station has been partial to Mann, so I figured we give them something different and see what develops."

Owens spotted some friends on the front porch of a house across the street. "C'mon. Let's say hello to some folks I know over there."

He led Temple to the small group while Cordis stayed with the van.

"Brothers. I want you to meet Jay Temple. The man is running for the New York Senate. Mr. Temple, this is Mr. Wayne, Mr. Thomas, and Mr. Morgan."

Temple stuck his hand out to shake and was greeted by smiles and 'high fives.' He caught on quickly and returned the hand slapping without missing a beat.

"All right!" the three men said, almost in unison. "All right."

"Brothers. I'm going to take Mr. Temple around the neighborhood and then stop in on Brother Jefferson. Would you be so kind as to let Brother Jefferson know that we should be at the club shortly?"

"Glad to, Reverend," the man named Morgan replied. "Good meetin' you, Mr. Temple."

"Glad to meet you, too."

234

The three men left the porch and headed north on Hudson. As they were leaving, a station wagon pulled in behind the van and Steve Adamson climbed out of the passenger seat.

He looked over at Temple and Owens, leaned down into the car to give the driver some instructions and then crossed the street.

"What gives?"

"Mr. Temple and I are taking a look at the forgotten people." Owens had his speech all prepared.

"That what you're here for?" Adamson asked as he looked at Temple with notebook in hand.

"Let's say I'm here to learn something, and Reverend Owens is here to teach."

"Great! I like it already. Let me get Arnie over here with the camera and recorder. We'll just follow along to get some footage and then do the interview."

"This ought to be real natural." Temple wasn't real excited about having a camera crew along for what he had hoped would be a natural exchange with people on the Southside.

"Don't worry. They're used to seeing me down here. It's you who are out of your environment," Adamson half–laughed.

"That's why I'm here. This is out of my environment, but it's in my District, and if I'm going to work for all the people, I need to know what their needs are first hand."

"Hey, I'm all for it. You do your thing, and I'll do mine." Adamson had the mike in hand and the cameras filming even before this exchange.

A woman came down the street carrying a baby. Owens walked over to her with Temple. "Mornin', Miss Tyler. How is Mimi today?"

The woman saw the camera and the two white men with Reverend Owens. She looked at her baby and shyly said, "Okay, Reverend Owens."

Owens turned to Temple. "Mr. Temple, I'd like you to meet Sissy Tyler and her little girl Mimi." He turned to the

235

young woman. "Sissy, this is Mr. Temple. He is runnin' for the New York State Senate."

The young woman looked directly at Temple. Temple smiled. "That's a fine looking little girl. What did you say her name was? Mimi?"

"Yes."

"Well, Mimi Tyler, you have a mother who really loves you. You are a lucky little girl." The baby couldn't understand what the white man was saying but her mother could. "Miss Tyler, if you could have one wish for Mimi, what would it be?" Temple returned the young woman's direct look.

The young woman glanced at Owens then Adamson and then back to Temple. Her shyness was gone. "A chance."

"Good! That's what I want for my children too. Let's both work to see that they get it." Temple touched the baby's head lightly with his hand.

"You're a good man," the young woman said. She looked quickly at the three men and went on her way.

Adamson followed Owens and Temple as they went door-to-door. Not every door was opened to the minister and the politician. But there was interest in this white stranger and as they walked the neighborhood they soon developed a following of young children.

Finally at the intersection of Hulbut and Gearson, Adamson asked Temple for his thoughts after touring the Southside.

Temple looked at the clean, young, black faces watching the cameraman and him, and said, "These people deserve a chance. We need to provide them with the opportunity to do something with their lives. For too long the white answer has been to give black people handouts. Welfare takes away their incentive and the sense of self-worth. The Southside needs business and jobs. I think the people in Albany need to see what I've seen today to appreciate what they have not been doing. I plan to bring the Southside to Albany."

Adamson smiled. "You don't sound like a Republican."

"This isn't about political parties. This is about doing what is right. I believe that people generally know what is right and what is not. Given what I've seen today, I have no doubt that the people in Albany would do the right thing if they can be made to see, as I have, what the Southside is all about."

Adamson checked the camera. "Do you plan to propose legislation to bring jobs to the Southside?"

"That and job training. I'd like to spend some of those Welfare checks on job training. As Mark Twain put it, '. . .then they'd be twice warmed. Once when they cut the wood and then again when they burned it.'"

Adamson turned to the cameraman and indicated that they had what they needed. He then turned to Temple. "Two questions off the record."

"Off the record?" Temple wasn't sure.

"Off the record. You have my word."

"Okay. Shoot."

"Did you ever work for Bobby Kennedy or John Lindsay?"

"Yes. I met Bobby Kennedy while I was in college and John Lindsay while I was in law school. I liked both men as individuals and thought that they had a vision for this country that was good. So I campaigned for, and helped out on each of their campaigns."

"And you are a Republican. Interesting! Second question. Do you think that we are not giving you fair coverage and is that why you are not buying equal time on our station?"

"Yes. I think that your station is biased in favor of my opponent and that the coverage leaves a lot to be desired."

"That's not true."

Temple could see that Adamson was truly affronted by what Temple had said. "Steve, I'll tell you what you should do. Go back and look at the political coverage of this race over the last two months and also the news stories involving Senator Mann. Then you tell me if she has been getting more air-time and better coverage."

237

"Well, she is the Senator, and she may be generating stories unrelated to the race."

"Steve, every other station has the same choices that you have. They have, in my mind, been fairer in their coverage. If your station has other reasons for not giving me the same unpaid-for time as Senator Mann, I can't do anything about that. But I don't have to pay for advertising time then, either."

"You may be losing a share of the market by not giving us more commercial time."

"I may be, but I like level playing fields, and your station has a decided tilt. That's the way it is, and until I see a fair shake from your station, our advertising budget will stay the way it is."

Adamson could see that Temple was set on this. He also wondered if, in fact, what Temple was saying was true. His manager had asked him to find out why Temple was not buying the kind of time he had bought with the other two networks and at least he had an answer. It wasn't going to go over big when he reported back.

Owens directed Cordis to the Pussy Cat Club, a Southside night spot that was not what Cordis and Temple pictured as the minister's typical parish place to visit.

As Cordis parked the van in front of the club, two black men who had been lounging near the entrance, stood up. Owens climbed out of the back of the van followed by Temple.

"Mr. Cordis, why don't you wait out here while I take Mr. Temple inside to meet Brother Jefferson." Owens turned from the open window of the van to the two men by the entrance. "Hi, boys! I have a guest of Brother Jefferson here with me."

The men nodded with a long look at Temple and then went back to their more relaxed positions against the wall of the building. One lit a cigarette and stared off into space.

Owens led Temple through the red wood door. Inside, the club was hot and damp. Several fans pushed hot air around a smoke-filled barroom. The smell of tobacco mixed with a sweeter smelling substance which Temple assumed was marijuana. There was the ever present barroom smell of beer.

Nine black men sat at tables scattered around the room, and a black man and a black woman stood at the bar. All of these patrons paid little attention to the two new arrivals.

Temple found it interesting that despite his presence, and obviously being out of place, very little notice seemed to be given to him.

"We will go back this way, Mr. Temple."

Owens took Temple through a door marked 'Office' and into a small room with a round table and four chairs.

There were three black men sitting in the chairs, two with their backs to the door and a third facing the door across the table.

"Brother Jefferson," Owens said as he led the way in. The two men with their backs to the door got up and turned to face Owens and Temple.

"Brother Owens," the seated man said. He was wearing sunglasses despite the darkness of the room. "I heard you was comin'. We don't see as much of you as we used to." He looked at Temple. "You the 'Great White Hope?'"

"I don't know about 'Great White' but 'Hope' sounds good." Temple stuck out his hand. "I'm Jay Temple."

Jefferson looked at Temple long and hard then at the outstretched hand. He thought for a moment then laughed and turned Temple's hand upward and gave it a slap. "Okay, brother. What'd ya want?"

Owens spoke up. "A good word on the street. This man is a good man. He wants to help us. Help our people. Maybe we'll get more than a handout with this Mr. Temple."

"Tommy," Jefferson took off his glasses and looked right at Owens. "You always was an idealist." Jefferson then turned to Temple. "You probably don't know it, mister, but there was a time when Tommy was on the streets. See them hands. Those ain't the hands of a minister. No siree. Ole Tommy could hit with the best. Then one day he gets this callin'. Damned if I

239

know who called him."

The two men along the wall laughed.

Jefferson went on. "He gets this callin', and I lose my man. Now, here he is askin' me to help a white man. Tommy, you're a fool."

Turning to Temple, Jefferson sneered, "White Mister Temple, you gonna make a fool out of ole Tommy?"

There was a tension in the room. No one moved or even seemed to breathe. Temple knew that this was a critical juncture in whatever it was that was to be gained or lost.

"Reverend Owens asked me to come here. To come and see things I've never seen before. I'm here, and I have seen." Temple looked at Owens then back at Jefferson. "Mr. Jefferson, you and I live in two different worlds. But I'm about to go into a third world, politics, and that world plays a role in both of our worlds. It can be a positive role or a not-so-positive role. The people on the Southside need help. If I get into this third world, I'll help."

"That simple?" Jefferson challenged.

"That simple," Temple replied.

In the silence that followed, there was an uneasy feeling by those who watched. The door was still open, and Temple had the notion that all those disinterested people outside the office were now very much interested.

Jefferson sat down at the table. He set his glasses on the table, looked at Temple, Owens, the two men along the wall, and then out the open door.

Finally, Jefferson smiled at Owens. "Reverend Tommy, any time you want to bring this white man back to my club. . ." he paused for effect, "call me. It's cool!"

Back in the van, Cordis waited for Owens and Temple to get in, then asked, "What happened."

The minister looked at Cordis very seriously and then with a confident smile said, "A miracle."

* * *

240

It was quite a contrast from the morning's walk through the Southside and the meeting at the Pussy Cat Club.

The General Humphrey Estate was a large private catering home sitting high on a hill, overlooking the City of Syracuse and Onondaga Lake. It had belonged to the Humphrey family dating back to a land grant given by the King of England before the American Revolution. For the last thirty years, the Estate had been opened to the public for private parties and weddings. It was here that the Republican Party in Onondaga chose to hold its annual meeting of 'The Club.'

'The Club' was the name given to an organization of large contributors to the Republican Party. Comprised mainly of business owners, entrepreneurs, corporate executives, and people with family wealth, the Club financed the Republican Party headquarters, staff, and occasional functions for committee people who worked each election cycle. Individually, Club members were also often supporters of individual candidates in their quest for election or reelection to public office.

The annual meeting was designed to parade candidates and office holders before Club members for their appraisal. It afforded politicians the opportunity to solicit financial support for their election. It was also a weeding out process for the limited number of dollars that would be available during the election cycle. Some candidates would make it, others would not.

Temple, Pat, Cordis, and Mary Tarkings, Temple's campaign coordinator for Onondaga County, arrived fifteen minutes after the scheduled start of the festivities. The main room of the Humphrey Estate was already filled with people.

"The Temples have arrived!" Arthur Gaines announced as they walked in the door. He rushed over to shake hands with Temple. Placing a hand on Temple's shoulder, Gaines directed Temple into the room and to a small gathering of familiar faces.

"Senator Barcliff, you know our next State Senator from the 48th Senate District?" Gaines stepped into the middle of the group, ushering Temple with him.

"Yes, of course. Hi, Jay. How's the campaign going?" Senator Barcliff was a tall, statesman-like man who always wore reading glasses. He had a habit of peering over the glasses at people when he talked to them and then pushing them up the rim of his nose when he was finished. Tonight was no exception.

Temple took all of this in and replied: "The campaign is right on schedule. With a little help this evening, we'll be giving my opponent the race of her life."

"That's what we like to hear," Gaines interjected. "Jay, you know Charlie White, Ken Mathews, and Doctor Carey?"

Temple smiled. Mathews and Carey were on his finance committee and Charlie White had already given a couple hundred dollars to his campaign. "Yes, I do. It's good to see you."

Temple shook hands with everyone as his wife walked up. "Pat, you know everyone." As Pat Temple was saying hello, Frank Pickering called the room to order by tapping his wine glass with his pen.

Pickering was the nominal head of the Club. A lawyer in Senator Barcliff's firm, he had been placed by the Senator in the Republican Party to oversee the operations and direction of the local party. He was both the Chairman of the Club and the parliamentarian.

"Thank you all for coming." Pickering noticed that there still was some conversation in the back of the room. He repeated in slightly louder and harder tones: "Thank you all for coming."

Having now gotten everyone's attention, Pickering continued, "Tonight, we celebrate a victory. The debt from our county executive race has been paid off, and we are ready to concentrate on this year's election."

Cheers came from most, but not all, of those present.

"We have a number of races to watch in the upcoming election." Pickering liked this part of his job. It gave him a sense of power to be able to cast the spotlight on different candidates and to be able to color that light as well. "Our Congressman is up for reelection. He's done a great job for us

242

in Washington, and we want to make sure that he continues to do a great job for us."

Pickering held his hand out in the direction of the Congressman. The Congressman had been talking to a group of businessmen. He broke away to acknowledge Pickering and the audience.

Pickering then introduced the newly elected County Executive. "In the history of county government, we have had only two county executives. I'm proud to say that both are Republicans and both are here tonight."

And so it went with all of the current office holders being introduced in descending order.

Cordis leaned over to Temple and whispered, "This crowd will be asleep before he gets to you."

Temple grinned. "I may be too!"

Pickering announced that before he got to the new faces in town, everyone should refill their glasses. This got the loudest applause of the evening.

About a half hour later, Pickering again tapped his wine glass. Somewhat less inhibited, he began, "And now for our fresh crop of new faces. We have a group of new candidates who plan on doing big things and making some big changes."

He took a quick drink and went on. "Not the least of which is our candidate for the 48th Senate District, vying to unseat one of our favorite Democrats, Senator Mann: our own Jay Temple, attorney, businessman, and community servant. Jay, come up here and say a few words."

Temple walked to the center of the room. There were a few conversations going on around the room, but as he turned to speak to everyone present, a quiet settled over the group. They had heard of, or knew, Temple, and they wanted to know what he had to say.

"Thank you, Frank, and thank all of you for this opportunity. Today, I did something I have never done before in my life. I walked through the Southside."

People who were only half-listening were suddenly

concentrating on what this Republican was saying.

Temple went on. "I talked to people who have a quite different lifestyle than you and I. A single mother, an unemployed construction worker, and probably a drug pusher or worse. I'm not sure."

He looked around the audience at the well-groomed, clean, and healthy faces staring back at him.

"You know what the bottom line was for these people? Self-respect and a job. That's what they were looking for." He paused, then went on.

"Whether it's the Southside in Syracuse, the air base in Rome, a farm in Madison County, or a factory in Onondaga County, that sums up what people are looking for in Central New York. Self-respect and a job.

"Over the next four months, I'll be talking about this and how we can ensure those things. New York State has lost too many jobs due to its high taxes and overregulation. We've taken away from the individual's self-respect by giving handouts instead of work. We've built a government structure based on a welfare state and have reached a point where the biggest employer in the state is government.

"Frank mentioned change. It won't happen overnight, but change is coming. If not this year, then next or the year after that. People are tired of high taxes, big spending, huge welfare rolls, and less personal income, fewer opportunities, and a lower standard of living, all because of government.

"I believe that a political revolution is at hand and that Republicans, both at the local and national levels, can and will lead the way. I hope you will join with me so that together, we will accomplish the change in direction so long overdue."

They liked what they heard and showed it by their applause. They also showed their support where it counted, both through their votes, and their financial support as the race drew ever closer. Temple was having an impact. His next financial filing demonstrated that in the race for dollars, he had pulled even with Senator Mann, a point not lost on the Senator.

Chapter XVII

Money Talks

Isaac Brody was a successful druggist and businessman. He had a chain of drug stores in the City of Syracuse which he had founded and made successful before the big chains had taken over the market. Now, at the age of sixty-two, he was the wealthy owner of a declining chain of six drug stores.

His stores had once been located in middle class neighborhoods, serving hard-working people who preferred paying in cash rather than by credit or worse still, by government subsidy. The stores hadn't changed but the neighborhoods had.

The middle class had moved to the suburbs, and in their place, the working poor and welfare recipients had moved in. They still required his services and products, but payment was a big problem.

Isaac Brody became a personal lobbyist for his own business. He developed relationships with local and state politicians. His goal was to keep government money flowing to his customers who, in turn, would keep his business profitable.

On this Tuesday morning in July, he placed a call to his State Senator, Laura Ann Mann.

"This is Mr. Brody." He told the secretary. "Would you tell the Senator that I have some information on Mr. Temple."

Senator Mann came on the line shortly. "Hi, Isaac. I understand that you have some news about my opponent?"

"Last night I did my good deed for the Republicans and

attended a meeting at the General Humphrey Estate. Very nice place, the Humphrey Estate. Food was only so-so."

"That's what I've heard." Mann always got a kick out of Brody's way of describing his reactions to different circumstances. She had known Brody for almost twenty years. He was a reliable individual when it came to providing information, especially concerning Republicans. She knew that he contributed to both political parties as a way of insuring access for his own interests. However, she also felt that he was especially attracted to her and as such, more forthcoming with her than with her Republican counterparts.

"Last night, after the usual nonsense, your Mr. Temple got up and gave a pretty good talk. Seems he had been down on the Southside yesterday morning and came away with some scruples. Imagine talking about the Southside and helping unwed mothers before a high class Republican crowd like that?"

Mann stared out her office window as Brody spoke. Picturing Temple giving the talk as Brody spoke she said, "Yes, I can."

Brody answered, "You can what?"

"I can imagine him doing that."

"Well, it sure surprised me. But what was more surprising is that I think he got a pretty good response out of that crowd when he was done. Laura, I like you. I want to help you with some advice. Take this Mr. Temple seriously. He's not like those other clowns that they ran against you."

"Thanks, Isaac. I know that you are trying to help. I am taking Mr. Temple seriously. I don't want to have the same thing happen to me that happened to Ahern when I ran against him. I've worked too hard to get complacent."

"Exactly. No one is going to beat you once you put your talent to work for you." Brody was glad that Mann took his advice as he had intended it to be taken.

"Isaac?"

"Yes."

"Thanks for your concern."

246

"You are welcome, Laura."

As the Senator hung up the telephone, she resolved that a news conference was in order — and sooner rather than later.

* * *

July was a time to plow into fund raising efforts. Temple and his people knew that as it got down to 'crunch time,' campaigning would have to have all of Temple's attention. But now, in July, personal contact with would-be contributors was all important.

Dave Yondle, with help from Ken Mathews and Dr. Carey, set up a rigorous schedule for the candidate to follow. Two to three hours a day, Temple was on the phone calling people and asking for a financial commitment. No one could sell Temple better than Temple.

When not on the phone, he was attending special luncheons set up by Don North, or dinner parties put together by Dr. Carey and other friends of Temple.

Mailings went out asking contributors to past Republican campaigns to consider giving to the new candidate in the Republican Party. The Congressman turned over his entire list of contributors to Temple. This was the single biggest viable list of names that was given to the Temple campaign and was second only to the list the candidate himself had developed.

The money began to flow. None too soon either, for Temple's television spots were now beginning to air and the pace was picking up.

In a small town or even a good-sized one like Syracuse, little happens that doesn't soon become widespread knowledge. The Temple campaign was becoming noteworthy and on Thursday, July 12th, Sally Notholm appeared at Temple's headquarters with her TV 4 cameraman in tow.

Laney Gardiner saw the reporter and cameraman enter the headquarters. Her desk was at the end of a fifty foot long room that was filled with telephones, desks, sorting table, folding chairs, and lamps. During the day, the main room of Temple's headquarters looked deserted. But at night, the place came alive as volunteers left their jobs to come and work on the campaign.

At this moment, Gardiner was the only person in the building. Yondle was expected back momentarily. Cordis and Temple had an earlier meeting at Republican headquarters and were also due back shortly.

Notholm and her cameraman saw the leggy, former model rise to greet them and immediately two separate reactions occurred. Notholm was envious and put on the defensive, while her cameraman looked on with admiration and desire.

"May I help you?" Gardiner smiled at the two television people.

"I would like to talk to Mr. Temple," Notholm spit out.

It was obvious to both Gardiner and the cameraman that Notholm was not being pleasant. Without the slightest hint of being intimidated, Gardiner responded, "Mr. Temple is not here right now but is expected back at any time. May I have your name."

She said it so evenly and simply that the cameraman had to check twice to see if Gardiner was serious or merely toying with his news lady. Notholm liked to think of herself as the Barbara Walters of Central New York. The apparent lack of recognition had to be biting into Notholm and throwing her off her usual haughty pedestal. The straightforward look on Gardiner's face gave no hint of her question being anything more than just that, a question.

Notholm blinked once, then, looking away from Gardiner said, "We'll wait."

Notholm walked over to an empty desk and sat down. Gardiner shrugged, smiled at the cameraman and returned to her desk and her work. The cameraman was amused. He busied himself setting up his camera and his lights. This was not something he wanted to get into the middle of.

Fifteen minutes later, Cordis and Temple walked through the front door of the building, laughing about their most recent

248

visit to Republican headquarters. They both saw the reporter and cameraman at the same time.

"Can we help you?" Cordis asked as he walked over to Notholm.

"I'm here to interview Mr. Temple." With a quick glance at Gardiner and then back at Cordis, Notholm finished, "I'm Sally Notholm with Channel 4 News Central."

Gardiner smiled to herself as did the cameraman.

Cordis looked at Temple as he walked up to Notholm.

"Hi. I'm Jay Temple." He held out his hand and Notholm shook hands with the candidate.

"Mr. Temple, I'd like to talk to you about your fund raising and your campaign. Do you have a minute?"

"Sure. Let's go over here and sit on the couch."

Temple led Notholm to the couch. She looked at the cameraman. "Is this all right for you, Fred?"

"Yeah. Great." The cameraman set up a tripod and turned on a bank of lights. He then walked over and placed a lapel microphone on Temple. Notholm was already hooked up.

The red light started to flutter on the camera and Notholm gave a forced smile as she gave her opening.

"I'm Sally Notholm, Channel 4 News Center, and today I'm at the opulent headquarters of Jay Temple, candidate for the New York State Senate in the 48th Senate District." Looking away from the camera, she half turned toward Temple. "Mr. Temple, you are a newcomer to the political world and yet you seem to be able to raise significant sums of money for your campaign. How much of your own money have you put into this campaign?"

Temple thought to himself 'This is a great way to start an interview!' He looked right at Notholm and answered, "One thousand dollars."

Notholm waited for more but it became apparent after a slight pause that Temple had given his answer. Direct and to the point. Notholm recovered and went on. "How much do you intend to spend on this campaign?"

"As much as we are able to raise. So far, the people in this Senate District have been very generous. I think that our message of reduced government spending and lower taxes has struck a chord and people are responding."

Notholm turned completely to face Temple. It went unnoticed by all except the cameraman who had worked with Notholm for several years. She never completely turned away from the camera. At least, not until now. She was speaking again.

"What do you think it will take, in terms of dollars, to win this race?"

"As you mentioned earlier, I'm new to politics, at least as a candidate. I've been told that my opponent, Senator Mann, will spend up to a quarter of a million dollars on her side and that as a non-incumbent, I need to raise at least that amount to have a chance at winning."

"A half of a million dollars is a lot of money for one race. Your financial report indicates that you and Senator Mann are running neck-and-neck in terms of dollars. Where is your money coming from?"

Temple smiled at Notholm. "Mostly friends and acquaintances. But it's interesting. This past week, I received a letter from a student at LeMoyne College. He enclosed a ten dollar bill. In his letter he said he wished he could contribute more but didn't have the money to do that. He also offered to help out on the campaign."

While they were talking, campaign workers were beginning to arrive and were gathering behind the camera.

Temple went on. "At the risk of embarrassing my new friend, I see that Johnny Wallace has just arrived and is standing behind the camera." Temple motioned in the direction of Wallace. "He's the student I was talking about. This campaign is about us giving people like Johnny and all of our children and grandchildren a future that's not so mortgaged by today's government that there isn't any opportunity for them to live happy, successful lives.

250

"Sally, if we continue to tax and spend and borrow as we are currently doing, no one will be able to live, work, or go to school in New York State. It's time for a change. That's why I'm running, and that's why people like Johnny are helping out."

Notholm didn't know where else to take this interview, so she thanked Temple and left Temple's headquarters with her cameraman in tow.

Cordis said to Temple, "I liked the last part best but that'll probably end up on the cutting room floor."

"Nothing is ever certain in life or politics."

"What about death and taxes?"

"Now there's a couple of morbid thoughts!"

Gardiner came up to the politician and the campaign manager. "I just wanted to remind you that we have a dinner party at six."

"Yes. Doctor Hailor's wife." Cordis checked his watch. "We've got about an hour."

Gardiner pushed her hair back from her forehead. "You have about an hour. Johnny, Patrick, and I are going to leave in a few minutes to help Mrs. Hailor set up." Turning to Temple, Gardiner smiled and said, "Do you need anything before we leave?"

"No. Thanks. Say, how was our reporter friend before we got here?" He motioned toward the door Notholm had recently exited from.

Gardiner replied, with a glint of mirth in her eye, "Slightly off balance."

Temple and Cordis thought they knew what Gardiner meant as they laughed, but they didn't.

On Friday, July 13th, Channel 4 News carried two stories of political interest. State Senator Mann announced that she was leaving on a seven-state swing to look into prison reform. Mann appeared on the newscast as Chairperson for the Governor's Task Force on State prisons.

"As Chairperson of the New York State Task Force On State Prisons, I feel that I have an obligation to bring our prison system into the Twentieth Century.

"Our prisons are not serving to rehabilitate, but rather are a breeding ground for AIDS, venereal disease, and more crime. Recidivism is high and individual worth low.

"We need to act. I am hoping that my visits to more enlightened programs will provide me with ideas that I can bring back to New York. Long term, the solution to crime is to rehabilitate those who are incarcerated so that when they are back in society, they can once again be productive citizens."

The second story opened with a picture of Jay Temple's headquarters. Sally Notholm was standing in front of the building.

"Here we are at the busy intersection of Thompson Road and Erie Boulevard in DeWitt at the campaign headquarters of Jay Temple. Mr. Temple, a wealthy lawyer from Fayetteville, is running a well-financed campaign to unseat three term incumbent Senator Laura Ann Mann. We spoke to Mr. Temple earlier today."

The scene changed to the inside of the headquarters building. Notholm was talking to Temple, ". . .you seem to be able to raise significant sums of money for your campaign. How much of your own money have you put into this campaign?"

Temple looked relaxed as he answered, "One thousand dollars."

Notholm then asked, "How much do you intend to spend on this campaign?"

Again a relaxed Temple answered, "As much as we are able to raise."

The camera cut in live to Notholm back in the studio. "Word on the street is that the big money in town is backing Temple's campaign to oust the outspoken Senator Mann."

Ron Clanton, Channel 4 news anchor, was sitting next to Notholm. He asked, "Sally, Senator Mann is kind of a maverick in Albany, isn't she?"

Notholm again showed her forced smile as she answered. "Yes. The Republicans would like to get rid of Senator Mann

252

and have made no secret about that. She has pushed for term limits, an open door on legislative debates and doing away with the "good old boy" system in state government.

"Temple is the alternative that the Republicans in Albany would like to see elected."

Clanton asked, "Is this another David and Goliath story?"

Notholm looked at the camera. "If the Republicans are the Goliath, then certainly Senator Mann is going to need a lot of arrows in her quiver to offset the flow of money to the Temple campaign."

The camera focused in on Clanton. "Thank you, Sally. This will certainly be a campaign to keep an eye on."

Cordis flicked off the television. "Damn! I'm going to call that station and raise hell with them. What kind of crap was that? Talk about one-sided coverage."

Yondle sat forward. "Well, look at the positive side."

Tarkings, Cordis, Temple, and Carey looked at Yondle.

"We did get equal time. Jay's name was tied to Mann's and people know that money is coming into our campaign. This may help as we look for more financial support. People like to be a part of a successful campaign and a successful fund raising effort."

Dr. Carey thought about this and said, "Dave may have something. Jay, you have said that there are two races that have to be won here: the election and the race to raise money. I think that you should push that concept everywhere you go. It takes money to run a political campaign. Everyone knows that. This might not have been as bad as it first appears."

Tarkings laughed. "If the power of positive thinking works, Senator Mann, look out!"

Following a day of campaigning door-to-door in Bridgeport, Temple wound up at the home of Frank and Sarah Schell of East Syracuse.

The Schells were a prominent couple in the East Syracuse community. Sarah was the president of the ESM Fire Department auxiliary and Frank was principal undertaker for the area. Neither had ever met Temple but had been encouraged by Temple's friend, Ed Thatcher, to invite Temple to a barbecue and introduce him to their friends.

Thatcher had told Temple that the Schells were not happy with Senator Mann and were very interested in what he had to say about tax relief for small business.

Temple arrived at 6:30 in the evening and was greeted by Sarah.

"Hello. I'm Jay Temple."

"Yes. I've heard a lot about you. I'm Sarah Schell," she smiled at Temple as she motioned him toward the hallway leading to the back of the house. "Everyone is in the back yard by the pool." She turned to him. "You didn't bring a bathing suit?"

Surprised, Temple answered, "No. Was I supposed to?"

"No. That's all right. Some of our friends did, but they always do. Barbecue at the Schells to them means a swim in the pool."

They reached the back door and met Frank Schell coming in with a chef's hat, apron, and empty plate with fresh blood from the hamburgers dripping off of it.

Sarah said, "Frank, this is Jay Temple. Mr. Temple, my husband Frank."

Temple did a mental appraisal of the couple during these introductions.

Sarah Schell was a petite and cute young woman with a quick smile and bouncy personality. Not what he would have expected of a funeral director's wife.

Frank Schell was a short, intense young man, with a quiet style and a studied disposition. He was what Temple would have expected. Handling the cooking chores at a barbecue, well, that was another matter.

The Schells immediately took it upon themselves to introduce Temple to their friends. There were approximately forty to fifty people at the Schell home at any one time. It seemed that people would come and go at will. In fact, that was exactly what was happening. Many of their friends were also neighbors who would leave for food and casseroles for the party or to check on their children. Some went home to change from their bathing suits into warmer clothes as the evening wore on.

Temple was impressed by how friendly everyone seemed to be. He also noted that everyone was quite aware of who he was before he had been introduced to them. The Schells had seen to that.

By the time that Temple thanked the Schells and said good night, he had been given advice on everything from how to run a campaign to bird watching. Three people had given him checks ranging from twenty dollars to seventy-five and two others had agreed to work on his campaign, including Sarah Schell. It had been a full day.

* * *

The week of July 16 proved that Yondle was right. The money flowing into the campaign did pick up. Temple got a lot of positive feedback on his brief interview with Notholm, especially from the business community. By the end of the week, the campaign had taken in an additional eighty-seven hundred dollars.

The campaign was getting another unexpected boost. With air time having been purchased on the commercial networks' news broadcasts for the last two weeks of July and first two weeks of August, Temple's ads were running along with the fast-breaking news story on the Middle East.

Iraq invaded Kuwait, seeking to annex this small country that was rich with oil reserves. The United States, with George Bush as President, thought differently. A joint Allied force, including an unusually large number of Arab nations, mounted a military effort to restore Kuwait's legitimate government and to oust the Iraqi military force occupying the country.

It was a huge military undertaking made for television. It not only bolstered the President's ratings but it jumped

255

Temple's ratings as well.

By the end of the four week run of commercial advertising, a Republican poll showed Temple's name recognition at 72% and Mann's at 73%. It was still too early for this to have an impact on voting, but it had a definite impact on contributions. In particular, the New York State Senate Republican Campaign Committee reclassified the Temple-Mann campaign as a 'watch race.' This meant that a real race was developing, and it also meant that money and/or help should be earmarked for the 48th Senate District.

Temple also noticed subtle changes in the people he saw and those whom he met. He had always taken the race seriously, even though it had been uphill from the outset. Initially, he had given himself a forty-sixty chance of winning. The State Senate Republican Campaign Committee had thought it more like a five to ninety-five chance of success against the seasoned Democratic Senator. But now, Temple was sensing a shift. People knew him, said hello to him by name, walked up to him to shake his hand, to wish him luck, or to talk about the election.

Temple was now on a roll. His door–to–door activity was stepped up a notch. In the last two weeks of July, he campaigned in Bridgeport, Cicero, DeWitt, Jamesville, Manlius, East Syracuse, Kirkville, Oneida, and Canastota. In populated areas, he would do every other street with his volunteers covering those areas he missed. In rural areas, he went to every door himself. Cordis was concerned about the amount of time this took and whether it would be more beneficial to hit high volume areas. Temple believed that he needed to get a sense of what these people were thinking about, too. He also felt that if he could talk one–on–one with anyone, he could win their vote. No precise measure of this was ever done but voting patterns indicated that Temple was correct in this assumption.

Temple closed out the month of July with an appearance before the Hamilton Rotary Club. This had significance for two reasons. First, because it was in the heart of one of Senator Mann's strongest geographic areas for support. Second, television stations, both in Utica and in Syracuse, sent camera crews to film the occasion. This meant that the entire 48th Senate District would have coverage.

There was a third factor which made it significant but Temple was unaware of this at the time. Mann had been given advance notice of Temple's trip to Hamilton. She already was reeling from her latest poll which showed a huge gain in name recognition for Temple. Not only had he stumbled into one of the highest rating periods of the year for commercial television due to the Gulf War, but now he was taking his campaign into her territory. She decided that it was time to take the gloves off and to carry the fight to Temple. She couldn't afford to ignore him any more.

Chapter XVIII

August: Month Eight
A Time To Debate

The lights and cameras were a distraction for the thirty-five Rotarians in the room. The Hamilton Rotary Club was an old traditional club that had met since its founding at the Colgate Inn. Most of its members were either on the staff of Colgate College or in businesses that related to the college and its students. They enjoyed the collegiate atmosphere of their lunches and saved the public relations for their community service activities. Suddenly being overrun with television crews was something they were not used to and weren't sure they approved of.

Temple concluded his remarks by saying, "Community service means a lot to each one of you as it does to me. I view politics as a form of community service. There are a great many needs out there to be met. The only sure way to take care of those needs is through elective office.

"Thank you for your time and for listening to my thoughts on this year's election."

The Rotarians applauded and the president of the club presented Temple with a token of their appreciation, a framed copy of the 'golden rule.'

Asked by a reporter about the meeting, one Rotarian who happened to be a close friend of Senator Mann, commented, "It was a circus!"

Another member who was a professor of history noted, "I liked the closing. . .tying politics to community service. Very

Jeffersonian."

* * *

That evening Mann met with her staff.

"I want to set up debates with Temple. He likes Hamilton so well, ask the League of Woman Voters there to set up something. I'm sure Betsy Collin would love to help out.

"Next, let's do something with the YWCA in Syracuse. Get their board to sponsor a debate downtown. We can push the funding for their unwed mothers program that I got for them last year.

"He's got a lot of nobodies running around Rome, so let's do one in Rome. Ask Lenny Tugston to get his union buddies out and have a question and answer forum. Have them put some labor questions to Mr. Temple.

"We'll rap it up in Utica. Get the teachers union representatives there to hold a debate on educational issues. We'll do a background briefing beforehand and knock him out on his lack of knowledge. They have a dislike for people that don't take the time to know their issues.

"Get his people to agree to these debates, and if they don't, we'll notify the media that Mr. Temple has refused to debate. Either way, we win." Mann looked at Johns and then Samuels. No argument came from either.

Samuels nodded. "It's early, but I think Mr. Temple has gotten to the point where we need to trim his ears back. If we get him thinking about debates, then maybe he won't be thinking about the campaign."

"Yeah. And if he blows it in one of the debates, he's done," Johns added.

"We need to make it a point that we've been there for these groups when they needed help in Albany," Mann voiced concern over the obvious. Samuels was seeing something in Mann that was unfamiliar. He thought to himself, 'maybe I have underestimated Jay Temple.'

259

Samuels said aloud, "We'll contact Temple's people first thing tomorrow."

The telephone rang. Mann picked up the receiver, talked for a few minutes and then hung up the phone. "Larry says Temple's appearance before the Rotary was a circus. Doesn't think anyone heard a thing that Temple said." She smiled and for the moment, the girl who had clawed her way to the top of a man's world thought that all was right with it.

The last Saturday in July was a record–breaking ninety-five degrees. Temple and Cordis were invited by Don Towelson, an Assembly candidate from Rome, to play in his golf fund raising outing.

Towelson's family had a history in local politics. His father had been an Assemblyman for eighteen years, representing the same district that Don was now running for. His brother was a city councilor and his sister was the county clerk. Don had been a State Police officer, a City of Rome Police officer, and Commissioner of Police for the City of Utica.

The Towelson name was well–recognized locally and the Towelson Open was sure to attract a crowd.

Cordis had agreed to play with some reluctance. He knew that Jay belonged to a country club and played golf and tennis. He did not know how well Temple played, but he guessed it was better than he did.

Cordis liked Temple's lifestyle. He admired the variety of activities and friends with which Temple seemed to be involved. Although Cordis didn't directly address the notion, he tied playing golf in with Temple's lifestyle and decided that this might be his avenue along the same path.

As Cordis steered the van into the parking lot of the golf club, he said, "I haven't played golf in a long time."

Temple responded without much thought, "I've only played once this year."

"Because of the campaign?" Cordis asked as he parked the van.

"No. Just my usual!"

260

"Your usual?"

"Yeah. I play about five times a year. My first game is always my best and then it is all downhill from there." Temple laughed.

"What kind of a handicap do you have?"

"Twenty-seven."

"Not bad."

"Not very good either. I just never want to spend the entire day playing golf. If you're going to be good, you have got to practice. Do you have a handicap?" Temple looked at Cordis.

Cordis nodded as he climbed down from the driver's seat. "Thirty-one."

As Cordis rounded the back of the van, Temple put his hand on Cordis' shoulder and said, "Well, from one duffer to another, let's have a good time and see if we can learn anything that will help my friend Allen Benair out."

Cordis asked, "What's Mr. Benair up to?"

"He called and suggested having a golf outing for our campaign at the Cavalry Club. He and Charlie Tossie want to set it up. Allen said that they already have a list of people to invite and would be happy to add any names that we provide to him."

"Hey, that's terrific. I'm going to approach today's activity with a whole new outlook." Cordis felt a lot better now about his being at the Towelson Open. It didn't improve his game, as it turned out, but it did provide some good observations which he and Temple would later incorporate in the Temple golf outing.

Temple had been encouraged to attend Towelson's golf tournament in order to meet people who might be active supporters for his campaign.

The two lessons that Temple eventually took away from this tournament, and one sponsored by the Congressman a month later, were that the time spent playing golf could be more wisely spent campaigning and the people who attend are interested primarily in the host for the event. They are not there to be solicited by other candidates.

On the positive side, it is good to be seen and to talk with people at the reception and banquet that usually follows the tournament. Temple made the most of this time without overtly asking for support for his own candidacy.

On the way back to Syracuse that night, Cordis asked Temple, "Why did you push Towelson so hard and never mention your own campaign?"

He was referring to Temple's remarks made at the banquet at the request of Don Towelson.

"It's a lot easier for me to talk about someone else than it is for me to talk about me. We were Towelson's guests among Towelson's friends and supporters. They wanted to hear about Don not about Jay Temple.

"The other reason is that I'm the State Senate candidate and Don Towelson is the Assembly candidate. In the order of things, I should be there to help Don. It was his day in the sun." Temple paused thinking as was Cordis of the ninety-five degree temperature. "No pun intended!"

They laughed.

The following evening, the Jewish community held a dinner honoring one of its most prominent fund raisers and community citizen, Barry Kohn.

Kohn was well-respected both within and outside the Jewish community. He had served on many boards of many charitable organizations and had been the primary supporter, and eventually the first president, of the new Jewish Community Center. He was someone, who once he had said that he would do something, you could be certain that it would get done.

The dinner in his honor was well-attended. Jay Temple had been invited not only because of his current race for the New York State Senate, but also because he had known and worked with Kohn in raising money for Onondaga Community College.

Temple worked a room as well as anyone. He was able to introduce himself to strangers easily by making a quick study

262

of the person's appearance, dress, apparent interests, or surrounding environment. The conversation was easy, and just as easily, Temple would excuse himself and move on to the next group of people or individual.

The lights flashed on and off twice, signaling that dinner was to be served shortly. Temple always found it amusing that no matter what the makeup of the audience, this was a universal signal for dinner and people would move en masse toward their assigned tables.

Temple was seated with Tom Mosby, Ken Mathews, Dr. Carey, Kevin Roth, and three members of the Jewish Federation; Karen Epstein, Conny Raymond, and Ada Cohen. Karen Epstein was also a committeewoman for the Onondaga County Republican Party.

Epstein leaned over to Temple, program for the tribute dinner in hand, and said, "Did you see who was at the head table?"

Temple looked at her and answered, "No. I haven't looked at the program yet. Anyone exciting?"

"Depends on your point of view." She had a mischievous look in her eyes as she held up the program pointing and saying, "State Senator Laura Ann Mann."

For the first time this evening, Temple looked first at the program and then up toward the elevated head table. Most of the audience of some eight hundred people had taken their seats as had the head table. Temple first noticed the Congressman talking with Kohn and his wife. He then looked down the length of the table, and for a brief moment, he locked eyes with Laura Mann.

Mann had been told that Temple was present, and through a friend had learned that Temple was at table 45 about halfway down the right side of the room. She had just found the table and her opponent when he looked up at her. Both flushed for a moment and then busied themselves with those around them.

Reflecting on the evening on their way home that night,

both Mann and Temple had foremost on their minds that brief instant of recognition. For both it was a recognition that each had sought out the other and each was taking the measure of the other. Politicians do that. They are not alone in this activity, but probably because of the competitive nature of their business, they feel a need to know what their opponent is doing and how they compare.

For Temple, it was an understanding of the advantage of being an incumbent. Mann was in the spotlight by virtue of her office. She carried it off well because of her poise and presence.

For Mann, it was a recognition that Temple was actually in there competing with her. He was working the same crowds that she was working. She, too, appreciated the advantage that she had being in office, but she also remembered another Senator who had the same advantage and had lost his seat to a Common Councilor from Syracuse. 'Temple was too comfortable politicking for a newcomer,' she thought.

At the Kohn residence that night, Arlene Kohn was recapping a wonderful evening with her husband.

"Our Congressman was certainly complimentary of your work this evening."

Barry Kohn smiled. "He should be. Our cocktail party for him raised nearly ten thousand dollars."

Arlene thought about this for a moment. "Politics makes strange bedfellows. Senator Mann has always been very helpful to you even though you are a Republican."

"I've reciprocated."

She smiled. "By inviting Jay Temple to your dinner?"

Kohn frowned. "Jay paid. Besides, he has been a friend and his daughter and our oldest have been friends in school."

"Who are you going to vote for?" she asked as she put her arms around her husband.

Kohn loved his wife and knew she was teasing him. He hugged her as they walked up the stairs to their bedroom. "That's why it's a secret ballot."

* * *

Dave Yondle and Laney Gardiner were working on the campaign financial records with Kevin Roth when the phone rang at the campaign headquarters.

"Good morning. Temple for Senate Headquarters," Gardiner answered the telephone.

At the other end of the line, a somewhat officious Joel Samuels asked to speak to Jay Temple.

"I'm sorry, Mr. Temple is campaigning in Madison County today. May someone else help you?" Gardiner said in an even tone of voice.

"This is Joel Samuels, Senator Mann's campaign manager. I would like to talk with someone about setting up a series of debates between the Senator and Mr. Temple." Samuels shifted an unlit cigar from one side of his mouth to the other as he talked.

"I believe you would want to talk to Mr. Ted Cordis," Gardiner answered, not being certain that the caller was really who he said he was. "Mr. Cordis is also campaigning with Mr. Temple. If you would like to leave a phone number where you can be reached, I will have Mr. Cordis call you upon his return."

Samuels left a number where he could be reached after five in the afternoon.

"What was that all about?" Roth asked.

Gardiner smiled as she looked from Yondle to Roth. "That was Joel Samuels, Mann's campaign manager. They want to set up some debates."

"Yes!" Yondle yelled. "They think that they're under the gun now, wait till Jay gets her in a one-on-one match. He'll have her for lunch!" Yondle blushed after recovering from his initial outburst. Roth and Gardiner laughed at Yondle's quick reactions.

"Have her for lunch?" Roth teased. "I don't think that they'd get along that well."

After a few more minutes of speculation about the

265

outcome of the pending debates, Yondle called the Canteen Restaurant in Chittenango. Temple and Cordis were scheduled to be there for a Republican Dinner that evening. Yondle wanted to get Cordis working on the debates as soon as possible. He left a message with the hostess to have Cordis call headquarters when they arrived.

Next, Yondle called Bob Berry, and filled him in on the latest developments. Berry said that he would call Tom Mosby and arrange to meet with Cordis that evening to discuss format and locations. Berry pointed out the obvious; that this offer was a big step for the campaign and must be handled well.

As things sometimes work out, Temple called in to headquarters in the late afternoon. Gardiner immediately told him about the interest in setting up some debates.

"Great. Laney, see if you can get someone to meet us at the Canteen in an hour. They can bring Ted back to headquarters and he and Bob, Tom, Dave, and you can get to work on the details before we call Samuels back. Also see if Ken Mathews and Jim Summers are available." Temple's mind was in high gear. These were all people he could count on to work out an effective strategy.

Temple continued, "We ought to have these debates spread out across the district and have a no–holds–barred debate on the issues. As soon as I am finished at the Canteen, I'll join the group to see what has been worked out."

Gardiner asked, "Should we call Samuels back before you get here?"

"No. Let's work out our plans first and then call. It's not going to make a difference whether we call tonight or tomorrow."

Temple filled Cordis in on what had happened while they drove to the Canteen. Cordis felt that tingle of excitement that comes periodically during a campaign when you know that something important is about to occur. His one comment as he thrust a clenched fist to the side was, "Kick butt!"

One thing that Temple had learned early was that

political campaigns did not allow the luxury of time in making decisions or dwelling on any one subject. You had to gather as much information as you could on any one topic, decide on a course of action, and then move on to the next demand on your time.

The general outline for the debates had been sketched by Temple to Cordis. Both realized that Mann would have her own ideas about this and that they would negotiate what they could. The bottom line was that Temple would take on the Senator in any format and at any event or location that was open for him. Temple felt comfortable with this and believed that the larger audience which the media would attract would far outweigh any stacked audience that Mann might have in mind.

It was also agreed that Cordis would call Samuels tonight as requested and arrange to meet with him at a later date to discuss details of the debates. This would buy time to get input from all those involved with the issues and strategy, and would set the stage for the debates themselves.

The van pulled into the parking lot of the Canteen. Kevin Roth and Dave Yondle were already there waiting. Yondle drove Cordis back to headquarters for the meeting while Roth accompanied Temple to the Madison County Republican Committee Dinner.

Jim Trout, chairman of the Republican Committee, met Temple at the door and took him around to meet a number of committee people who had not yet met the Senate candidate personally. Temple was impressed with the warmth and sincerity of the group.

The dinner was excellent. Temple appreciated a good Black Angus steak, and that was one of the hallmarks of the Canteen. After dinner, Jim Trout introduced the guest speaker for the evening, Assemblyman Lyle MacKay.

MacKay knew everyone in the room, their children, and their grandchildren. He had been the local veterinarian and had seen to their cats and dogs, cows and horses, in good times and in bad. He'd been paid for his services in cash, jams,

267

vegetables, and beer. He enjoyed being a politician because he enjoyed people.

MacKay stood up with microphone in hand and said, "This has been a great evening. Jim here has been filling me in on all the latest gossip since I left for Albany. He tells me that Aggy over there," MacKay pointed to an elderly woman at a back table, "drove Harvey's pick-up through the back wall of their garage and nearly killed Emma Lou Harris' cat. Harvey told Jim that Aggy was sorry about the wall, concerned for the cat, but praised heaven that the machine stopped before it ruined her garden!"

The entire room exploded with laughter. Temple enjoyed this. MacKay was the politician of yesteryear. He knew his audience and could spin a yarn just beyond truth, but close enough so that even those about whom he was talking weren't quite sure that the situation he was describing wasn't what actually happened.

MacKay went on. "Aggy, there's this guy named Ken Slater walking around. I sure hope the next time you start old Harv's pick up, he's around."

Again laughter at MacKay's reference to his opponent.

"Folks, you've known me most of my life. Except for a couple of years with Uncle Sam during WW II, I've been right here in Chittenango. I took care of your animals and now I'm trying to take care of you. The Governor sure isn't helping any. He'd like me out and my opponent in."

A few people shouted, "No."

"He'd like to get a Yes-man back in Albany in my place."

A few more 'No's' came from around the room.

"Old Cuomo says 'out with MacKay and in with some more of my *tax everybody* boys.' But we're not going to let that happen, are we?"

Now, everyone shouted, "No."

"You said it. I plan to work just as hard in this election as I did fourteen years ago when I was first elected to the

Assembly. I've got a good campaign manager in Johnny Benders and between us and with your help, I'll be back in my seat in Albany come January giving Old Cuomo and his New York City crowd a piece of my mind."

Everyone cheered and clapped for their aging Assemblyman and friend.

"Just as you have supported me, I want to introduce you to a fella who I think could really make a difference for all of us. This guy's from just down the road in Onondaga County, but he knows a lot about the things that are bothering us. I'd like you to meet Jay Temple, our State Senate candidate."

MacKay handed the microphone to Temple as he shook his hand. Temple thanked MacKay for the introduction and told him how much he enjoyed his comments. Then putting the microphone up close to his mouth Temple began, "I can't tell you how much I am enjoying this evening. The food has been sensational. You have all made me feel right at home, and it's like talking to old friends."

People smiled at Temple as he reached out to them.

"I would like to thank Aggy for offering to drive our campaign van for us for the remainder of the race," Temple paused as the laughter came after the recognition, "but I'm a little concerned about my own garden."

The audience applauded. Temple checked Aggy to make certain that she was taking this in the way he had hoped. She was laughing along with everyone else.

Temple went on. "We have a real opportunity this year to make a difference in the way business is done in Albany. My opponent has been telling you for years that she is opposed to the Albany spend-and-tax program. Yet her voting record shows that she voted the same way every other politician in Albany voted 97% of the time."

Temple paused to let that number sink in before he went on again. "Ninety-seven percent of the time she voted for the tax-and-spend policies that have cost this state jobs, money, livelihoods, and a decent standard of living. Ninety-seven

269

percent of her votes were on policies that have increased your taxes.

"I think we need a change in the Senate. We need someone who will say this is right and that is wrong. We need someone who will not compromise principle for expediency. And we need someone who will say 'no' to tax increases and spending increases more often than three out of every one hundred votes on the Senate floor."

The audience at the Canteen stood up and cheered their Senate candidate. They knew they had two winners. One, an old line politician who knew them by name, and the other, a well-spoken newcomer who talked about what concerned them most, being able to afford to live in New York State.

MacKay and Temple left the Canteen with a strong base to build upon over the next two and one half months. That's exactly what they were planning on doing.

Chapter XIX

The Issues

The pace of the campaign was picking up for both candidates. It was only mid-August but Temple was now in his full campaign stride. His typical day began at six in the morning with either staff meetings or factory visits. Factory visits meant standing outside a plant gate as workers arrived, introducing himself and shaking hands while a campaign volunteer would hand out his literature, buttons, and pencils. Temple often thought the real selling point here were the pencils.

Next would be a round of solicitation calls usually beginning around ten in the morning and lasting an hour or more depending on how successful he was and the responses that he received.

At noon it was speech time. Women's clubs, service clubs, church groups, civic organizations, company lunches — anywhere where three or more people gathered, Temple was ready and willing to discuss his views on various issues.

Afternoons were spent on door-to-door campaigning and areas of the district were targeted to get as broad a coverage as possible. Temple had promised himself that no section of the district would be left out in his race to represent the interests of every constituent. His staff discovered the meaning of 'seasonal roads' during this part of the day. On more than one occasion, they would get lost on roads that were essentially impassible during winter months. But they would always find people living on these roads. Temple would say hello and sometimes spend more time than Cordis would have liked talking to people who really struggled to survive.

On one occasion, Temple met Jake Muller, a recluse who made baskets for money, and raised vegetables and fished to eat. Muller had worked in a foundry that had been closed when the owners moved south. He couldn't find work that paid anywhere near what he had been making so he moved to 'the country.' His wife couldn't take it so she left him and moved to Pittsburgh. They had one son who was in the service. Muller didn't know if his son was part of Desert Storm or not. He hoped not.

Muller told Temple that the state had gone 'to hell in a hand basket.' He said politicians had ruined the state and that it would never change. "The only thing that changes are the people that go there. You people mean well, maybe. Once you get there you change. You're more concerned with stayin' there than doin' what's right. Business is leavin' because of that."

Over the next few months, Temple thought about what Muller had said. He wondered if politicians do change. 'Maybe most do go to Albany or Washington with the right ideas and values but somewhere along the way the system changes them.' It was something he'd have to remember.

A quick dinner, usually McDonald's or Burger King, would be followed by a fund raiser or other event for more handshaking and talk about the campaign and the issues of the day. By eleven at night, it was back to headquarters to thank the volunteers who had been working all day on other aspects of the campaign, and then home by midnight.

He and Pat would have tea. He would tell her about each detail of the day, and she would bring him up to date on their children's activities.

It was a pattern that would be repeated almost daily until Election Day.

* * *

Laura Ann Mann followed a similar schedule except she would add visits to her Senate Office to take care of any matters

272

that could not be handled by her staff. She would also call her contacts with the media on a regular basis to feed them some information which might generate a news story. This in turn would translate into free campaign advertising for the Senator.

Mann knew the type of stories that would turn on each reporter in her Rolodex. She had Tork Johns constantly creating releases she could use as she worked the reporters. It was a technique she had developed as a common councilor and had now perfected as a Senator.

Johns had been studying issue statements that Temple had been putting out. He discovered that there was one issue that Temple had not talked about yet, and it was an issue that had always been the backbone of his Senator's support.

"Laura Ann," Johns called out as he saw the Senator enter her office. He hustled over to her doorway. "I think I have something that will slow down Mr. Temple."

Mann immediately turned to her aide. "What?"

"Abortion."

"Abortion? What do you mean?"

"He's never said where he stands on abortion. He talks about being an issue guy and yet on this issue, I can't find a single word." Johns smiled as he saw that the Senator recognized the same opening that he had.

"You're right! I've studied his news releases, and I don't recall that he has said anything about where he stands on pro-choice either." She thumped her desk. "We won't let Mr. Temple off that easy." She called Annie Wilson, her secretary, into her office and asked her to arrange a lunch appointment with Sally Notholm.

* * *

Temple had returned from a luncheon given by a Rome couple he knew through his Rotary activities.

The Pinticos were a very community-minded family who had devoted many hours to improving the quality of life for the

273

people of Rome. Mike Pintico had been president of the Rome Rotary Club and had played a major role in the development of an Erie Canal Museum in Rome. He had also chaired the local United Way Campaign and worked on the Rome Hospital Fund Drive. His wife had been active in the Women of Rotary and had brought an emergency care program to the community. She had also been an active school board member and served on her church board of deacons.

The Pinticos had never been involved in politics and political races outside the non-partisan school board races. They had friends in both parties and thought the best way to keep them was to not get involved in political campaigns.

Their friends knew that the Pinticos stayed away from the political arena, so when they received invitations to have lunch at the Pinticos' home to meet a political candidate, they were interested. Thirty people were invited and twenty-six people joined the Pinticos and Jay and Pat Temple for lunch.

Jay and Pat were introduced by Mike to his friends while his wife served salad and soup to the assembled guests. Temple had then given a brief talk expressing his gratitude to the Pinticos and his admiration for what they had done for the City of Rome. He said that he hoped he could someday look back at his time in government and be able to say that he had done as much.

Temple's talk was well-received, and he had been given many positive indications of support.

Back at headquarters, he sat at his desk looking out the showroom window at the setting sun. Cordis walked over and said, "How did it go in Rome?"

Temple wheeled around in his chair to face his campaign manager. "Great! The Pinticos are nice people. Their friends seemed truly interested and were very kind to Pat and me."

"Did you come away with any suggestions we can use in Rome?"

"Actually, I did. Something that we can use not only in Rome but throughout the district."

"What's that?"

"Billboards. Signs." Temple looked out the window again. "Look out there across Thompson Road. See those billboards for the car dealership?"

Cordis looked out the window at the billboard. "Yes."

"I drive by that sign every day and because I do, I know the name of that dealership. I think we need to get some signs up around the district."

Cordis turned to Temple. "Bob Berry is planning a yard sign blitz the last two weeks of the campaign. Says that way you'll be fresh and on everyone's mind when it counts."

"I need to be on everyone's mind now. The State Committee won't give me money for the campaign without the name recognition and voters won't relate unless it becomes almost second nature to remember who I am and what I'm running for. With all due respect to Bob, I think we need the signs now."

Cordis could see that Temple thought that this was an important part of the campaign strategy. He kicked himself for not coming up with it on his own. Cordis had never been involved in a campaign of this magnitude before and wanted to do everything to perfection. As much as he wanted Temple to win, he also wanted to establish his own credentials as a 'king maker.' If Temple were to win, Cordis knew that he would be in high demand. If Temple came close to winning, Cordis knew he would still come out ahead because no one else had gotten near to Laura Ann Mann. In fact, most Republicans were afraid to even run against her. The top Republican officeholders in the county were constantly in fear that she would leave the Senate, where she was in the minority party, and run against them.

"Ted, are you still among the living?" Temple laughed as he brought Cordis' thoughts back to the present.

"Sorry. I was just thinking about the next step for your signs."

"Give Ken Mathews a call. He might be able to help out." Temple walked over to his desk and took out a piece of paper and a pen. "Here's the idea I have for our billboards and signs." He started to draw a campaign sign. "We want them all to look the same. Some will be larger in size, but I want them recognized as mine."

The colors were as Cordis would have guessed, knowing Temple: red, white, and blue.

* * *

Sally Notholm had never been to Albert's before. Fortunately, it was on the main street in Cazenovia and not difficult to find. It was one-thirty in the afternoon, a time arranged to fit both Laura Ann Mann's schedule as well as Notholm's.

"Hi, Sally," Mann shouted from the bar as Notholm walked in. Mann had been talking to the bartender, a long time friend and manager of the restaurant.

"Hi, Laura Ann. Is this a liquid lunch or do we actually eat something?" Notholm said as she joined Mann.

"Whatever." Mann smiled a friendly grin.

"Let's eat, I'm famished."

Mann led Notholm to a booth in the back of the restaurant. There were very few people left in the room this late in the lunchtime. No one seemed to pay them much attention.

Notholm opened the conversation, "How's the campaign going?"

"You tell me."

"Well, I don't care much for your opponent. Typical male ego. Thinks every woman can be won with politeness and manners. Did you catch my piece on his finances?"

"Yeah. I question how many of the little people have contributed to his war chest."

Notholm picked up a pickle and bit into it. She talked as she chewed. "Rumor in Albany is that the Republicans in the Senate may kick in big for this guy." She watched Mann for a reaction.

"They would kick in big for any 'guy' that ran against

me. They hate my guts!"

"Well, Kris is going to go over the campaign finance reports when they come in to see who the big givers are. We'll run another story on campaign spending then." Notholm finished her pickle.

As they ate they talked about a number of races other than Mann's. They also talked about Notholm's work on a murder case and her upcoming series about the case. She felt that this might be her big break.

Over dessert, Mann said, "Getting back to Temple for a moment. He talks about taking stands but have you heard where he's coming from on the pro-choice issue?"

Notholm looked up from her cheesecake. "Hey, you know I don't think he has said anything about abortion." Notholm was thinking now. "If he had, I would have remembered it."

"Well, if you find anything on that, would you let me know? It's an important issue for me, and I think the public should know exactly where he stands on the Republican position of reversing the present law." Mann knew that Notholm would not let Temple off the hook on this one. Notholm was an avid pro-choice advocate. She supported the programs of Planned Parenthood and had been on their board. She had covered all the rallies and had even gone to Washington, D.C. for the nationwide rally a few years ago. 'So much for objective coverage,' Mann thought.

As Mann and Notholm were leaving Albert's, a group of Cazenovia College students were passing by. A brief look of recognition crossed the face of one of the girls as they continued past the Senator and the reporter.

* * *

Bob Berry had scheduled a number of news conferences since the announcement of Temple's candidacy. The topics for each conference had been different. Temple had addressed the

277

issues of taxes, crime, spending, budgets, education, welfare reform, business incentives, higher education incentives, help for the handicapped, the aged, and for the urban and rural areas. The news conferences had been held at Republican headquarters, at factories, on farms, and in front of schools. Temple had been disappointed by the apparent lack of interest by the media in these subjects and the low turnout by reporters. For Temple, these were all key issues.

Berry had arranged for an Editorial Board with the newspapers during the second week of August. He and Tom Mosby met with Temple the day before to go over possible questions that might come up during Temple's meeting with the press. Berry assured Temple that he would have the papers' staff there in force.

Temple had never done anything like this before, and his two advisors made it sound like an interrogation. Halfway through the session, Terry Levin called. Terry had been in state government as a legislative aide and knew a lot of reporters in Syracuse.

"Jay? This is Terry."

Temple recognized his old friend's voice.

"Hi, Terry. What's up?"

"Just a bit of advice for you. My resources tell me that Sally Notholm has been snooping around asking where you stand on the abortion issue. I think you ought to have a response for her and soon."

"Thanks, Terry. Your call is timely. I'm here now with Tom Mosby and Bob Berry getting ready for the Editorial Board tomorrow."

"Well, it's not my place to tell you how you should think on this issue, but I will tell you that this is not a great topic for Republicans."

"I know." Temple had been thinking about this subject for a long time. He had stayed away from it for a number of reasons. First and foremost he believed that to have or not to have an abortion was a very personal decision. He had always

278

worked to preserve life, and it was hard for him to justify taking a life, even if it was an unborn baby.

But he had prepared a paper on the subject while in law school and had seen the brutal methods women and girls had resorted to in order to abort pregnancies before the law had been changed. Temple thought that there must be a balance, but he did not know where it was.

After he hung up the phone he told Berry and Mosby what Levin had said. They both offered alternative approaches to the subject, either pro-choice or pro-life. They pointed out that Assemblyman Howard White was pro-choice and that Senator Lansing was pro-life. Both advocated that Temple take a stand, "one way or the other."

Temple asked, "What gives 400 plus representatives the right to decide on a law that will govern the millions of people who live in New York State, when it comes to an issue of life and death? An issue that involves ethics, health, and religion?"

Mosby answered. "You said it. Four hundred representatives. They are elected to make those kinds of decisions."

Temple shook his head. "Abortion is both a medical question to be dealt with between a doctor and a patient, and a religious question of when life begins. There are too many different circumstances dealing with both these questions to answer in one law saying that abortions are legal or illegal."

Berry spoke up. "If you don't answer one way or the other, the press will crucify you as a wishy-washy candidate who cannot make a decision."

Mosby said, "Worse than that, Mann will have a field day accusing you of being pro-life and ready to cast the deciding vote in the Senate. You'll be labeled whether you like it or not."

Temple concluded, "Well, it's something I'll have to wrestle with and answer as I believe."

No one knew what that answer was, but Temple would continue to search within himself for some direction.

279

At ten in the morning on the following day, Bob Berry and Jay Temple walked into the offices of the Syracuse Gazette for the Editorial Board. They were greeted by Dave Brickyard, the chief political editor, who led them into a nondescript conference room of institutional gray walls and curtainless windows. An ashtray piled high with cigarette ashes and butts sat on the otherwise empty conference table.

Brickyard motioned to Temple to take a seat at the head of the table as he spoke. "Have a seat, Mr. Temple. Bob, you can sit in by the wall if you'd like."

"Okay, if you don't mind," Berry said as he took a seat behind Temple.

"We don't mind. I'll call the others in." Brickyard left the room for only a few minutes and returned with George Hague, Gerald Blakesley, Tom Shraider, and Bert Peters. All four men were seasoned reporters. They had gone through hundreds of Editorial Boards with other politicians and were pretty much set on the idea that the faces changed, but what came out of the mouths did not. The lack of esteem they shared for politicians was evident in their lackluster greetings to Temple.

Chris Stanley, a young female reporter, came rushing in just before the questioning started. She immediately apologized for being late and said hello to Temple with a handshake and a smile. Temple thought to himself 'Well at least we have one person with some enthusiasm.'

Brickyard opened the questioning. "Why are you running for the New York State Senate?"

"I'm not happy with the direction that our state is going, and I believe we are not getting the proper leadership to make the changes that are necessary."

Hague interrupted, "That's typical political rhetoric. What specifically do you think needs changing, and who is not providing proper leadership, to use your words?"

Temple smiled. "Well, obviously I don't believe that Senator Mann is providing the leadership we need or I wouldn't be here today."

Brickyard and Blakesley quietly laughed at that comment.

Temple continued, "But leadership comes from the top. The Governor has not been able to build a consensus in Albany. Both houses of the legislature go their own way. The Governor can't get his programs or budgets approved. The result is that New York is tops in crime, taxes, and spending and at the bottom of the list in education, development, and a growing agricultural and industrial base."

Temple then gave a litany of statistics without referring to any notes on the state's finances, educational standings, depletion in agriculture, loss of jobs by industry, and spending bills aimed at feathering the nests of current officeholders or their constituents, with no real benefit to the state as a whole.

Blakesley lit his pipe in a contemplative way that signaled to the others that the senior political reporter with over fifty-five years of experience was about to hold forth.

"Mr. Temple. It seems to me that you have done your homework and know the numbers on your issues very well. Do you honestly believe that the public will be interested, much less understand, what you are talking about?"

Temple had never really considered the question, but he was certain that issues were what the race was all about.

"Yes, I do. I've covered a fair amount of distance already in this race. The people I have talked with do understand the issues and are interested. In fact, they have helped me to frame some of the issues by their thoughtful comments."

Blakesley took a long drag on his pipe, exhaled, and said, "Mr. Temple, you are an idealist. People don't care. They don't listen, at least not for long. In the end, they act on their emotions, not their brains."

Temple was taken aback by Blakesley. "I disagree with you, sir. I think that you are selling the public short."

Blakesley smiled at his pipe. "Could be, but in fifty-five years I've yet to see a politician elected because of his or her brains. Emotions are what win or lose an election. We in the press know it because we cover it."

"Wouldn't it make more sense to deal with the issues that are impacting the well–being of the people who read your papers?"

"It might make sense, but it wouldn't sell newsprint." Blakesley eyed the new candidate with interest. It had been some time since he had sat in on an Editorial Board with anyone who sincerely believed in people and issues. It was a kind of innocence that would no doubt have to reckon with the real world at some point. Blakesley knew that Temple would come to face this reality sometime between now and November. The question was how and when.

Temple fielded a variety of questions from the other reporters. But after the Board had been concluded, he only remembered the exchange with Blakesley. He had always been a fan of Blakesley and had in fact gained much of his initial knowledge of state politics and issues by going through old newspapers and reading Blakesley's weekly columns.

Temple wondered if Blakesley was right. If emotions do govern election outcomes, he'd have to inject emotion into the issues. That would be his assignment. He would have to work the emotional in with the factual to get his message out to the public.

Within two days, Temple had spent the time necessary to bring his facts home with real life situations. People stories that captured the attention and the hearts of those he spoke to.

The race continued to tighten.

* * *

The local manufacturers had their own political action association which covered a large part of the senate district in which Temple and Mann were competing for votes.

282

Every election cycle, they hosted a round of interviews with candidates who would be interested in their endorsements, and financial support.

Temple felt comfortable seeking their support in as much as one of his main campaign themes was the need to bring manufacturing jobs back to New York State.

The director of the association was Bill Brown. Brown had really pulled the organization together after he became director. He had worked for a similar organization in Maryland and knew the right things to do to build consensus. The politics of the organization was strictly limited to what was best for manufacturing in Central New York. Brown believed in winners. He had seen his organization blow it in the three prior elections by supporting Mann's opponents. All had lost and each time he had to go, hat in hand, to the Senator for help with legislation. He was hoping his board had finally seen the light and would support Laura Ann Mann in November.

Mann had had several conversations with Brown, mostly off the record. Brown had promised that his association would be appreciative of her vote in opposition to the Industrial Liability Bill that would increase workman's compensation costs by fifty percent for most members. Mann had come through, but to no avail, as the Republican majority passed the bill. Mann knew that the manufacturers owed her for that vote. The bill never stood a chance of being defeated because it had been sponsored by the majority, but her vote was contrary to her usual support of labor.

Robert Anderson was a past president of the Association and very influential with its board. He was an outspoken advocate of the manufacturing industry both in Syracuse and in Albany. He and Bill Brown were friends, and in fact, Brown had been hired by Anderson.

Chester Pickney called the Association meeting of the Board to order. "Today, we will be interviewing both State Senate candidates for consideration of our support in the upcoming election.

283

"Our candidates will be Jay Temple and Senator Laura Ann Mann. We will follow the same procedure that we have followed in the past. They will give an opening and closing statement, and we will ask whatever questions we feel appropriate. Try to ask the same questions of both. Our goal is to find out which of the two we feel will best represent our interests.

"Now, is there any discussion before we start?"

Brown spoke up immediately. "I'd like to remind the Board that Senator Mann came through for us on the Industrial Liability Bill. She has shown a willingness to work with us. Despite our not having endorsed her in her previous three races, we have developed a good relationship. The very fact that she is coming in this morning to talk with us indicates her interest in us. I would hope that you will give her a fair hearing and consider the importance of having supported an elected official when it comes to looking for help after the election."

Brown was barely done speaking when Anderson stood up. All eyes went to him.

"Bill is absolutely right. It is important to support the one who gets elected if you hope to have any influence with that representative after the election. But there are two things we need to think about. Principle, and who is going to win in November.

"This race hasn't been decided yet. In fact, I'm hearing that it's a real horse race at this point. Second, sure Laura Ann supported us on the Industrial Liability Bill. It was a vote against the Republicans that went party line, and it was a throw away. We lost that vote before it ever got to the floor. Why? Because none of our Republican friends would break with the leadership.

"We need to ask these candidates about where they will be for us next year and the year after. We need to ask where they will be if their party has an opposing position. It's a matter of principle to me and I hope for all of you."

Anderson sat down.

284

"Anyone else?" Pickney asked. He turned to Brown. "Please bring in Mr. Temple."

Temple had known going in that Bill Brown wanted the Association to support Mann. He had also known that the primary argument for the Association in its support of Mann was her vote on the Industrial Liability Bill. Predictably, this had been one of the first questions asked of him during his interview.

"The Republican Senate, in a party line vote, passed the bill. The pressure to tow the line is immense. If you don't go along, that member item, that committee assignment, the plush office, the support staff, all of it may be withheld. How are you going to deal with that, Mr. Temple?"

"I campaigned for ten months telling the people, whom I now represent, that I'm going to make New York State more attractive for business and at the same time create new jobs for the fifteen thousand workers who were displaced by the failed policies of state government and now you want me to support a bill that will only continue to force more companies and more jobs out of New York.

"Senator, you've been in politics a lot longer than I have. Tell me how I explain that to all those people who believe in me. . .believe that the Republican Party is the answer to Cuomo and the Democrats. No, I'm not going to vote for that bill, and I would like you to reconsider your support.

"Part of the problem in Albany is that there are so many bills that many representatives don't take the time to understand what they are voting for and the long–term effect of their vote. I hope that with my experience and background I can help educate my colleagues on issues just like the Industrial Liability Bill.

"As long as the Republicans control the Senate, Senator Mann will not be able to have that kind of influence. One question you should be asking is, 'Will the Republicans retain control of the Senate?' If the answer is yes, as I believe it is, then even a Freshman Republican Senator would have more influence than a four–term Democrat with a history of attacking the other side of the aisle."

Temple thought that he had given the committee a lot of food for thought with that answer. He was right.

As he walked out the door of the Association building, he saw Mann and her aide Tork Johns walking up the sidewalk toward him.

"Good morning, Laura."

Mann looked at Temple searching for some indication of how he thought he had done with the Association. Seeing no outward signs, she smiled, "Hello, Jay."

Temple nodded to Johns and crossed the pavement to his campaign van.

He watched Mann confidently walk through the front door of the building followed by Johns. He couldn't help but admire the way she carried herself. She always held her head high, eyes alert, and had a commanding presence, especially where Tork Johns was concerned. He thought to himself that had she been a Republican Senator, there would have been no race.

A week later, the Association announced its endorsement of Jay Temple for the New York State Senate.

The local electrical workers union announced their endorsement of Senator Laura Ann Mann the following day.

* * *

Temple found that one of his biggest obstacles was the power of incumbency. After a particularly good speech and reception at the Canastota Fire Department, the chief told him that they liked what he had to say and certainly the community needed more jobs and business but that his people had to support Senator Mann.

"That's the great thing about this country. You can vote for the candidate of your choice," Temple said and then asked, "Can you tell me why you are supporting Mann?"

"Yeah, I can do that. We've been working with a 1954

pumper for years. No way we could afford a new one. Senator Mann got us Number Three over there last year. We owe her." The chief smiled as he looked at the latest version of a Hydropumper gleaming in the light of the station house. He went on. "You're a good man, Temple, but if she hadn't found the money, well, we'd still be using old Number Three."

"What happened to Old Number Three?"

"Traded it in on this." The chief pointed to the new truck. "They probably re–outfitted the old pumper and put her back to work somewhere else."

Temple thought about new and old Number Threes as he drove back to Syracuse that evening. 'A member item by the Senator bought a new fire truck. The old truck that was still being used somewhere else. Member items are tax dollars everyone pays and then politicians use at their discretion to buy constituents things they desire, whether actually needed or not. No votes, no public disclosures to speak of. Yet billions of taxpayer dollars are spent every year on band uniforms, library books, kitchens, playgrounds, parks, buildings, ponds, practically anything that means votes.'

There may be merit in all this, but Temple guessed that there would be a lot closer scrutiny of the expenditures if the Senate and Assembly had to approve and publicize the expenditures each year.

Temple found that there was a pattern of how member items were used, not just by Mann but by most state legislators. They were usually given to places where support for the legislator was high, where there could be good coverage by the press, and usually timed to be fairly close to an election. Temple concluded that this had to partially account for the fact that ninety-six percent of incumbents get reelected.

Temple knew that he could not address the specific member items given, or their merits, but he also decided that this was an issue that deserved public discussion. It became part of his platform of reform. Publicly approved and disclosed expenditures of taxpayer dollars for member items.

287

* * *

The last weekend in August was devoted to the more rural areas of the Senate District. Temple and his volunteers attended a Gas and Steam Engine show in Vienna, a Dairy Show in Clockville, and the Farmer's Parade in Morrisville.

At the Morrisville parade, Temple walked in front of his antique MG, shaking hands and talking to kids who had been given the now traditional, handful of candy from Temple's volunteers. It was a big hit both with parents and children.

Mann rode on top of a Chevy Impala convertible, wearing her broad brimmed straw hat and flowing flowered dress. Temple's rolled-up shirt sleeves and loose tie were a stark contrast to the Senator. Temple had to, again, give Mann credit. She looked great but each had decided how they wanted to be perceived and each had accomplished what they were hoping for.

At the field days following the parade, Mary Tarkings caught up to Temple.

"Jay, you won't believe this, but Mann came over to me. She knew I worked for you and said she'd like to get a picture of you with the MG."

Temple thought about the strange request. 'Not so strange. The press keeps playing up the wealthy insurance executive angle in this race. She probably would love to have a picture of her opponent with his antique MG.'

"I think we'll pass on that request," Temple told Tarkings. "Besides, we are scheduled to be at the Chiefs game in Syracuse at seven p.m. We'd better get back."

Temple shared his thoughts with Cordis on the way back to Syracuse.

Cordis reacted admiringly. "It's like a chess game. Only the Senator has met her match with you."

"Well, I may be overreacting, but why risk things when you don't have to."

They dropped the MG off at Temple's home, picked up

his family, and went on to MacArthur Stadium for the baseball game and more campaigning.

* * *

Photo-ops are considered an integral part of the political campaign process. These are opportunities for candidates to have their pictures taken with someone of celebrity status. The photographs are, in turn, used to show support of the candidate by the celebrity.

Temple wondered about the value of these pictures. Obviously, it was a rare occasion when the celebrity actually knew the candidate. Yet here he stood, in a line of politicians, waiting to have his photograph taken with the Vice President's wife.

Temple and Cordis had driven from Syracuse to Albany for this opportunity. Berry had made the arrangements. Berry planned to issue a press release indicating both the Vice President and his wife supported Temple's campaign for the New York State Senate. The White House had approved the release as it did for all Republican candidates.

Temple was next in line now. As he stood by the entry to the curtained room, he noticed how poised the Vice President's wife was. She was either very used to this sort of arrangement, or a natural politician in her own right. Possibly both.

The photographer signaled to the man at the entry and Temple was taken in to meet his hostess.

"Good evening, I'm Jay Temple."

"Yes, Mr. Temple from Syracuse. I understand you are running a good race for the Senate."

"It'll be a close race. My opponent is a woman with a good sense of politics. But, that's a topic that would take more time than we have to talk about."

The photographer arranged his two subjects for the picture.

"I heard your talk earlier about the need to provide opportunities for children with handicaps. I know something about this. As President of the Easter Seal Society in New York, I know we do a lot of work in that area. I'm glad that someone on the National level is willing to lend support." Temple smiled as the picture was taken.

"Actually, Easter Seals got me started on this. Their theme 'give ability a chance' is very important. If we can only see to it that they are given a chance, we will have taken a big step." She smiled at the camera as she responded.

The camera clicked, there was a flash, and it was over. Temple moved on, taking with him the belief that the Vice President had married the right person. She was sincere, and she wasn't afraid to speak out.

A week and a half later, Temple received a note from Mrs. Quayle, wishing him luck in the campaign and enclosing an article on her speech to Congress about children with disabilities. He concluded that she was genuine. 'You meet a lot of good people through politics despite what may be the popular perception.'

Chapter XX

September: Month Nine
Crunch Time

September became the month for endorsements, debates, and major fund raisers. At one point Temple counted over thirty fund raising events just for Republicans.

Dave Yondle and Laney Gardiner were the mainstays of Temple's fund raising events. They solicited, arranged, and carried out a series of events that included lunches, dinners, cocktail parties, and social teas with people from all three counties. They saw to the printing and distribution of invitations, coordinating the guest lists, having volunteers at the event to handle everything from decorations to serving, and mailing out the thank-you letters for those who attended and contributed to the campaign.

Temple attended each of the functions, mingling with the guests, thanking the hosts and hostesses, and speaking to the groups at some time during the event.

September was a good month for the Temple campaign as it neared the two hundred thousand dollar amount in total dollars raised. It was also a good month for Mann, who now realized that she was in a real political fight and that she could lose her seat in the Senate to Temple if she did not throw herself into the race. She closed out September with one hundred and twenty-two thousand dollars.

The newspapers and television networks picked up on the financial battle going on in this senate race and began giving it headline coverage. The Syracuse papers assigned a reporter to review the financial reports of both candidates and to interview candidates and their supporters. By the time October arrived, it would become clear that this was the most expensive political campaign ever waged for a Senate seat in Central New York.

Mann's major fund raising event for the year was to be a dinner cruise with a blues band on Onondaga Lake. Price: $75.00 per person.

Temple, Cordis, and Yondle discussed a function at the Hotel Syracuse with a big name speaker. It meant putting money into the event up front. Roth was brought into the discussions by Temple. He indicated that they had a surplus of twenty-one thousand dollars in the campaign chest.

It was agreed that ten thousand would be the maximum they would spend on a speaker. Yondle obtained a list of celebrities in that price range, made arrangements for a dinner at the Hotel Syracuse, and lined up a local television personality to act as emcee.

The Syracuse Gazette covered the story:

Dinner Politics — If you want a dinner guaranteed to bring out the political big wigs in the Democratic Party, try Senator Laura Ann Mann's evening cruise on Onondaga Lake, October 16th. Shrimp, beer, salad bar, and music by blues group, the Downbeat, all for $75 per cover.

On the other hand, Republican Jay Temple has taken local political fund raising this season outside the local area. At $125 per cover, you can sit down for dinner with guest celebrity, sportscaster Ted Lane, and emcee Dan Lanagan of Channel 4. The place is the Hotel Syracuse Ballroom on October 18th.

Arthur Gaines, chairman of the Onondaga County Republican Party, was asked about having an outside celebrity speak at an individual candidate's fund raiser. He said, 'Hey, this is

292

politics. If it gets people's attention, why not!'

Jerry Binnery, chairman of the Democratic Party, had this to say, 'Temple couldn't fill the Hotel's coffee shop, he needs someone like Ted Lane. If he paid me ten to fifteen grand, I'd be tempted to speak at his fund raiser, too. Of course, Mr. Temple wouldn't like what I had to say.'

Dinner politics is the crowning event of this, the most expensive political campaign this fall.

* * *

Labor Day offered Temple's campaign team one of the great logistical challenges of the entire campaign. It was time to capitalize on the name recognition that Temple had been building through his television commercials. They wanted Temple to cover the entire geographic area of his Senate District by marching in as many parades as he could.

Laney Gardiner and Mary Tarkings planned the schedule and timing along with Dave Yondle so that Temple would hit six separate parades throughout the district.

At 9:00 a.m., the Fayetteville parade would lead off the marathon of parades. Next, they would go to Chittenango for a 10:30 starting time. This would be followed by an appearance in the Syracuse parade starting at 11:00. Because of Temple's placement in the parade, his time would be closer to 11:45. Rome was a good forty minutes from Syracuse, but Temple was scheduled for its 1:00 pm start. Again, positioning was all important to a timely arrival of the candidate. At three in the afternoon, Bridgeport would have its parade, and then Boonville at 5:00.

Boonville was actually outside of the 48th Senate District but many voters from the 48th went to the Boonville festivities. The parade was followed by tractor pulls, chain saw carving contests, eighteen-wheeler races, and the roast. It was a parade and field day like no other, and it was a good way to end the day.

Mann's campaign team scheduled the Syracuse parade, Cazenovia parade, Bridgeport parade, and Hamilton parade for their Senator. West, east, north, and south was their thinking. This schedule also allowed for two hours between each parade. Experience had taught them that this was about the right spread to insure proper time between parades. Johns informed the Senator that her opponent would be in the Syracuse parade and the Bridgeport parade but that she had been given a lead position and that he was way back in the pack. Mann appreciated Johns' work.

Mann would use her famous Chevy Impala and a dress she had picked out especially for the Labor Day parades. Temple opted for the campaign van over the MG, now being sensitive to the labels the newspapers were trying to pin on him. This also gave his team the room they needed. Six volunteers, his wife, and son would be traveling the parade routes with him.

Signs were ready, as were leaflets, buttons, candy, and pencils. The candidates were anxious to get started, but they would have to wait for morning.

It was a warm September morning as Temple's campaign team arrived at his home for a pre-parade breakfast. It had been agreed upon that everyone accompanying the candidate would meet at his home at seven-thirty in the morning. It would give them an opportunity for a final review of the day's plans and the only good meal they'd probably get before nightfall.

Dave Yondle, Laney Gardiner, Ted Cordis, Mary Tarkings, Patrick Fitzgerald, and Mary Price all had volunteered for the caravan. Doctor Carey and Kevin Roth also arrived unexpectedly to join the group.

Pat Temple had more than enough food to take care of the two newest arrivals.

While they all ate, Cordis reviewed the assignments. Dave and Kevin would carry the banner, the two Marys and Laney would hand out candy to the children followed by Kevin,

294

Patrick, and Dr. Carey with leaflets, buttons, and pencils all advertising 'Temple for the New York State Senate.' Temple, his wife and son, Tyler, would walk behind the banner shaking hands and saying hello to the parade watchers. Cordis would drive the van and operate the loudspeaker system. The van had been decorated with flags and banners and was the closest thing to having a float in the parades.

At 8:30 they all left in the van for the Fayetteville parade. It was a tight-knit, happy group that pulled onto North Manlius Street for their assigned spot in the parade.

Tyler was nervous about this whole parade idea. He had never been in a parade before and was shy to begin with. Temple knew that his six-year-old son was having a hard time with all the commotion.

While waiting for the parade to start, Temple picked up his son and said, "Hey, Tyler, let's go take a look at those fire trucks. Do you want to?"

Tyler loved fire trucks and immediately shook his head, yes.

Temple took Tyler to the spot that had been assigned to the fire department. Most of the firemen knew Temple and one was Tyler's gym teacher.

"You fellas need an extra volunteer?" Temple said as he walked up to a hook and ladder truck.

"We sure do," Tom Button, the assistant chief, said as he walked over to shake Temple's hand. "Who have we got here?"

"This is Tyler." Temple introduced his son. "Tyler, this is the assistant fire chief."

Tyler looked at the man in the blue uniform with silver buttons. He smiled. "Hello."

One of the younger firemen came around the truck with a fire hat and asked Tyler if he'd like to put it on.

"Yes!"

"Let me just adjust these straps," the young man said as he reworked the head straps inside the helmet. "There we are. That should fit." He placed the helmet on Tyler's head and was rewarded with a big smile.

"Daddy, can I go on the fire truck?"

"I don't know. Tom, would you mind if Tyler climbed up on your truck?"

Button smiled. "As long as he wears his official firemen's helmet."

Tyler immediately grabbed hold of both sides of the helmet with both hands and held it firmly to his head. Everyone laughed.

"Looks like he'll be wearing his helmet!" Button turned to Temple. "How about the two of you riding along with us in the parade?"

Tyler turned to his father. "Can we, dad? Can we ride on the fire engine?"

Temple looked at Button then at his son. "Sounds like fun to me."

"Great," Button said. He showed Temple where to sit with his son.

Cordis smiled and shook his head. He turned to Mary Tarkings and said, "Jay just falls into it. Everyone will see him up there. What a break."

"What should we do?" Mary asked.

"Stay close to that fire engine." Cordis answered.

He told Yondle and Roth to move the banner up in front of the fire truck. Everyone else would follow behind the truck and in front of the van.

Fayetteville was a great start for Temple and for Tyler. Tyler's friends all saw him and shouted to him. By the end of the Fayetteville parade, Tyler was ready to move on to the next five parades.

In Chittenango, Temple walked the route with his wife and son. They knew a lot of people along the parade route, having already made a number of trips to the small town. They were also regulars at the Canteen, site of July's Republican Dinner. Chittenango was a friendly town and made Temple's little caravan feel welcome.

296

The Syracuse parade was completely different. It was run in a very business-like manner because of its size. There were over three hundred entries in the parade. Bands, fire departments, boy and girl scout troops, military units, clowns, cowboys, Indians, radio stations, floats, and many other groups, not the least of whom were politicians, all lined up along the route for the big parade.

The crowds were large, the bands were loud, and the wait was longer than expected. Temple concluded that he didn't gain much by being in the Syracuse parade. Cordis reassured him that the appearance was important.

Neither Temple nor Mann saw each other in Syracuse. Both knew that the other was in the parade. Both were too busy to go out of their way to actually go looking for the other.

Mann counted Syracuse as a success. Her off–the–shoulder, pale blue dress caught everyone's eye and was captured on film for both the evening news and the next morning's edition of the Syracuse Gazette. As a State Senator, she was invited to attend the formal ceremony following the parade. Once again, she stood out in the crowd.

Because of the length of the Syracuse parade, Temple's people were put under the gun to make the Rome parade. Dave Utley, a Syracuse policeman and friend of Temple's, caught up with him at the end of the parade, and after a brief conversation about Rome, offered to drive the candidate separately to that parade. It was decided that this made sense. Cordis took the van and the rest of the entourage while Utley whisked Temple away in his unmarked car.

In Rome, Cookie Talbot, Lou DiMatino, and Patty Stuto waited nervously for Temple to arrive. They had all met Temple on his first visit to Rome and all liked him. They were organizing Republicans to work for him, and his appearance in the Rome Labor Day Parade was a way of confirming that he would not forget Rome when he was in the Senate. It was even more important now that his opponent Senator Mann had declined an invitation to be a part of the parade.

The parade marshal gave the signal to Cookie that her section should prepare to pull out.

"Where can he be?" Stuto asked in a plaintiff voice.

"I wish I knew," Talbot answered.

"There's Mr. Temple," DiMatino said.

They all looked in the direction DiMatino was pointing. Temple was shaking hands with a man in a plain black car. He looked up, saw Cookie, Lou, and Patty, and hurried over.

"Sorry for the delay, but the Syracuse parade got off to a late start."

"Well, you are here. That's what is important," Cookie summed up everyone's thoughts.

"Yeah, Mann isn't even coming," Patty added.

"Mr. Temple, I know you care for Rome, and by the time we are done here Rome will care for you."

"Thanks, Lou. Well, what do we do now?"

"You and I are going to ride in that Ford convertible. Let's go." Cookie was a take–charge kind of a person. As Temple had learned, she was well known and liked in Rome. She would be a great ally for him and a loyal worker.

As their part of the parade pulled out and passed the K-Mart parking lot, Temple's campaign van arrived. The entire group poured out of the van and came on the run to join with Temple and Cookie. DiMatino and Stuto were in the front seat with Stuto driving. She slowed down to let the others catch up. In seconds the banner was in front of the Ford and all the others were alongside. Dr. Carey handed Tyler up to Temple. Pat Temple decided to walk by the car and hand out candy to the children along with the two Marys.

Rome gave Temple a warm welcome. He could feel the tie with this Canal city. He truly liked the people and knew their needs. Rome would be an important part of his district if he were to be elected.

Bridgeport was a small town on the shore of Oneida Lake. Labor Day was the official closing day for boating season, even though many boaters would stay on into October.

298

The parade was always late afternoon to accommodate those who were pulling boats out of the water or closing up camps.

It was a small parade and Mann knew that she and Temple would meet. She had met Tony Melow at previous Bridgeport parades. He was the leader of the local VFW color guard and always had the honor of carrying the American flag at the head of the parade. Mann arrived early and sought Tony out for a special request.

The color guard wore black plumed hats with one side pinned up. Their shirts were a deep yellow silk and their black pants had a matching deep yellow stripe running down the outside of both legs. There were three flag bearers, three drummers and six trumpeters in the group.

Cordis pulled the van up in front of the P&C Grocery Store. One of the parade organizers came over, checked the banner on the side of the van, and looked inside. "Mr. Temple?"

Temple was in the passenger seat. "Yes," he said as he leaned forward.

"Oh, hi, Mr. Temple. You are to follow the East Syracuse High School Marching Band. They are over there." The man pointed to a gathering group of teenagers in blue and white uniforms.

"Thanks, we'll pull the van in behind them."

"Right."

The man went on to the next arrival in the parade. Cordis drove the van to where the high school band was lining up and parked.

About a quarter of a mile down the road, Senator Mann climbed out of her car. She was wearing a deep yellow cowgirl shirt with black fringe, a short black fringed skirt, black cowgirl boots, and a black cowgirl hat. She gave Tony and the color guard a big smile.

"Hi, guys!" she said as she walked toward them.

"Pretty sharp get-up!" Tony exclaimed.

"Thanks. I'm looking forward to joining you for the

299

parade."

"When they see you, they aren't even going to notice us!" Tony and the rest of his group laughed.

A cameraman from Channel 7 arrived and wanted to get some footage of the color guard for the evening newscast. Tony lined everyone up and as the drums and bugles played 'America,' the Senator stood at attention, saluting the flag.

The last stop of the day was Boonville, New York.

Temple had driven past the Boonville turnoff from Route 12 on many trips to the Adirondacks. Until now, he had never taken the turnoff and did not know what to expect. As it happened, Boonville was a turn of the century town that had been kept up nicely. Victorian styled homes lined both sides of the main street and ornate buildings of brick and stone made up the center of the village. The people were warm and friendly and came from hardworking families who believed in self-sufficiency. Temple felt very much at home.

Temple's caravan was placed between an eighteen-wheeled log hauler and an eighteen-wheeled paper company truck. The campaign van and Yondle's station wagon were both put in the parade. Yondle had agreed to take the volunteers back to Syracuse, as Temple and his wife and son had planned a weekend in the Adirondacks.

Tarkings, Yondle, and Price hurriedly decorated the station wagon while Temple and Cordis went over the parade route.

The driver of the log hauler climbed down from his cab and walked up to Temple. A burly, dark-haired man in his late forties, he was dressed in a Woolrich plaid shirt and jeans.

"You Jay Temple?"

Temple looked up. "Yeah. I am."

"I'm Bud Salley. I drive for Cordelle Logging. That's my rig in front of you."

"It's nice to meet you, Bud."

"I got a question for you. What's your position on closing down the Adirondack Park?"

300

Salley gave no hint as to what his position was but the fact that he worked for a logging company and that most logging companies would be the direct beneficiaries of a Park closure, led Temple to conclude that he probably was in favor of closure.

"Well, Bud, you and I may not see eye–to–eye on that one. I spent many summers camping in the Adirondack Park and I've brought my family up here many times to enjoy the woods, mountains, and lakes. I favor keeping the Park open." Temple was thinking to himself that he'd better be prepared to duck.

Salley looked hard at Temple and then gave him a big toothy grin. "You're okay." Salley extended his hand to Temple. As they shook hands, Salley said, "Most politicians think because I haul logs I favor doin' away with the Park. No way! My boys and I spend a lot o' time fishin' here. Won't be a decent spot left if they take away the Park. Hope you win."

Temple introduced Salley to Cordis, his wife, and son.

"We're heading up to Big Moose Lake right after the parade," Temple told Salley.

"Nice place. Lousy fishin'!" was Salley's response.

Temple was well–received in Boonville. To his surprise, people knew him and shouted out his name as he walked by. "Hi, Mr. Temple, saw you on television." "Mr. Temple, we're from Rome and we're for you." "Mr. Temple, hope you win." People he had never met were reaching out to him. It struck a chord deep inside of him, and he knew that if he won, he would not forget these people.

The only scare came as they were walking along the route and throwing candy to the crowds. Pat's throw was short and the parade had picked up speed. A throng of small children ran into the street to pick up the candy directly in front of the paper company truck.

It was a close call, but the driver of the truck was alert and slowed down to avoid any injuries. The children never knew that anything was wrong, but Pat relived that episode for many months after the campaign.

The parade wound its way along the main street and out

301

to the fairgrounds on the west side of town. Once around the dirt racetrack and it was over.

Temple thanked his volunteers who had stuck with him now for over fourteen hours. They all had dinner at the local McDonald's where more people came over to talk with Temple.

Cordis smiled as he and the others left the Temples for Syracuse. "Laura Ann Mann watch out. Here comes Senator-elect Temple!"

As they drove along Route 12 on their way to Big Moose Lake, Pat looked at her husband. "What are you thinking?"

Temple looked at her quickly then back at the road ahead. "I still can't get used to the idea of people I have never met supporting me."

"You mean those people who called to you in the parade?"

"Yeah, those and the ones at McDonald's and the ones who send contributions to the campaign, and the ones who volunteer. It's really quite humbling."

"You're a good man." Pat Temple smiled at her husband. "People are seeing that. Everybody likes to help someone who is really good and who cares. They're finding out what I have always known."

Temple blushed and then laughed. "You sure it's not just your rose–colored glasses?"

* * *

The following week, plans had been made for more fund raisers, door–to–door campaigning, a news conference, and a trip to Long Island for a meeting with a private publisher.

The two fund raisers were a great success. The first was held at the Cazenovia Lake home of a well–known doctor and business entrepreneur. The doctor and his gracious wife opened their home to about thirty friends and business associates. The meal was catered and the wines came from the doctor's private cellar. Once again, someone whom Temple had never met before not only entertained Temple and his wife, but also raised over five thousand dollars for Temple's political campaign.

The second fund raiser was hosted by an oil company executive who knew Temple socially and who believed that Temple's proposal to prioritize spending was the right answer for state government.

Before a group of twenty guests, Temple's host introduced him as "a man who is right–thinking about government. He believes that you don't spend more than you take in, and you prioritize how you spend what you do take in."

This fund raiser netted twelve hundred dollars, again from people Temple had never met before.

On Thursday, Temple flew down to Long Island. He met with Jake Barens, a private publisher and friend of Temple's father.

"So, the political bug bit you?" Barens walked over to a map of New York State that hung on his wall. "See these red and blue pins?"

Temple saw that the entire state was covered with one or the other of the colored pins. "Yes."

Barens looked back at Temple. "This is the balance of power in New York State. Just four changes in elected officials and the balance shifts. Each pin is an elected Assemblyman or Senator. Blues are Republicans, reds are Democrats. No hidden meaning." Barrens laughed.

Barens and Temple talked for over two hours about the current state of affairs in New York. Both agreed that the lack of borrowing power by the state, the low credit rating, and the high taxes were all contributing to the decline of the Empire State.

In the end, Barens offered to print a special edition newspaper devoted to Temple's campaign, the issues, and the candidate. Twenty thousand copies of the eight–page paper would be published and delivered to Temple's headquarters. For his part, Temple had to provide the copy and take care of the distribution. It was a novel idea but one that appealed to

Temple. The Syracuse Gazette had not been his friend, and he liked the idea of publishing his own views for a change. Finally, people could get both sides of the issues.

The two men shook hands and Temple flew back to Syracuse in time to make his six o'clock news conference at Republican Headquarters.

Bob Berry met Jay Temple at Hancock Airport at 5:15pm. On the way to Republican Headquarters, Berry went over the list of expected attendees from the press and the main subjects to be covered in the press conference.

"Smith Parsons announced that it is laying off another three hundred employees this week. This ties in with your comments on the unfriendly job environment in New York State. They have indicated that they are going to North Carolina," Berry said as he reviewed his notes.

"Three hundred more people whose families now have to deal with how to survive without their breadwinner's income." Temple shook his head. It was becoming an all too common story in Upstate New York.

Temple had now seen, firsthand, what the loss of a job means to a family. His campaigning door–to–door had revealed a part of Central New York that had been unknown to him. People who lived in his own area were suffering because of loss of jobs. It had nothing to do with how they performed. It was an economic decision that companies were making because of the huge tax and regulatory burdens placed on them by New York State.

"Education is another area you will want to touch upon. Your proposal to cut state mandates and put more money back into the classroom and more teachers into the system." Barry flipped through his notes.

Temple thought about the classes he had visited both in Rome and in Syracuse. Some had in excess of thirty students per teacher. He was told that this was due to cutbacks in state aid and state mandates in other areas. 'No wonder New York's scores on standardized testing were so low. How can one teacher possibly meet all the educational needs of that many students.' He looked at Berry who was still pouring over his handwritten notes.

"Bob, you know the part of being a politician that still amazes me?"

Berry looked up. "What's that?"

"The wide–ranging topics and issues about which you are expected to be an expert. Tonight, I'm going to be talking about tax reform, spending cuts, education, crime, the drug problem, environmental issues, and long–range needs for our state's infrastructure. Things that we all talk about but now that I'm running for the Senate, it becomes newsworthy."

Berry smiled. "Hey, if people are going to vote for you they've got to know where you're coming from. You may have talked about these things before, but you were never in a position where you could've done anything about them. Come November, you may be."

Republican Headquarters had drawn a pretty good crowd of reporters. All three commercial networks from Syracuse, five Syracuse based radio stations, one from Rome, one from Oneida, one from Oswego and two from Utica. The Syracuse Gazette had its political reporter there along with a reporter from the Madison Daily and the editor of the New Deal.

Berry thanked everyone for coming, and as the television camera lights were turned on, he introduced Jay Temple.

"I'd like to add my thanks to Bob's for having you join us today."

Temple looked out at the reporters and at the camera. He continued.

"Today Smith Parsons announced the layoff of some three hundred employees. Smith Parsons executives attribute the layoffs to the high taxes and over regulation in New York State.

"Smith Parsons is another in a growing list of businesses that is pulling out of New York State and opting for states, such as North Carolina, where taxes and regulation are not so overbearing."

305

Temple paused and looked at the 'keepers of the public trust.'

"You know, too often we see or read stories like Smith Parsons and the three hundred people whose lives were just changed dramatically, and we miss the real drama of the moment in the numbers and words.

"Three hundred families, wives, husbands, children, parents, all will have their lives altered by this layoff. Some will recover, some will not. But all will be marked for life. Marked by the fear that something like this could happen again.

"These layoffs were not because of poor performance by the employees. These layoffs are because of poor performance by New York State.

"We need a change in Albany. A change in direction and a change in leadership. How many more people are we going to cause to suffer the hurt that the employees of Smith Parsons and their families are suffering?

"New York State needs to get its house in order. We need to reduce the tax burden, reduce spending, promote the use of our skilled work force by business, and set priorities at the state level that will be met within the means that are available."

Temple went on to list actions that the state could take to accomplish his goals. He then talked about crime and the need for more police officers in the field and an education program in the schools. "The time to stop the criminal is in the schools before he or she gets started."

Temple detailed the rest of the issues he wanted to cover at the news conference and then opened up the floor for questions.

Sally Notholm quickly stood up and with a quick smile asked, "Mr. Temple, abortion is a major issue in this state and yet we have not heard where you stand on this. Are you pro-life or pro-choice?"

Temple had known that at some time during the campaign he would be faced with this issue. He had rehearsed in his own mind how he would respond. Still, the suddenness and unexpectedness of the question threw him off his stride for a moment.

"Abortion is not a black and white issue. I have given this a lot of thought, and I'm not sure that I can put a label on where I stand."

Notholm started to interrupt, but Temple held up his hand. "Let me finish. My wife and I had a child a little later in life than is normally the case. Tyler has turned out to be one of the great gifts of life to both of us. Personally, I would not make a decision to abort a life, because to me, life is too precious. Every activity that I have involved myself in has had at its basic thrust, the betterment of human life. Personally, I will always strive to save lives and to make life better for people.

"But, at the same time, I realize that as a legislator, I have a responsibility to the people who have elected me to office. There are arguments on both sides of this issue that have merit.

"Pro-choice advocates talk about the tragedies of back-alley abortions before New York's current law was enacted. They argue for those who have been raped or become pregnant through incestuous relations. These are hard matters to deal with.

"I don't believe that 432 legislators in Albany have the right to decide these issues for the millions of people in the State of New York.

"My solution," Temple paused for effect, "is a state-wide referendum. Let the people decide if they support the current law permitting abortions. If a majority can come to a conclusion on this, then as a legislator, I would support that decision."

Notholm was not to be put off without another try. "Mr. Temple, aren't you side-stepping the issue? If you are elected to the Senate, you could very well be called upon to vote on a bill banning abortions without the benefit of a referendum. What would you do then?"

"I would hope that I would have enough influence with my colleagues that I would be able to show them that my suggestion of a referendum is not only the appropriate ethical response, but also the appropriate political response."

Notholm dug in her heels. "But what if you did not have enough influence to keep the issue from a vote. How would you vote?"

Temple smiled at Notholm. "I appreciate your persistence on this, but I have told you my thoughts, and I think you will find that I'm pretty persistent, too, when it comes to having others, in this case the legislature, consider alternatives that make sense."

That evening, on the Eleven O'Clock News, Notholm characterized Temple as 'wishy-washy' on abortions and the next morning, the Syracuse Gazette followed the same pattern, stating that Temple who claimed to be the only candidate to talk straight on the issues, refused to give his position on the abortion issue.

Temple thought he had been very clear on how he would handle the question of abortion in New York and where he stood personally. He could not understand why the newspaper and Notholm did not carry what he had said, rather than paraphrasing and actually misquoting him. He was also amazed that none of the other issues which he had talked about got any coverage at all.

The Syracuse Gazette closed its column with a quote from Senator Mann. "When told about Jay Temple's lack of response on the abortion issue, Senator Mann said that elected officials should not have the luxury of sitting on the fence. That's the real problem in Albany today and that's what I've been fighting all these years. I support pro-choice. It gives everyone the right to choose and that's the way it should be."

It was not a high point for Temple and his campaign team.

Chapter XXI

Money Matters

Money was increasingly becoming an issue of concern for Temple and his campaign team. The constantly slanted stories in the Syracuse Gazette and Mann's use of her franking privilege, the ability to send out mailings to the entire district at taxpayer expense, was taking an unwarranted toll with the voters.

Temple needed vehicles to get his message out to the voters. The personally produced newspaper was one, but he needed to be able to get back on the air, and that kind of advertising would cost a lot of money.

On September eleventh, the New York State Senate Republican Committee held a fund raiser aboard a New York City cruise liner. Temple and Cordis were invited to attend.

Every New York State Republican Senator was on board along with the party's biggest backers. At five thousand dollars per person, the trip offered a boat ride around Manhattan and a chance for contributors to meet one on one with elected representatives and enjoy good food, wine, and views at the same time.

Temple's goals were simple. He needed to work the crowd and to gain financial support for his candidacy. Senator Valli was the driving force behind the cruise. He was also the starting point for Temple's activities.

Temple and Cordis had no sooner walked onto the ship when Valli and Toby Hagan came down the stairs leading from the upper deck.

Valli saw the two men approaching and immediately

walked toward them with his hand outstretched. "Jay, how's it going in Syracuse?"

"I think we are giving her a run for her money," Temple answered. "You remember Ted Cordis?"

Valli and Cordis shook hands. "Of course I do, and you know Toby Hagan?"

"Yeah, hi, Toby." Temple shook hands with Valli and Hagan. "I wanted to talk to you about the campaign tonight. "

"Better do it now. I'm going to be up to my ears in conversation later on." Valli seemed interested as he led the small group to a table on the lower deck. A waitress took their drink orders and disappeared inside the ship.

"Well, how much are you looking for this time and what do you need it for?" Valli got right to the point.

"We need about twenty-five thousand for another round of TV commercials and some radio spots," Temple answered.

Cordis leaned into the conversation, "Channel 4 and the Syracuse Gazette are painting a bad picture up there right now, and we need to offset their spin."

"Yeah, I read the Gazette's coverage of the abortion issue. It's a dumb issue. Not more than one in every thousand families in New York has to deal with abortion. Yet the papers want to make this a cause for celebration. I don't get it. Never did. But as a politician, you have no choice!" Valli was right, but that didn't change things for public consumption. Temple knew that this would be an uphill battle, but he knew that he was right.

Valli turned to Hagan. "What do the polls say? Temple still in the race?" Valli asked.

"Very much so," Hagan responded. "Temple's do–able."

"Give him his twenty-five," Valli ordered. "Gotta get to the others. Good to see you, Jay. You too, Cordis. Toby will take care of you." And with that, Valli got up from the table and joined a group of noisy Senators just coming around the deck.

310

Cordis and Hagan worked out the transfer of funds and timing while Temple greeted people along the deck.

The cruise ship slid silently through the East River, past the Empire State Building, past the United Nations Building, and on toward the Consolidated Edison plant.

Temple now leaned on the railing and watched the city glide by.

"Pretty from here, isn't it?" Cordis asked.

"Yes, it is. I've always liked the lights of the City at night. I used to have an apartment in Brooklyn overlooking the East River. I spent many a night marveling at all the people, all the lights, all the activity."

"Now you have an opportunity to have an impact on all of that as a State Senator."

"I was just thinking that before you came over. It's quite a responsibility."

Cordis looked at the candidate. He admired the way Temple always looked at things. This wasn't an ego thing with Temple; it was a desire to improve things, a desire to help. Cordis said, "It's a responsibility that should be in good hands. Yours."

* * *

Arthur Gaines called the meeting of the Onondaga Republican Finance Committee to order at seven thirty in the morning. Charles White, Ken Mathews, Joseph DiNagro, Howard White, Tom Mosby, and Dr. Richard Carey were also present.

Gaines stood up from his seat at the head of the conference table. "Gentlemen, Ken Mathews has asked the committee to put some more money into Jay Temple's campaign. We are here to discuss that request this morning."

Gaines looked around the room. He counted four of the committee members working directly for Temple and four, including himself, who were not.

"The polls show Temple with a possibility of winning this seat. But, I have to be honest and say that I think he blew it on the abortion issue. He came off in the press as if he were hiding something. I think that has given Mann an edge."

Mathews stood up. "That's exactly why we need to give Temple some more money. He's got to get out there with a PR blitz to get his story told. Five thousand more at this point is a good investment for us."

DiNagro spoke up. "Are we setting a precedent that whenever one of our politicians make a political mistake, we will bankroll him to a renewed career?"

Mosby spoke up. "I wouldn't classify this as a political mistake. It's more a case of one-way coverage. Everything I've read in the Gazette has leaned in Mann's favor. This is more of the same. Jay needs some avenue to get his side of the story out. At this point that means commercials.

"I spoke to Bob Berry and he thinks that they can do something to knock out the 'wishy-washy' label. He and Ophidia are working on it now. But they do need money."

Charles White had been listening. He asked, "How much does Jay have now?"

"About twenty-nine thousand, total," Mathews answered.

"Is the state going to give him any help?"

"Yes. They are very committed to Jay at this point because of the polls. They are planning on dumping in twenty-five thousand in contributions or 'in kind' help," Mosby said.

"What is 'in kind' help?" White asked.

"Commercials that they produce, mailings that they send out, stuff like that," Mosby responded.

"So what you are really looking for then is five thousand with no strings attached. What I mean is no 'in kind' help?"

"That's right." Mathews looked at White. "I think the message here is that we, the Onondaga Republican Party, have the wherewithal to help a candidate win a tough race. Jay Temple is a winner."

The committee concluded that they would give the five

thousand to Temple for his race.

* * *

Temple was often surprised by events which seemed to happen without any direct activity on the part of his campaign staff or himself.

It had been a long week of campaigning. Cordis had acted as his driver and had kept him company as he had crisscrossed the district on his door–to–door campaign.

They had campaigned at every junction where there were one or more people. Temple shook hands and handed out pamphlets at malls, McDonald's, Burger Kings, church socials, and grocery stores. He canvassed neighborhoods from Erieville to Minoa to Verona Beach.

They stopped for ice cream at the Stockbridge Eatery and talked about the campaign with its owner and his wife. The owner liked Temple, but his wife was Senator Mann's local representative. She pointed out the new library room in town that the Senator had funded as a member item less than a year ago.

On the way out the door, Temple turned to Cordis with a smile and said, "Well, the ice cream was good!"

At Verona Beach, Temple and Cordis met with Tommy LaPora. Tommy was the top Republican in the area and by all accounts, had a pretty tight grip on the committee there.

After the initial introductions, LaPora went right to the bottom line. "Laura Ann Mann is a regular Joe! She comes into my bar and sings with the band. No pretense about being Senator. Last year the 'Beach' needed some new water pipes. You know what the Republicans in Albany told me?"

Temple said, "No."

"They told me to see my Senator. Me, a Republican, and they tell me to see my Senator, a Democrat! So I did just that, and she comes through for the 'Beach.' So, my friend, you may be a good Republican. You may be a great candidate. You

313

may even be a good person. But the 'Beach' is going to support Senator Mann. Good Republicans didn't cut it when we needed it."

Temple could see that this was an emotional issue for LaPora, and he understood his sentiments. He nodded his head and said, "If I were in your shoes," he paused as LaPora waited to rebut whatever Temple was about to say, "I'd do the same thing."

Temple stuck out his hand and shook LaPora's. "Thank you for your time and honesty."

LaPora shook Temple's hand, not quite sure of what to make of this politician. He watched Temple and Cordis walk out of his bar, thought for a moment, shrugged his shoulders, and went back to work.

On the way back to Syracuse, Temple made a mental note to talk to Senator Valli about how to, and how not to, handle local Republican leaders.

That night, a dinner had been scheduled at Nikki's Restaurant in Syracuse. Edward Landar, a philanthropist and highly successful business man from New York City, had requested a small get together in Syracuse with Temple and a few other local Assembly candidates. Temple had been told that Landar was interested in making some political contributions to the Upstate candidates for state office.

Cordis and Temple picked up Temple's wife on the way to the dinner.

"I guess I don't understand politics," Pat said as she checked her hair in the vanity mirror. "Why would Edward Landar be interested in your campaign?"

"He likes honest politicians," Temple offered.

Cordis laughed. "I could offer a lot of other alternatives to that choice, but I can see that this is the wrong crowd for that."

When they arrived at Nikki's, they noticed a white stretch limousine in the 'no parking' zone outside the restaurant.

Cordis observed, "It looks like our host for dinner has

arrived."

Temple and his wife were no sooner inside the door when Arthur Gaines hurried over to them. "Mr. Landar is anxious to meet you. Come on, I'll introduce you."

Gaines led the Temples over to a tall, thin man of about fifty years of age. He had thinning sandy colored hair and deep-set eyes. He was well dressed and soft-spoken.

"It's a pleasure to meet you," Landar said as he shook hands with Pat and Temple. "I've been hearing good things about you and your campaign. You are running against one of the most formidable Democrats in the state and making some serious gains."

Temple smiled. "It's our pleasure, I assure you. I only hope that your source of information is accurate."

"Comes directly from the NYSSRC. They've got an impressive bank of political computers, and they are putting out some great numbers on your political efforts."

"You must have met Toby Hagan."

"Yes, as a matter of fact I did," Landar said, somewhat surprised.

"Toby is impressed with his own equipment and is quite a good salesman when it comes to selling his end product."

"This is true. But he is also part of the reason that I am here."

"Well, we're happy that he brought you Upstate. You said 'part of the reason.'"

"Yes. The other part is that I like what you have to say. I've seen some of your news clips and read your reports, which I understand you write yourself?"

"Yes. If I'm going to be quoted, I want to be sure that it is what I have said."

Landar nodded. "I know the feeling. Politicians have enough trouble with being misquoted without someone else writing their work.

"I intend to get involved in state politics in the next year or so. I am hoping that we can begin to make needed changes

315

now so that when I do become more directly involved, there will be some good people in place who will work with me." Landar watched Temple closely for his reaction to his words.

"If by working with you, you mean doing what is best for the people in this state, then you have come to the right place. If you are looking for someone who will rubber–stamp everything that you do regardless of the outcome, then I hope that you enjoyed your trip to Syracuse." It was Temple's turn to gauge Landar's reaction.

Landar looked at Temple for a moment, then reached inside his suit coat pocket and pulled out an envelope. He handed it to Temple with a note that said 'Good luck in November and beyond. Edward.'

"We'll work well together, Mr. Temple"

Later that evening, after much talk of politics, needs, and changes of direction, Temple opened the envelope and found a check for one thousand dollars, payable to his campaign. He was pleased until Ted Cordis raised the possibility that there may have been a bigger check in his other pocket had Temple given a different answer.

Temple had never thought of that. But he had answered truthfully, and he knew he could live with that.

Finally, at home that night, Pat made them tea, and as she brought the cup to her husband, she said, "I still don't get it. Why would Edward Landar give you, a stranger, one thousand dollars?"

"Dad used to say, 'politics makes strange bedfellows.'"

Chapter XXII

Counterintelligence

School had been in session for about two weeks. Temple would pass several bus stops in the City of Syracuse on his way into work every morning. He enjoyed seeing all the young faces, eager to get to school with their friends after a long summer.

On the morning of September seventeenth, he had just turned the corner at Hawley Avenue when he noticed a rusty, black van pulled up to a stop at the next intersection. This was also the corner where a little blonde–haired boy waited each day for his school bus.

Temple had seen the boy every day for the past two weeks and had made special note of him because he was about Temple's son's age.

In less than a second, Temple also took in two men behind the van. One was opening the back doors of the van, while the other was talking to the little boy.

Temple's heart jumped. He pushed down on the accelerator of his own van.

The man talking to the little boy reached for the child, who was now screaming. Temple saw another man running down the street toward the corner where the rusted van was parked. He was yelling frantically and waving his arms as he ran.

Temple sensed this was not right. All of this had happened so quickly that Temple's reactions were working almost ahead of his thought processes.

He sped to the corner. The man by the rusted van's doors yelled something to the other man who was now trying to drag the little boy to the rear of the van.

As Temple's van came even with the parked van, he swerved in front of it to block its way. He slammed the shift lever into park and jumped to the street.

Two cars passed him as he ran toward the little boy. The man who had been at the back of the rusted van was now in the driver's seat. The other man, holding the boy, looked up, saw Temple, and jumped into the back of the van, releasing the boy as he did so.

Temple was at the boy's side as the van lurched backward in reverse.

The boy jumped back onto the sidewalk next to Temple. The driver of the rusted van stripped his gears as he jolted into forward and sped off around Temple's van and down the road.

The man who had been running down the sidewalk reached the little boy and picked him up. "You all right, son?" He asked the little boy twice more before the boy was able to shake his head 'yes' between sobs.

"Is he going to be all right?" Temple asked the man.

"I think so. Thanks, mister. I was watching my boy from the house. When I saw those two assholes stop, I wasn't sure what was happening. If you hadn't stopped, I don't know if I'd have made it in time." The man heaved a long sigh. Tears formed in the corners of his eyes as he thought about the unthinkable. Suddenly he fell to his knees sobbing along with his son.

"You going to be all right?" Temple put a hand on the man's shoulder.

The man nodded, but appeared to be embarrassed at his own uncontrollable crying.

Temple said, "Okay." He climbed back into his van and continued on to work. He debated calling the police but had no way to identify the men or the van. It had all happened too quickly.

When he arrived at his office, word of his actions had already started to circulate. One of the cars that had passed had been a secretary with his company, and she had seen some of what took place in her rear view mirror. She, too, had not thought to get a plate number on the van, even though it had roared past her at a stop sign. She had been too frightened by the men's proximity to her to react quickly.

Temple concluded that he would have to settle with the thought that he had at least stopped whatever it was that was happening, and that was a good thing.

In another part of the city, two members of the special military task force on drug interdiction reported Temple's actions to their commanding officer.

"You wouldn't believe the way he went at them!" one said.

"Geez, he had them both back in the van like jack-rabbits!" the other said.

The commanding officer smiled a wide grin. "I guess we have found our man!"

* * *

Arthur Gaines wanted to insure his involvement in each of the campaigns in Onondaga County. As Chairman of the party, he knew that the success of the candidates would reflect his own success. He liked sharing the limelight, and he liked having a platform from which he could hold forth.

"Nancy, I've decided to hold weekly meetings of the Chairman's Council from now until Election Day."

Nancy Sandlin was the secretary and assistant to the Party Chairman. Her husband Bill Sandlin was the Chairman of the County Legislature. Both were well-respected, and both took their jobs very seriously.

Nancy turned in her chair to face the Party Chairman. "Every week?"

"Yeah. Maybe we can generate some excitement if we

319

get the town leaders, candidates, elected officials, and campaign contributors together more often. "I've been thinking about this, and I think it would help solidify the party. You know, everyone pulling the wagon in the same direction." Gaines thought for a moment and then continued. "Call Charles and ask him if he goes for the idea."

Nancy looked up Charles White's phone number and placed the call. As soon as she was connected to him, Gaines signaled to her that he'd take the call.

White was perhaps the most influential Republican in Central New York and Gaines had second thoughts about having his secretary asking White questions that he should be asking.

Gaines outlined his thoughts to White. White added a few modifications, including who should be invited and what the format of the meeting should be. Both agreed that the sooner they got started with the idea the better.

The first Chairman's Council was held a week later with a standing–room–only gathering of the party's faithful.

Gaines loved it. He finally had center stage and was being backed by the 'who's who' of Republican politics in Onondaga County. He gaveled the meeting to order.

"Ladies and gentlemen. Welcome. This is a fantastic turnout, and we have some terrific candidates to support this year! "I hope you all got some doughnuts and coffee. If not, help yourselves. Tom Ebert supplied them for us. Thanks, Tom." Gaines waved a hand to Ebert who nodded.

"I think it would be a nice idea if we went around the room and introduced ourselves. Most of you know each other, but for the few newcomers, it might be helpful."

Eighty-three people introduced themselves, each a politician in one way or another and each with a vested interest in the outcome of the fall elections.

Gaines and White had it planned that first the current officeholders would speak, and then the candidates for office.

"We are privileged to have with us this morning, a person who needs no introduction: the son of former State

Senator John Wales, a former City Councilman and former President of the City Council, and currently our Congressman from the 27th Congressional District, the Honorable Thomas P. Wales."

Loud applause followed the introduction of Wales by Gaines. Wales smiled as he walked to the podium. The room settled down as Wales began to speak.

"Ladies and Gentlemen, what a great day for the Republican Party. What a great election year.

"We have an outstanding line-up of candidates this year, and I'm proud to be on this ticket with them."

Again applause filled the room.

"Senator Al D'Amato is a great campaigner and has promised to spend a lot of time in Central New York this fall.

"Hank Palermo has proven to be one of the best county executives in the country, and he's running again this year and should lead all of our local candidates to victory.

"Howard White and Tommy Bright are again running for the Assembly and have some tough competition, but when the going gets tough, they get going, and I know they will win big!

"My friend, Senator Lansing, is unopposed, except by our friends over at the Gazette." Wales referred to the recent series of articles the Syracuse newspaper had run on Lansing and other Republican Senators who had met behind closed doors to work out a budget resolution with the Governor. Wales got the laughter that he had expected.

Wales looked around the room and then fixed his eyes on Temple who was standing in the doorway. "There is one race this year that I am particularly interested in. As most of you know, I spent six years in the City Council and during that time fought continuously with Laura Ann Mann over what was best for the City of Syracuse.

"As you also know, she went on to the New York State Senate where she has continued to be an obstructionist and has made some very insulting remarks about our own Senator Lansing. In fact, I wouldn't be surprised to find out that she had

321

something to do with the recent newspaper stories that have been running in the papers.

"Well, this year we have a candidate who is giving Mann a real run. The polls show that he is closing in fast, and I think that after November sixth, we'll be introducing this candidate as Senator Temple!"

The room again was filled with applause as the Congressman motioned for Temple to come forward.

Temple was a little embarrassed by this attention, and also sensitive about the feelings of the other candidates in the room. However, Temple did appreciate the comments and support of the Congressman.

Gaines leaned over the Congressman's shoulder as Temple came forward. "Let's have a few words from our next State Senator."

There was more applause as Temple stepped to the podium.

"Congressman Wales is too kind. We have a long way to go before November sixth. Laura Mann is just getting into high gear, and I know that we will have a real race to run between now and Election Day. I hope that all of you will support me and all the other fine candidates we have in this room. I think Congressman Wales said it best when he said that this year we have some outstanding candidates. Let's all go out there and work to get the entire ticket elected."

After the meeting was over, Gaines and White congratulated each other on a great idea. The Chairman's Council would now be a weekly event.

Through the remainder of the election cycle, the Council met weekly. Some meetings were better attended than others. The attendance averaged out at about forty. But it set a precedent and gave the Republican Party a forum for discussing issues and races. It drew some less active people back into an active role. It also helped increase the revenue for Party coffers as contributors discovered that they could have direct access to the politicians by attending these gatherings.

322

Temple benefitted from the Chairman's Council meetings, gaining valuable insight about the party members. He found himself impressed with the common sense, good judgment, and political smarts of Bill Sandlin, the Chairman of the County Legislature.

Tommy Haines, the Republican candidate for County Clerk, had been a top sergeant in the Air Force. He was hard working, straightforward, and possessed an uncanny ability to relate to the 'man on the street.' Tommy and Temple respected each other, and found opportunities to help in each other's campaigns.

For Temple, the Chairman's Council meetings were a success because of his having time during the campaign to actually sit down for an hour or more with people like Spelling and Haines and get to know them. As a result, Temple concluded that despite popular beliefs, there were politicians out there who worked hard and had principles.

* * *

Temple, Cordis, Tarkings, Price, and Roth were all working on putting together a District-wide mailing when the phone rang at Temple's Campaign Headquarters.

Laney Gardiner had been going over the donor's list, adding the most recent contributors to the computerized listing. She answered the phone.

"Temple for New York State Senate Headquarters, may I help you?"

There was a pause as she listened and then she said, "Please wait while I check to see if Mr. Temple is available."

Gardiner pressed the hold button. "Jay, there's a Captain Twining on the phone for you. He says he is with the United States Army!"

Everyone looked up.

Cordis smiled at Temple. "They've called your draft number."

"Too late. I have my retirement papers." Temple walked over to his office and picked up the phone.

"Hello. Jay Temple."

"Mr. Temple, this is Captain Twining of the United States Army, Special Intelligence Unit. Sir, I was wondering if I might meet with you privately?"

"Is there a reason for this meeting, Captain?" Temple wondered why he was receiving this call.

"Yes, sir. Sir, we have been working on a special operation in Syracuse and would like to brief you on it."

"What kind of an operation, Captain?"

"Sir, I can't get into details over the phone but will fully explain when we meet."

Temple thought for a moment. "All right, Captain, how about meeting me at my Campaign Headquarters tomorrow at ten in the morning?"

"Sorry, sir, but that would be too public and too late. May I suggest the Wegman's parking lot in DeWitt at three o'clock this afternoon?"

"How do I know that you are who you say you are?" Temple asked suspiciously.

"That is an appropriate question. I'll give you two numbers. First the local FBI number and second, the Armory number, where we are currently headquartered. Call one or both and verify who I am. You'll find both numbers in the phone book as well." The Captain was pleased that Temple was careful with how he handled sensitive situations.

"Very well, Captain. If I verify that you are who you say you are, I'll meet you at three today at Wegman's."

"Will you be driving your blue van?" the Captain asked.

"Yes."

"Park in the back of the lot, and we will join you."

"We? Who else will be there?" Temple asked.

"Sergeant Kingsley."

"I'm going to bring my campaign manager, Ted Cordis."

"You may if you want, but he cannot be present at our

meeting."

"Okay. He'll find something to do nearby."

After the call, Temple called Roth and Cordis into his office and relayed the conversation. Roth agreed to do some grocery shopping around two-thirty and to stay near the window of the store in case something went wrong.

At three that afternoon, Cordis pulled the van into a space near the rear of the parking lot. As he stopped and turned off the ignition, a dark blue Dodge sedan pulled alongside the van. Two men climbed out of the sedan. Both wore green sweaters and slacks with a black stripe running along the outside seams of their trousers. Both also had short brown hair, sunglasses, and gave quick glances around the parking lot before climbing into the side door of Temple's van.

The first man into the van immediately removed his sunglasses and with a quick smile, introduce himself.

"Mr. Temple, I'm Captain Twining and this is Sergeant Kingsley."

He held out his hand and Temple shook it. Temple introduced Cordis.

"This is Ted Cordis, my campaign manager."

"Yes, I know." Twining shook Cordis' hand. "And I believe Kevin Roth, your campaign treasurer, is doing some shopping inside the store." Twining smiled.

"Who are you?" Temple asked.

"Sir, we need to talk privately." He looked at Cordis. "I don't mean to insult you, Mr. Cordis, but I have orders from the Pentagon that I am to talk only to Mr. Temple. If you would like to wait in our car, here are the keys."

Cordis looked to Temple for direction.

"Okay, Ted. Please wait in their car."

Cordis took the keys from Twining and waited in the Dodge sedan.

"Mr. Temple, Sergeant Kingsley and I are part of a special strike force set up by the Federal Government to stop the flow of drugs into the United States.

325

"We have been assigned to the Northeastern Department and are working with the FBI and the Air Force SIF in a joint effort to keep drugs from being brought in over the border from Canada.

"We have been successful in shutting down a large drug ring in Buffalo, but have reason to believe that the cartel behind that operation is now moving to the Syracuse area.

"AFSIF has intercepted two light aircraft flying into the area with two thousand pounds of heroin, and we believe that their destination was a small airstrip near Canastota.

"We have been trying to work with the local police agencies but are encountering resistance."

Temple looked at the two men. It was an interesting story, but why were they telling him. "Does all this have something to do with me?"

Twining went on. "We pulled your two-o-one file. An Armor office, OCS, One hundred Forty-second Armor, served with distinction, first place in Army ATV at Fort Drum, honorable discharge.

"As a civilian, your record is equally impressive. We've been watching you over the last several weeks, and the incident with the rusted van and the child confirmed that you were what we are looking for."

Temple sat up straight. "Rusted van and child? Explain."

Kingsley pulled out a notebook and opened it. "Seventeen September, 0800. While observing subject under consideration, his blue van suddenly swerved to the right, effectively cutting off escape route for rusted van. Subject jumped from blue van and sent two unidentified men running. They apparently were trying to kidnap a young boy and were prevented from doing so by subject's actions. No injuries reported."

Kingsley looked up at Temple with admiration. "Nice work, Mr. Temple."

Temple had different thoughts. "You were both there

and didn't do anything?"

Twining stirred uneasily. "First, it all happened pretty fast, as I am sure you recall. Second, we were under orders to observe, not take action. I am sure you can understand what it means in the Army to be under orders not to take any action. And finally, we would have tried to get the Syracuse police to help, but as I said, the locals are resistant to working with us on anything."

Temple wasn't totally convinced. It had been a while since he had worn Army green, and there had been times when he had stretched his orders based on his own judgment. But he knew that there were many who didn't and wouldn't. Obviously, Twining was one of those.

As if reading his mind, Twining said, "If it makes you feel any better, Sergeant Kingsley wanted to go after the van. But I told him that our orders were to stick with you."

"Not much better, but you do have half an argument. What do you want from me," Temple nodded to Kingsley.

Twining went on. "What I am about to tell you must not be repeated, for your sake as well as ours."

"Agreed."

"We have reason to suspect that the cartel we are trying to shut down has friends both locally and at the state level who are blocking our efforts. I can't tell you how we know this, but it is based on fairly reliable information.

"That same source has indicated that the next step will be to use the Hell's Angels and other motorcycle groups to bring in illegal drugs from Canada. The RCMP is working with us to prevent this from happening. Unfortunately, our side of the border is not as cooperative.

"We believe that you are going to win your race for the New York State Senate. When you do, our analysis is that you will be a force in Albany and locally.

"We want to have you help us shut down this drug cartel."

Temple thought to himself that this was too unreal to

327

believe. "What can I do?" he asked.

"You will be able to open doors to the local and state police agencies. We don't have the manpower to do all that needs to be done. A combined force would. If state government forces a joint action, we can clean the streets and get these hard cases behind bars where they belong."

Temple still was having difficulty understanding the magnitude of what Twining was saying. Temple asked, "Are you telling me that right now, state and local police agencies are not cooperating with the Federal government on this drug task force because there are politicians blocking a joint action?"

Twining shook his head. "Sir, it's hard to understand the reasoning, but yes, that is exactly what I am saying."

"Do you have proof?"

"Some, but not enough. That's why we need someone within the system to help us."

"Well, if what you are saying is true, I'll help in any way that I can."

Twining smiled with relief. "Sir, it will be our pleasure to work with you."

After the meeting, Temple shared what he could with Cordis and Roth. Cordis summed up their reaction best when he whistled and said, "Holy shit!"

* * *

Three days after the Wegman's parking lot meeting, Temple had another unusual encounter.

He had spent three hours touring a factory and finding out how hard it was for the manufacturing industry in New York to compete with companies in other states. It was four in the afternoon when he returned to his campaign headquarters.

Upon arriving, Cordis and Gardiner came quickly over to him and motioned for him to keep his voice down. Temple looked at the two concerned faces and then beyond them to Dave Yondle. Yondle had his eyes fixed across the room and out the window facing Thompson Road.

"What's going on?" Temple said in a hushed voice.

"Those Army guys said that they had been watching us. Well, now we have someone else who I think is tapping our phone lines." Cordis was visibly shaken.

"What are you talking about?" Temple had had a rough day and was ready for bear.

Gardiner spoke up. "About noon today, this guy appeared on Thompson Road with a headset. I thought he was hitchhiking, but he has just been sitting on the guard rail, and he's been there for more than four hours."

Cordis took Temple's arm. "Come see for yourself. Dave, is he still there?"

Yondle turned quickly to face Temple. "Still there. I think he has some sort of box on the ground by his feet."

Temple, along with Cordis and Gardiner, joined Yondle.

"That guy has been there since noon?"

"Yes!" Gardiner shivered. "It's spooky."

"It's crazy."

"Maybe he's working for Mann?" Cordis said.

Temple took one last look and then turning, said to his staff, "There's only one way to find out." He walked out the front door, up the street and down Thompson Road to where the man still sat.

As Temple approached, the man got up from the railing. Temple walked right up to him and said, "My staff has been worrying about you. I understand you've been here since noon. Can I help you?"

The man pulled off the headset and looked nervously at Temple. "Help me? Ah, no. Actually, I'm counting cars."

"Counting cars?"

"Yes. The state pays me to verify the traffic counter. He pointed to a device by his feet. It counts vehicles that pass through a beam and sends impulses to the telephone line over there." He pointed to the telephone pole at the intersection of Erie Boulevard and Thompson. "My job is to do a manual count as well." He held up a hand held counter.

Temple noticed that the headset was attached to a recording machine around his waist. Satisfied that the man was either harmless, or at least put on notice that they were watching him, Temple offered, "Well if you need something cold to drink, stop in."

By the time Temple walked back to his headquarters, the man was gone.

Cordis was unnerved by the events of the past few days. He suggested to Temple that they request that the phone company check the phone lines for possible wiretaps. Temple thought about this and concluded that everyone was overreacting. He suggested that they call it a day and take the night off. Cordis agreed. He called Tarkings and Price and told them that the meeting for signage was canceled. He and Yondle then left together to get some dinner.

Gardiner stayed a while longer to finish up some thank-you letters for Temple to send to his latest contributors.

In his office, Temple thought about the man with the headset. There was one other possibility. He placed a call to the unlisted number that Twining had given him.

"Sergeant Kingsley. How may I help you?"

"Sergeant, at ease. This is Jay Temple."

"Hello, Mr. Temple. I didn't expect to hear from you. What can we do for you?"

Temple told Kingsley about the man with the headset and suggested that if they had a concern about security they may want to check it out.

"We have, sir."

Temple smiled. They were still on the job. "Sergeant, I will assume from your short answer that if it were something I should be concerned about, you would tell me."

"Yes, sir."

"Sergeant, have a nice day." And with that call, Temple put the incident out of his mind forever.

330

Chapter XXIII

State and Local Help

One of many new views of politics that Temple was seeing began in earnest in the fall. Fund raising went into high gear. Every candidate suddenly had needs for unlimited cash and the political parties also had an insatiable appetite for raising campaign funds.

Temple was receiving three to four solicitations a week. Some came with an invitation to be a guest and others expected the candidate to contribute. On the low end, the price per ticket was fifty dollars and on the high end, the price was five thousand dollars.

Temple made a concerted effort to attend those functions for which invitations were extended. He understood that these were usually from other candidates who wanted to either be helped by his presence or who wanted to help him in his quest for the State Senate seat. He appreciated both. He also remembered this lesson when he had his own fund raising events and wherever possible included other candidates without asking for money.

After much thought, Temple also concluded that he might better spend his money on his own campaign than on fund raisers for other candidates, especially those that were in the thousands of dollars. Fortunately, he had friends who were committed to buying tables at some of these events. Very often they thought to include him at these occasions.

Arthur Gaines had created another first for the Onondaga County Republican Party. It was the First 'Annual' Republican

Sports Celebration. A banquet with the coach of the Syracuse University Basketball Team and one guest coach from another nationally ranked team as the guests of honor. The price per ticket ranged from one hundred and fifty dollars up to five hundred dollars. The five hundred dollar tickets included meeting the coaches and having your picture taken with them.

James Tolling was the owner of a commercial construction company founded by his grandfather and which, up until two years earlier, had been run by his father. James had taken over the business, and with it, the commitments of three generations. Tolling Construction had always been and continued to be, a major contributor to the Republican Party.

Tolling's father had heard Temple speak at the Chairman's Council meetings and was impressed. He had suggested to his son that they include Temple and his wife as their guests at the 'Sports Celebration.' James called Temple. They had met socially a few times but had not known each other well. Temple accepted the invitation with gratitude. On the evening of the event, he and Pat arrived at the Hotel Syracuse for the private 'Coaches Reception.'

James Tolling and his father along with Arthur Gaines, greeted their guests at the door to the Persian Terrace in the Hotel. Tolling Construction had underwritten the entire reception.

As the Temples entered, they were immediately approached by several friends. Temple made his way toward their hosts while Pat talked with two women who were working on her husband's campaign.

"Good evening, Jay," the senior Mr. Tolling said as Temple approached.

"Good evening, Mr. Tolling. It was very nice of you and James to include Pat and me in this evening's events." Temple shook hands with both Tollings. "Hi, James. Looks like a big party!"

"Yeah. Art kept coming back with more people and we finally had to move the reception from the Blue Room to down here. At five hundred dollars a head, Art's beside himself!" Tolling slapped Gaines on the back.

Gaines had the look of a man who had just won the lottery. A perpetual smile on his face and constantly in motion, he shook Temple's hand. "Senator Temple, how are we doing?"

"Great!"

Gaines took Temple by the arm. "Come with me. I want you to have your picture taken with Jim and Rollie. You can use it for your campaign."

Gaines led Temple to the back of the large reception area and up onto a stage. A photographer had set up his cameras and a curtain for the purpose of taking pictures of the coaches with each of the guests at the function.

A line of people were being ushered to where the coaches stood, given a quick introduction, had a picture snapped, and then ushered off the stage at the far end. It was a smooth and quick way to give everyone a memento of their five hundred dollar–a–plate dinner.

Gaines led an embarrassed Temple past the line of guests waiting for their turn with the coaches.

"Excuse me, people," Gaines said as he stopped the procession. "We've got to get our next State Senator in here so he can get around and say hello to everyone."

Gaines brought Temple up to the spot where the Syracuse University and Villanova Coaches were standing. "Jim Boeheim, Rollie Massimino, I'd like you to meet Jay Temple, our candidate for the State Senate."

The Syracuse coach smiled. "Jay and I go way back. We were classmates at Syracuse."

The Villanova coach held out his hand. "I won't hold that against you, Mr. Temple. Good luck with your campaign."

Temple shook hands with both coaches as the camera clicked away unnoticed. "It's nice to meet you," Temple said to the Villanova coach. "I hope you have a great season," then looking at the Syracuse coach," but not as great as Syracuse!"

Massimino laughed. "You gotta be a great politician;

333

you know where your votes are coming from!"

The camera continued to click, catching all of the bi-play. "I've taken up enough of your time," Temple said looking back at the other paid guests waiting to meet the coaches. "I'll look forward to hearing your talks after dinner."

As Pat was watching her husband, talking to the coaches, James Tolling walked up to her to say hello.

"Think he'll win?" Tolling asked.

She turned to the tall blonde–haired man. "Oh, hello."

"Well, do you think Jay will win?"

She smiled. "Yes, I do. I'm Pat Temple."

"I know," he said. "I'm your host, James Tolling."

Pat could feel the color in her cheeks. She should have at least known who her host was, but she had only met him once before and had been sidetracked by friends when Jay had gone over to say hello. She had not recognized him until he had told her his name.

"I know," she said. "It was nice of you to invite us."

"Well, I think Jay has a chance to win this race, too. Dad and I both like what Jay has to say. It would be nice to have someone in Albany who really understands business."

"It'll be nice to have someone there who is honest," Pat Temple added.

* * *

418 Broadway, Albany, New York was the coordinating headquarters office for the New York State Senate Republican Campaign Committee. It was a nondescript building off a small alley, finished in brick, and under renovation.

The top two floors, however, were quite remarkable given the location. Equipped with the very latest computer technology, the NYSSRC could analyze voting patterns by household anywhere in the state and provide interested parties with names, registrations, household income, voting history, and a variety of other information by street address and by family.

This information, in turn, could be used for very sophisticated polling practices in current races and could minimize the percent of error in the results. At least that was the basis for the very substantial investment the NYSSRC had made in hardware and manpower.

Toby Hagan, the director of the NYSSRC operations, smiled at the printouts in front of him. He was waiting for Arnold Ophidia and Senator Valli to arrive. Both wanted to see the state–wide results of the most recent poll conducted on State Senate races.

Ophidia had at least seven races that he and his firms were handling. One in particular was most amusing to Hagan.

The elevator door slid quietly open and the Senator and the Campaign Manager stepped out. Valli was talking while Ophidia chewed hard on his cigar.

"Toby, how we doin' with our boys?"

Hagan knew Valli's chief concerns were the incumbents because they were his power base. "Reelection looks good for all but Howard and Sickles."

"I told you those shit-for-brains were in trouble. Howard is pushing birth control in a Catholic district and Sickles thinks he's the Secretary of State. Talks about bringing the PLO to the peace table. Geez! He's a damn State Senator in a Jewish district. Any kid on the street would have more sense!" Ophidia had definite opinions.

"Arnold is right. Our polls show that those are the issues hurting both Senators," Hagan confirmed. "We've worked out some models that, if followed, should win back the support that they have lost by Election Day."

Valli nodded. "Get that information over to Senator Manto. I'll talk with him about Howard and Sickles. How's our bullpen doing?"

Hagan laughed at Valli's reference to the new faces in this year's election. "Three races to watch. One may surprise you." Hagan handed copies of the printouts to Valli and to Ophidia.

335

Ophidia was the first to react to the latest poll results being shown to him. "This is the damnedist thing I have seen. The stiff in Syracuse is making a race of it."

"He likes you, too!" Valli said as he smiled at the printout. "How do we insure a win?"

Ophidia looked up. He had predicted that Mann would easily knock off Temple. "No contest," he had said. Now the guy was actually drawing within sniping distance of the toughest Democrat in the field. "I'll call my partner Bob Berry. If we can slide a professional campaign manager in there, the jerk might get elected."

"I don't want 'might.' If we can get Mann out of the Senate, you're worth every dollar we've paid you over the years. You'll be on permanent retainer!" Valli was serious in a kidding sort of a way. Ophidia saw the possibilities, both good and bad.

Hagan broke in, "Our models suggest that Temple appeals across party lines and is running strong in traditional Mann strongholds. He's weak in the City of Syracuse and strong in the City of Rome. His organization is weak in Syracuse."

"Can he win without Syracuse?" Valli asked.

"Only if he carries the suburbs around Syracuse."

"What are his odds at this point?"

"We're projecting 52% Mann, 47% Temple. We are a long way from Election Day!"

Within an hour, Ophidia was on the phone to Berry.

"Bob, the poll results put the race at 52% Mann, 47% Temple."

"All right! That's great news." Berry was excited. He liked Temple and saw a potential that could lead to great changes in the future. He was getting caught up in the race.

Ophidia brought Berry back to reality. "Great news if he wins. We've got a winner only if we get rid of the Ted Mack Amateur Hour and get a pro to run the campaign. So far it's been blind luck!"

Berry agreed that Desert Storm had played into the success to date. They had gotten a big boost in name recognition due to their air time buys and the huge viewership.

Ophidia went on. "Listen. I want you to talk to the Congressman. Temple listens to him. Explain the facts to him and get him to get together with Temple for a pow-wow. You know. The importance of first winning the race, and then worrying about who wears what hat. Temple has the chance of a lifetime. He could knock off a real force in politics. If he beats Mann, he can write his own ticket in Albany." Ophidia paused, "We could too!"

Berry was thinking. "Arnold, I hear what you are saying but I have to tell you, Temple, from what I have seen, is a very loyal and principled fellow. He's not going to be receptive to dumping anyone."

"Shit! My dog's loyal. That ain't going to get him elected. The Congressman will understand. You talk to him. Valli made it clear that if Temple has a chance, we are to go all out."

* * *

Temple was working on his next press conference when Tom Mosby's phone call came into campaign headquarters.

"Jay? This is Tom. Ken and I would like to get together with you at Republican Headquarters tomorrow morning at eight if you are available."

"Let me check." Temple turned to his campaign schedule to confirm that the morning meeting was okay. Behind his desk was a large three foot by five foot calendar showing the entire month and his three county schedule. "Looks good. What is the reason for the meeting?"

"Your campaign is going into high gear, and we want to have you sit down with the Congressman and Larry Kent, his campaign manager, to talk about some strategic planning issues."

"Good idea. I'll listen to all the advice I can at this point. Should Ted or Kevin come along?"

"No. I think we want to keep this small. The

337

Congressman may want to say some things to you that he'd rather not share with too many people."

Temple heard a warning bell sound somewhere inside of himself. "Tom, is there something more to this than you are telling me?"

Mosby hesitated. He was told not to get into it with Temple until the meeting. On the other hand, he had volunteered to help Temple. He liked Temple, and he owed him a straight answer. "Yeah. There's concern about putting you over the top. The most recent state poll shows that you could possibly win this race. We want to tell you how we see you doing this."

Temple sensed the struggle within his friend. He also knew that Mathews was not fond of Cordis, and putting it all together, he knew what tomorrow was all about. "Thanks, Tom. I'll be there, alone."

As Temple drove to Republican Headquarters on the following morning, he thought about the upcoming meeting. The Congressman would be there, along with Larry Kent, Tom Mosby, Ken Mathews, probably Bob Berry, and Arthur Gaines.

It was a stacked deck against Ted Cordis. Ted had devoted practically every hour of every day to Temple's campaign since he had joined the team. Temple had talked to Cordis about this huge commitment of time on more than one occasion. Temple did not want Cordis's business to suffer because of the campaign.

Cordis had assured Temple that his business would not be hurt by his work on the campaign. "I have it all under control. My day care center is run by an excellent woman. I only have to do the books once a month, and she takes care of the rest. My brother and I have some interests overseas, and he's agreed to handle things until after November. My secretary handles the day–to–day stuff, so I'm in good shape. I can spend as much time as needed on the campaign."

Temple had expressed his apology to Cordis for not being able to pay him for the work he was doing. Temple knew that he had a full time campaign manager and that it was not uncommon to pay for a manager. But both had agreed, early on, that any money raised would be spent on the campaign, and that if Cordis had to cut back on time because of his personal financial needs he would do so.

As Temple pulled into the parking lot next to Republican Headquarters, he knew what he would do. Most people would not be comfortable going it alone in this situation. Temple actually was looking forward to the confrontation. He knew inside himself that he liked working against the odds.

It would start out at five or six against one: himself. He believed he could win them over to his way of thinking. As he climbed the stairs to the second floor offices, the arguments took shape in his mind.

Tom Mosby greeted him in the outer office. Nancy Sandlin, the chief assistant to Gaines, looked on with some anxiety.

"Hi, Jay. Thanks for coming this morning. The Congressman, Larry Kent, Bob Berry, Ken Mathews, Arthur Gaines, and Tim Sullivan are going to be with us. They're in the conference room."

Temple smiled. 'Not bad, I had everyone accounted for except Sullivan,' Temple thought to himself. 'This works better. Sullivan will understand my arguments and buy in.'

Tim Sullivan was the Congressman's public relations person. Temple liked Sullivan. He had come to Temple's initial campaign team meeting and had offered several helpful suggestions. He had also arranged for the Congressman's public endorsement of Temple's candidacy.

Temple thought of Sullivan as a friend. Sullivan also had a side business with his brother selling ice cream in Skaneateles. Temple had stopped at their store on more than one occasion to enjoy their product and just to talk with the Sullivans. They were both down–to–earth and interesting people.

Temple said to Mosby, "Well, let's go in and have our little talk."

Mosby knew Temple was ready. He admired Temple's

self-assured nature. 'This guy will make a hell of a State Senator.'

Everyone stood up to greet Temple as he walked in. Temple started with the Congressman and shook hands and made small talk with each person in the room. He would refer to either family, sports, or business, depending on their mutual interest as he said hello. This drew them in and took the obvious edge off of the meeting.

The Congressman spoke first. "Jay, you've done a really fine job with your campaign. We have the most recent polls and they show only a five-point spread between you and Mann."

"We are all working hard, and I have a lot of great people helping me."

"You do. The point is that you can win this race. Larry and I have been through a lot of these campaigns. We have a pretty good idea of how the voters think, especially in Central New York. We also know that experience is what pays off down the stretch. That last five percent is hard to manage, and you need a pro in there to hold what you have and to build the winning margin of victory."

Temple watched the Congressman as he spoke. He maintained eye contact until the Congressman looked away to his own manager, Larry Kent.

Kent picked up the conversation. "Jay, you are working hard. People tell me that you are everywhere. Dinners, parades, door-to-door, you are doing exactly what you need to do. But there is no way you can cover a hundred and eighty square miles and meet every voter in person before Election Day. That's where you need professional help."

Berry spoke up. "Jay, I have worked on the Congressman's last four campaigns with my partner, Arnold. Arnold actually served as campaign manager during the first race and helped bring Larry along. Larry also attended a National Republican Party Manager's Training Program in Washington for four weeks and has since attended two refresher programs."

Kent smiled at Temple. "The point is pretty clear, Jay.

340

If you really want to win this race, and I am sure that you do, you need to bring in a professional campaign manager."

Ken Mathews cleared his throat. "Jay, as you know, I have not only been raising money for you but have been keeping an eye on finances for your campaign. You have been concerned from day one about not spending more than you take in." Mathews laughed, "That's a novelty in politics in and of itself! Your campaign is now generating enough money that you can afford to hire a professional. In fact, with these latest poll results, the NYSSRC will probably be willing to help with more dollars if they know that it will be spent wisely."

Gaines said, "That's affirmative. I spoke with Senator Valli this morning. He is very pleased with the poll results. He said that the state would be willing to help out if you decide to go with a professional campaign manager. This is great! We can finally get rid of Senator Laura Ann Mann."

Temple had purposely waited for everyone to say their piece. He knew that they would. Mosby and Sullivan had not said anything. Temple noted this as a positive sign. Mosby the lobbyist and friend and Sullivan the PR man and friend, would be the first to come around.

When no one else said anything further, Temple leaned forward, looking at the Congressman. "You actually provided me with the inspiration for forming my campaign team." The Congressman looked at Temple and knew that Temple had his own thoughts on the subject matter at hand.

Temple continued. "I have always been impressed with your campaign team. They are totally dedicated to you. Larry has given up his insurance business during each of your campaigns to do whatever you needed of him. Tim and I have talked. He has been your friend, as has Larry, since you three were kids, and they'd both walk through fire for you." He paused as he looked at Larry and Tim. Then Temple continued.

"I approached my friends to work on my campaign early on. I was looking for that same kind of friendship, dedication, and 'people smarts' that your people have. Unfortunately, the time commitment was too much for my friends."

Temple shifted his gaze to Gaines. "Arthur, you recommended Ted Cordis to me. Remember?"

Gaines nodded but said nothing.

"Your thinking was that here was a young man, interested in politics, hard working, and with a ready source of manpower with his Young Republicans. I took your advice and Bob Berry and I met with Ted shortly thereafter."

Temple now turned to Berry. "You remember that meeting, Bob." It was a statement not a question. "We had breakfast together, discussed the upcoming campaign, and what we were looking for. After Ted left, you said that you thought he was perfect for the job. Isn't that about the way it happened?"

Berry nodded, his eyes looking down at the conference table.

Temple went back to the Congressman. "I have a guy now as my campaign manager who lives at our campaign headquarters. He has motivated all those Young Republicans I mentioned to spend countless hours volunteering to do everything from cleaning our offices, to making phone calls, marching in parades, handing out literature from door–to–door, to making yard signs, and countless other necessary jobs connected with political campaigns."

Temple paused and looked at each individual around the table. Then he went on. "Loyalty runs two ways. Ted and his people have given me the same loyalty and friendship that Larry and Tim have given to you. I can't turn around now that we are closing the gap, and be disloyal to them." Looking directly at the Congressman, Temple finished, "You wouldn't."

The Congressman looked at Temple, thought for a moment, and said, "You're right, I wouldn't."

Temple stood up. "Thanks." He looked around the silent room. "Gentlemen, I appreciate your concern and your interest. I know that you are most concerned that I win this race. Two months ago, there are not many who would have said

342

that I would get this close. We've come this far doing the right things. If I can't continue doing this the right way, I'd just as soon not win.

"Ted Cordis is going to be my campaign manager. I hope I count on all of you to continue to give me the great support that you have given me up until now." Temple left the room.

That day, everyone who had been at the morning meeting called Temple to express and reaffirm their support for his position on Ted Cordis.

The Congressman told Larry Kent after the meeting, "You've got to like that guy. He's a straight shooter." Kent agreed.

Chapter XXIV

Made For Media

September through the first week in November became a blur of activity for Temple. It was both the longest period of time in his life and the shortest. He would comment to his friends on more than one occasion, "So much to do, so little time."

On Thursday, September sixth, Temple was invited to speak at the Syracuse Monarch Club. A businessmen's club since the early 1900s, it was the type of group that should have been supportive of Temple's ideas and directions.

As he entered the tenth floor meeting room at the Hotel Syracuse, he noticed a couple of reporters from local radio stations talking with members of the Monarch Club. Jill Towers of WKBL walked up to Temple with cassette player in hand.

"Good morning, Mr. Temple."

"Good morning."

"I'm Jill Towers with WKBL. I've been assigned to cover your race by the station."

"Great! It'll be nice to have you along."

Towers was in her mid-forties. A working mother of two children, she and her husband both struggled to maintain their home and send their oldest daughter to college.

Temple's campaign had interested her husband first. He had heard Temple speak at the plant where he worked. He had been impressed both with his sincerity and his ideas for reducing taxes and getting the state back on the road to recovery. Ted Towers had encouraged his wife to cover Temple.

A week later, without any urging by Jill Towers, the station manager had called her into his office.

He said, "Jill, I think the race to watch this year is going to be the Senator Mann — Temple race. Mann has had her way in the last two elections, but I sense that this time it's not going to be so easy. I want you to cover this race and give it some air time. Let me check what you get, and we'll go from there."

Two days later and she found herself talking to the tall, dark-haired Senate candidate in the Hotel Syracuse. "May I ask you a few questions?" She studied Temple's body language as they talked. He was relaxed, confident, and maintained eye contact as he answered questions and asked some of her.

"Why are you running for the State Senate?"

"Bobby Kennedy once said, 'Some people see things as they are and ask why, I see things as they might be and ask why not?'"

"I see things in Albany as they are and as they could be. I think that a change in direction is something that all New Yorkers want, and I think I can play a role in making those changes come about." Temple smiled at Towers.

"Can you give me some examples?"

"Sure. Don't spend more than you earn. Three years ago, New York State government spent one point five billion dollars more than it raised. Two years ago, it spent two point nine billion dollars more than it raised, and last year the deficit climbed to three point five billion dollars. I think that the direction of the current government is clear and that a change is called for."

"Mr. Temple, aren't these just numbers that the average voter has a hard time understanding?" Towers was impressed with the ease at which Temple cited statistics but wasn't sure that could be translated into votes.

"Possibly, but now there is a proposal working its way from the governor's office through the legislature that would increase taxes in New York State by seven point nine billion dollars. I think everyone in the state can understand that. I haven't met anyone yet who thinks his taxes need to be increased." Again the easy smile from Temple.

They were interrupted by Carl Jorning, the program chairman for the Monarch Club. He wanted to get the program underway.

Halfway through lunch, Jorning introduced Temple to the fifty or so members present. Temple walked to the podium and began his talk.

"Thank you for your kind invitation to speak with you today. As business people, a lot of what I am going to say you already know first hand. It's no surprise to you but it seems to have come as a surprise to many in state government.

"New York is in a financial crisis. Rated as one of the ten worst run states in the country, Standard and Poors and Moody's have given New York the third worst credit rating of all fifty states.

"This in turn means that when New York has to borrow money to cover its deficits, we pay premium dollars for that borrowing. It also means that when it comes time for the state to pay back the money that it has borrowed, our taxes climb to the highest in the nation.

"Mrs. Towers of WKBL asked me before the meeting where changes needed to be made in state government. Before we can tackle any other problems as a state, we've got to get our financial house in order.

"If you or I continued to spend more money than we took in, we'd be forced into bankruptcy. Well, that's the direction the state is going in, and I'm running for the Senate in the hope that I can change that direction."

There was loud applause as the business people responded to Temple's appeal to their longstanding complaints about state government.

Temple continued. "New York State has lost two hundred and thirty thousand manufacturing jobs over the last eight years. Factories have left our state and moved south, where the business climate is less burdensome and the taxes are anywhere from three to ten times less than here in our state.

"We can not afford the spend-and-tax philosophy of this state. The Governor has proposed seven point nine billion dollars in new taxes for the coming year. Part of that proposal includes a twenty percent increase in corporate taxes and one hundred and fifty new commissions to further regulate your businesses.

"These are not solutions to the problem of the mass exodus of businesses and jobs from the state, these are contributing factors!"

Again there was loud applause.

"The Governor's programs do not help business. They do not help the employer who bears the burden of the ever-increasing taxes and regulations, and they do not help the employees who lose their jobs when a business decides that it has had enough and leaves the state.

"What these programs do is spread the burden of taxation on a smaller and smaller base, making it even more burdensome for those businesses that remain in New York."

Heads nodded in agreement as Temple brought the members of the Monarch Club to the point of his talk.

"I'd like to ask you a question. Who in the 48th Senate District is providing the leadership on these important issues? Have you ever heard my opponent, Laura Mann, speak out on these issues? How effective has she been in changing the direction of state government?

"We need change. We need focus. We need to get our priorities straight. We need effective leadership at the state level if we are to survive the financial crisis that we are in. Thank you for your interest."

The members of the club again gave their enthusiastic applause to Temple. Towers noted the support. She interviewed several members after the meeting and, to a person, they said that they would vote for Temple on Election Day.

WKBL carried portions of the speech and the exit interviews during its hourly news reports for the remainder of the

347

day and evening. Temple was appreciative, Mann was not.

That night, Jill Towers told her husband about her experience with Temple and the reaction to his speech. He nodded his head and said, "I've never voted for a Republican in my life, but this guy may be my first."

Later, as she lay in bed thinking, Jill Towers thought about her own voting record. She had always voted for the female candidate if the choice had been between a woman and a man. She wondered how she would vote this year.

* * *

By mid–September, news coverage of the Temple–Mann race was picking up. The Temple Campaign was again running his television 'promo' showing the candidate as a coach with his youth basketball team, talking with a farmer in LaFayette about the burdensome regulations farmers faced in New York State, talking with a shoemaker in Cazenovia about the economic hardships that small business had to deal with daily, and with his family celebrating Tyler's birthday.

Temple had visited a nursery school in Minoa accompanied by photographers. As he knelt to talk with several preschoolers, the cameras snapped and the following day, the weekly newspapers carried a photo essay of his visit and described his educational priorities for the state.

Joel Samuels knew that now the race was for real. Lacking time and money to produce a new spot for television commercials, he pulled the old 'Rhythm and Blues' commercial and convinced Channel 4 to add a trailer from one of the Senator's recent news conferences to the commercial.

Mann's piece was placed with all networks in the same time frame as Temple's. This didn't go unnoticed by the political reporters, and they began focusing on the race that was beginning to dwarf all others in time, money, and effort.

Even the Syracuse Gazette began covering the race with short front page clips. Campaign comparisons were drawn, still

348

favoring the Senator, but at least acknowledging Temple's run.

Stewart Ropespear called his political reporters together for an early morning discussion of the local political scene.

The reporters sat around the Editor's spacious mahogany office, each hoping that someday lightning would strike and they'd occupy a similar office. Finally, the boss entered and walked over to his padded leather chair and sat down.

"Wales is in a closer race for his Congressional seat than we thought. I want some attention paid to his race. Get some issues out there that highlight the differences between the candidates." Ropespear shifted slightly and smiled at his favorite hatchet-man, George Hague.

"George, I want you to cover Senator Mann's debate with Temple next week at the Hotel. The YWCA is sponsoring this one, and I would guess that there will be some discussion of women's issues. The Senator will be in her element. You'd have to be an ignorant bastard to agree to take her on, one-on-one, in that setting. Anyway, it should give you plenty of copy."

George Hague and the other reporters in the room got the message.

Ropespear discussed possible endorsements by the paper and their timing, and then adjourned the meeting. He had an appointment with former Senator Barcliff. He did not want to be late.

As the reporters filed out of the Editor's office, Mike Flynn, a young reporter with the paper, leaned over Hague's shoulder and said, "Temple is not as dimwitted as some may think. You may have a hard time spinning your piece."

Hague looked at the young reporter and grinned through his graying beard. "Just watch me."

* * *

Bob Berry was ecstatic. Arnold Ophidia had written Temple off as a loser who wouldn't get to first base. "He's not

349

tough enough for this business.' Ophidia had said after Temple had refused to wage a personal battle with Mann. Berry had asked his partner if he could stay with the campaign. Ophidia looked at him in disbelief. "It's your funeral. You aren't goin' to make it as a king maker if ya work losing campaigns."

Now the race was closing. Temple was pulling substantially ahead of Mann in the fund raising area, and the media was finally coming around. It was time for Berry to show Ophidia what he could do. He wanted this campaign to win and he wanted to pull in the 'big bucks' for his agency. He shared some of Temple's dislike for Arnold, and he relished the thought that he could prove his partner wrong.

A meeting was set up for outlining the direction of campaign advertising down the stretch. On September nineteenth, Berry, Temple, Pat, Mathews, Cordis, and Mosby met at Temple's home to plan the campaign strategy from that point through Election Day.

Berry had brought flip-charts to give the group a clear picture of how he believed the campaign should go.

"Jay, you've got a real chance to win this race!"

Cordis smirked, "Tell us something we don't know."

Berry ignored the comment. "The latest poll shows you only fifteen percentage points behind. And that's with her commercials running opposite yours and her concentrating on this race. You're in the driver's seat. The race is yours to win or lose."

Mathews leaned forward placing both of his hands on the table. "Jay, I think that you are going to win this race. You've got the momentum, you've got a great team of volunteers, and you've got the money now to do some good things.

"Bob has put together an outline that I think we need to take seriously."

Temple said, "Well, you've obviously seen it, and if its that good, why don't we all take a look at the entire proposal and then comment afterwards."

"Good." Mathews leaned back in his chair having given

his stamp of approval up front for Berry's offering.

Berry nodded to Temple. "Okay. First the polls show that people like you. The first promo that we did has gotten the message over that you are like everyone else: a family man, interested in children, farmers, the small businessman, and the state of affairs in New York State.

"The polls also indicate that there is some concern that you may be too nice a guy to handle the toughness of Albany politics. So, I suggest that we tape another promo showing you as a no-nonsense guy who will go to Albany and get the job done."

Cordis interrupted, "Do we have enough time to get this produced and on the air?"

Berry smiled. He was well ahead of everyone with planning and implementing his strategy. "I have arranged to hire the Channel 7 studio for the spot. One week turnaround, and in a format that will be ready for on air use."

"Great!" Cordis conceded.

Berry went on. "Next, we want to get a letter out to the voters from Pat telling them why she feels Jay would be the right choice on Election Day."

Pat exclaimed, "Me? Why me? I'm not good at writing, and I'd be embarrassed."

"We did this two years ago in the Wales campaign and found that it was very effective among women voters. It reinforces the family image with the feminine touch. It is particularly important in this race because Jay is running against a woman."

Pat turned to her husband. "What do you think?"

Temple knew how uneasy his wife was with public scrutiny. She would be very happy if she could just work in the background and help out behind the scenes. Both he and his wife also knew that in politics that's a luxury that few political families can enjoy.

"I guess I'd have to go along with Bob. I think that once you get into it you'll be fine. On the positive side, you can say whatever you want. That's a rarity in politics, too!"

Everyone laughed except Pat. She tried another tack. "Wouldn't it make more sense to have you write a letter to every voter. You're a great writer and I would think that they would be more interested in hearing what you had to say as the candidate than what I have to say as your wife?"

Berry fielded this question. "Pat, you'd be surprised at how many people are interested in what you have to say as the candidate's wife. Jay is going to have ample opportunity to get his message to the voter. We need you."

She looked at Cordis, then Mathews, and then Mosby. All said that they agreed. Reluctantly, she agreed to do the letter.

Berry flipped the page on his easel. "The debates will generate a lot of coverage. Starting next week, we do a news conference a week. The NYSSRC will be pumping out releases for us, and we can generate some of our own. Jay, you can look them over and pick out what fits for you. Next week we'll do one on the Governor's proposal to pull one hundred state policemen from Upstate to go down to New York City. We lose protection for the benefit of the City."

Berry turned another page. "Talk shows are now interested in having you discuss the issues at their studios. We'll try to spread those out through October so that you do one a week. Channel 7 wants to air a debate but Mann's people have said no. I think that's another good sign."

Mosby nodded, "I've known Laura since she got into politics. She's never not appeared for a debate with her opponent. I agree with Bob, you've got her worried. If you do well in the upcoming series of untelevised debates, she may fall apart."

Cortis laughed, "We should be so lucky!"

Berry offered several additional public relations opportunities and then concluded, "Last but certainly not least, I've gotten commitments from a number of Republican Senators to come in and speak to the district on your behalf. We need to provide them with a forum for their appearances."

After a lot of discussion, the group bought into Berry's outline. He left the Temple home that evening feeling very good about himself and his ability to make kings. He started thinking about his own possibilities once Temple was elected.

The 'Do Me A Favor' letter that Pat Temple agonized over for three weeks was a tremendous success. It not only promoted her husband in a way that only a wife could do, but it showed a caring, loving wife who supported her husband and believed in him as someone who could truly make a difference.

Pat's letters went out the second week of October. Three days later, people were asking to see the wife of the candidate. Invitations to events included a special request that Mrs. Temple join her husband. Wherever they went, the women in particular, wanted to talk with Pat and listen to what she had to say.

She slowly realized that if her husband were elected, she could have an impact on certain of her own pet projects as well.

One night after dinner, she turned to her husband. "Jay, if you do get elected to the State Senate, I'd like to use what influence you and I have to help children."

Temple looked at his wife and saw a spark kindling in her dark brown eyes. "I've been thinking along the same lines. Ever since that parade in Madison County, I've had this thought about helping hungry kids who can't help themselves. In America, no child should go hungry."

Pat listened. She and her husband had always been pretty much on the same wavelength. "I'm glad you agree. As the wife of a Senator, I could probably do some things that you wouldn't have time to do. I could look into what New York is currently doing to help these children and then come up with some ideas that might provide more direct help where it was needed."

"I think that would be terrific! In a year, you'll be the belle of Albany!"

"Are you making fun of me?"

"No. I think that you would bring to Albany politics a

353

new image. Someone who takes the high road and who does the right things for the right reasons. That's what this state and this country needs. I'd never make fun of you for that."

Temple got up from his chair and walked over to his wife. He bent over and kissed her gently on the lips. He thought to himself that regardless of the outcome of this race, he already was a winner.

Chapter XXV

The Taste Of Victory

The campaign was quickly taking on new dimensions. Temple and Mann were in full stride by late September. Both campaigned with a purpose and took advantage of every opportunity to meet people and to try and win votes for the November election. Surprisingly, their paths crossed only during their debates. When they did meet, it was as cordial as two combatants could be, knowing that the other was the main focus of every waking moment, and that only one would walk away with the prize that each of them sought.

During the last week of September, the State Republican Committee sent in an 'observer' to watch and advise Temple's campaign team. Butch Carroll had worked for the Committee for a number of years. His specialty was Senate politics. He knew all the players and had done much of the same work for them as he was now assigned to do for Temple.

Carroll was a forty–year–old former track star from Cal-Tech. He was very regimented. Up at five–thirty in the morning, out jogging by six. He ran twelve miles every day before a shower and breakfast. Breakfast consisted of orange juice, one egg, and toast.

By nine o'clock he was in the office reviewing plans and statistical information. His specialty was analyzing political polls. He had worked with Toby Hagan at the request of Senator Manto and had concluded that Temple would be the newest Republican State Senator come Election Day.

In a meeting with Manto and Senator Valli, Carroll

outlined his reasoning and backed up his opinion with solid poll information. Hagan had confirmed the results by conducting three separate polls. The race was going to be close but the projection was clear.

Manto looked directly at Valli. "We need to bring Mr. Temple into the fold. If he beats Mann," he paused and smiled at Carroll, "I mean *when* he beats Mann, he will be someone to be reckoned with. We need to have some control over his actions. I suggest that we get into his campaign organization with money, advertising, and manpower."

Valli knew that this was not a suggestion, but a directive from the Majority Leader. Valli, as head of the NYSSRC, also knew that it was his job to carry out the directive. "I have asked Butch to go on sight with Temple's campaign, three days a week. Arnold Ophidia has been working on a few other campaigns, but he's on the payroll, and we can direct him to get some power pieces out on Temple."

Manto nodded, "Good. Ophidia knows how to win and should have a field day with Senator Mann."

Carroll cleared his voice. "Excuse me, sir. There might be a hitch there."

"What do you mean, a hitch?" Manto demanded.

"Well, I've heard that Temple and Ophidia don't see eye to eye on how to deal with Mann. Ophidia wanted a campaign that goes for the jugular, but Temple nixed the idea. Temple's focus is on issues."

Manto flushed. "An idealist. Well, he's gotten this far I guess. Okay. Have Ophidia prepare an alternative plan and, Butch, you be our eyes and ears with the Temple people. If you think he can do it without playing hardball, we'll go along with Temple. But if he falters, we bring in the heavy guns."

Carroll left the meeting considerably less buoyant than when he had entered. The responsibility for calling the shots had fallen to him. If Temple lost because he had made the wrong call, it would be his head. He liked the idea of Temple making it with his new politics. But he was working for the NYSSRC, and he knew their way was different. Manto wanted a winner to add to his slim majority in the Senate. Temple was an unexpected bonus baby for the Republican majority. Carroll would have to deliver.

* * *

Bob Berry felt his adrenalin surge as he talked at length with Arnold Ophidia. After he hung up the telephone he could still hear Ophidia's voice. "Your boy is a cash cow for us. Valli is pullin' out all the stops on this one. Whatever it takes."

Berry rolled the words around in his mind. 'Whatever it takes.' The NYSSRC was sending in Butch Carroll to help out. He was a top gun for the Committee. Republicans and Democrats alike knew Carroll. He had been highly successful in Albany politics, working the back rooms. That meant they were projecting Temple as a winner.

Berry leaned back in his leather chair and turned to look out his fourteenth floor office window. He could see the hills of LaFayette looming in the distance. He thought, 'Temple is out there campaigning right now. He doesn't even know how far reaching his influence is.'

Berry swiveled back to his desk and said aloud, "Let's get to work!"

He phoned Mosby and filled him in on the most recent developments. Mosby was pleased. "This is good. Very good. Bob, call Ken and tell him. I'll talk to Jay about Butch. I think he'll understand the benefit of having Butch help if I talk to him."

"Okay, Tom. I'll call Cordis and let him know that Carroll will be spending some time at headquarters."

"Good. Bob?"

"Yeah."

"We better start thinking about what we are going to do after."

"After?"

357

"After Jay wins. He's going to need a lot of help getting acclimated to Albany."

"I'm ready to go!"

The two men laughed and hung up to follow through as they had agreed.

Cordis was not pleased with having Carroll come in to the campaign. He did not trust Berry or Mathews, or Mosby, for that matter. This was his show, and he did not like their growing influence with Temple.

Temple had lunch with Mosby and was given a full summary of Butch Carroll's background and position in Albany. He appreciated the fact that Carroll was willing to take a leave of absence to spend a few days a week offering suggestions to the campaign. Mosby and Berry had been the closest things to professional politicians involved with Temple's campaign. Carroll brought in real experience and could offer another perspective to the campaign decision process.

Temple had no sooner walked into his headquarters when Cordis approached him.

"Jay, we need to talk."

"Sure, Ted. What's the matter?" Temple could see the strain on Cordis' face. They had campaigned together, day and night, for the last five months. Cordis had become a part of Temple's family. Jay was sensitive to his campaign manager's feelings.

They walked into Temple's office and sat down.

"I don't like this deal with this guy from the NYSSRC. We're doing well without him. They didn't give us the time of day before now. We suddenly jump in the polls and now they want to get into bed with us. I think we should politely tell them that we don't need their help."

"What's really bothering you?"

"What do you mean?"

"I think that there is more to this than having someone from Albany come in to help out."

Cordis looked at Temple. He thought, 'this guy sees

right through me.' He moved uncomfortably in his chair. "Aren't you happy with the way I'm running your campaign? If you're not, tell me and I'll go quietly right now."

Temple was taken by surprise with Cordis' response. He had never questioned the way Cordis was running the campaign. In fact, Temple had felt guilty about the amount of time and energy that Cordis had devoted to him. Cordis had driven Temple from one end of the District to the other. Cordis had recruited the core group of volunteers that handled all the daily work and a lot of nighttime duty as well. He had lived the campaign twenty-four hours a day since he had signed on. Temple had offered to compensate Cordis for his work but Cordis would not take any money. He had said that they might better spend it on the campaign. Now Cordis was feeling unappreciated by the candidate.

Temple looked directly at Cordis. "Ted, let me tell you something. You could walk away today, and I'd never say a bad word about you. You have given me everything since you joined the campaign, and I am totally appreciative of what you have done and are doing. I couldn't have had a better campaign manager if I had tried.

"Carroll is coming in to observe and make suggestions if he can see anything that may help us. We decide whether what he has to offer is of any benefit. It's no different than advice we receive from any other person working on the campaign.

"The bottom line is that you and I call the shots. It's been that way all the way through this and will continue to be. I have confidence in your judgment and know that you will be looking out for my interests. You are the campaign manager and won't be replaced."

Cordis looked at Temple. His thoughts were swirling through his head. Temple could see this but had no idea of what they were all about. Finally Cordis smiled a tired smile. "I guess I've been pushing too hard. If you think Carroll's okay, I'll go along. Sorry for what I said."

Temple stood up. "I'd be worried if you weren't concerned. Any time you need to talk, see me."

Cordis stood up, nodded, and said, "I will."

* * *

On Saturday, September 22, Congressman Wales had arranged for a joint appearance with Temple at the Josh Moore farm in Madison County. Wales had invited the Secretary of Agriculture to his Congressional District, and the Secretary had agreed to come. About two hundred farmers would be in attendance, and Wales wanted to help Temple pick up support in this area.

Temple, Pat, and Tyler arrived at the Moore Farm around noon. There was already a large crowd gathered together at the farm including Larry Kent, the Congressman's campaign manager, and Tim Sullivan, the Congressman's public relations man.

"Hi, Jay." Kent walked over to the Temples as they came up the stone and gravel driveway.

Temple stuck out his hand and shook Kent's. "Larry, I don't know if you have ever met my wife, Pat." Temple paused, "Pat this is Larry Kent, a good friend of Congressman Wales."

"Pleased to meet you, Pat," Kent said as he looked from Pat Temple to Tyler. "And who is this?"

Temple picked his youngest son up in his arms. "This is Tyler."

Tyler Temple looked down at his hands as he leaned against his dad's shoulder. "Hello."

Kent patted Tyler on the shoulder then looked at Temple. "C'mon, I'll introduce you to our hosts."

He led the Temples over to a spit where a pig was slowly being turned over a hot bed of coals.

"Josh, I'd like you to meet Jay Temple and his family. This is Pat Temple, Jay's wife and his son Tyler." Kent stepped aside to let Temple and Moore shake hands.

360

"Nice of you folks to join us. I'm just checking out our porker. Think it's about ready." Moore made a few more cuts in the roast and then turned to Tyler. "Son, you hungry?"

Tyler nodded as he answered, "Yeah."

"Good, well, you can start the line. Get a plate over there and c'mon back."

As Tyler went with his mother for the plates, Temple said to Moore, "It sure was nice of you to include us. I hate to admit this, but this is the first real pig roast that we have ever been to."

"Well, then I'm glad you came, Mr. Temple."

"Call me Jay."

"Okay, Jay, call me Josh. Say, you haven't met my wife, Marie." Moore called to a woman wearing a bright green apron with apple designs sewn on it. "Marie, c'mon over here. This is Jay Temple."

Marie Moore came over with a welcoming smile. She had green eyes, red hair, and was in her early fifties. An attractive woman who took an active part in the farm's operations, Marie was the perfect hostess.

"Mr. Temple, I've heard a lot about you. We're so glad you could join us today."

"Thank you, Mrs. Moore. The pleasure is ours." Temple turned to his wife and son as they walked up. "Mrs. Moore, I'd like you to meet my wife Pat and my son Tyler."

"Please, call me Marie. Mrs. Moore makes me sound too old." She laughed as she exchanged greetings with Pat and Tyler Temple.

"Tyler, do you like farm animals?" Marie Moore not only knew about farms but she knew about children as well.

"Yep."

"Would you like to see some Holstein cows?"

Tyler looked at his father. "Can I, dad?"

"Sure." Temple smiled at his youngest son.

Tyler immediately set his plate down and looked at his mother. "You're coming too, aren't you, Mom?"

361

Marie winked at Pat. "Of course she is. Let's go. I'll give you a quick tour of the Moore farm."

"Mind if I tag along?" Temple asked. "I'd like to see your farm too."

"Sure. Josh, take care of our other guests while I show the Temples around."

Mrs. Moore led them around the entire building complex explaining equipment and how it was used, and showing Tyler their prize winning herd of Holsteins, the chicken coop, and the horse corral.

Tyler, in turn, amazed Marie Moore with his knowledge of the animals and the farm equipment. Tyler loved to read non-fiction, and his favorite interests were animals and equipment. He had a sound basic knowledge of almost everything he saw and his retention was remarkable. He took in every additional piece of information that Marie Moore offered and, no doubt, would use it later on.

When they got back to Josh Moore, Marie told him about young Tyler with great admiration. She concluded by looking at the boy and saying, "Tyler, any time that you want to come and work for us, just let us know. We'd be happy to have someone who knows all that you know working on our farm."

As the Temples were again going to join the others now at the food line, the sound of a large engine came circling in from above. A helicopter landed about twenty-five yards away. The hatch opened and out stepped a pilot, then Congressman Wales followed by the Secretary.

Josh Moore looked at Temple with a big grin, "You may never get to eat."

On the way back to Fayetteville, the Temples talked about their first 'pig roast' and their son.

"Marie and Josh sure enjoyed Tyler." Temple smiled as he drove.

"Isn't he something else?" Pat laughed.

"Why am I something else?" Tyler asked as he listened to his parents.

Temple looked in the rear view mirror at his son. "Tyler, there are not a whole lot of boys your age whoknow as much about farm machinery as you do."

"Or farm animals either," Pat said.

Temple asked his son, "How come you know so much?" He loved to hear Tyler's explanations about things.

"I don't know, I'm just smart I guess," Tyler said very matter of factly. "I like farms. If you like farms, then you got to know about them, dad. So I do."

Both parents laughed while Tyler just smiled and shrugged his shoulders.

Temple went on. "The Moores were very nice to take us around and introduce us to all of their friends."

Pat looked over at her husband. "Do you ever wonder why people are so nice to us?"

"Yeah, quite often. Congressman Wales has been very good to me. At first I thought that he thought he would use me."

"Didn't that bother you?"

"No. Because when I thought about it, I was using him too. He gave me some exposure that I would not have gotten otherwise. He was also the first elected official to support my candidacy. He's still giving me more help than any other elected official, and he doesn't have to. He has his own race to run."

Pat Temple smiled at her husband. "He knows a good man when he sees one."

"I think he respects me, and I even think that we are becoming friends. That's a real positive in this campaign."

"What? Becoming friends with our Congressman?"

"More than that. I've met a lot of very nice people and a lot of people have gone out of their way to help me. I think I appreciate people more because of this campaign.

"It's the Congressman, the Moores, Ken Mathews, Ted Cordis, Kevin Roth, everyone. They are all willing to lend a hand for something that they believe in and sometimes just to be nice people. Win, lose, or draw, this has been a great

363

experience and something I will never forget."

Pat shook her head. "You love being with people."

"Yeah. I guess I do."

"Me too, dad!" Tyler's voice drifted up from the back seat.

Temple looked at Pat, "Just smart, I guess!" and they both laughed along with Tyler as they drove the rest of the way home.

* * *

On Monday, September 24, Temple headquarters received word from the YWCA that the debate between Temple and Mann had been postponed until October 18th. They agreed to the postponement.

Temple spent the morning at the regional headquarters of a large insurance carrier, talking with many of the over five hundred employees working in the office.

Every election cycle, the carrier extended invitations to all candidates to come and meet their employees. It was an informal gathering in the company cafeteria. There were no speeches, no organized program. It was just an opportunity for politicians to mingle with company employees during the three lunch shifts. It was an opportunity that several candidates took advantage of.

As Temple was going from table to table, saying hello to the people he met, a familiar voice called out his name.

Mary Pasternak was a former New York City Legal Aid counsel who had moved to Syracuse and had established a thriving practice. Smart, untiring and driven to achieve, she was now running for a seat on the Supreme Court bench. She, too, was working the crowded lunchroom.

Temple looked up and saw Pasternak coming toward him. It had been a while since they had seen one another. Four years earlier, Temple, Pasternak, and five other candidates for the United States House of Representatives had appeared together

364

in a televised debate. The debate had been an unwieldy event complete with name calling and shouting, but out of the pandemonium Temple and Pasternak had met and had formed an unstated mutual admiration society.

Temple had been impressed with Pasternak's intelligence and knowledge of the subject matter that had been addressed. Pasternak had been struck by Temple's sincerity and his concern for others despite his Republican label. She had told him after the debate, "You are in the wrong party. You should be a Democrat!" Temple had laughed and asked her if that was an endorsement. In the end, neither had won. Temple lost the Congressional nomination and Pasternak lost in the General Election.

Now here they were again. Politicians on the campaign trail.

"Hi, Mary."

"Hi, Mr. Temple. I've been reading about you."

"Anything good?"

"Yes. I'd say you are doing a good job of getting your name out there. It also sounds like you are raising a lot of money for your campaign."

"It takes a lot of money to run against an incumbent. You may recall that. I think I read somewhere, about four years ago, that you were complaining about the unfair advantage that an incumbent has."

"Do you believe everything you read?" she laughed.

"Only if it's good news."

"Speaking of incumbents, I'd better not get caught talking to you. They'll throw me out of the party."

"I didn't think Mary Pasternak worried about those things."

"Mary Pasternak doesn't. It's just politics. Say, it's good to see you. Good luck!" She smiled with an encouraging look on her face.

Temple returned her smile. "Good luck to you, too."

Several other politicians came and went during the lunch

shifts. Temple stayed the entire time in order to meet as many people as possible. He talked about the election, campaign issues, basketball, both at the college level and professional, and about business. He heard the complaints of constituents and also their suggestions. In the end, he concluded that this was a very worthwhile way to spend a half day.

Back at his headquarters, he commented to Dave Yondle as they worked on their upcoming major fund raiser, "It's interesting, Dave, every time one of the opposing candidates would come into the cafeteria, his or her opponent would leave. You'd think that since they are running against one another and comparisons are going to be drawn anyway, that they would stay just to hold up their end of the action."

"*You'd* think that way but not many others would," Yondle said.

"Why not?"

"Most politicians I have known are insecure. They hide their insecurity in different ways but basically they are never sure of themselves. It's understandable given the fact that how they are perceived has a lot to do with whether they get elected. But they are always conscious of how others see them. They want to be seen in the best light. It's a real risk to stand toe–to–toe with their opponent. Who knows how they will be compared."

Temple sat back and looked at Yondle. "Dave, that's pretty astute! I never gave that much thought, but you probably have something there."

"You never gave it much thought because you don't think like that. Your strength is that you are yourself, take it or leave it. You'll never lose in politics because you have nothing to lose. You're a rare commodity!" Yondle laughed. "If we don't get these invitations out, I may make a liar out of myself."

It was Temple's turn to laugh.

Later that day, as he drove to the Rome Republican Dinner for Assemblyman Towns, Temple thought about what Yondle had said. What would he lose if he lost the race? Money? No. Prestige? No. Time? Not really. He was enjoying what he was doing, and he had his family and friends with him. He actually was gaining there because in reality he was seeing more of both family and friends than he would have had he been working.

In the end, he concluded that what he would lose would be the opportunity to help change the world he lived in. There were other ways to accomplish change, and he knew that. But he also believed that potentially the most powerful people of influence when it came to accomplishing change, were the politicians. They controlled both the mechanics of change and the purse strings to get the job done. He hoped that with the coming of November, his opportunity to change the direction of things would also come.

Temple had spent a lot of time in Rome, getting to know its people and its problems. He had made a lot of friends, and there were many who attributed in part Rome Hospital's survival to his efforts.

The Towns' fund raiser was also to be the occasion for the Assemblyman and Mayor Eiles to endorse Temple's candidacy. Local news reporters were on hand as the party faithful began coming through the doors.

Towns and Temple were talking when the Mayor arrived in a jogging suit, sweaty, and with a towel thrown around his neck.

"Hi, guys," the Mayor said as he walked over to the two candidates for state office.

Temple was thinking it, but Towns gave their mutual thoughts expression. "Are you going to issue your endorsement like that?" Towns looked at the Mayor's clothing with a combination of shock and disapproval.

"Well, actually no. I have to apologize to both of you, but I completely forgot about tonight. I just happened to be jogging by and ran into Frank Catallana. He reminded me about tonight, and I thought I'd better at least come in and face the music."

Towns looked puzzled. "Then you are going to endorse

367

Jay and me tonight?"

"Hey, I'd like to guys, but I can't, like this. We'll reschedule something. I'll have Allan Gant set it up."

"But what about tonight?"

Temple felt sorry for Towns. This was his big night and he had had it all planned out in his mind. Now the plans were unraveling.

Eiles saw the look on Towns' face. He said, "You'll be all right. You got all these people here to back you. Besides, Mr. Temple is one of the great stand-up speakers of the day. Let him put the power of the New York State Senate behind you. You know? An unbeatable team for Rome, Towns and Temple."

After a few more words of encouragement, the Mayor left. He went without giving an endorsement and or making a commitment.

Eventually, he would announce that "As the Republican Mayor of Rome, I support everyone on the ticket." But the real support for Temple came from Mrs. Eiles, who worked tirelessly to unseat Laura Ann Mann.

Temple concluded that Mayor Eiles was ever the politician, and like so many who held office, he was always aware of the fact that after the election, he would have to work with whomever was in office and that it was much easier to do that if you hadn't gone too far out on the proverbial limb. When they started cutting the limb off, Eiles wanted to make sure that he could get back to the main trunk.

Towns complained to Temple about his view of the Mayor's backing out of his promise of support.

Temple looked at Towns and said, "In the end, you and I are going to win or lose. The Mayor, the Governor, no one else is going to really make a difference. We either win it or we lose it based on our own actions. The endorsement would have gotten some headlines, but what we need in November are the votes. And that's something only you and I can earn."

Towns listened and understood. He worked hard and, in the end, won a very tough race for the State Assembly.

368

Chapter XXVI

A Rising Star

Temple's campaign staff tried a wide variety of ways to raise money for the campaign. Dave Yondle was particularly good at taking suggestions and then running with them.

From the end of September through the third week in October, Yondle coordinated a golf tournament, a celebrity dinner, six private dinner parties, six executive luncheons, a pizza party, a boat party, and eight cocktail parties, all designed to raise money for the campaign.

In addition, he and Laney Gardiner did all of the follow-up work on solicitation letters and phone calls and kept track of the expenses associated with each fund raising effort along with Kevin Roth.

Roth and Gardiner also helped out on the events. Gardiner was the liaison person for Temple at each of the functions. She introduced the candidate to those who did not know him and usually briefed him on the people involved before he arrived at the particular function. She also ensured that the host or hostess had sufficient help by bringing in volunteers from the campaign to work the functions.

By the end of the campaign, they had a well-run machine at work on the fund raising side. Everyone knew what needed to be done and the best way to do it. After the election, Yondle would use his skills to manage a large charity's endowment program. Gardiner would become the development director for a major non-profit corporation. Both had received valuable experience in the political arena and both used their

369

contacts and experience to develop a career path.

Fund raising for a political campaign is not done in a vacuum. It takes a lot of help from the outside to really be successful. One of Temple's strengths was his ability to attract people who were willing to go that extra mile for him. Allen Benair was one of many who did just that.

Benair and another friend of Temple's, Chad Goodson, decided that they would sponsor a golf tournament for their friend's campaign. They arranged with Twin Oaks Golf Course to hold a golf outing and steak dinner at a cost of one hundred dollars per person. They arranged for door prizes, carts, decorations, and tee times. They also solicited friends and acquaintances to support the outing.

Fifteen foursomes were fielded for the event, grossing almost six thousand dollars. The day was sunny and warm, and spirits were high. The golfers all had stories to tell as they watched the last foursome chip onto the eighteenth green.

Temple was about thirty yards off the green and his chip shot went right, landing about twenty–five feet from the pin. Ken Mathews was about twenty yards from the green, and his chip shot rolled to within six feet of the pin. Alice Mathews, Ken's wife, was on the edge of the green, in the rough. She putted her ball to about eight feet from the pin.

Pat Temple had waited her turn in a sand trap at the edge of the green. "You all had some great shots. I'm going to hate having to follow you from here." She looked down at her ball sitting on top of the white sugary sand. "Well, here goes!"

She hit through and under the ball with a clean swing and follow through. Sand flew in the direction of the pin and momentarily obscured the ball. Suddenly, the ball appeared in the air among the sand. The ball arched high in the air and then slowly descended to the green, landing on the grass and rolling toward the pin.

Benair, who had been watching from the clubhouse, yelled to his wife and Chad to come and look at Pat Temple's shot. They arrived on the deck just in time to see her ball slide neatly into the cup.

Pat yelled, "I can't believe it."

"Great shot!" Mathews said.

Benair shouted from the deck, "Hey, Jay, I bet I know where Pat has been while you were out campaigning!"

Temple laughed as he waved at Benair and walked over to his wife. "That was terrific! Your timing was perfect. Right in front of the clubhouse. I wish I could do that."

Alice Mathews joined in, "You and everyone else in the clubhouse. Nice shot, Pat."

"Thanks. I don't think that I have ever done that before. I still can't believe it."

Mathews turned to Temple. "Maybe it's a lucky sign?"

Temple answered, "I think it's a sign that it's time to eat."

That evening, they all cooked their own steaks over an open fire. Prizes with lots of humor and imagination were awarded to everyone. Benair's and Goodson's wives had seen to every detail, right down to the table decorations. But the real talk of the evening was the chip shot on the eighteenth. It was a light spot in an increasingly demanding campaign.

* * *

Mann called Joel Samuels on the telephone. "Joel, this is Laura. Why did we postpone the YWCA debate with Temple?"

Samuels expected the call. He had made a strategic decision to back off the debates to as late as possible in the campaign. He wanted to limit Temple's exposure and hope for something to come along in the interim to derail an even stronger campaign by the Republican newcomer.

"Laura, I've always been straight with you. Temple's showing me more than I expected."

Mann thought to herself, 'I could have told you that.' She said, "What does that mean?"

371

"It means that I want to limit his free press time. If we debate him now, that's coverage that he doesn't have to pay for."

She had just read his most recent campaign finance report. "I don't think he's worried about buying time."

"Politicians always worry about buying time. They never have enough money."

'So, now he's been upgraded to a politician.' This may have had negative connotations to most, but Mann knew that in Joel's mind, a politician was a worthy title. It meant someone who was smart in the ways of the world and in the ways of handling people and information. Politicians, for Samuels, didn't have to take a back seat to anyone. He had a professional respect for politicians. It was evident that he had now gained some respect for her opponent.

Samuels interrupted her thinking, "The other possibility is that he will do something between now and the debates that will open a good avenue of attack. Something that will allow us to turn the tide away from Temple, and toward you."

"Do you think that the tide is running against me?" This was not an easy question for Mann to ask. But she, too, had seen the polls. Her polls! There was no question that Temple was gaining on her. The real question was whether or not he had the time and wherewithal to overtake her by the election.

"Laura, this is going to be a photo finish unless he blows it. I hate to have to tell you this, but, as I said, I always call it the way that I see it."

She thought for a moment and then said, "I've known that, too. You get a sixth sense about politics after you have been in it a while. I'm worried, Joel."

"If I were a betting man, and I am, I'd still put my money on you!" Samuels had liked Laura Ann Mann from the very first day that they had met. There was no pretense to her. You may not like her, but what you saw was what you got. 'A diamond in the rough!' as he would describe her.

"Thanks, Joel. I'm putting my money with yours."

372

Temple arrived at his headquarters early. It was the last Saturday in September and time was becoming critical as he still had a ways to go in the polls. He believed that he could do it if he could just get his message out to everyone.

Gardiner was already there when Temple arrived.

"Did you spend the night?" he asked her half-jokingly as he checked his desk for messages.

"I thought about it, but my boyfriend, Dan, wouldn't let me." She yawned.

"What time did you leave here?"

"About three."

"Three? Hey, you need to get more sleep than that or you won't be able to hang in there to the end."

She looked up at him with a determined expression. "I'll be here to the end. You don't have to worry about me. I come from hardy stock!"

"Me too!" Patrick Fitzgerald had come in through the front door and had picked up on the conversation.

Temple laughed and said to him, "What? Be here to the bitter end, or come from hardy stock?"

Patrick shrugged, "Both."

Robert Anderson walked in next, smiling and asking, "Say, is there a fellow named Temple around here, running for the State Senate?"

Temple looked up at his old friend. "Depends on who's asking."

Anderson smiled a big, toothy grin, "A guy who wants to give some time to the campaign of our next State Senator."

Temple remembered back to those early days of the campaign. Anderson had been advised that Temple didn't have a chance. Now he was here offering his time. He'd be a great addition because Temple knew that when Anderson committed to something it was a one-hundred percent commitment.

Temple asked half in jest, "What are you offering?"

373

"Not a lot. Just my life from now until Election Day."

"Doesn't sound like much, but we'll take it." Temple shook Anderson's hand and introduced him to Gardiner and Fitzgerald.

Yondle, Roth, and Dr. Carey arrived next, and they all decided to get some breakfast at the diner next door. Cordis had called and left a message that he had some business commitments that were going to tie him up for a while. Temple noted the call but was quickly caught up in the campaign's demands of the day and of the weeks that followed.

Temple was scheduled to campaign in Oneida, Sylvan Beach, and finish at the Polish Hall in Rome that evening. Anderson, Roth, and Carey all agreed to travel the campaign trail to Oneida and Sylvan Beach with their friend. His wife also joined him that evening in Rome.

Roth tolerated the campaigning but was more interested in helping Temple out with the finances. Temple relied on Roth to keep him out of trouble both with expenses and with the campaign filing requirements.

Anderson and Carey, on the other hand, loved the campaign trail. Both were very good with people and people, in turn, warmed up to them quickly. After the Saturday in Oneida and Sylvan Beach, both would work hard through October campaigning for Temple. This helped Temple to reach out to more of the voters in the district in a very positive way.

Butch Carroll had spent a week and a half at Temple headquarters. He had gone over every aspect of the campaign, meeting volunteers, reviewing fund raising, watching commercials, getting an understanding of the organization, and witnessing the candidate's public-speaking ability at several speaking engagements.

Carroll was a professional. He'd seen a lot of candidates come and go, and he had seen a lot of organizations, good and bad.

Temple's operation impressed him. People were happy and committed. They ranged in age from the very young to the very old. There was a scarcity of minorities, but the candidate had worked the predominantly black neighborhoods of Syracuse twice during the ten days that Carroll had been in the district. That was something else that impressed Carroll, and he thought to himself, 'That takes guts!"

On October first, Carroll went back to Albany for a meeting with Toby Hagan, Senator Valli, and Arnold Ophidia. The meeting was held in Hagan's office at the NYSSRC.

"So, where are we at with Temple?" Valli asked through the cigar clenched between his teeth. Ophidia always provided Valli with a Havana knowing the Senator's weakness for a good cigar. With the embargo placed against Cuba by the U.S. government, Havanas were not easy to come by. Ophidia hated the premium that he had to pay for the cigars, but he loved them, too, and he could write it all off as a business expense. Valli controlled the purse strings, and it was worth a good cigar now and then to 'feed at the public trough.'

The question was directed at Carroll. He pulled out his notebook and after a quick glance, looked up at Valli. "Temple's got one of the best organizations I've seen for a newcomer. He's got all the areas covered with people who know what they are doing. Fund raising is coming along nicely. They have raised about two hundred and fifty thousand dollars to date and should hit three hundred thousand by Election Day. He has a full time day staff of three and about two hundred volunteers who fill in at various times and days as needed.

"They start every morning at about 7:30 and work until about two or three the following morning. This goes on seven days a week.

"Temple is a savvy guy. He handles people well. Understands them and genuinely likes them. He has very good speaking abilities. He's clear and unequivocal. He's at his best when he adlibs.

"Temple knows the issues and is a quick study. He can spout off numbers and relate them to personal circumstances with great ease. He's an independent thinker with a mission. My read is that people in the district are listening."

Hagan spoke up at this point. "I can back up what Carroll is saying. Our weekend poll was quite remarkable."

"What'd ya get on the Temple race?" Valli asked as he leaned forward with his cigar in his hand.

"Bottom line, ten percent difference if the vote occurred today."

"Ten percent! With a month to go. Shit, we should be able to knock that bitch off in style!" Ophidia grinned as he thought about the money he could make with this race.

"What weaknesses did your polls show?" Valli asked Hagan.

"Mann still ranks high with bluecollar workers."

"Men and women?"

"No. Just men. Temple's doing all right with women."

Ophidia jumped on the opportunity just opened to him. "Senator, I can tell you where the problem is and what we can do to solve it."

"I'm listening."

"I've met Temple, and I think Butch will back me up on this. Temple comes across as too nice a guy." Ophidia looked at Carroll.

"He is a decent guy," Carroll confirmed.

"'Decent' is the word," Ophidia almost snarled. "Decent doesn't equate to tough. And when you are dealing with the 'boys' in the factories and on the trucks, they want a tough son-of-a-bitch representing them, not a 'decent' guy!"

"What would you suggest?" Valli asked.

"I'd suggest that we do a commercial that shows our Mr. Temple as a no-nonsense, take-charge kind of a politician. We can script it out, tape it, and get it on the air within a week. Then we follow up with some hard hitting mailing and, bingo, the bluecollar crowd becomes Temple supporters." Ophidia looked from one to the other to see if he had gotten his point across.

Valli looked at Hagan. "Do you think that would do it?"

376

"Wouldn't hurt."

Valli turned to Carroll. Carroll didn't report to Valli, but Valli knew him well and knew that he had good political sense. "What do you think?"

"If you can get Temple to buy into the script, it might help."

"How much is all this going to cost?" Valli asked Ophidia.

"Fifty, maybe sixty, depending on how much you want to insure that you knock the broad off."

"Toby, make sixty thousand available to Mr. Ophidia." Valli paused and gave him a long stare. "Get receipts."

* * *

Temple spent the entire day on Monday, October first campaigning with Sam LaGuzzi in Rome. LaGuzzi liked Temple. He liked his honesty. He liked his interest in Rome. And he liked the fact that Temple had helped keep Rome Hospital open.

"You ever been to a Boccie Ball Game?" LaGuzzi smiled maliciously.

Temple recognized the look. "Sam, I'm afraid that there is a hole in my education."

"Okay. Let's fill it!" LaGuzzi took his car at about sixty miles per hour around the Fort Stanwyck loop. It was posted for forty-five. He then headed north over the railroad bridge to a factory field on the northeastern side of the track. He pulled into a crowded parking lot and said, "Welcome to the National Boccie Ball Tournament courtesy of the City of Rome."

Temple discovered that boccie had its own following and that it was akin to baseball within certain groups. He met hundreds of enthusiasts that day and picked up an appreciation for both the skill and the history of the sport.

The following day, Temple met with representatives of the six county judicial conference in which Onondaga County

377

was a part. Temple, in addition to being a candidate for the State Senate, was also a delegate for the selection of judicial candidates.

Many of the delegates to the judicial conference were acquaintances of Temple and were anxious to discuss his campaign for the Senate. Those who were in his Senate District offered their support.

From the Conference meeting, Temple went to a fund raiser for Senator Lansing. Lansing had at first not been sure of Temple but over the last few weeks had picked up the level of his activity on behalf of Temple. He had called Temple personally to invite him to his reception as his guest. Now, midway through the function, Lansing signaled for the hundred-plus supporters to quiet down so that he could thank them.

"I want to thank all of you for coming out and supporting this little gathering for my campaign. Many of you have been with me since I got started in this business of politics. For your sake and my own, I am not going to mention how long ago that was." Lansing paused as the assemblage laughed at the Senator's humor.

"I rarely invite another candidate to these affairs because I don't want them to be too political. But this year, there is a young man running for office for whom I have gained a great deal of respect. His name is Jay Temple. I'd like to ask Jay if he would say a few words to you."

Temple moved through the group of people to join Senator Lansing.

"Jay, would you say a few words to my friends?" the Senator asked.

Temple smiled at Lansing. "Very few. Senator Lansing is a very generous statesman. I sincerely appreciate his kind invitation to be with all of you this evening and for his offer to let me speak with you. But this is his night. He has been a true friend and representative of the people of Central New York. The good things that he has done for this community are too

378

numerous to mention. He has touched a great many lives through his work in public office. I only hope that if elected, I will be able to do as much for my constituents as he has done for you. Congratulations, Senator." Temple shook Lansing's hand, and for the first time, Temple noticed a receptive look in Lansing's eye.

"Thank you for your kind words, Jay." Lansing was impressed with the brevity and tone of Temple's remarks. Later that evening, Lansing went home and wrote a memo to his campaign committee treasurer to send a thousand dollars to the Temple campaign.

Lansing thought to himself, 'if he does get elected, we will make a good team.'

* * *

On the third of October, Bob Berry met with Temple and Cordis for lunch at Reilly's restaurant. Berry had arranged for a private booth in the back section of the restaurant.

"Jay, we got some great news on the results of this weekend's survey and poll!" Berry was an enthusiastic PR man. He could make hell sound like the place for a vacation. Temple knew this and was always amused by Berry's lead-ins.

"How much is this 'great' news going to cost us?" Cordis asked in a flat voice.

"Nothing!" Berry said and then waited for the effect of his words to sink in.

"Nothing?" Cordis questioned.

"That's right, nothing! Butch Carroll gave a glowing report to Valli on your campaign, and Toby Hagan followed up with his polls showing that you are only ten percent behind Mann and still closing."

Cordis smiled at Temple. "Ten percent! That means if you can swing six percent, we win!"

Temple thought for a moment. 'I've been going at this for almost ten months, and I'm still only at forty-five percent.

379

What can I do that will put me over fifty percent in a month? Any suggestions?"

"As a matter of fact there are. Hagan's polls indicate that you are still weak among male bluecollar workers. They want someone who is strong enough to take on the Albany scene and get some changes made. They still aren't convinced that you are the one." He checked Temple to see how his words were coming across. Berry couldn't read Temple, so he went on. "The NYSSRC has authorized the funds to produce a commercial where we show you as a forceful and committed individual ready to take on the Governor if need be to see that there is a change in direction of this state's government."

Cordis interrupted, "The NYSSRC is going to pay for this?"

"Yes. The entire production and the air time."

Cordis looked at Temple with a smile. "They think you can win. This is the opportunity that we have been waiting for."

Cordis then turned back to Berry. "Will they help out with the rest of the campaign?"

"Yes. They also plan on paying for the production and mailing of several brochures. Mostly canned stuff put out by the Senate Republicans, but crediting the local candidate with its direction."

Temple sensed that this was coming a little too fast and too easy. "What kind of control do we have over the material?"

"You have to approve or it won't be used," Berry answered.

"You're sure that we have the final approval?" Temple asked.

"Absolutely."

"Well, I guess that we have nothing to lose," Cordis offered.

"Just the election," Temple half joked.

This was a turning point in the campaign, both financially and politically. Temple was now poised to win the election. The party pros were talking about staffing the new

State Senator's office, and the party regulars were beginning to line up for whatever handouts they might be able to get.

Within a week of meeting with Berry, Temple had shot a professionally directed campaign commercial. It showed Temple in his law office, surrounded by books, talking about the dire financial straights that New York was in. Temple was seated on the edge of a table. Halfway through the commercial, Temple stood up and asked his viewers to stand up with him and tell the Governor that they had had enough. That it was time for change. That it was time to make the Empire State an Empire once again.

Temple, Cordis, Mathews, Carey, and Berry previewed the final version. They concluded that it was a very strong message. Temple was privately amused by his performance. It wasn't really him, though the issues and arguments clearly were his. They all concluded that it made Temple look strong and would appeal to the one group that he was having trouble with. Male, bluecollar workers.

That first week in October established a torrid pace for Temple. After spending Monday in Rome and Tuesday in Syracuse, the campaign swung to DeWitt, Fayetteville, Minoa, East Syracuse, Cicero, and Jamesville from Wednesday through Friday. Temple spoke at Women's Clubs, Lions Clubs, Gun Clubs, Church Associations, Fire Stations, and in high schools about the need for change and the new priorities that he hoped to achieve for state government. Tax reduction, more jobs, better education, and crime control became his major themes. Government waste, mismanagement, and the inability to keep in touch with the people of the state were the sub-sets of his speeches.

On Saturday, Temple received a call from Don Crawford, the news anchor at Channel 7. Crawford wanted Temple to appear live on his Sunday talk show 'People In The News.' The plan was to interview Temple on October fourteenth and then Senator Mann on October twenty-first. Temple agreed.

That afternoon, Temple brought his parade team to the

Eastwood Columbus Day Parade. It was a bright, sunny day and a good crowd was on hand for the festivities. As was usually the case, all the incumbent public officeholders were given spots at the front of the parade and all the challengers were given positions at the rear of the parade. Temple took this in stride and often kidded his less–than-appreciative staff, that they were merely saving the best for last.

Cordis was complaining bitterly that Senator Mann had been picked as an Assistant Marshal, and they had not been told about the selection.

"Well, we're here, and we can't very well back out of our commitment now," Temple said as he listened to the complaints. "Look. There are people all along this parade route who aren't going to care who is first and who is last. They came to see a parade, and we are part of what they came to see."

Cordis frowned. "I'm glad you feel that way because I just got our position assignment. We're second to last!"

"Who's last?" Temple asked.

"Ted McCord and his horse, Topper."

"Let's go find Mr. McCord." Temple smiled.

"Why? You'd rather be in last place?" Cordis asked with a note of sarcasm.

"Absolutely!" Temple answered.

They found McCord and Topper in a field next to the Victory Market parking lot. Temple talked to McCord for a few minutes and then shook his hand.

When Temple walked back to Cordis and the others who had arrived to walk the parade route for the campaign, he said, "Well, it's all arranged. I'll be the last one in the parade."

"And you're happy about that?" Cordis said in disbelief.

"Ted, I think you'll find the arrangement just perfect. I'm going to be riding Topper."

The Eastwood parade gave Temple a huge surge in local recognition. The Temple - Topper team was a big hit all along the parade route, and Cordis had to admit that last place, at least in a parade, was not all that bad.

382

The first weekend in October was also Apple Festival in LaFayette, New York. The biggest event of the year for the tiny hamlet, LaFayette drew in over twenty-thousand people each fall to sample apples in everything from pies and cider to doll heads and wall hangings. Farm families in particular took advantage of the Apple Festival to sell their homemade crafts and canned fruits. It was a politicians' playground and everyone running for office put in at least an appearance.

Temple had divided his volunteers for the weekend into two groups. The first group consisting of Ted Cordis, Mary Tarkings, Patrick Fitzgerald, and Mary Price covered the Eastwood Columbus Parade. The second group consisting of Pat Temple, Robert Anderson and his wife, Fred Childs, Kevin Roth, Laney Gardiner, and Dave Yondle and his wife took on the assignment of the Apple Festival.

Both groups were given a huge supply of 'We Back Jay' bumper stickers, pencils, buttons, flyers, and yard signs to hand out to would-be supporters of the newcomer to politics.

Patrick Fitzgerald picked Temple up at the end of the parade route in his 1973 Ford sedan. The campaign van had been used to carry the Apple Festival crew and handouts.

Temple climbed down from Topper and gave the Palomino a pat. Ted McCord had been riding in the white LaBaron convertible that had been meant for Temple. McCord walked up to Temple with a smile and said, "How'd Topper treat you?"

"He's a great horse. How old is he?"

"Five. Got him as a colt. Smart little guy! Had him trained within four weeks. Can't say that about any others I've had." McCord took the reins from Temple. "Where'd you learn to ride like that?"

"Believe it or not, Bayport, Long Island," Temple laughed.

"Long Island! I thought that all they had down there were ducks and potatoes."

"No. There's a horse or two. Mrs. Robins ran a horse

383

riding stable of sorts in Bayport. She had maybe six or seven horses. I was a big Roy Rogers fan as a kid and wanted to learn how to ride a horse. So my mother arranged lessons for me."

"Well, whoever taught you to ride, knew what they were doin'."

"Mrs. Robins was the owner and instructor. We had to learn to ride bareback before she'd let us try our hand with a saddle. She always said, and I agree, that if you can ride bareback, you can ride anywhere."

Temple thanked McCord again for the use of Topper and then drove off with Fitzgerald to the Apple Festival.

An hour later they located the van amidst about four thousand other cars. Fitzgerald found a parking spot about three rows behind the van. They climbed out of the Ford and headed toward a field where hundreds of people were milling about among seventy to ninety tents. There was a huge midway set up on the far side of the grounds and more people jammed their way in to enjoy the rides and food. Here and there 'We Back Jay' buttons were seen and Temple commented to Fitzgerald, "Someone must be here somewhere."

Temple and Fitzgerald finally found Temple's wife and Sue Yondle in one of the craft tents.

"Pat," Temple called out, "where is everyone?"

Pat smiled guiltily. "They all went over to the Midway. Sue and I decided to mix pleasure with business."

Temple looked at Sue Yondle. "Hi, Sue. Dave must be losing it to let you shop alone with my wife. We'll both be broke by sunset!"

"That's what Dave said when I told him I was going to chaperone your wife." Sue was a pretty blonde from Pennsylvania and had grown up at craft fairs. She and Pat were having a good time so Temple decided to let them continue to browse while he caught up with the rest of his campaign helpers. They agreed to meet at the van in two hours and Temple and Fitzgerald headed toward the midway.

As Temple approached the gates to the midway, he was

surprised to see ten to fifteen political candidates standing at the entrance greeting people. Fred Childs, Dave Yondle and Laney Gardiner were also standing there, handing out Temple's literature, pencils, and buttons.

"Hi, Jay! How'd the parade go?" Yondle shouted as a few people stopped to see the new politician coming up to the gate. One older woman came forward. "You're Mr. Temple?" she asked.

"Yes, ma'am," Temple answered.

"Listen young man, you're a nice guy. I've read about you and heard you on the radio. But that TV commercial you've got running now is terrible. I hate it every time you point that finger at me. You ought to take it off the air." She nodded her head in agreement with the advice that she had just given.

"I appreciate your advice" Temple said with sincerity. "I'll take another look at that ad. I think I know what you mean."

"Good! You do that. I want you to go to Albany and do something about all these politicians! They're a troublesome lot!" Again she nodded in agreement with what she had said.

Temple smiled at the woman. "Troublesome is a good word. We'll see what we can do."

Later that night, Temple and his wife watched the evening news. Temple's new 'strong' commercial ran much to the displeasure of Pat.

"That's awful" she said. "That's not you."

Temple had to agree. It was a piece of acting, but it was not him.

"I think that you should call Berry right now and tell him to take those ads off the air. If you don't want to, I will."

One thing about Pat, Temple thought, you always knew where she was coming from. "I'll call first thing in the morning," he said.

He called Berry early the next day.

"Bob? This is Jay."

"Good morning."

"Good morning. Listen. I got some feedback on our newest ad, and it's not being received well." Temple described his meeting with the old woman and his wife's reaction.

"Geez, Jay. It's only running this week, and we've already paid a non-refundable fee for its play." Berry knew that the NYSSRC and Ophidia had already heavily committed for the time.

"What about running our family values ad?"

"Not tough enough. Remember who we are after with this."

"Yes, but think of who we might lose if we continue with it." Temple countered.

"You're the boss. I'll pull the ad tomorrow and run your values ad in its place."

"Thanks. I felt uncomfortable with it from the beginning and should have said something. I think it amused me to see me playacting but that's really not my style."

"I know," Berry admitted. Berry wondered how Ophidia and the Albany boys would take all this.

Berry called the TV stations running the commercial. They were reluctant to pull the ad for two reasons. First, it had been placed out of Albany. The Syracuse office had no connection with the placement and payment. And that led to the second reason for their reluctance. The time slots were bought and paid for. They couldn't stick something in those slots without approval of the purchaser, Arnold Ophidia.

Berry next placed a call to Ophidia and told him about his conversations with Temple and then with the TV stations.

"Listen, you dunce," Ophidia's temper flared, "the NYSSRC wants to pay us to run ads that will take care of the bluecollar vote. They want tough ads not mom and pop and apple pie ads. You tell that overgrown boy scout that these ads are just what his campaign needs. In fact, he should be going after Laura Ann Mann with a butcher knife! Tell him that politics is a rough and dirty game. If he wants to play and win, he'd better learn the rules and play along with them."

Berry listened but concluded long before he hung up that that was one message he wasn't going to deliver. The old saying about 'killing the messenger' crossed his mind.

The 'get tough' message was on the television constantly for the next two weeks. Despite calls from Temple, Cordis, and even Pat, the ads ran their course and Temple had a second image for the public to consider. As one of his friends said, only half in jest, "Everytime I turn on my television, there you are, yelling and jabbing your finger at me."

Neither of the Temples were happy with Berry's handling of the commercial, but in the end Jay Temple had no one to fault but himself on that one. He had filmed the commercial. He had acted out the part. And he had given the initial okay after talking with his advisers. As Truman had said early, "the buck stops here." Temple had to get on with the campaign and not get hung up on one ad.

And get on with it, he did.

Chapter XXVII

October: Month Ten
Judgments

On October tenth, the Syracuse Gazette invited Temple to appear before their editorial board. The meeting was to be held in a conference room at the newspaper. All the political writers for the paper would be on hand and given an opportunity to ask the candidate about his views on any subject. The purpose of the meeting was allegedly to give the writers a chance to pass judgment upon the candidate and to determine which of the candidates running for office would receive the newspaper's endorsement.

On the ninth, Temple met with Mosby, Berry, Summers, and Terry Levin to review the issues and to discuss possible areas that the editorial board might get into. Cordis had been invited but had another commitment. Tim Sullivan and Larry Kent agreed to participate via conference call. For convenience, the meeting took place at Berry's office.

A wide variety of issues were discussed. Levin seemed to have the most to offer having talked with one of the reporters scheduled to attend the meeting. He indicated that the biggest issue in the Senate race was who could do more for the area: an incumbent Democrat in a Republican controlled Senate or a political neophyte running against the system.

Temple knew what his choice was, but now he had to convince them.

It was agreed that Temple and Berry would attend the editorial board. On the tenth, Temple met Berry in the lobby of the newspaper, and they took the elevator to the second floor.

Gerald Blakesley met them as they were coming out of the elevator. He carried a cup of coffee in one hand and a pad and pencil in the other. His tie was loose around his neck, and his glasses hung on the end of his nose. He looked over the frame at Temple.

"Good morning, Mr. Temple," he said in a crisp clear voice.

Blakesley and Temple's grandfather went way back. Temple had known the Blakesley name long before he ever met the man. Blakesley was a legend in the newspaper reporting business. He lived up to his reputation and enjoyed it.

"Good morning, Mr. Blakesley," Temple answered.

"Are you here for the editorial board?"

"Yes, I am."

"What time are you scheduled for?"

"Ten o'clock."

"Good. Then you are first up, and you're right on time. Follow me." Blakesley led Temple and Berry to the conference room.

Blakesley had ignored Berry until they reached the room. He then turned to Berry and said. "Still with Ophidia. What a waste of a good Harvard education."

Turning to Temple, Blakesley continued, "I'll get the rest of the staff. Make yourselves comfortable."

After Blakesley left the room, Temple asked Berry, "What was that all about?"

"In college, I worked one summer with Blakesley here at the Gazette. He wanted me to become a newspaper reporter. I didn't, and he never has forgiven me."

"Did you ever talk to him about it?"

"Yeah. Once. I told him that I could make a lot more money in advertising than I could in newspaper writing."

"What did he say?"

"He said that I was wasting a God-given talent for writing."

"It's still not too late!"

"If you don't do well today, I may have to consider it."

They both were laughing as the reporters filed into the room.

Ed Curry had run the editorial boards for the paper for over twenty years. Next to Blakesley, he was the senior political reporter. He considered himself to be a nonpartisan observer of the political scene and tried to run the editorial boards according to the way he pictured himself.

"Mr. Temple, thank you for accepting our invitation to join us this morning," Curry said with genuine interest.

"It's my pleasure," Temple responded.

"My name is Ed Curry, and I will be the catalyst for what I hope will be a good exchange of ideas." Curry turned to each of the reporters present as he introduced them.

"You already know Gerald Blakesley, our senior statesman on the Albany desk. Next to Jerry is Tom Penderson. Tom covers the financial side of political campaigns. Next to Tom, we have Al Pesky. Al has been assigned to cover several candidates including Senator Mann. Finally, we have Chris Blayton. Chris also has been assigned to cover several candidates including you, Mr. Temple." Curry looked over his reading glasses at Temple and smiled.

Temple had nodded to each of the reporters as they had been introduced. When Curry finished with his introductions, Temple again looked around the table as he spoke. "It's a pleasure meeting you today. I have met some of you before today and have read columns by all of you at one time or another. I have to admit that a good part of my political education on state politics came from articles that each of you have written." Temple finally focused his attention on Chris Blayton.

"Ms. Blayton, I thought your article on closed-door politics in Albany was particularly well done."

Blayton sat up in her chair. She had graduated a year and a half earlier from college with a degree in Journalism and had immediately impressed Stewart Ropespear with her portfolio of stories from her college newspaper.

Blayton had been given some challenging assignments upon her arrival at the Syracuse Gazette. She had measured up to the expectations of her performance. She was a product of her times. A young woman who believed in equality of the sexes, ready to compete on any playing field, well educated, and armed with a belief in her own invincibility.

She also had the ability to put 'spin' on a story. This was newspaper jargon for taking the facts and directing the reader to draw certain conclusions based upon the way the facts were presented. Ropespear particularly liked this talent and especially coming from someone with the other traits that were so in evidence with his newest political reporter. With this in mind, Ropespear had seen to it that Chris Blayton was assigned to the Temple campaign.

Blayton looked at Temple. She had seen his photo file at the paper and had also seen his television commercials. She knew that neither would give her what she was really looking for, the real Jay Temple. She had confidence that their face-to-face meeting would fill in the blanks. "Thank you, Mr. Temple. If you don't mind, I'd like to start off with a couple of questions?"

Temple smiled, "Go ahead."

"You mentioned my article on closed-door politics in Albany and that surprises me. A good portion of that article had to do with the New York State Senate and the Republican majority. You have criticized Senator Mann as being ineffective because she is outside the power loop. If you are elected are you going to be inside or outside the power loop?"

Temple watched Blayton as she talked. Her eyes never left his, never flinched in the stare even during the point she was driving home. A tough but honest question. He decided the best way to handle her direct approach was to be just as direct.

"Ms. Blayton, I am not familiar with the term 'power loop' but if you mean dealing with the Republicans who are in power in the Senate, your analysis is right on target.

"Senator Mann cannot deal effectively with the Senate Republicans, due in part to being a member of the opposition party, but also because she has been too confrontational in her dealings with, not only the Republicans, but also the Democrats in the Senate.

"I believe in open discussions of all issues that come before the Senate. Senators are elected by the people, and the people have a right to know how their representatives think and what they are doing. Closed doors mean back room deals and benefits for special interests. I oppose any decisions made by a public body without public discussion."

Gerald Blakesley weighed in at this point. "My experience has been that there are some issues which are either too inflammatory to discuss in public or which might never get resolved if discussed in public. I think that you will find that you will have little support for your views in Albany, Mr. Temple."

"Mr. Blakesley, I know what you are saying and there was a time I might have even agreed with you. But times have changed, and the circumstances that New York State finds itself in now is one of financial crisis. Much of the blame for this crisis can be attributed to back room deals and closed–door politics. You pay for my project, and I'll take care of yours. If deals like that are being struck, then the public should know about them and about the people who are making them."

Blakesley looked seriously at Temple and asked, "Mr. Temple, do you think that the public really cares? That they would even pay any attention?"

"Yes, I do. I have been impressed with the knowledge and interest of the people to whom I have talked as I have campaigned throughout the district. They know what is wrong with the state, and they are keenly aware of the needs of the state. I think that the people are ready for change."

Blakesley shook his head. "I think that you are naive, Mr. Temple. Three weeks is about the longest attention span the

392

public has on any issue, and that's being generous."

"I respectfully disagree. I think that you are selling the public short."

"On the contrary, I think that you are giving them too much credit. Your whole campaign is an appeal to an intellect that isn't there."

Temple was questioned on a number of specific issues by the other reporters in the room, but Blayton was taken aback by her exchange with Temple, and in turn, his with Blakesley. In truth, she had pictured Temple as another male chauvinist out to take back a man's work from a woman who, because she was a woman, couldn't do the job as well. Temple did not come across this way at the editorial board. She wasn't certain any more about how she saw this politician.

There was something else about him that bothered her. It took her a week and her next encounter with Temple at a news conference before she realized what it was. His eyes. He looked at people the way she did. Unflinchingly. Her ability to do this had been an inner strength for her. Now, she was covering a man who had that same power. She needed to know if it was an act or if he was for real. Was he sincere? That was the real question that she needed to answer before she could put her now famous 'spin' on her story.

Temple finished his editorial board with the Syracuse Gazette by thanking each of the reporters and shaking hands. On the way out, he asked Berry, "Well, how do you think it went?"

"I think that they have to give you serious consideration based upon what you said and your obvious ability. Whether it's enough to win an endorsement against an incumbent, I don't know. This paper hammers incumbents all year long and then come election time, endorses every damn one of them! And they question my character for being in advertising? Unbelievable!"

* * *

Sam LaGuzzi was on the phone to Temple early on

393

October eleventh.

"Mr. Temple, are you coming to Rome tomorrow?"

"As a matter of fact I am, Sam. Why? What have you got in mind?"

"Well, Mr. Temple, there is someone here you should meet. His name is Mr. Medina. He can be of great help to you if he likes you."

Temple was intrigued. "What does Mr. Medina do for a living?"

"He's a wine importer."

"Well, Sam, I have a ten o'clock editorial board with the Observer Dispatch and then a two–thirty appointment with the Utica papers for an editorial board. How about meeting at eleven thirty with Mr. Medina. Do you think that time would be convenient for him?"

"He said he would be available any time tomorrow."

"Where should I meet you, Sam?"

"I will meet you at the Dispatch parking lot when you are finished with the editorial board."

"Great. I'll look forward to seeing you tomorrow."

"Okay, Mr. Temple. By the way, my wife, Maria, sends her regards."

"Say hi to Maria for me."

"I will. Goodbye, Mr. Temple."

After he hung up the telephone, Temple wondered about Mr. Medina. But his thoughts were quickly interrupted as Bob Anderson walked in to pick him up for a tour of the Anderson Company plant and a meeting with its one hundred and three employees.

Bob Anderson was spending much more time on the campaign now. A long time friend of Temple's, he now believed that Temple had a real shot at winning the election. Despite earlier reservations and hesitation to commit a large amount of time to Temple's political race, Anderson regretted not being involved and was determined to make up for lost time.

For Temple, Anderson's timing couldn't have been

394

better. Ted Cordis had devoted five months of his life to Temple's campaign. Cordis had worked day and night on all the little details that don't make headlines in a campaign but that make the campaign machine function. Now, Cordis was having to cut back on his involvement and his time committed to the campaign. With less than a month to go and with round–the–clock commitments by Temple, he needed all the help he could get.

Anderson picked up a part of the load with Laney Gardiner, Dave Yondle, Kevin Roth, Patrick Fitzgerald, Mary Price, Mary Tarkings, and Doctor Carey rounding out a strong campaign team for the finish.

Anderson had never taken Temple on a tour of his factory. Temple had been in the office several times, but this was the first time he actually went down on the lines with Anderson's employees. It was a worthwhile learning experience for Temple, and Anderson was a good teacher.

"We put the safety of our people first," Anderson explained. "We are working with heat, electricity, open flame, and volatile chemicals. I took this place over twenty-two years ago, and we've had only three accidents causing serious injuries during that time. All three were careless accidents that could have been avoided. Two were related to drinking, which we now monitor, and one was a guy who was in a hurry to get out for lunch, and he left his torch on. His replacement didn't realize it and when he picked up the torch he severely burned his arm."

Anderson introduced Temple to each of his people by name and explained what they did. Sometimes Anderson would throw in a story about the individual or his family and get a laugh or a nod. By the time the tour was finished, Temple had two impressions. First, Bob Anderson knew his business very well and second, he had the respect of his employees.

At eleven that morning, Anderson called his entire company staff into the company cafeteria. When everyone was accounted for, he introduced Jay Temple.

"You people know me. I tell it like it is. This is my friend Jay Temple. He is running for the New York State Senate against Senator Laura Ann Mann. I think that Mr. Temple can do a better job for all of us than Senator Mann has done.

"You all know that I would like to expand this plant. I would also like to give all of you more money. You'd like that too, wouldn't you?"

The people laughed, raised their eyebrows, and nodded their heads.

"Well, I can't do it because I'm paying too much money in taxes. New York would rather have me support people who are not working, than to hire more people and to pay a better wage to those who are working." Anderson paused to let his words sink in. Then he went on, "Mr. Temple here, stands for change. I strongly recommend that if you live in his district, you vote for him." He turned to Temple and said, "Jay, you have met most of these people earlier. Maybe you have something that you'd like to say to them."

"Thanks, Bob." Temple looked around the room at the mixture of bluecollar workers and office workers. "A newspaper reporter told me that the people in this state don't have any real interest in the issues of high taxes. In fact he said that three weeks was about the limit of your attention span on any issue. I told him that I thought he was wrong! That he was selling all of you short!

"I believe that you know that you are paying taxes that are way too high.

"I believe that you know that over eighteen thousand manufacturing jobs, like yours, have left the state because of high taxes and overregulation.

"And I believe that given the choice you and a lot of other hard working people would rather earn a good living than be given a handout for a mediocre existence.

"But the people in Albany don't seem to have gotten that message. They think the way that newspaper reporter thinks. They think that you don't care. That's why I am running for the

396

Senate. To take a message to Albany that the people do care, do understand, and do want change.

"Right now we offer welfare to new people who come into our state thirty days after they arrive. The cost is in the billions of dollars, and you and I are paying for it.

"Did you ever hear of 'member items?' These are expense dollars that every legislator gets to spend in any way that they choose. No one has to account for the value of what the money is being spent on, and it costs you billions of dollars every year.

"When we talk about billions of dollars, the number is so big that you and I have a hard time relating to it. But when our friends, our neighbors, and our families are losing jobs because New York State is just getting too expensive a state in which to do business, we can understand the impact that government is having on our private lives."

Temple then went on to talk about education, crime, and health care. He answered questions and talked about his ideas for a new way of running government in Albany. Anderson's employees responded very positively and many indicated that he had their support in November. They thanked him for coming and Bob Anderson for having him. Temple felt good about a morning well spent.

At noon, Anderson and Temple drove to Cazenovia for a twelve-thirty luncheon with a group of Madison County business people. Allen Stablemeyer had arranged for the luncheon at the Lincklaen House.

The Lincklaen House was an old historic stagecoach stop in the center of Cazenovia. Governors, Senators, and Congressmen had dined there and occasionally spent the night. It was an appropriate spot for a political luncheon.

Stablemeyer had worked for a major employer in the Syracuse area, taken early retirement, and had begun his own entrepreneurial business immediately upon retirement. He was an avid tennis player and had met Temple at a local tennis club. Both were competitive in whatever they undertook. Stablemeyer recognized this trait in Temple and admired him for it. He lived in Cazenovia and wanted to help. When he had asked Temple what he needed most, Temple had indicated that financial support from Madison County would be a great help. A review of past election contributions showed that little financial support had been given to the past three Senate races. It is to be noted that the 48th District is made up of parts of Oneida and Onondaga Counties, but that Madison County is entirely within the District.

Stablemeyer agreed that he would get support for Temple.

The luncheon was beautifully served by the staff and the food was excellent. About forty business people attended. Stablemeyer introduced Temple as a friend, an honest businessman, a thinker, and an innovator. "Four things we really need in Albany!" The group laughed but in the end, after a lengthy question and answer session, a total of eleven thousand dollars was raised at the luncheon.

On the evening of October eleventh, Jim Summers and a group of attorneys who were friends of Temple hosted a fund raiser at Nikki's Restaurant in downtown Syracuse.

One of the interesting rules in politics is that judges cannot take part in partisan politics except for the year in which they themselves run for office. As an extension of this rule, most judges opt not to contribute to political campaigns.

Sensitive to this rule, Summers sent invitations to the 'bench' to be the guests of Temple at the fund raiser at no charge. Six judges took advantage of the invitation to join with fellow attorneys for a night of fraternal intercourse.

Eighty-three attorneys and their spouses also attended the fund raiser contributing an additional six thousand two hundred and twenty-five dollars to the campaign.

Temple always enjoyed the opportunity to be with other attorneys. There were always 'war stories' to be told and to listen to. Temple had heard some of the same stories on more than one occasion, but somehow they got better with age.

One particular story was always a favorite with Temple.

Judge Manley, a widely respected legal scholar with a penchant for history, had been a trial lawyer with one of the large corporate law firms. Many years earlier, at a Bar Association meeting in New York City, one of Manley's partners thought it would be a great opportunity to introduce a then young trial lawyer, Manley, to a family friend of the partner who was then Chief Judge of New York's highest court, the Court of Appeals.

The partner called Manley over to where he was standing with the Chief Justice and said, "Harold, I'd like you to meet Chief Justice Bitmer. Judge, this is Harold Manley, one of our up-and-coming trial lawyers." Turning to Manley, who had had a few drinks, the partner whose family was from Bath, New York, said, "Justice Bitmer is from Bath, New York."

Manley looked the Chief Judge straight in the eye and said, "Only shitheads come from Bath, New York!" And with that, Manley turned and walked back to the bar.

The story again was being told among a group of attorneys at the bar in Nikki's, including Judge Manley. Temple asked Judge Manley if there was any truth to the story.

Manley looked at Temple and in his recognizably deep voice said, "Jay, the bad things that men do live on long after they're dead, the good things are often interred with their bones." He laughed along with everyone else. Temple concluded that years after both the Judge and he were gone, the story of Bath, New York, would be told at legal gatherings and lawyers would laugh at the chutzpah of that young attorney.

Temple made it a point to get around and talk with each of the people who had come out to support him. He caught up on their practices, their families, and their outside activities. One thing that always impressed Temple about his profession and the men and women who peopled it was that they were involved in their communities, volunteering their time and talent at no cost to make their village, town or city a better place in which to live.

Finally, in a short speech to the entire group, Temple thanked everyone for their support and for spending some time with his wife and him during a busy fall.

As they drove home that night, Temple said to his wife, "You know, there never is enough time to see all the people that I'd like to spend some time with."

Pat Temple looked at her husband. "What do you mean?"

"There were a lot of people at the reception tonight that I would love to see more often. Just to talk. But my schedule is always so full that I just never seem to have the time."

"Well, with the campaign, no one expects you to have a lot of time."

"Yes. I know. But I'm not talking just about the campaign. So many people have come out to help me with this thing. People I haven't seen in years. It's not just the ones tonight. I've been so busy these last few years that I have lost touch with some people I consider close friends."

"What can you do about that?" Pat understood what her husband was saying. In some ways she felt that she, too, had not been given the time that she would have liked from her husband. She missed him when he was not with her. He had given a lot of himself to the community over the years. Now he was going to be giving even more of himself to others if he was elected. It was a mixed blessing. She believed that he could bring a lot of positive changes to state government but she also knew that it would mean even less time with the family and friends. She said, "As a State Senator, you are going to have even less time for those you care for."

Temple looked over at his wife then back at the road. His thoughts ran quickly through the sequence of considerations that brought him to where he was at this point. "If I do win this election, you've got to promise me that you will remind me often that I need to spend time with our family and friends."

Pat smiled at her husband. She knew the importance he placed on his family and how much he loved his children. Inwardly, she half hoped he would lose the election, but she knew this meant a lot to him. This was something he always wanted to do. He was alive and enthusiastic and loved being out

400

with people. She was torn between wanting him all to herself and wanting him to do the things she knew he was capable of. She resigned herself to accepting whatever the outcome of the political race. She put her hand on his, "I will."

That night, Temple went into his youngest son's room and looked down at the small head lying on the pillow. Tyler was a beautiful little guy. Temple remembered other nights when he would go into his other two children's rooms to kiss them goodnight long after they had gone to sleep. Time has a way of slipping quietly away. He had been busy, too busy. He knew that there had to be a balance, but he had already lost time with his older children that he could never recover. All he had was the time he had left. Somehow, he would have to make more of an effort to spend some quality time with his family. Later in bed, he thought about the day, the campaign, his family and his friends. 'So much to do and so little time.'

* * *

On Friday, October 12th, Cordis arrived at the Temple home at seven-thirty in the morning just as Temple and his family were starting breakfast. Temple invited him to join them before they started out for Rome and Utica for the editorial boards with the local papers in both cities.

Cordis had become a surrogate member of the family over the last several months. He had spent many hours working on Temple's computer, entering campaign records dealing with contributors and volunteers. Many nights, he would work well past midnight on the data and then be ready to go early the next morning. Temple had missed his friend's company over the last few weeks and was glad to have the chance to catch up with Cordis and his personal news during their trip to Rome and Utica.

Pat put together a breakfast of eggs, bacon, and toast for the travelers and then got her children off to school.

Temple and Cordis made short work of breakfast and

were on the road by eight o'clock.

"How is your business going?" Temple asked as Cordis drove the van onto Route 5.

"I'm getting things back in order. My brother is helping out with some details in California."

"California! What are you working on?"

"Well, it's pretty complicated." Cordis paused as he put his thoughts together. "I've been doing some investments in foreign currency. I have two corporations involved in this and my brother is the president of our California operation while I am president of the Delaware corporation. The Delaware corporation has been buying options in the European market and then having the funds flow into the California company for investments in real estate.

"My partner in Belgium disappeared with some of our profits, and so we're trying to unload the California real estate so that I can pay back our investors."

Temple listened to Cordis and watched his friend as he described his business problems. Temple then asked, "This didn't happen because of all the time you have spent on the campaign, did it?"

Cordis glanced quickly at Temple. "No. This problem was developing long before the campaign. I just didn't realize it. If my partner in Belgium hadn't taken off, I'd be fine."

"Is there anything that I can do to help?" Temple offered.

"No. It'll all work out. But you can see why I haven't been around as much lately." Cordis again glanced at Temple.

Temple looked thoughtfully out of the front car window. "Yeah. That's too bad." He turned to Cordis and said, "Take whatever time you need to get your business back in order."

"I will."

"Is this trip today a problem?"

"No. I asked Dave Yondle to get in touch with me if my brother calls. I'll have to be back tonight, though. I'm expecting a call from Europe."

"Do you have enough money to get by?" Temple was

willing to give Cordis some financial help if he needed it.

"I'm all set. I have other resources that I haven't touched. Most of the money at risk belongs to investors. I'm trying to salvage something for them, not for me."

"Okay, but if you need anything, we could probably help you out a little," Temple again offered. He sensed that Cordis was uneasy with the conversation. He attributed this to Cordis' sense of pride. Temple decided that he had made the offer and that if Cordis wanted to take him up on it, he would know that he was able to. Temple decided that he would not bring up the subject again. He did not want to embarrass a guy who had given so much of himself to his campaign.

At the Observer Dispatch, Temple met with Madeline Reynolds, wife of the paper's editor. They had met at the beginning of the campaign and on two other social occasions in Rome.

"Good morning, Madeline."

"Good morning, Mr. Temple," Madeline Reynolds smiled and then looked at Cordis.

"Madeline, this is Ted Cordis, my campaign manager. Ted, this is Madeline Reynolds."

"Nice to meet you, Mr. Cordis."

Reynolds turned back to Temple. "Let me remember. The last time I saw you was at General Granger's Base Party for the Secretary of the Air Force."

"Right. That was a nice function."

"Mr. Temple, I have to admit, you have done a remarkable job of getting known in Rome and elsewhere. Whether you win or lose this election, you've run a good race."

Temple was surprised by Madeline Reynolds' comments. He knew she was a friend of the Governor and a supporter of the Democratic Party. This was a meaningful compliment and meant a lot to a candidate who had devoted so much time to overcoming what many had said were insurmountable odds. Temple looked directly at Reynolds and said simply, "Thank you." It was enough. They understood one another.

"Mr. Temple, you will be meeting with Edna Saint Lever and Joe Tyser. They do our editorial boards. My husband said to say hello and to apologize for not being here. He's at an editor's meeting on Long Island."

"Tell him that I said hello and send my best."

"I will."

Madeline Reynolds signaled to the two reporters, and they led Temple into the conference room. The interview lasted for an hour and forty-five minutes, and went well. Excerpts of the editorial board appeared the following day in the newspaper along with a picture that a staff photographer had taken during the interview. The photograph showed a smiling Jay Temple, gesturing with his hands, while answering a question. He looked the part of a politician.

Temple joined Cordis in the waiting room after the interview. As they left the newspaper's office, they found Sam LaGuzzi waiting for them in the parking lot.

"Good morning, Mr. Temple," LaGuzzi said warmly.

"Good morning, Sam. You remember Ted Cordis."

"Yes. Good morning, Mr. Cordis."

"Hi."

"Mr. Temple, Mr. Medina is waiting for us at his home. Why don't you follow me. That way you can leave right from Mr. Medina's home for Utica."

"Good idea, Sam. We'll follow you."

As Temple was getting into the van, Cordis asked, "Who is Mr. Medina?"

"A wine distributor Sam thought I should meet."

Cordis raised one eyebrow but said nothing as he looked at Temple. Temple shrugged. "Sam knows Rome. It's his call."

Ten minutes later, they pulled through a gated driveway that led to a beautifully landscaped Tudor home. As Temple climbed out of the van, a gardener nodded to him.

Sam LaGuzzi led Temple and Cordis to the front door. Mr. Medina answered the door and led them through a well appointed living room into a library complete with floor to ceiling bookcases, leather chairs, and hand carved desk.

"You admire my desk, Mr. Temple," Medina said, noting Temple's interest. "It is a fourteenth century masterpiece. It has been in my family for that long. That is why I have this library. It is a fitting place. Don't you think?"

Temple smiled at the old man looking at him from behind silver framed glasses. "Very fitting. This is a beautiful library. Quiet. Not too much sunlight. I suspect it is a good place to come and think."

"You're an understanding man, Mr. Temple. Mr. LaGuzzi said you were. I think that you would make a good Senator."

"Thank you, Mr. Medina. I'm going to try to be."

"You have my blessing." The old man closed his eyes as he sat down on his heavily padded armchair. "Life holds many challenges. Mine is to live out my life in comfort and peace." He opened his eyes and again looked at Temple. "What are your challenges, Mr. Temple?" he asked.

"Right now, to learn what people in my district need. Later, to do what I can to take care of those needs."

"Have you learned, Mr. Temple?"

"Some things. Mr. Medina, I think you know that the real challenge is to continue to learn. Too many people forget that. I hope that I never forget the need to continue to learn."

"If you are sincere, you won't."

Cordis and LaGuzzi listened but weren't sure they followed what was being said. It was enough for them that Temple and Medina seemed to understand one another.

On the way to Utica, Cordis asked Temple what he thought about Mr. Medina. "He's a man of some influence in Rome. He is also smart enough to know his limits," Temple answered.

"Know his limits?" Cordis asked.

"Yeah." Temple paused. "He didn't ask anything of me."

405

Chapter XXVIII

Face to Face

The weekend of October 13th and 14th was spent at a variety of functions. Saturday morning, Temple, Fitzgerald, Tarkings, Price, and Doctor Carey went to a shopping center in Oneida for two hours of shaking hands and handing out brochures. At lunchtime, Temple appeared at an Elk's Club reception for Republican candidates in Oneida while his volunteers went to the Oneida High School football game to hand out campaign material. At two o'clock, Temple joined his volunteers for an hour at the game.

Temple was a personal friend of the principal. The football game gave him an opportunity to catch up on his friend's career since leaving the Jamesville-DeWitt school system.

At three-fifteen, they were back in the van heading back to campaign headquarters for a meeting with some people from the press.

Mike Flynn of the Syracuse Gazette was doing a profile of each of the candidates for state office. He had requested photographs of Temple's family and was waiting for Temple when he arrived from Oneida.

The two men talked for about an hour enjoying each other's shared family experiences. Temple talked about his two sons and his daughter, about his wife and their many moves from apartment to home to four more homes before finally settling in Fayetteville. He talked about his work, his community activities and his church. It was a different look at a politician, and it was a comfortable topic for both reporter and candidate.

Flynn related to the moves, the dog, and the stories about Temple's children, having gone through similar experiences. Both concluded that they had a lot in common.

At five o'clock, Fitzgerald picked up Temple and took him to an opening reception for Bonwit Teller's at the Carousel Mall. This would be replicated the following night, only for the J.C. Penney Department Store. Temple knew the managers of both stores and was their guest, not as a politician, but as a friend. No buttons, brochures, or speeches. The crowds both nights were large and Temple found that recognition of what he was doing politically and who he was, was high among those in attendance.

On Sunday, Temple attended a brunch at Bob Anderson's in his honor. In the afternoon, he and Anderson went to Sylvan Beach for a political fund raiser with Senator D'Amato. The Senator was a popular figure in Sylvan Beach. He had helped them get Federal money for a harbor expansion. This meant more money for local merchants and more votes for the Senator. The evening was spent at the Penney's Store.

Temple knew the clock was ticking and that every minute was important now. There were just three weeks left until Election Day. He wanted to make the most of the time remaining.

Late that Sunday evening, Temple retired to his study to prepare for the upcoming round of debates with Senator Mann. As he worked through his material on the issues, he wondered how his opponent was holding up. She obviously was going through the same kind of hectic round–the–clock schedule. She was a seasoned politician. He thought that she was probably accustomed to the pace. Then he changed his mind and concluded that you never really got used to the pace. You just took it for what it was and got on with what you could do to make the most of it.

* * *

Senator Mann was well aware of the fact that Temple had raised more money than she had, or would, at this point. He had purchased more air time and more radio spots than she could afford. But she had two things going for her which she knew that he did not.

First, the power of incumbency. She could use her franking privileges for state funded newsletters to every voter in her district. As was true for most legislators, she was allowed six free mailings a year, and in an election year, she and her fellow incumbents would use at least four of those free mailings for the campaign.

The second advantage that she had was her ability to deliver the ten second sound byte. She could give the press exactly what they needed for their TV, radio or newspaper spots: a ten second statement around which they could build their own story. She did it neatly, with feeling, and better than any other politician in office or running for office.

Mann had studied Temple's speeches and TV spots. He was good if given the time, but in a fast-paced world where everything is measured in seconds and by the word, Temple was too detail-oriented. He gave the media too much to work with. They weren't interested in having to digest what he said and then try to reduce it to something that would fit within their time or space limits. They wanted the story handed to them, short and simple. This is exactly what Mann did and did so well. The result: she got more coverage on the news and in the papers than any other politician in the area.

Falling far behind Temple in the matter of fund raising, Mann still needed to raise money. She was slipping in the polls from what had been a huge lead down to where now it looked as though her race would be a photo-finish.

Her campaign committee put together several last minute fund raisers. The featured event was a boat trip around Onondaga Lake with the sitting Democratic United States Senator for New York. Senator Daniel Patrick Moynihan was the senior United States Senator from New York and had recently shown some interest in helping to clean up the toxins in Onondaga Lake. He had promised a huge package of Federal financial aid to Onondaga County for the project. He would be a big draw for Mann.

It was a cool, overcast day on October fourteenth as the boat pulled away from the dock. It had a capacity for two hundred, but was not completely filled for this October afternoon. Tickets had been sold at seventy-five dollars a piece. One hundred and thirty-five people joined the two Senators for the cruise. Mann netted seven thousand thirteen dollars after expenses and Senator Moynihan took away with him a cold that lasted for two weeks.

On Monday, Mann spent the day traveling from one studio to the next, talking about her new initiative as a member of the Senate Committee on Crime and Corrections.

"I've had a longstanding concern for the lack of coordinated treatment for sex offenders in the New York State Prison System." Mann looked directly into the cameras or at the radio announcer and went on. "It's not a rehabilitation program. It's a program designed to teach these people to control their behavior. In New York the rate of recidivism is close to fifty percent. It costs the taxpayer $26,000 per year to keep these people in jail. My program will reduce the incidents of repeat offenders and save the taxpayer money."

Her time proved to be well spent. Every TV and radio station she visited picked up the story and featured it in their broadcasts. The next day, news reporters from fifteen local and statewide newspapers called or appeared at her office for further details of the Senator's new proposal. It was a story that captured the media and the public's attention.

Stewart Ropespear read the Gazette's coverage with appreciation for both the Senator's and George Hague's way with words and with a story. 'This is a block buster! Sex, violence, fear, punishment, compassion, and resurrection, it's all here.' Ropespear thought to himself. He called Hague on the phone.

"George, good job on the Mann sex offender stuff! Get

out and do some follow-up work. Talk to offenders. Get their views about the hope this program offers them. Find some victims with the angle that had this program been in place earlier, they might not have gone through their ordeal. Find someone who wants to forgive and help these sick people get well. You know the picture."

Hague knew the picture and did just as was suggested. The Gazette ran a series of articles on Mann's proposals, the success that similar programs had in other states, and the courage it took for the Senator to speak out on the issue. Interviews with offenders who admitted they had a problem stemming back to their own childhood followed. They wanted help but never had a place to turn to. They liked Mann's proposal.

The victim angle was harder to pin down. Hague finally found a woman who had been victimized as a child but who now thought kindly of her assailant. She said that through prayer and meditation she had come to realize that the man needed help. She hoped that the Senator's proposal would give the help that was needed to those who suffered from uncontrollable sexual impulses.

There was wide disagreement with Mann's approach to the problem of sex offenders. Mann, herself, knew that the Senate would never pass a bill that would adopt all of her proposals. But the story generated widespread coverage and ate into the impact of Temple's paid advertisements.

Temple didn't agree with Mann's approach to the problem. When interviewed about Mann's proposals, he said there were other priorities more important, such as the huge state deficit, but his view was that the laws were too lenient and sex offenders were too quickly put back on the street. "I have little sympathy for people who hurt children and would be more concerned with helping the victim than the offender."

The line on this issue was clearly drawn, but Temple's remarks got scant coverage. His paid commercials continued to hammer away at the financial failings of state government and the Democrats' tax-and-spend philosophy.

410

* * *

As the eighteenth of October approached, and the first live debate between the candidates, both Mann and Temple were fine-tuning their intended direction.

Temple's people weren't satisfied with just winning the race for campaign dollars, they wanted to win big. Dave Yondle had been working for months on bringing in a big name celebrity for a gala dinner event. Eventually, he had made contact with Ted Lane, a former baseball player and coach who now had his own sports program on CNT TV.

It cost ten thousand dollars to bring Lane in, but it also assured a large attendance. The Hotel Syracuse Grand Ballroom was booked and Yondle hoped to fill it to capacity, eight hundred people, with a cover charge of one hundred dollars per person. The date was October eighteenth, the same day as the first debate between the candidates. Temple would square off against Mann at noon in the Imperial Room of the Hotel Syracuse and then share the podium with Lane in the Empire Ballroom that evening.

Invitations went out to every Republican in the District as well as to every friend and acquaintance Temple had met over the years. Guest invitations were sent to the Majority Leader in the New York State Senate, the Chairman of the NYSSRC, and the County Executives for Madison and Onondaga Counties. Five hundred and sixty-five people attended the function bringing in thirty-four thousand five hundred dollars after expenses.

The Majority Leader and the Chairman of the NYSSRC did not attend but did send the Majority Whip in the State Senate as their representative. Senator Giles was well known in Central New York and was well received as a stand-in for the party leaders in the Senate. Later, Giles would give Senator Manto and Senator Valli glowing reports of the evening, the news coverage, and the candidate. It would be the impetus that propelled the NYSSRC to flood the campaign with literature and mailings during the closing days of the campaign.

The other piece of information that gave added strength to Temple's campaign was the results of the most recent poll done in the district. It showed Temple receiving forty-six percent of the vote, Mann receiving forty-nine percent, and just five percent undecided. This meant that Temple was solidifying his support and could win if events and circumstances fell just right.

Valli attributed the latest results to the TV advertising that had shown Temple as a tough politician ready to take on the Governor, if need be, to help his constituents.

Temple attributed the results to the hard working team of volunteers who were now spending countless hours and their own vacation time working on his behalf.

Others attributed the rise in the polls to Temple himself. He had turned out to be much more of a politician than anyone would have imagined. Whatever the chemistry, it was working.

* * *

October eighteenth was a day that had been long awaited by the Temple campaign team. It was the first head–to–head confrontation between Temple and Mann, and it was coming at a critical time in the election cycle. Both candidates were virtually in a dead heat in their race for the senate seat. Both candidates now had the name recognition. And both candidates were prepared on the issues. The delay in this first meeting had actually worked to Temple's benefit. Had the debates occurred in August or sooner, his knowledge and positions on the issues might have been less than they now were. He also would not have been coming into the debates carrying the same political stature that he now had.

The Imperial Ballroom at the Hotel Syracuse had been set up to accommodate an estimated seventy-five members of the YWCA board, their guests and other interested parties. By eleven that morning, it became apparent that the room needed to be rearranged.

All three local TV stations had sent camera crews and reporters to cover the debate. By eleven-thirty, seven radio station reporters and three newspaper reporters had joined the media coverage. The podium was covered with microphones, taped in clusters, so that every word could be picked up and recorded for later use.

Jean Hanold, the chairperson of the political forum, was running from one spot to another getting the hotel staff to take care of the minute by minute changes being made. Somehow, she managed to have everything in place and the media accommodated by the time the first guests began to arrive.

Senator Mann, accompanied by Tork Johns, Joel Samuels, and Annie Wilson arrived promptly at twelve noon. Hanold showed Johns, Samuels, and Wilson to a table just left of center and in front of the podium. The Senator was brought to the head table where she was introduced by Hanold to Dorothy Winthrup, the President of YWCA board of trustees.

Temple arrived a few minutes after Mann. Cordis, Anderson, Tarkings, Price, Roth, Doctor Carey, and Pat Temple arrived along with Temple. Hanold went to greet them and to show Temple's guests to a table just right of center and in front of the podium. Temple was amused by this as he saw Mann's staff on the left. He wondered if the seating was intentional, and if so, who had the good sense of humor.

Hanold then brought Temple to the head table where he said hello to Mann and was introduced by Hanold to Dorothy Winthrup.

"Mr. Temple, this is our president, Dorothy Winthrup."

"Mr. Temple and I know each other." Winthrup smiled as she offered her hand to Temple.

Temple shook hands with the President. "It's been a long time, Dorothy. It's good to see you."

They were interrupted by Sally Notholm. "Excuse me. We'd like to get a mike check. Could someone speak into the microphones?"

Winthrup excused herself and did the requested testing

413

for the media.

Temple looked over at Mann who was now seated and reading some notes that she had brought with her. His advisers had always made her out to be a demon in female clothing. Looking at her now, studying her notes, it was a hard image to hold onto.

"Jay."

Temple turned toward the person calling his name. There was Patrick Fitzgerald with Laney Gardiner and Dave Yondle.

"Hope you don't mind that we closed headquarters down. We wanted to come over to hear the debates," Fitzgerald said.

Temple smiled at his staff. "I'd be here too if I were you."

He sat down in his chair and surveyed the room, saying hello to those he recognized and to those who were watching him.

Lunch was served and after everyone had finished, Dorothy Winthrup stood up and spoke into the microphones.

"I'd like to thank all of you for joining us today for this candidate's forum, sponsored by the YWCA in conjunction with the League of Women Voters. I would especially like to thank Jean Hanold and her committee for organizing this program. I think this is the first time that we have had this much media attention, and it is kind of exciting.

"I would also like to thank Senator Laura Ann Mann and Mr. Jay Temple for agreeing to participate in our forum. We know that this is a busy time of the year for both of you."

There were some chuckles in the audience at this last comment. Winthrup continued. "The format today is that each candidate will give a brief opening. This will be followed by each posing a question to the other and a response and then a rebuttal if appropriate. Responses will be limited to three minutes and rebuttals to one minute. Jean Hanold will be our timekeeper and will signal when there are ten seconds left to a speaker.

414

A coin was tossed and Senator Mann won. She elected to go first.

"Senator Mann has served in the New York State Senate for three consecutive terms and is now seeking her fourth. Will you join me in welcoming Senator Laura Ann Mann?"

As Mann stood up and approached the bank of microphones, she was greeted by loud applause. She smiled briefly, looked at Temple and said, "Mr. Temple," then turning back to look directly at the cameras in the back of the room, she said, "Ladies and gentlemen. It is my pleasure to be here, at this YWCA - League luncheon, to talk about this year's race for the New York State Senate."

She glanced quickly at her notes then back at the cameras.

"The League of Women Voters has always focused on election reform. I think that my race this year is a prime example of the importance of election reform!"

Temple noted a twitch in Mann's temple as she increased the intensity of her remarks.

"Mr. Temple and his people have misled, misinformed, and outright lied to the public about my voting record and the things that I believe in. His 'bought and paid for' television commercials have repeatedly said that I voted to raise taxes. The truth is that I voted against the budget and that it was the Republican Majority in the Senate that voted to increase your taxes. The truth is that Republican Majority is the same Republican Majority that is helping to pay for these commercials and is the same Republican Majority that Mr. Temple wants to become a part of.

"If Mr. Temple is elected, we will have added just one more boy to the 'good ole boys' network that has put down campaign reform at every turn.

"Closed door sessions, midnight bills, and back room deals, I've been fighting these abuses for years. Now, Mr. Temple would have you believe that I am a part of all this. I think you know better, and I think the public knows better.

415

"I plan to continue to fight the type of politics that Mr. Temple and the Republican majority represent. They will find that all the money in the world, spent on this campaign, won't hide the truth.

"We need a fresh approach to government. We need to throw the good ole boys out and elect progressive candidates. Mr. Temple and his cronies in Albany do not represent the sentiments of today's voters. I believe that I do represent the voters in Central New York. I am willing to stand on my record. Thank you."

Again there was loud applause. Temple had to admit that Mann was a master at putting spin on a story. TV cameras had captured her performance. It was convincing. Now it was his turn.

As Mann sat down, Dorothy Winthrup stood up to introduce Temple.

"It is my pleasure to introduce to you Mr. Jay Temple. Mr. Temple is an attorney and Vice President of a local business establishment. He has served on many community boards. He is the Republican - Conservative candidate for the New York State Senate. Please join me in welcoming Mr. Jay Temple."

Temple stood to slightly less applause than Mann had received. Owing to her remarks, he thought that he was lucky to have any applause at all. He approached the podium telling himself to stay with his own game plan. So far in the campaign he had Mann on the defense. He wanted it to stay that way.

Temple placed both hands on the podium and began.

"Thank you, Dorothy, for the introduction. It's nice to see so many old friends here today."

Mann looked up at Temple trying to understand what he meant by old friends. Temple continued.

"I appreciate the opportunity to talk to you this afternoon about the problems that we all know exist in our state.

"We have, in Albany, a group of career, professional politicians who have a tax-and-spend mentality. Their policies have cost us jobs and a higher standard of living. They have reduced the quality of life that we might otherwise be enjoying. Unemployment in New York State is at an all-time high. Manufacturing and farming business have left the state in droves. The educational achievement of our students has dropped to one of the lowest levels in the country. Crime has risen to all time highs. Drugs can be purchased on almost any street corner in this state, and we do not feel safe in our own homes at night. If you doubt any of these statements, open the newspaper when you go home tonight or turn on your radio or TV.

"Do I blame Senator Mann for all this?" Temple let the question hang in the air as reporters focused on the Republican - Conservative candidate. "Yes, I do." Mann flushed, there were some undercurrents of comments around the room.

"Senator Mann indicated that I said she voted for tax increases. That is not true. What I have said is that she voted 'yes' over ninety-three percent of the time during her last two years in office. A look at her voting record will show that she voted 'yes' on every spending bill that came to the Senate floor but that when it came time to pay for these spending bills, she voted 'no.' It was a safe bet on her part because the majority would have to vote 'yes' or they would have no source of revenue to fund their spending programs.

"That would be like you or me running up a huge charge account and then saying that we weren't going to pay for what we had charged. The law won't let us do that and our State Legislators shouldn't be allowed to do it either."

There were nods of agreement around the room.

"If you want true reform, I will tell you what I favor.

"First, a twelve year term limitation and four year terms.

"Second, public referendums on important statewide issues.

"Third, no closed door deals, and that includes something the Senator uses along with all other legislators, a gimmick known as member items. Do you know that five billion dollars a year is given away by legislators in the form of gifts to constituents. Five billion dollars of our tax money without a vote and without any public record. That's one reform the Senator could undertake."

Jean Hanold stood up indicating that Temple had ten seconds to complete his opening.

Temple concluded his opening. "It's time for change in Albany. We need to set priorities and legislate accordingly."

Winthrup again went to the podium. "Well, we never said this would be dull!"

There was laughter around the room. She went on. "For the next twenty minutes the candidates will ask and answer questions from each other on a rotating basis. Mr. Temple, you will ask the first question."

Temple went to the podium. "Senator Mann, you have served in the Senate for six years now. Three terms. Since you took office, the state has continually been operating with a deficit. Last year the deficit was three billion dollars. This year you and your Senate colleagues voted to increase spending by another three billion dollars. That's a six billion dollar swing. How do you intend to pay the state debt and raise the additional spending money?"

Mann walked quickly to the podium.

"This is another example of how my opponent and his public relations people twist the truth.

"The truth is that it was the Republicans in the Senate who voted for the big budgets that have caused the deficits.

"I have been in the minority in the Senate since the first day I took office. And not just the Democratic minority. I'm also an outsider because I am one of very few Senators who is also a woman.

"I'm not part of what they call 'the club.' It's the club that is the problem in Albany and somehow I don't see Mr. Temple upsetting the old boy network the way I have.

"I have spoken out against the abuses of the system and am on public record for campaign reform. To indicate otherwise is nothing but dirty politics."

Mann went back to her seat without looking at Temple

418

or the audience. She sat down and folded her arms in front of her.

Temple stood for his rebuttal. "The question was how they intended to pay for the three billion dollar deficit of last year and the three billion dollar increase of this year. Obviously by increasing our taxes. That will mean more jobs leaving the state, more unemployment, and a state credit rating that will be close to the worst of any state in the country. This is exactly why we need change and why I am running for office."

Mann was next up with a question for Temple.

"Your campaign financial report shows that the NYSSRC, a Republican Senate Election Committee, has given you almost thirty thousand dollars in contributions. This fund is controlled by the Republican majority in the Senate. Do you expect us to believe that you will go to Albany and vote against the same people who financed your campaign?" She frowned at Temple and smiled at the audience as she returned to her seat.

"I don't vote against people. I vote for or against specific bills.

"I mentioned earlier the need to set priorities for legislative action. Mine are jobs, education, crime reduction, health care, and tax relief.

"If there are bills offered that go to solving these problem areas, I will vote for them and for the funding to implement the proposals. All other bills will have to be weighed carefully in the context of what we have to spend.

"It's kind of like running a household. You have a budget. You know that you have to pay for food, the mortgage, and utilities. Once they are taken care of, then you determine where the rest of your money will be spent. What you and I don't do, but what the state has been doing, is spending money that they don't have."

Mann rebutted Temple's comments by saying that he was naive and that compromise was what politics was all about. His priorities were too simplistic.

Temple asked his next question. "Senator, the Governor

has said that this is the year of the child, yet he has proposed to cut twenty-three and a half million dollars from the State University System. Do you support this cut, and if not, what are you doing to help improve education in New York?"

"Yes, I support the Governor. The State University System is one of the least expensive college education systems in the country and one of the largest.

"This is really a small cut in terms of the System's overall budget. It would mean a tuition hike of about one hundred dollars a year for the average full-time student. Tuition has not been raised in at least the last six years while I know most colleges review tuition increases at least every two years.

"There are also some internal cost cutting measures that could be adopted which may eliminate the need for a tuition increase. I think the Governor has seen the studies and is acting appropriately."

Temple commented that the large majority of students in the State University System were working people who were trying to get ahead by increasing their education. They were people, who for the most part, would be long term residents of New York. They were the people that the state should help with their education. Temple said that he would vote against any such cut.

Mann played what she believed to be her strongest card of the day.

"Mr. Temple, you have criticized my voting record. Recently a bill came before the Senate that would create shelters for unwed mothers and also provide state funding for abortions. I voted for this spending bill. How would you have voted?"

"Senator, my vote was cast for shelters back in the early seventies."

Mann again frowned but this time without smiling at the audience.

Temple turned to Dorothy Winthrup. "Dorothy and I were on the YWCA Board back then, and the 'Y' was trying to find a way to fund a home for unwed mothers. They had started the program in our local building, and it had quickly outgrown its space.

"Dorothy and I put together the thrift shop which I believe is still going strong to this day. A used clothes shop with low prices, volunteer workers, and enough profit to amply fund the home that the 'Y' now runs for unwed mothers."

Temple looked out at the audience. He pointed to different women in the audience. "Martha, Sandy, Amy, Mary, and many others out there worked with Dorothy and me on that project and in doing so helped a lot of women in our community.

"I'm supportive of those programs, Senator. I have less interest in band uniforms, park benches, tractors to rake beaches, and a variety of other member items that have been spent without voter approval or knowledge. The only benefit that I see with member items is a possible buying of votes by the legislators."

Mann rebutted by saying that she resented the remark about buying votes and that she believed that she had done a lot of good with her use of her member items.

The time passed quickly. After several more exchanges, both candidates were called upon to give their closing remarks.

Mann was first in order for the closing.

"I appreciate the time and effort that the 'Y' and the League put into arranging this forum. I think that all of you have a pretty good picture of how my record has been distorted by my opponent.

"We need to clean up politics. We need to change the 'business as usual' way of doing things in Albany. I have fought to do both during my last six years in office. I plan to continue to fight against dirty politics and back room deals and to expose both wherever and whenever they occur.

"I hope you will continue to support me in this effort."

Mann sat down to the applause of the audience. Temple walked to the podium for his closing remarks.

"I, too, want to thank the YWCA and the League of Women Voters for arranging this political forum between Laura and myself." He looked briefly at Mann who obviously didn't like being called Laura.

Temple continued. "I don't believe that accurately stating what the voting record of a sitting Senator is, is dirty politics. In fact, I think that it would be wrong not to disclose that voting record. We send people to Albany to represent us and to vote for us on bills that impact our daily lives. In an election year, we should be told how they voted and how those votes effect all of us.

"Senator Mann voted 'yes' on ninety-seven percent of the spending bills. That means that we are paying more in taxes so that the state can pay for those expenditures which she, and a majority of the State Senate, approved. That's not dirty politics, that's fact.

"We need to hold our government accountable to us. We need someone in Albany who is willing to do that. Hopefully, with your support, I will be that person. Thank you."

Temple received a good round of applause as Sally Notholm made her way through the well wishers to where Temple was standing.

"Mr. Temple. Could we get an interview with you in the back of the room?" Notholm interrupted Tarkings who was talking to Temple.

"I'll be right there," Temple responded as he turned to two other women who had just come up to talk to him.

Notholm returned to her own camera crew and announced, loud enough for all the crews could hear, that Temple would be right back to do a post–debate interview.

It was fifteen minutes before Temple could finally break away from the group of people who had stopped by to say hello to him. As he walked back toward Notholm and a cluster of reporters and camera lights, he saw Mann, Johns, and Wilson standing in the far corner. There were no reporters interviewing her. Temple didn't know if this was a good or a bad sign. He'd soon find out.

Notholm took his arm and led him into the center of the lights. All three TV station crews were going to film this while radio and newspaper reporters looked on. Mann was watching too.

Politicians always have a personal vision of themselves and where they fit into the scheme of things. Sometimes their vision is accurate but more often than not, it doesn't come close to reality.

Temple had a vision of his campaign before he committed to run for the New York State Senate. He could see himself surrounded by cameras, microphones, and the news media, talking about the important issues of the day. He had prepared himself for just that experience.

During the first eight months of his campaign, Temple received only sporadic coverage of his press conferences by the TV networks and daily newspapers. The radio stations had been better, as had been the weekly community newspapers. But it was far from what Temple had initially envisioned.

As he now stood in the center of a ring of reporters, all asking questions at the same time, with a half dozen camera lights shining in his face, he reached another milestone in his political career. The attention was what he had been hoping for. He knew that it was important to make the most of it.

Notholm zeroed in on the candidate. "Mr. Temple. Senator Mann said during your debate that she voted for state funding of abortions. How would you vote on that issue?"

Temple looked into the camera behind Notholm. As the tape whirred through the reel, he answered, "My personal belief is that abortions should be available for three different circumstances. Rape, incest, and the health of the mother. If a doctor certifies that a woman needs an abortion in order to save her own life, and the woman could not afford the necessary medical attention, then, yes, the state should provide for the saving of the woman's life."

Temple noticed that Notholm was not only taken aback by his unexpected answer but that she also glanced quickly toward where Mann was standing. He thought to himself, 'this is a setup.'

423

Temple went on. "The problem with the abortion question is that it is very difficult to draft any legislation that will deal with all of the issues involved.

"At what point are you destroying a child's life to save the mother? Some argue at conception. Some say not until after the first three months. And some will argue not until the child can survive on its own, free of the mother.

"I don't have the answer to those questions. I do know that the State Legislature should not be the body that resolves this issue."

Notholm recovered from her initial shock and asked, "If not the legislature, who? The courts?"

"No." Temple again caught Notholm off guard. "The people. If this is as important an issue as it seems to be, then a statewide referendum should be held where every New York resident can participate in the decision-making process."

Notholm gave a sly smile. "Referendums are not allowed in New York State."

Temple looked knowingly at Notholm. "I know, and that's one of the reasons I'm running. We need to give the people of this state more of an opportunity to have a voice in government. I would propose that we make referendums a part of the political process in this state. I am surprised that our legislators haven't sponsored a proposal to that effect before now."

Terry Davis of TV 7 had been waiting patiently. She spoke up. "Mr. Temple, you have talked about the problem of drugs being available virtually on every street corner in America. How would you propose we combat this problem?"

Temple looked at Davis. "That's a good question. Let me tell you first what I would not do. I would not pull one hundred state policemen from upstate New York to go down to New York City. The Governor is doing that as we speak and without objection from our local representatives.

"We need to maintain a strong law enforcement presence in our communities. I think that the problem is serious enough that we should create a joint task force between all law enforcement agencies and perhaps the military to interdict the drugs before they reach the streets. We need to beef up our court systems so that they can intelligently handle the caseload. They need to be able to separate the users from the pushers and have appropriate actions to be taken with both.

"But an equal partner with the law enforcement side has to be an educational component. We need to put more money into our schools to educate our children to the tragic consequences of drug use and addiction. We also need to funnel more money into after school programs so that kids will have places to go and things to do. An active student is less likely to get involved in drugs than one who has a lot of nonproductive time on his or her hands."

Steve Adamson of TV 4 asked, "Mr. Temple, all these ideas are going to cost money. A lot of money! You say that you want to cut spending and reduce taxes. How do you justify what you have just said with your spending and tax reduction campaign?"

"Steve, New York State had a fifty-seven billion dollar budget last year. Fifty-seven billion dollars! With no increases. That is a lot of money to spend in one year.

"I mentioned during the forum that what this state government needs to do is to set priorities and then fund qualified programs with available resources.

"Every voter and every group that I have talked to about the issues that are of concern to them, list the drug problem as one of their greatest concerns. It's one of mine too. Let's put our tax dollars to work in areas of importance to the people rather than in areas of special interest to our legislators!"

Temple fielded several more questions with direct answers. He motioned to different reporters, giving everyone the opportunity to ask about whatever was on their minds.

As he talked, he noticed one reporter in the background who seemed to shy away from the lights and cameras. Temple did not recognize the man but felt sorry for him and thought that he was probably intimidated by all the lights.

Finishing with a question, Temple turned to the bearded man in the background and asked him if he had any question that he would like to ask.

The man looked up and said. "Maybe one. It was mentioned that you have received a lot of money from the Republican majority in the Senate. Do you feel that you owe them anything for their support?"

Temple thought, 'that's a fair question.' He answered. "If the question is, do I appreciate their help, the answer is 'yes,' and I will thank them for it. If the question is, will they control how I vote on any, and I mean *any*, issue or bill that comes before the Senate, the answer is 'no!' I've made it clear to everyone who has contributed to my campaign that I'm my own man and will not be politically indebted to anyone because of their support in this election."

Mann was pleased with her part in the forum but upset with the lack of attention that followed. Clearly, Temple had been the focus of the coverage following the debate. She had never experienced this before. She had always had more attention paid to her, often to the exclusion of her opponents. George Hague had come over to her shortly after the interviews with Temple had concluded and told her not to worry. He smiled at her through his scruffy beard and told her to read his next article. She did, and it made her feel much better.

* * *

Temple's staff was jubilant over what they considered to be their candidate's finest hour. He had met his opponent, and unlike past Republican challengers, he had not been vanquished by her. Their enthusiasm spilled over into the second highlight of the day, their fund raising gala at the Hotel Syracuse.

As people gathered for cocktails on the tenth floor of the hotel, the three major news networks were replaying parts of the debate between Temple and Mann. Reporters' comments were,

426

for the most part, very favorable for Temple.

Terry Davis, reporting on Channel 7, said, "Jay Temple, appearing very relaxed, fielded tough questions both from Senator Mann and from the reporters covering the debate. He did not hesitate to express his views and cited facts and statistics to support his positions. Here, now, are the issues he addressed and his positions on each."

The television screen then displayed a series of issues along with Temple's position on each. Davis did a voice–over while this was being shown. Temple thought that this was particularly effective coverage.

Sally Notholm was not quite as kind to Temple as she reported on Channel 4. "Today, Senator Mann debated her Republican challenger, Jay Temple, before a forum sponsored by the YWCA and the League of Women Voters.

"Mann stressed her record in office as a champion for open government. She also took Temple's campaign team to task for what she viewed as a distortion of her voting record and dirty politics."

The television screen excerpted Mann from the forum. "Mr. Temple and his people have misled, misinformed, and outright lied to the public about my voting record."

Notholm came back on the screen. "Mann went on to say that contrary to Temple's paid commercials, she has voted against raising taxes. She said it was the Republicans in the Senate who had actually voted to raise taxes that she opposed.

"Mr. Temple then responded to Senator Mann." Notholm smiled as the television screen now excerpted Temple's response. "Senator Mann indicated that I said she voted for tax increases. This is not true. . .she voted no."

The screen again showed Notholm. "The forum quickly became a contest of who could outdo the other. Neither candidate gave any ground. The big question is whether or not this race will become another political mudslinging contest as we have seen in the past. If today was an example of things to come, it will be dirty politics as usual."

427

Chapter XXIX

All That Glitters
Is Not Gold

The biggest fund raiser of the campaign was well-attended and well orchestrated by Temple's staff.

Dave Yondle had been in touch with Ted Lane throughout the day. Lane was flying in from Florida and had problems with his connecting flights. There was a brief moment when it looked like Lane would be a no-show for the dinner. Yondle, with the help of a friend at USAir, immediately went to work on the problem and was able to re-route Lane. His flight would arrive at 7:30 in the evening, but at least he'd be there. Yondle met Lane at the airport and drove him to the hotel.

Laney Gardiner had made all the arrangements with the hotel caterer. She had enlisted the help of a number of volunteers to staff the reception area and had gotten the Young Republicans from Syracuse University to decorate both the reception area and the cocktail lounge.

Allie Anderson, Bob Anderson's wife, took responsibility for the table decorations in the ballroom. She, along with several friends, put together over fifty centerpieces and decorated the head table.

The hotel provided a dark maroon backdrop for a twenty-five foot long sign that stood eight feet high and read, 'Jay Temple For The New York State Senate.'

Everything was in place as the guests filed into the ballroom for an evening of politics and humor.

The emcee for this occasion was local sportscaster, Dan

Lanagan. His voice was well known to the audience, and he was well-liked by local sports fans.

Lanagan and Temple met just outside the ballroom with Senator Giles and County Executive, Hank Palermo.

"Hi, Jay!" Lanagan said as he shook Temple's hand. "Where is our guest speaker?"

"You may be the one!" Temple laughed. Temple could see the color drain from Lanagan's face. "Just kidding. We had some logistical problems with a faulty plane engine, but I've been assured that Ted Lane is on the way and is being picked up at the airport by my aide, Dave Yondle. Lane should be here by eight o'clock."

"Gee, I hope so." Lanagan looked at Giles and Palermo. "I didn't come prepared for an entire program."

Giles smiled, "That's why you've got all these politicians around you. Give us a microphone and an audience, and we'll be good for hours!"

Lanagan wasn't convinced.

Temple excused himself to do a sweep of the reception area, greeting his supporters and thanking them for attending the fund raiser.

The mood was upbeat, and there was a sense of victory in the air.

Once again, the television and radio stations were on hand trying to get a sense of where the Temple campaign was going. Reporters interviewed guests and other politicians in attendance. Their responses to questions were uniformly positive. They were supporting the man who would be the next State Senator from the 48th Senate District. Some of the respondents volunteered that this was just the beginning of a rising political star and that they expected bigger things in the future.

The lights and cameras added to the festive atmosphere in the ballroom. As the guests at the head table made their way to the raised platform, the crowd applauded and some pushed forward to shake hands with Temple and the others.

In addition to Senator Giles, Oneida County Executive Don Pern, and Onondaga County Executive Hank Palermo, Congressman Wales and Dan Lanagan joined Temple at the head table. Lanagan introduced those seated at the head table and then read a list of other politicians and notables in the audience.

The invocation was given by Temple's friend and minister, Hal Worden. A contingent from Temple's older son's Boy Scout Troop led the audience in the salute to the flag. Dinner was served and the conversation poured forth on the election, the candidates, and the issues.

Lanagan kept a close watch on the main entrance to the ballroom and was relieved when Ted Lane finally appeared at eight ten. Lane was brought up to the podium by Dave Yondle and introduced to everyone sitting at the head table. He sat down in the empty seat next to Temple.

"Rough trip?" Temple smiled.

"Sure was. First the plane engine malfunctioned in Florida, and they scratched my flight. Then we hit some turbulence over Pittsburgh, and I thought that I was going to buy the farm! Then I get to Syracuse and my luggage is nowhere to be seen. Say, you've got a gem with that Yondle fellow."

"He's a good friend."

"Good friend? He's a Houdini! He got me here tonight. He never gave up."

Temple nodded with appreciation. He knew that Lane was part of the draw for the people who had paid to come to his fund raiser. Yondle had worked hard, not just today, but throughout the planning of this event. He was a very important part of the whole campaign effort. Temple thought to himself, 'There's no way to thank people like Dave adequately.'

Late that evening as Yondle, Lane, and Temple shared a drink in the hotel lounge, Temple turned to Yondle and said, "Dave, I want you to know that I really appreciate all that you are doing for my campaign. Sometimes I get so tied up in the minute–to–minute activity that I may not seem as appreciative as I should be. But I sincerely appreciate your work."

430

Yondle smiled at his friend. "I know you appreciate what I do. That's why I'm doing it. Just do me a favor, get elected!"

Temple thought about Yondle and all the others who had worked so hard. They'd all be disappointed if he didn't win. Especially now that they were this close to winning.

He made a renewed vow to himself to work even harder, if not for himself, for them and for all those people who had shown their support over the past several months. 'Seventeen days left and many roads left to cover in between.'

At home, Pat gave her husband a hug. "What a great night for you! Everyone was so supportive. I think that you are going to win."

"Well, if I can get over fifty percent of the rest of the district to feel that way, we'll be on our way."

* * *

Everyone was impressed with Temple's big show.

Ted Lane commented to a reporter as he left the ballroom that night that he had spoken at a lot of dinners and this was as well organized and run as any he had attended. Lane went on to say, "I don't know anything about local politics, but two things impressed me. First, the people involved with Mr. Temple's campaign. They're well organized and hard working.

"Second is Mr. Temple. I don't know what kind of politician he is. But he's straightforward, and what you see is what you get. I like that."

The reporter asked him if he thought Temple would win.

"I can't answer that, but Jay Temple is willing to step up to the plate for the things he believes in. In my book, that's what makes a player and that's what wins ball games."

Senator Giles had lunch with Senator Valli and Senator Ryan the following Monday.

Valli asked, "How was Temple's affair?"

Giles put his glass down on the table. "That young man

431

is a winner. He has great support. Hell, I even enjoyed Ted Lane, and I usually can't stand to listen to him."

They all laughed. Valli was already planning the NYSSRC push to help the Upstate New York Republican with his campaign.

After the Temple fund raiser, the Syracuse Gazette carried two stories. The first by Chris Blayton reported:

Some five hundred Republicans attended a $125 a plate dinner for Jay Temple, Republican candidate for the 48th Senate District.

Ted Lane was the guest speaker and Dan Lanagan was the emcee. Both indicated that they were not endorsing Temple. Both were paid by Temple's campaign committee for speaking. Lanagan said, 'They paid me my normal fee for my services. This was strictly a business arrangement.'

Lane confirmed that he, too, was paid for his appearance. 'Politics is like show biz. I told Temple that if he doesn't make it in politics, there's always news reporting. I wanted to be a coach and look what I'm doing.'

Lane's normal fee is fifteen thousand dollars. We could not confirm what Lanagan is usually paid.

Cordis threw the newspaper down on Temple's desk. "This town needs another paper!"

"Hey, at least they spelled the names correctly," Temple laughed.

Mike Flynn wrote the second article for the Gazette. It appeared in the Friday morning edition. It read, "Last night, Republican Senate Candidate, Jay Temple, filled the ballroom of the Hotel Syracuse with supporters to hear Ted Lane talk about sportsmanship as a winning tradition.

"Over five hundred people contributed to Temple's campaign event that included a cash bar and dinner. Temple's campaign treasurer, Kevin Roth said, 'We will clear about thirty thousand dollars on this event.'

"Joining Temple were Congressman Wales, County Executive Palermo, County Republican Chairman Gaines and many other Republican politicians and officeholders. Gaines indicated that this was the biggest Republican fund raiser of the season by an individual candidate. He said, 'It takes guts to bring in a big name speaker like Ted Lane. Not everybody can afford to do that.'"

The story made the front page.

Temple's campaign team liked it as a recognition piece.

Stewart Ropespear liked it because it pointed out the big money at work in a local campaign.

Laura Ann Mann did not like the coverage or the message. Temple was attracting big names and big money to his campaign. It was beginning to be a lot for her to deal with. This was a different race than any she had been in before. It was clear that Temple would out-spend her significantly.

Saturday's edition of the Syracuse Gazette had a different focus. George Hague had his own weekly column on the front page of the paper. This week his story dealt with the Temple-Mann debate.

"Who is this wealthy insurance lawyer, Jay Temple? That's the question I aimed to have answered and so I went to another one of those political rituals for which the League of Women Voters is notorious.

"There was Jay Temple dressed in a blue pin-striped suit with red power tie and white starched shirt. This is the dress that all really successful businessmen wear nowadays.

"Temple is running against State Senator Laura Ann Mann. Over the last six years, Senator Mann has been a thorn in the side of the Republican controlled Senate. She has defiantly confronted the old boys network over their back room deals, blatant discrimination against women, and their political payoffs.

"During the debate, the Senator charged Temple with

433

receiving money for his campaign from the Republican back room gang. Later, I asked Mr. Temple if he felt that all this money from his possible future Republican colleagues would give them some influence over his voting. He said, 'Absolutely. I have to listen to all those who support me.'

"I think we have too many good old boys in Albany now. Senator Mann has been a bright ray of hope in an otherwise shadowy world of politics. She is for open government by the governed not by those who can pay the highest price.

"Yes, I found out who Jay Temple was. Now you know, too."

The story ended, but the reaction was swift and strong.

Temple called Ropespear, and was in his office early Monday morning.

"Thank you for seeing me, Mr. Ropespear." Temple sat down in a deep leather chair in the editor's office.

It was a spacious, well-appointed office with original paintings hung and lighted over mahogany walls. The Persian carpets were thick and Ropespear's desk was made of a highly polished mahogany wood as well.

Temple thought to himself, 'and they call me a wealthy executive.'

Ropespear leaned back in his chair and stared at Temple. "What can I do for you, Mr. Temple?"

"You have a reporter by the name of George Hague. He wrote an article in Saturday's paper about me that was completely untrue. I would like your paper to print a retraction."

Ropespear sat up in his chair. His stare hardened. "I don't like being told what to do, Mr. Temple. The fact is all my reporters have professional standing and have the liberty to write stories exactly as they see them. I don't interfere."

Temple sat forward and returned Ropespear's stare. "Are you telling me that if your reporters print untruths, you will let those lies stand?"

Ropespear was red with rage. No one talked to him like

this. "Listen. First, I don't know that the story that George wrote about you is untrue. George has been with this newspaper for many years and is a good reporter. I certainly am not going to have him retract a story just on the word of an unknown politician."

Temple was ready for this. "You don't have to take the word of an unknown politician. How about a videotape of your reporter asking me the question that I responded to and my answer. Channel 7 has the tape and is willing to let you see it."

Ropespear stood up. "Mr. Temple, I'm not trotting off to some TV station to look at some out-take of a news conference. You need to understand something, my friend! We own the ink! We can do whatever we want!"

Temple stood also. "So you are unwilling to see the tape and unwilling to print a retraction?"

"You got it!"

Temple turned and walked to the door of Ropespear's office. At the door he turned and said, "Now I know how the game is played and where you are coming from. Oh. . .and I'm not your friend." With that, Temple turned and walked out of the office and never looked back.

Temple left the Syracuse Gazette building and returned to his campaign headquarters. He needed some time to collect himself and to get back on track for the campaign. He knew that without the Gazette's support, these last few weeks would be all uphill.

As he pulled his van into the parking lot of his headquarters, he saw an eighteen–wheeler being unloaded. The tractor trailer had brought ninety-five thousand newspapers up from Long Island. These were special edition papers which Temple and his staff had designed, edited, and prepared for distribution to the public. Regular newsprint had been used in three tone color and the idea was to distribute them as a special insert with the Gazette. Obviously, this wasn't going to work now.

Kevin Roth came over to the van to find out how

435

Temple's meeting with Ropespear went.

"Don't ask," Temple responded as he climbed out of the van. "He told me that he owned the ink and could print whatever he wanted to."

Roth was shocked. "You mean that they'd print lies even if they knew that what was being put out was untrue?"

"That's about the size of it."

Roth immediately went on the offensive. "Let's sue the paper."

Temple shook his head. "I thought of that, but we can't win a battle with the paper. They have a lot more access to the people than we do. This is a grin–and–bear–it situation."

"There's got to be something that we can do."

"If you come up with something let me know. In the meantime we have to find a way to get all these newspapers out to the public."

Temple picked up a copy of the paper. It looked good. The campaign logo appeared in bold print across the top of the first of four pages. Pictures and stories followed showing the candidate visiting a school yard and kneeling down to talk with children. Another showed Temple delivering a speech to a group of seniors at a senior center. There was a picture of Temple shaking hands with black residents on Syracuse's south side and a family picture showing Temple with his wife and three children.

The articles dealt with the candidate's positions on education, state spending, taxes, health care, farming, drugs and crime, the environment, and open government. It was a clear and direct communication designed to flesh out the candidate and let the reader know who they would be voting for.

Temple's staff and advisors met that afternoon to discuss the problem of distribution. A door–to–door blitz was planned for the last week and a half of the campaign. It was decided that the blitz would be the method of delivery. In the end, only about half of the papers got out to the distribution points, and there was no way to monitor how many actually reached the voters of the district.

Temple concluded that it was a good idea and a good way to offset the negative, or at least paucity, of coverage by the newspapers, but that it failed to have a significant impact because the delivery system was not in place.

That Monday evening, Temple attended an ice cream social held in his honor at the Manlius Town Park. About two hundred people turned out for the event that offered music by Tommy Trumpet and the Magic Five along with ice cream, soda, and beer.

Toward the end of the event, Temple was helping the band load their equipment into their van when he noticed a plaque on the side of the park pavilion. The plaque read: "Donated to the Town of Manlius through state funds provided by Senator Laura Ann Mann."

Temple smiled to himself and said, "Thank you, Senator.

On Tuesday, Temple traveled to Madison County to meet with area farmers. Mann was long touted as the friend of the farmer in the New York State Senate. Her voting record showed that in her six years in the Senate, she had not sponsored a single piece of farm legislation. Temple was ready for his meeting.

Ted Carson was the local leader of the farm community. He had a large dairy farm in Canastota. He was also the local Grange Master and had made the arrangements for Temple to address the farmers.

Carson introduced Temple. "We are pleased to have Jay Temple, a candidate for the New York State Senate, with us today. Mr. Temple is running against Senator Laura Ann Mann and has agreed to talk to us about farm issues."

Carson turned and nodded to Temple who was given polite applause as he stood up. Rather than go to the podium, Temple walked around the table that the podium was resting on and sat down on a corner of the table. It was a casual pose, and at once, some of the tension in the hall disappeared.

"I've been told that you wonder what a lawyer and a businessman knows about farming." Temple saw several heads nod in agreement. "The truth is, not much! But, I do know a few important things!" Temple paused as they waited to hear what the few important things might be.

"I know that the cost of farming in New York continues to climb every year, making it more expensive for you to do business. I have had the same experience with my business.

"I know that property taxes on farms has jumped disproportionately compared to other property owners because of the large number of acres under cultivation and their development potential.

"I know that between 1978 and 1987, one point two million acres of valuable farmland have been taken out of production.

"I know that more than seventy-five hundred farms have gone out of business in the last five years.

"And I know that farming is a vital resource that must be protected and preserved if this state and this country are to survive."

There was spontaneous applause from the farmers in the room. They liked what they were hearing.

Temple went on. "I'm not a farmer, but I can appreciate these problems. I'm trying to be a politician who offers more than words to people who need action.

"I would propose the following:

"First, the creation of an agricultural district to stabilize tax assessments.

"Second, the authorization of municipalities to purchase the development rights from farmers for their land. This would take the pressure off the farmer to sell valuable farmland for development.

"Third, use of scientifically approved methods of increased farm production.

"I ask you to look at my opponent's record on farm bills and compare her record to the bills I am offering. I promise to have a bill dealing with each of these proposals before the Senate Agriculture Committee within ninety days of my taking office."

His audience stood and applauded his remarks. A no nonsense group had just been given a no nonsense talk. They liked what they heard. Temple hoped that this would translate into votes at the polls.

Carson thanked Temple for coming. Others came up to him to introduce themselves and discuss their individual problems. Temple learned more that day about the plight of farmers than he had learned in his entire life. Later, he was given a tour of Carson's farm and met several of the workhands on the farm. It was a tough life with low pay and a high risk of injury. Temple vowed he would work hard to help the farming community.

Chapter XXX

All Is Fair In Love,
War, And Politics

Arnold Ophidia was never one to be called a shrinking violet. After he was given the go-ahead by Senator Valli to produce support pieces for Temple, he cranked up his public relations firm. Two people were assigned to do layouts for a series of one page advertisements. Postcards were printed with Temple's face on them asking for support. Message cards were also printed which directly attacked Mann as a do-nothing Senator. In fact, the heading on everything that went out dubbed Mann as 'The do-nothing Senator.'

Ophidia got a message from the Mayor of Rome that Mann, in a fit of rage over growing support for Temple in his city, said that she didn't care about Rome because it represented only fifteen percent of her district. Ophidia smirked at the message. This was perfect.

Ophidia called Berry. "You've got to get the boy scout to buy this!"

Berry liked the idea and told Temple that he could use the idea to push the fact that he represented everyone.

Temple wasn't comfortable using rumored conversation. "Get it in writing, check out the report and make sure those who heard her say this will come forward when and if needed."

Berry agreed. He reported back that both the Mayor of Rome and the Police Commissioner heard the comment.

Temple still felt uneasy about using it. He didn't think he needed to at this point. The polls showed the race to be in a dead heat. He wanted to win it his way. The following day he told Berry that he was not going to make it an issue.

Berry reported back to Ophidia. Ophidia lost his composure. "You tell the boy scout that he's got to use this. It'll insure that he wins! Tell him that in neck-and-neck races, the incumbent always wins. Tell him that Valli and Manto want to get this out. Geez! Tell him it's the damn truth! He ought to understand that."

Berry went back to Temple with Tom Mosby.

"Jay, everyone in Albany thinks that this will put you over the top. They want you to win. It's all true. Eiles and Catallana swear that she said it."

Mosby joined in. "Jay, if she's not willing to represent a portion of her district, they should know about it. Rome and Syracuse are the two biggest cities in your district. This will cement Rome and offset whatever we lose in Syracuse. It'll offset the fifteenth ward vote."

Cordis had come back to headquarters that day. Temple asked what he thought.

"Well, this isn't something that you are saying. It isn't even something that you heard. If Catallana and Eiles say it happened, it's their word against hers. I'd print it that way."

Temple thought about the advice he was being given. He was still reluctant but saw that a compromise was needed. He turned to Berry. "If the NYSSRC wants to put this out on its own, I can't stop them. But my campaign team isn't going to get involved. This is between Eiles and Mann."

Berry looked relieved. "Right. You won't be involved. Jay, you made the right decision."

"It's not my decision. If the Rome officials want to make this an issue, it's their call."

Berry called Ophidia right after the meeting. "Arnold, I got Temple to okay the Rome piece."

"You're a magician!"

"Just one thing. He doesn't want to be brought into this. It's to be a state thing."

441

"No problem." Ophidia smiled to himself. "It is a state thing."

* * *

Thursday, October twenty-sixth was the day of the big Celebration of the Arts in downtown Syracuse. All of the museums and arts centers were to be open to the public from five to ten in the evening.

For a price of fifty dollars a person, people could attend a special cocktail party in Hanover Square. Berry had done the promotional materials for the event and had told Temple that it was a good place to see a lot of people.

He was right. Temple and his wife arrived at five-thirty along with Cordis, Mary Tarkings, Dave Yondle, and Laney Gardiner. While the others handed out campaign buttons, Temple and his wife made the rounds.

There were over a thousand people at the open-air cocktail party. At one point, Temple turned and found Captain Twining and Sergeant Kingsley standing right behind him.

"Mr. Temple, how are you?" Twining asked.

"Fine." Temple wasn't sure how to proceed with the two men. Both were in civilian clothes. He knew that they were part of a special drug task force and that their own safety depended upon not being identified with their activities. "How are you?"

"We're doing okay. We just wanted to wish you good luck. It looks like you're going to win." Twining smiled knowingly, and the two men disappeared into the crowd.

Pat returned to her husband's side. "Who were those two men?" she asked.

"I guess you could say they were well-wishers," Temple answered as they made their way over to Cordis.

Later, Temple told Cordis about the two Intelligence Officers appearing. Neither were quite sure why they would be there or why they came over to talk to Temple.

Temple and Cordis then discussed the Rome debate which was scheduled for the following evening. It would be the second of three face–to–face confrontations with Mann.

* * *

October was the month from hell for Laura Ann Mann. She was in a race for political survival. She had known deep down inside that it would be like this, but she had not really understood what it would mean. She had never really envisioned herself in this kind of a political contest. She had always controlled the races that she had run in in the past. Temple had taken that control away. He had dictated the direction of the campaign up until now. She knew that if she were going to win, she had to get control.

Joel Samuels listened to his protégée as she vented her frustrations with the campaign. When she was finished he said, "Laura Ann, I know what you are feeling. This is a lot tougher than I thought it would be. But I have faith in you." He walked over to Mann and placed a hand on her shoulder. "I have faith in your appeal to the voters in this district."

She looked at him and felt reassured. "How are we going to get out in front this last month?"

Samuels turned, walked back to a chair next to a coffee table, and sat down. Mann followed, sitting down opposite her campaign manager.

Samuels pulled some papers out of a briefcase on the table. "This is our strategy down the home stretch. My research indicates that a majority of the voters in this district are satisfied with the state's current law on abortion. You are on the right side of that issue; Temple's waffling. That's your first issue.

"You are best known, according to the polls, for your fight against the old boys and your push for open government. People like that. You need to pump up that idea. That you are the champion for honest, open government. Against the back room deals.

443

"And that leads us to Mr. Temple. You've got to tie him to the good old boys. You do that by accusing him of dirty politics. That's the image the good old boys have, and you need to paint him with it.

"His TV commercials say that you voted 'yes' ninety-seven percent of the time and that your voting record has cost the taxpayer. They go on to talk about the high taxes in New York because of the spending by the state government. There is an inference there, or at least we will draw it, that you voted to increase taxes. You didn't. That's misrepresentation and that's dirty politics."

Mann thought for a moment. "Isn't that a stretch?"

"It's a spin. Some people will think that you did vote to raise their taxes. He's saying that your 'yes' votes cost the taxpayer. You're going to tell them that you voted against the budget. You did. The papers will love it. We need to find Temple's Achilles heel. We've got nothing else, so this is it."

Mann listened to Samuels. She pushed her pro-choice platform everywhere she went. She held a news conference and accused the Senate Majority with trying to get her out of office by financing Temple's campaign. She painted herself as a lone voice fighting the Albany political machine. And she accused Temple of distorting her voting record. "This is the lowest form of dirty politics, and I intend to expose it for what it is," she told the press.

Some of the media people bought into the tack that Mann was taking and reported that the Temple-Mann race was turning into a mudslinging contest. Editorial comments condemned the practice, and attention on the race for the New York Senate heightened.

At a fund raiser for the Onondaga County Executive, reporters cornered Temple and asked him for a response to Mann's charges of distorting her voting record. Temple answered, "Truth is not a distortion. She voted 'yes' on ninety-seven percent of the bills brought before the Senate this past year. She claims to be the maverick. Jousting with the good old

444

boys. In reality she has a better voting record for the majority than some Republicans do.

"These bills cost money. She says she voted against the budget. She did. But the budget simply provides the money to pay for all those 'yes' votes. She voted 'no' on how to pay for the bills, but she voted 'yes' on almost every expenditure."

Temple realized almost at the outset that Mann was trying to put him on the defensive. It was a good tactic. He tried to counter with issue oriented news conferences, but the press was more interested with the dirty politics charge. The coverage ebbed and flowed with the issue throughout the month of October.

Both candidates worked around the clock during the last two weeks of the campaign. They got what sleep they could between two or three in the morning until six or six-thirty and again as they traveled from one campaign stop to the next.

For Temple, it was an effort to try to keep his clothes from looking as though he had slept in them. For Mann, it was a constant battle with her hair. Both quickly found an answer. Temple carried extra changes of clothing in the van and Mann learned to sleep sitting upright.

Chicken barbecues, rib roasts, and Burger King hamburgers became a steady diet as the two politicians criss-crossed the 48th Senate District. Fire departments, schools, shopping centers, grocery stores, church dinners, civic meetings, factory gates, and plain old fashioned door–to–door campaigning filled their every hour.

It amazed Temple that he and Mann never seemed to be in the same place at the same time. Only once did they meet briefly at a fire department raffle and dinner in Tully. They said hello to each other and then went about the business of campaigning.

After the Tully meeting, Anderson and Temple were driving back to Syracuse when Temple turned to his friend and said, "You know something interesting?"

"What?"

"I don't think you ever appreciate what someone else is all about until you walk in their shoes."

"What do you mean?" Anderson was trying to catch up to Temple's thoughts.

"I mean, seeing Laura at that auction today. . .working the crowd, I know what that's like now. I actually admire the way she carries it off."

"Well, you should. That's why she has won all those other elections. But do you want to know something else?"

"Okay, I'll bite. What?" Temple laughed.

"You're as good as she is. Maybe better. I've watched you. You not only do it well, working the crowd, but you look like you're enjoying it. I could never do that. You're a real politician!"

Temple laughed again, "Give me a break."

"No! No! I'm serious. To be successful in politics, really successful, people have got to have a sense that you're for real. One on one, you are one of the best."

Temple smiled at his friend. "Well, that's nice of you to say. I appreciate it."

Anderson laughed. "Good! Now the bad news. That TV commercial of you waving your finger and talking tough is lousy. That's not you, and I don't think it helped you at all."

Temple turned serious. "I agree. It was a mistake. I tried to pull it, but I guess I wasn't demanding enough with my PR people. They let it run its course."

Temple thought about the commercial for a moment longer. "I can't dwell on that now. In this game you have to take your bumps and bruises and move on. Even when they are self-inflicted.

"Friday night I'll be debating Laura in Rome. Right now, I have to focus my attention on that. After the election, you and I can sit down and talk about the pros and cons of what we have done. Right now. . .we just have to keep on doing!"

"Amen." Anderson turned the van into the parking lot of Temple's headquarters. It was late in the afternoon. There

446

were twelve days left before the election. The parking lot was full, so Anderson parked in the lot of the restaurant next door to the campaign office.

* * *

Sergeant Kingsley looked concerned as he entered Captain Twining's office. It was 0800 on twenty-seven October.

"Captain?" Kingsley saluted out of habit even though he was not in uniform.

"Yes, sergeant," Twining replied as he looked into the worried face of his aide.

"Sir, we just got a report indicating that our Mr. Temple is in for some rough going over at the debate tonight."

"What do you mean?" Twining asked as he reached for the papers in Kingsley's hands.

"Seems a couple of the local unions are sending some people over to try and force a confrontation."

Twining scanned the reports. They indicated that Union Local 118 in Rome and 122 in Utica planned to send men to the Temple-Mann debate to cause a disruption and embarrass Jay Temple before the media.

Twining looked up at Kingsley. His thoughts took him back to Vietnam for a brief instant. "Sounds like a job for the 'Lone Ranger and Tonto.'" Both men laughed at the reference to their call signs as Green Berets in Vietnam. "I think we'll plan on attending the meeting in Rome tonight."

The Rome debate was held in the auditorium of City Hall. Noticeably absent was the Mayor of Rome. Politically, he decided not to get cornered into having to declare his support for his fellow Republican or the sitting State Senator for his district.

Temple had long ago concluded that the Mayor was not going to publicly endorse his candidacy. On at least four other occasions the Mayor had had the opportunity to help Temple, and on all four he had skillfully avoided any endorsement. It was too close to the election now for the Mayor to tactfully avoid the

447

obvious question from the press. 'Who do you support for the Senate race?' So he took the only option left — not to show up!

Temple's people were in high gear at this stage of the campaign. Polls predicted a nail-biter, the press called it dead even, and Albany insiders were already talking about who would staff Temple's Senate office.

Temple arrived by van at City Hall with Gardiner, Yondle, Cordis, Tarkings, Price, Fitzgerald, and Pat. They were met at the front door by Allan Gant, Mayor Eiles' assistant, who hastily explained the mayor's absence. Much to the surprise of Temple, however, was the appearance of Jenny Eiles, the Mayor's wife. It quickly became apparent to Temple that Jenny did not share Eiles' appreciation of the current State Senator.

"Mr. Temple, I've been working with the Catallanas and Corey Urban on your campaign to unseat that woman, and I can tell you this: you are going to win here in Rome." She had a very satisfied look on her face as she spoke.

"Jenny, I hope you're right. I know that Corey has been working hard on my campaign since the very first day I came to Rome. With people like you and Corey and the Catallanas out there, I'd like to think that my chances in Rome are pretty good."

"Count on it!" she said with authority.

Gant added, "I think Jenny is right. You'd be surprised at how many people know who you are. That's something none of the past people in this race had going for them."

Temple nodded. "Well, I've spent a lot of time in Rome, and I feel that I know the people here pretty well myself. I like the people here. They are good, hard working people who have really made me feel that this is my second home. I'm looking forward to helping Rome when I get to the Senate."

Temple and his entourage went up the stairs to the auditorium. It was already full of people, and there were still twenty minutes more before the debates were scheduled to begin.

Temple immediately saw Mann and Johns talking to a group of men directly in front of the stage. He could tell by what he saw that these people were her supporters.

Mary Catallana came over to Temple. "Hi, Jay."

"Hello, Mary."

"I've been doing a little spying for you." She looked at him with a hint of mystery in her eyes. "See those men Mann is talking to?"

"Yes."

"They are from the local steel union. They're being given questions to ask you during the debate."

Cordis leaned over to Temple. "We can put some good questions together to ask Mann if you want us to."

Temple looked at his two campaign workers. "No. I'd rather let things develop naturally. I'm not worried about questions from the floor. I'll just give them the best answer I can and let the chips fall where they may."

Cordis would rather have had Temple go for Mann's throat, but he admired Temple's attitude. "We ought to fight fire with fire."

Temple looked at Cordis. "I'd rather fight a fire with water!"

Laney Gardiner had been standing behind Temple listening to the conversation. "I like it," she said.

Temple turned and smiled. "Thanks."

Temple used his twenty minutes before the debate to shake hands and say hello to the one hundred and seventy some people in the room. He made it a particular point of shaking hands with each of the men who had been talking to Mann when he arrived. It was his way of relaxing.

Madeline Reynolds was the hostess and moderator for the debates. In addition to all of her other accomplishments, Madeline was the President of the Rome League of Women Voters, the sponsor of the evening's debates.

The candidates were asked to take their seats. Laura Ann Mann and Tess Arnold, a Democratic candidate for the Assembly, sat to the left of Madeline Reynolds. Temple and the Republican candidate for the Assembly, Dave Towns, sat to the

449

right.

As the talking subsided, Madeline rose to her feet with microphone in hand. "We'd like to welcome all of you to tonight's debate sponsored by the Rome League of Women Voters. We are happy to have both the candidates for the New York State Senate and for the Assembly with us this evening."

She then introduced the candidates giving a brief biography of each as provided by them.

The format was simple. An opening statement followed by questions from the audience addressed to a candidate with any other candidate being allowed the opportunity to respond as well. All candidates had agreed ahead of time to stay until every question had been answered.

Madeline Reynolds explained all this and then turned to the openings as selected by a random drawing of names. Temple had been selected to go first.

Temple stood and thanked Madeline Reynolds and the League for the invitation to speak to the people of Rome in the closing days of the election.

Local radio stations carried the debate live and reporters from the Dispatch, the Madison Daily, and the Utica Observer took notes for the next day's edition of their respective papers.

"This has been a busy ten months for my staff, my friends and my family as we have traveled back and forth across the 48th Senate District.

"Personally, I have met so many great people and have had such a warm reception by everyone that I will be sorry to see this campaign come to an end. There are probably not a lot of politicians who would say that!" Temple laughed along with his audience.

He continued, "I'm sure Laura, Tess, and Dave all know something about what I am saying. There are experiences that you have as a candidate that you no doubt will remember the rest of your life. It's the farmer whose door you knock on at eight in the morning and he invites you in for breakfast with the family; it's the little child who looks up at you during a parade and says 'thank-you' for a piece of candy; it's the single mother working two jobs to feed and house her children, or the steel worker who has lost his job because the plant has shut down.

"There are a million faces out there, each with a different story. And when you run for office, they share their stories with you. More openly than they would if you were just a stranger, more openly sometimes than if you were a family member or a friend. You see, they want you to help them and that's why I'm running for the Senate. I want to help these people and all the ones I haven't met.

"I suspect that is why Laura, Tess, and Dave are running too. I think most politicians, at least, start off running for all the right reasons. They want to help. I also think that somewhere along the way something happens that changes elected officials. I don't know if they lose touch with their times, the people, or the issues. But something happens and they no longer are traveling down the same road that led them to be elected in the first place. At that point, it's time for a change.

"You, as voters, are the ones who determine when that point is reached. Each of us can only offer you the best we have. We tell you how we would handle issues. We tell you what is important to us and what isn't. We offer our solutions. But you must decide.

"I think that my experience both before I got into this race and also, since I have been campaigning and meeting the people of this district, offers an opportunity to vote for a change in direction.

"I look forward to answering your questions this evening and thank you for being here."

Laura Ann Mann was the next to speak.

"I have represented you in Albany for the last six years. I have spoken out on the issue of abortion; I'm for free choice. I have spoken out on the issue of open government, the midnight sessions, the back room deals, and public hearings on bills that effect you.

"I have brought money to Rome. This past year, I

provided state funds for the school library, a new fire truck, and an addition to the museum. I have met with representatives of Rome Labs and have written to the federal agencies involved with the Rome air base.

"I know your problems and your concerns, and I believe that you have had good representation in Albany. I am hopeful that you agree with me, and that you will continue to support me as you have done in the past.

"Mr. Temple talks about politicians losing touch with their constituents. If this is a reference to me, I resent it. I work hard at staying in touch with the people in my district. If he is talking about the wealthy businessmen and industrialists who are supporting his campaign, then he's probably right. I haven't been bought off by them, and they probably aren't very happy with my steadfast support of labor. But I believe that everyone is entitled to work. I will continue to support labor as I have in the past, and I will continue to push for jobs here in Rome."

Temple thought to himself, 'She sure can put a spin on any statement that she wants to.'

As Tess Arnold was giving her opening, Temple saw Twining and Kingsley slip into the back of the auditorium. He wondered what the drug task force was doing in Rome and appearing here tonight.

Arnold and Towns each reiterated the biographical sketches that Madeline Reynolds had outlined in her introduction. Arnold dealt at length with her experience on the school board and Towns, likewise, went into great detail about his work as a state policeman and as a member of the police commission for the City of Rome. Both felt that they had the experience to represent Rome in the New York State Assembly.

Reynolds then opened the meeting for questions from the floor. One of the four union men in the front row stood up immediately to ask Temple a question.

"Mr. Temple. A lot of people in Rome used to work for Corning or for the steel mills. Management of those businesses decided to pull out and leave a lot of us unemployed. How do you feel about that?" The man continued to stand, folding his arms across his chest, as he waited for the answer.

Temple stood up and looked directly at the man with the folded arms. Their eyes locked in a stare that dared the other to look away. Temple answered, "Corning and the steel mills of Rome are not the only manufacturers who have left this state.

"In the last eight years, 230,000 manufacturing jobs have left New York State! Where have they gone? South. Why? Because of taxes. Cuomo is proposing a twenty percent tax increase for business this coming year. For every one hundred dollars paid this year, next year we'll pay one hundred and twenty dollars. Business can't afford this state.

"I talked with one of the manufacturers still here in Rome. He told me that his business is struggling. The out–of–state competition is fierce because of cheaper labor and a lot lower taxes. His business is a fourth generation company here in Rome. A lot of his people are third and fourth generation workers at his plant. He feels he owes those people and their families something. Something for the loyalty they have shown over the years. But he may not be able to compete if state government continues to raise his business tax by twenty percent a year.

"Think of it in terms of your own income. If I were to take twenty percent more in taxes out of your paycheck every year, how long could you last? Just because it's a business and not an individual doesn't make the end result any different.

"I think New York State should encourage business to stay in New York. I think we should be looking for ways to bring new businesses into New York. It's become obvious to me that those in government today have no clue as to how to go about doing that. If they did, you wouldn't be asking that very good question of me tonight."

Mann moved to the microphone in front of her seat. "I'd like to say something about this man's question. There is a bill that has been moving through the Assembly and that I have cosponsored in the Senate that would prohibit any manufacturer from leaving the state without first giving the state five years advance notice. This would allow the state to work with the manufacturer over a reasonable period of time to try and save it as a going concern in New York.

"The Republicans in the Senate have blocked any progress on this bill." She sat back and smiled at Temple.

Temple was still standing. The man with folded arms had sat down. Temple answered the statement by Mann. "It sure would make me anxious to come to New York if I were an outside business, and I knew that once I got to New York I couldn't leave for five years!"

There was some laughter in the audience. Temple continued, "This is just the kind of thinking that encourages business and industry to leave. That kind of bill doesn't address the real problems, which are taxes and state spending. Somewhere in that bill there is probably a new commission or agency waiting to be formed to administer the bill. The result; more spending, more taxes, and more regulation.

"I've been there. I know. If we move as a government to support industry, we will save jobs. If we create a business climate that is positive, we will bring new business to the state. We need people in Albany who will do that."

Another one of the "front row four," as Cordis would later dub them, stood up to ask a question. "Mr. Temple. You are always talking about business and taxes. But what about people? If the state makes all these cuts you talk about, it's the people who will suffer. I have a seventy-two–year old mother who is dying from cancer and has no money. What do I tell her about you?"

Temple again stood up and looked the man directly in the eye. Only this time it wasn't a look of challenge, it was one of sympathy and compassion. "Tell her that I'm very sorry.

"One of the things we do as a family is set priorities in how we spend our money. Obviously, health care is at the top of our lists. It should also be at the top of our government's list.

454

"Being involved in the insurance industry, I am familiar with a new idea which I think has merit and which I would be willing to put into legislation if elected. It's called living benefits. Essentially, living benefits means that if I have a fifty thousand dollar life insurance policy, for example, and I have a doctor's determination that I am going to die, I can get the proceeds of the policy during my last illness to use as I see fit. I don't have to be dead before the life insurance is paid.

"This would free up a substantial amount of money for the care of those who are in the most need.

"The other idea whose time has come is that of managed care. Medical costs are rising so fast that we need a way to contain those costs. I believe that managed care is the wave of the future."

A third member of the 'front row four' stood up. "Mr. Temple. The newspapers say that if you get elected you will take your marching orders from the Republican big shots in Albany. Will you or will you turn on your own party?" He smiled and sat down.

Temple stood again. This time he didn't even look at the man who had asked the question. He looked out at the audience. "The article that he is talking about appeared in the Syracuse Gazette. 'It was not true, and I have told the Editor that it was not true.

"People who know me well would laugh at the idea that anyone would dictate how I would vote on a given issue. If elected, it will be because you have faith in my judgment. I will never do anything that will dishonor that trust."

Temple sat down. There was a quietness that settled over the room. Then someone in the back applauded and instantly everyone else in the room joined in.

The debate went on for about two hours before Madeline Reynolds thanked everyone and closed the meeting.

The candidates were surrounded by the usual well-wishers as they made their way out of the auditorium.

As Temple reached the outside door, he saw the 'front

row four' waiting outside the door. "Our friends," he said to Cordis as he motioned in their direction.

"Maybe we better wait for the others to catch up with us," Cordis suggested.

"If we did, they'd know it. Come on." Temple walked through the door and headed right toward the four men.

One of them stepped forward and directly in front of Temple. "Mr. Temple." He hesitated. "You're okay. We came here tonight to rattle your cage, but you're okay." The others nodded their agreement.

Temple smiled. "I knew what you were doing. I saw you with Laura before we started. You took your best shots and so did I. Actually, they were pretty good questions." Temple laughed and they joined in. Another added, "I work for the Senator on her campaign here in Rome. No hard feelings?" He stuck out his hand.

Temple shook the man's hand and said, "No hard feelings."

As he and Cordis turned toward the parking lot, he saw Captain Twining and Sergeant Kingsley leaning on the hood of a truck. Both were watching Temple and the group.

Twining smiled and waved as he and Kingsley turned and climbed into the truck.

Cordis said, "Weren't those the two guys from the armory?"

Temple watched the truck pull away from the curb. "Guardian angels!"

As Kingsley turned the truck down the road leading to the Air Base, he said to the Captain sitting in the passenger seat, "I like that guy."

Twining looked over at Kingsley as if he had read his mind. "I was just thinking the same thing."

Kingsley went on as they passed through the gate. "The way he walked right over to those guys. Hell, they could've punched him out as easily as not."

"Yeah," Twining agreed. "But they didn't. He handled

them well inside. I'd like to find out if any of those boys vote for him on Election Day."

"You sorry that we didn't get to mix it up?"

"No. Maybe. No, I guess it worked out for the best. It wouldn't have been too good for Temple if things had gone bad."

"Wonder how he'd be in a fight?"

"I think he'd be okay."

"Between tonight and that incident with the kid, he sure as hell doesn't look the other way!" Kingsley pulled into a parking spot marked, 'D.O.D.I.U.'

The men climbed out of the truck and walked away. The night was quiet and all was right with the world.

Chapter XXXI

November: Victory And Defeat

On November first, the two candidates met for the last time before the election. A debate sponsored by the New York State Teachers Union had been set up at the Ramada Inn in Utica. A panel of three, one union member, one school board member, and one administrator had been designated to ask questions of each of the candidates.

To Temple's surprise, the Ramada had a series of rooms that had been blocked out for, not only his debate with Mann, but also for debates on education issues between candidates in ten other contests. Each group had been assigned a different room, all small, with a capacity of twenty to thirty people per room. Union members and other interested parties could walk from room to room listening to those debates in which they were interested.

It wasn't what he had expected. He thought that there would be a larger audience and that the debate would be more open. He wondered what Laura's expectations were of this meeting.

Temple, Cordis, Tarkings, and Fitzgerald had made the trip together to Utica. They were directed by one of the union members to room 110. Laura Mann and Tork Johns were already there and seated in the front row of chairs facing three individuals at the front of the room. Two were men and one was a woman.

Temple was introduced to the three people who turned out to be the panel for the evening's debate. He was then asked to take a seat in the front row next to Laura Mann. He thought to himself, 'this is a very polite gathering.'

Mann and Temple exchanged quick hello's and the questioning by the panel began. Mann cited specific statutes and regulations in response to questions concerning union activities and what role the government should play in policing union action.

Temple was impressed. He didn't have code sections to rely on but did have an opinion on the general topic.

"Senator Mann has given you the citations; I cannot. But I think that it's important for you to know where I am coming from on educational issues.

"I do not believe that public employees should have the right to strike. I feel especially strongly about this where the teaching profession is concerned.

"A teachers' strike sends thousands of children home from school. The time that they miss in the classroom can never be replaced. The educational opportunities can never be fully replaced.

"Add to this the fact that now you are also causing a disruption in the family routine which places tremendous hardships on some families, and you have a situation which I do not believe should be tolerated.

"When I was a school board member, roughly one quarter of our district was comprised of single parent families. These parents had to not only meet the demands of their families in the home, but also had to maintain a job to support their families as well. These parents count on the school day to give them the time to work.

"My views may not be popular here but that's where I am coming from and you should understand that. Our most important asset in this state are our children. As teachers you have a tremendous responsibility. You play a key role in the development of every child whose life you touch. That role should be given the respect that it deserves, but it also requires a certain amount of sacrifice on your part. The inability to strike

459

is, in my mind, one of the sacrifices."

Temple's comments didn't win a lot of votes among those in the room. Cordis would later comment that there weren't enough people in the room to worry about it. But Temple believed that he had been straightforward with everyone throughout the campaign, and he wasn't going to hedge on the issues now.

Temple also had a chance to watch Laura Mann up close as she answered questions. She looked tired. Her answers were not as crisp as they had been at the outset of the campaign and she was not as combative as he had seen her on other occasions. An hour after they had begun, the debate was over. Mann actually seemed relieved to be able to leave the room even though Temple had thought her answers were what the limited audience was looking for.

Temple's last glimpse of Mann came outside the Ramada Inn. As his van with its small band of campaign workers pulled out of the Inn's parking lot, Mann was standing alone at the curb waiting for Tork Johns to bring the car around. She looked really tired and alone.

Cordis commented, "She looks beat, and she is."

Temple looked at Mann for the last time during the campaign and said, "I feel sorry for her."

No one in the van could believe that Temple had said that. To them, she was the enemy. The fight was still on and no quarter should be given. But to Temple, Mann was a politician who was giving her best to a tough campaign. Whether he won or lost, she was a worthy opponent who did what she believed in. She was no different than he was when it came to that. Their approaches and beliefs might be different, but he could still respect her effort and her desire to win. She did look beaten as she stood there alone. It was a very sad sight for Temple.

* * *

Friday, November second was another big day for the Temple campaign. The results of a district wide poll of thirty-five hundred voters, randomly selected, showed Temple leading for the first time. Forty-nine percent of those polled said they would vote for Temple, forty-eight percent said they would vote for Mann, and only three percent were undecided. The polling agency said that this was a very rare result, having that definitive a picture of the outcome of a race less than a week from Election Day. They also pointed out a margin of error of three to five percent.

The poll heightened the sense of victory and excitement among Temple's volunteers.

Arnold Ophidia met Senator Valli at the Desmond for breakfast. Both had seen the poll results.

"I still can't believe it! We're finally going to be rid of that bitch!"

"Hey! You can't believe it? I can't believe it. I didn't think that the boy scout would ever take her. The great thing about this is the mail drop today. When those postcards hit Rome, we'll add a few points to the difference and lock the election."

"Well, now we've got to start planning where to place Mr. Temple and with whom we'll staff his office."

"Do yourself a favor. Put someone on him that knows the ropes. He's got some strange ideas that need to be curbed quickly."

"We'll handle it. He owes us. Hell, we sank a bundle into his campaign."

"Just commenting. The guy needs watching."

"Whatever happens, just not having Mann running around like a loose cannon will be worth it. I really didn't think anybody could beat her."

"Hey, I blanketed that damn district with paper these last two weeks. Every damn dog in the three counties gotta know Temple's name by now!"

"Yeah. But dogs don't vote."

461

* * *

Mann called her office staff into a meeting at seven-thirty on Friday morning. She looked tired and drawn. Annie Wilson was concerned.

"Laura Ann, are you all right?"

"Just tired, Annie."

"Can I get you some coffee?"

"That would be nice," Mann exhaled.

Wilson left the room as the others were filing in. She returned with the coffee in time to pick up the conversation that Mann was having with the others in the room.

"This has been a long, tough campaign. I have been told that the Republicans have just gotten the results of a poll done on Tuesday and that my opponent has a one percent lead at this point."

There were looks of concern exchanged between those in the room. Someone said, "That's impossible!"

Mann smiled. "I hope so. But I've always been honest with you, and I want you to begin thinking about what you may want to do if things don't go well on Tuesday."

Wilson said, "That's a Republican poll."

Mann looked at her long time associate. "I know how they do these things. It's pretty accurate. Three or four percent error rate either way. The point is that this is going to be close. I don't want this conversation to leave this room, but I also don't want you waking up Wednesday morning to something that is a total surprise."

They all offered positive words of encouragement as they left her office. Only Tork Johns stayed behind. "Was that smart?"

Mann looked at Johns. "Probably not, but I had to do it. Imagine waking up, turning on the radio, and finding out that you didn't have a job?"

Johns looked at his boss. She really looked tired. "It's not over yet. I don't believe that you will lose. You're the best thing that ever happened to politics. You are a product of the people and the times. Temple can't beat that with all the money in the world."

She laughed as she walked over and put her arm through his. "Tork, you are worth every dollar you don't get paid."

That afternoon Joel Samuels interrupted Mann's campaign schedule. "Meet me right away at your office in Syracuse."

"What is it?" she said, half in panic, over the pay phone.

"He's done it. He's self-destructed!"

"Who?" she wasn't following the conversation.

"Temple. I told you that he'd do something that would blow the race. Well, he just did."

Her heart pounded so fast that her ears were ringing. "What did he do?" she shouted into the speaker.

"A postcard in Rome about you. No identification about who sent it. Actually, it came out of Albany. But it'll sink his ship as surely as if he'd mailed it from his home. Now get down here so we can win this race."

Mann practically jumped into the air. "I'm on my way!"

It was three-thirty in the afternoon by the time Mann got back to her office. Samuels was waiting with Rick Mellton, a public relations professional.

"Tell me what's happening," Mann said as she hurried into her office.

"This!" Samuels said as he handed her a postcard.

The front of the postcard displayed a not very complimentary picture of Mann and a caption that read, 'Rome is not important to me, it's only sixteen percent of my district.' The reverse side read, 'Jay Temple cares about Rome. Vote for Temple for the New York State Senate.' The only other notation was a post office box number in Syracuse.

As Mann studied the postcard, Samuels explained its significance.

"This is a clear violation of the Election Law. Any political advertisements must identify who the sponsor is and, if printed, it must contain the address of the sender."

"I can't believe this! Who got this thing?" Mann was clearly angry.

"As far as we know, everyone in Rome," Samuels answered.

"Geez. We have to get something out to counter this!"

Samuels smiled. He was ever in control. "Rick has worked out a little scenario for you. You are scheduled for the eleven o'clock news on Channels 4 and 7."

Mellton handed Mann a script. "This will put Temple on the run. We'll also get a couple of the League people on the news so that it's not all coming from you. You'll show your indignation at this latest dirty trick by the Republicans and then let others carry on the battle." Mellton could see the whole thing in his mind. "The media will have a field day with this. Temple will have nowhere to go."

Samuels joined Mellton in his assessment. "He's finished. The press is hungry for this kind of news. They'll all be on him. At that point you take the high road. You're hurt, but they've gone after you like this before. Your job is to represent the people of Central New York. Despite the dirty politics, you are going to go back to Albany and fight for clean government. That's your line from now until Election Day."

Channels 4 and 7 broadcast their interviews with Senator Mann on their eleven o'clock news programs.

Samuels watched with admiration. Mann gave a great performance. Indignant, strong in the face of adversity, yet somehow vulnerable. He knew she had the race won.

One of the quirks of fate in this campaign was that none of the Temple people saw or heard about Mann's interview until Saturday morning.

As Saturday, November third, dawned, Temple was up early and getting ready to go to the big rally in Manlius for his volunteers from the three counties. Over three hundred people were expected to help out with his newspaper door–to–door campaign.

464

To offset the one-sided coverage he had experienced, he and his staff had put together their own newspaper on the stories and issues that they felt were important. It looked and read like a weekly newspaper, but it was clearly a political paper. In bold print across the banner, it proclaimed 'Temple For New York State Senate.'

This was to be his climactic communication to the voters. It represented everything that he stood for and was about. Pictures of family, friends, and businesses filled its pages with accompanying stories. It was different than most political pieces because of the format. Temple liked it. He hoped that they could get the twenty-five thousand pieces out before Election Day. Rallies similar to the one in Manlius were scheduled in Rome and Syracuse. It was now or never. Tuesday was the final day, and there would be no more opportunities after Monday.

Temple believed that with the paper, he had done all that he could have to run a good campaign.

At eight o'clock, he received a call from Cordis.

"Jay, this is Ted Cordis. We have a problem."

"What kind of a problem?" Temple asked with concern.

"Sally Notholm is here at headquarters. She wants a response from you on Mann's charge that you are guilty of dirty politics. Remember that postcard that the NYSSRC was talking about sending? The one on Mann's statement about Rome?"

"Refresh my memory." Temple was trying to place the conversation on a postcard.

"Berry and Ophidia had gotten some feedback from Mayor Eiles and Frank Catallana that Mann had said Rome didn't matter to her because it was only sixteen percent of her district."

Temple suddenly remembered the conversation. "Didn't we say 'no' to that? I thought I told them that that was between them, Eiles and Mann."

"You did, but they didn't. They sent the postcard out of Albany. They didn't indicate who sent the card. They did put our P.O. Box on it. You know what that means?"

Temple knew only too well. He knew the rules, and he knew that this was a big mistake. "I'll be right there."

Cordis warned, "You should know that the TV stations interviewed Mann on the news yesterday, and she's denying ever having said that bit about Rome."

Temple couldn't believe this. "I want you to call Eiles and Catallana and get them to be available to verify their statements."

"You got it." Cordis hung up the phone. He saw Notholm sitting on the sofa in the entry. He had an empty feeling in the pit of his stomach. He knew this wasn't good.

By the time Temple arrived at his campaign headquarters, more of the press had also arrived.

As he walked through the door, he was approached by fifteen to twenty people with cameras, microphones, and note pads. He held up his hands as they all began to talk at once.

Temple said, "Please give me a chance to make a statement, and then I will answer your questions."

Cordis came over and handed Temple a postcard that had been given to him by Notholm. Cordis looked at Temple but said nothing. Temple saw the forlorn look in his campaign manager's eyes.

As Temple looked down at the card, he realized the quandary that he was in. If he admitted that the NYSSRC mailed it, it would raise the question of who was controlling this race and ultimately who would control him if he was elected. If he indicated that his people sent this, he was guilty of a campaign law violation. He looked up at the quietly waiting press and made his decision.

Temple walked over to a desk and sat down on its edge. "This postcard was sent by my campaign. I see that it does not have the proper identification on it. We made a mistake, and I apologize. What questions do you have?"

Notholm was the first to ask the question that everyone wanted to know. "Senator Mann says that you lied. She says

466

that she never said that she didn't care about Rome because it represented only sixteen percent of her district. How do you respond?"

Temple shifted uneasily. This wasn't his battle, yet he was stuck with it. "Mayor Eiles and Commissioner Catallana both indicated that the Senator did say that. No part of this Senate District is too small not to be represented. They were understandably upset with the Senator as would be a lot of other small communities that make up this District. I suggest you contact them to verify the statement."

The rest of the questions were variations of the same theme. All agreed that Eiles and Catallana were next on the interview list.

Temple left his headquarters for the Manlius rally with the understanding that Cordis would contact Eiles and Catallana. Cordis was to alert them that they could expect a call from the press to verify their statements about Mann's comments on Rome.

* * *

The rally in Manlius was a huge success. More people than expected turned out for this last major push by Temple to reach out to the voters.

Temple's spirits rose as he said hello to everyone and caught the positive excitement everyone had for the campaign. Congressman Wales was there to lend his support and to introduce Temple.

"It's my pleasure as your Congressman to introduce to you, your next State Senator, Jay Temple!"

Temple shook hands with Wales and thanked him for coming. "This is a great crowd, and I appreciate the fact that every one of you came today to help me out in the final stages of the campaign.

"You have all worked hard for me." He paused. "It's hard to find the words to express how much you all mean to me.

467

All I can say is thank-you. Thank you very much for being here and for all that you have done."

The crowd of partisans cheered their candidate. Bob Anderson then explained the details of what was to happen, and maps were distributed to everyone. The maps showed the area of distribution each volunteer would be responsible for. Cars and trucks began streaming out of the town hall parking lot. The final drive for victory was underway.

Cordis had tried unsuccessfully to reach Mayor Eiles. He did talk with Frank Cattallana and Frank told him that it would be no problem.

The interviewing did take place, but only with Catallana. Eiles was out of town for the weekend and not available for comment. Catallana indicated to the press that he and Eiles had met with Mann to discuss her lack of support for Rome Hospital. He then stated, "She may not have said those exact words, but that's what we thought she was getting at."

Notholm, followed by every other reporter covering the Rome postcard, jumped on Catallana's statement. That evening on the six o'clock news, Notholm said, "The Temple campaign committee sent an unmarked postcard to every voter in Rome. The postcard indicated that Senator Mann did not care about Rome. Mann denied this allegation calling it a lie and the dirtiest trick yet in a mudslinging campaign for the New York State Senate.

"Jay Temple, when interviewed, admitted that the postcard was sent by his committee. He stated that the comment was made by Mann to Commissioner Catallana in Rome. This reporter contacted the Commissioner and he said, 'She may not have said those exact words, but that's what we thought she was getting at.'

"It's too bad when political campaigns have to sink to the level of distortion and character assassination that this race has reached.

"Campaign law requires honest advertisements and a statement by the political committee doing the advertisement

468

identifying the committee and giving their address. This postcard misses the mark on both requirements."

The TV camera focused on the post card then cut away to Notholm. "The people of the 48th Senate District will decide the outcome of this race on Election Day, this coming Tuesday."

Temple watched the television broadcast of the news at his headquarters along with Gardiner, Roth, Yondle, and Cordis. Fitzgerald, Price, and Tarkings joined them. Channel 4 was the worst coverage, but it was evident that all of the networks were critical of the Rome postcard fiasco.

Cordis looked at Temple. "I can't believe Catallana just didn't say that that's what she said."

Temple shared Cordis' disbelief but offered, "Well, he's probably not used to giving interviews and being put on the spot like that."

"Yeah, but he's the one who told Albany what she said," Cordis shot back.

"It was a bad idea to begin with. I didn't like it, and I should have just said 'no' to the whole thing. I shouldn't have let Albany get involved."

Cordis could see that Temple was taking this very personally. "Hey, you were busy then. You said 'no' to our doing it, and you told them that if they did it, that was between them and the Rome people. They're the ones that screwed this up. They had no right putting our P.O. Box number on that postcard."

Temple smiled at his campaign manager. "I should have stopped it."

Cordis looked down at the floor. "No. You're wrong. I should have stopped it. I'm the campaign manager."

Temple knew that the timing and content of the postcard fiasco would impact the election. He hoped that the audience for all of this was limited, but with the extra coverage being given the postcard to Rome, the chances of a limited effect were not great.

Temple also knew that this was not the time to give up

the effort. Sunday morning he attended church and accepted all the good wishes from his friends and acquaintances. Then he hit the campaign trail again.

His first stop was a church chicken and biscuit dinner in LaFayette. Thankfully, no one mentioned the Rome letter. Many of those present recognized him and wished him well in the election.

From Lafayette, he and Pat drove to Cicero for a fire department rib roast. Several politicians were already there when they arrived.

Howard White, a Republican Assemblyman, immediately walked up to Temple. "Hi, Jay, Pat. They sure took you over the coals on that postcard." White looked right at Temple as he talked. "I'll bet you Laura Ann said just what you printed and is now trying to get out of it. It sounded like something she would say."

Temple looked at White. He had known him for a long time and knew that he was trying to be positive. Somehow, it wasn't working.

Temple said, "The postcard was a mistake. It should never have been sent. But with two days left to campaign, I'm not going to let that take away from all the other things that we need to do. Whether she said it or not at this point is irrelevant."

White looked confused. Finally he said, "Well, I'm with you all the way!" With his head tilted slightly downward, he gave Temple two thumbs up signs.

Temple chuckled to himself at White's Nixonian antics. He clapped him on the back and said, "Thanks" as he moved on through the crowd. The Temples spent about twenty minutes working the crowd and then headed for the parking lot.

Back in the van, Pat asked her husband, "Is it worth all of this? The press coverage, the glad handing, the politicians?"

Temple looked at his wife. She really didn't enjoy politics. He knew that deep down inside he really did enjoy the political game. Even the tough time he was having now. It was

470

all part of the process. If you got through it and learned something from it, you'd be better the next time. If not, at least you stepped up to the plate. That's more than most do. Politicians, Democrats and Republicans, do step up to the plate.

He recalled a line that he'd heard somewhere and answered Pat. "It's better to have tried and lost than never to have tried at all. If given the same choice, to run or not, I'd still choose to run. This state does need to change direction, and I really think that I can do some good."

Pat looked at her husband. She worried about how he would take losing if it came to that on Tuesday. She said, "What if you don't win?"

The question hung out there in the air for a few moments. Finally, Temple answered. "I haven't given it much thought. I guess I go back to doing the things I've been doing and spend the rest of my life thanking all those people who did so much for me over the last ten months."

"No regrets?" she asked.

"No. It's really been a great experience. The people I've met. I never really appreciated how giving people are in Central New York. Hasn't it amazed you that people we have never known go out of their way to help or even just to say hello?"

"I guess that you've seen more of that than I have."

"Think about the Polish Hall dinner we went to a few weeks ago. I've never done the polka in my life, but we had a great time with people we had never met before."

Pat laughed recalling her husband stumbling around the floor at the Polish Hall. "Yeah! You had fun! I'm not sure everyone else did," she chided. "They thought you were a good sport but that you didn't have much rhythm!"

They both laughed. As they drove to their next stop, each of them thought of other things that had happened throughout the campaign. Both concluded that there were a lot of bright spots to remember.

* * *

Monday, November fifth, was a cold, clear day. It was also the get–out–the–vote day. Volunteers for all campaigns, including Mann's and Temple's, spent the day going door–to–door, phoning supporters, reminding them to vote, and generally getting ready for the celebrations expected on Tuesday, Election Day.

Temple's headquarters overflowed with people. Channels 4 and 7 were running television cables across the floor for live broadcasts on Election Day. Reporters from the newspapers, radio, and television stations were shuffling in and out of the campaign headquarters all day looking for personal interest stories and projections on the outcome. Campaign workers were calling for more volunteers and inviting supporters to attend the Election Eve celebration.

Amidst all of this, Temple was making his own calls to people who had given him help since the beginning of the campaign. He thanked them for their financial support, for placing yard signs, for sponsoring and working on mail drops, for their advice, for their time, and for their involvement.

About twelve o'clock on Monday afternoon, Temple took a break to go out for lunch with Kevin Roth, Dave Yondle and Bob Anderson. On the way out, Steve Adamson of Channel 4 asked Temple, "What do you think about Callahan's prediction?"

Temple hadn't heard about Callahan's prediction. He knew that Callahan worked as a pollster and was a professor in the Political Science Department at Syracuse University. "What prediction is that?" Temple asked.

Adamson smiled. "He's predicting that you win in a close race."

Temple was surprised. "I hope he's right!"

Yondle congratulated Temple. Roth shared Temple's thought about hoping that Callahan was right. Anderson said with tongue in cheek, "Was there ever any doubt?"

Temple looked at his old friend. "Then or now?" they

472

both laughed.

The luncheon conversation was lively thanks to Adamson's comments.

As he was sitting down at the table, Anderson said, "They wouldn't be here setting up all those cables if this wasn't going to be a close race. They like the excitement as much as any of us."

Roth added, "Wouldn't that be something? Beating Laura Ann Mann."

Temple looked at Roth as he pulled a chair out to sit down. "You sound like you were expecting a different outcome?" He said it with mock indignation.

Roth didn't catch Temple's tone. He quickly responded, "I thought you could do it. But a lot of people out there thought that you were jousting with windmills."

"You're kidding!" Temple said again with mock surprise. "I can't imagine anyone thinking that I was wasting my time."

Roth caught on, and they all laughed.

Temple interjected a serious note. "Whatever happens tomorrow, I want to thank you all for what you have done. I have to be very thankful for all the help I've gotten in this race. It's still mind-boggling to me the way you and a lot of other people have responded." He paused to share with each a look full of the feeling of deep appreciation and friendship which had developed between them during the campaign.

Temple then turned to another subject as their lunch was being served. "I often wonder how effective all of our traveling was, as well as our door-to-door campaigning. We probably saw or met only about ten percent of all the people who are going to vote tomorrow."

"That's a fair number of people," Anderson answered. "Then you figure that each of them goes out and tells ten of their friends about you and suddenly you've covered the entire district!"

Roth laughed, "I like your math!"

Yondle asked, "Does that work with contributions? If

you get ten percent to contribute, can you expect that they will go out and get ten of their friends to contribute? Does that mean that one hundred percent of the district will contribute?"

"I think we'd better eat our lunch," Anderson said as he picked up his fork. "It was just a thought."

Roth added one more thought for the group. "Your name recognition in the district went from zero to over ninety percent in less than six months. I'd say all of your hard work paid off."

Yondle added, "Think of what we could have done if we'd had a couple of years to plan and get ready for this race. Wow! That would have been something."

Temple appreciated their input. "This has been a case of our hard work.

"Yeah, I guess more time would've helped, but I'll bet every candidate has said that, no matter how much time he or she has had. Frankly, I've done just about everything that I wanted to do in this campaign. I could've done some things sooner with a little more time and a little more money up front, but all in all we did get it done. Thanks to you."

Anderson asked, "No regrets?"

Temple thought for a moment. "Not about running. I like campaigning, debating, meeting different people. A couple of things though. The TV commercial with me waving my finger at the camera, that wasn't me. I knew it, and I should've canned it. The other thing is the Rome postcard. Beyond those two, I can't say that there's anything else that comes to mind. Maybe not doing the billboards. I still think that that's a good way to get people thinking about your name."

Roth looked up at Temple. "It's hard to argue with the name recognition result. You did something right."

"Yes, I guess so. Hey! Maybe with billboards, I'd have hit a hundred."

Roth laughed, "You're a greedy politician!"

Anderson shrugged his shoulders. "Take what you can get. If you can top out on the name recognition polls, do it.

Next time, we'll do the billboard thing too."

They finished their lunch and went back to work on the campaign.

Temple and his family went to a huge Republican campaign rally at Long Branch Park that evening. Every candidate, their families, and friends turned out for the event. It was estimated that over fifteen hundred people were on hand to hear Arthur Gaines introduce the candidates.

Banners, pamphlets, buttons, and bands were the order of the evening. The news media was also there in force. Everyone was interviewed by someone during the two hour production that culminated with a short fireworks display. Now the long wait would begin.

Chapter XXXII

Unsung Heroes. . .
And Villains

The unsung heroes of any campaign are always the family members of the candidates. They suffer through the grueling campaign schedule, the long absences, and the publicity (good and bad), and the public scrutiny of their own lives, even though they are not the ones running for public office.

Temple along with Pat, and Tyler, went to their polling place early Tuesday morning.

It was located in the local fire department station house. The same five women had been poll watchers for over twenty-three years. They knew everyone of the nine hundred and eighty-three voters who voted each year, and they enjoyed their contribution to democracy.

As Temple walked through the doors of the fire station, he suddenly realized that this particular year, things were different. There was a blaze of lights, coupled with several flashes of light from cameras close by.

Terry Davis of Channel 7 News held up a microphone to Temple. "Good morning, Mr. Temple." She smiled.

Temple blinked under the glare of the lights. He smiled back. "Good morning, Terry. How are you?"

"I'm fine, Mr. Temple. What we all want to know is, how are you?"

"Great!" he again smiled. Tyler reached for his father's hand. Temple smiled down at his young son. "Neither of us are used to this much attention this early in the morning." Temple laughed.

476

Tyler looked from his dad to the reporter. "Hello," he volunteered.

Davis smiled. "Another politician in the making. Is this the beginning of a dynasty?"

Temple answered without hesitation, "Depends upon today."

Sally Notholm worked her way up to Temple. "Who are you going to vote for today?"

Temple looked at her and answered, "Which race?" He laughed; she didn't.

Zig Clayton of the Madison Daily asked, "Is your son going to vote too?"

"He'd like to," Temple turned to Tyler. "Who are you going to vote for today?"

Tyler pointed at his father. "You."

Temple and his wife registered at the desk as they had done for many other elections. Mrs. Jennings, the Democratic poll watcher, looked up at Temple and smiled. "We haven't had this much excitement around here, ever! Good luck, Mr. Temple."

"Thanks, Mrs. Jennings." Temple felt very good inside that Jennings, who had been a Democratic stalwart forever, would offer her good wishes.

After he and his wife had voted, Sally Notholm approached Pat Temple with her camera crew. She held up her microphone and asked, "Mrs. Temple. You took one minute and thirty-seven seconds to vote. Your husband only took forty-two seconds. Why were you in there so much longer than he was?"

Pat didn't care for Notholm before this meeting. She had seen her at other events and had also seen the kind of coverage that Notholm had given to her husband. Now she was asking her a question that Pat thought bordered on imbecilic.

She squelched her initial response and instead said simply, "I wanted my son Tyler to see his father's name on the ballot. I explained to him what this was about and showed him

477

how people would cast their vote for his dad. I didn't keep track of the time."

She gave Notholm a quick smile and turned to leave the polling place with her husband and son.

Notholm stood there staring at the retreating back of Pat Temple. The cameraman chuckled to himself, "Good show!"

Outside, the wind had picked up. The Temples walked to their van as several voters said hello to them and wished them "Good luck!"

* * *

The unions had done their usually efficient job of circulating Mann's political literature. The week before the election, every union hall had been paid a personal visit by Mann, and every union steward had voiced their support for her reelection.

Pro-choice advocates had also rallied to her call. They helped with the door–to–door campaign and made calls to their supporters to vote for Mann. Planned Parenthood published Mann's credentials in their October newsletter and strongly endorsed her candidacy over Temple's. Temple was labeled as a Pro-Life candidate.

The teachers' union was split over their endorsement. The rank and file members usually voted Democratic, but this year their President was from the Jamesville-DeWitt School District and knew Temple. She had worked with him while he was on the school board and had argued that he was very supportive on the educational issues that were important to the union. In the end, each local was allowed to act independently, although the New York State Teachers Association endorsed Mann.

The newspapers were another story entirely. The Syracuse Gazette endorsed Mann saying that Temple was too naive for Albany and had run a typical mudslinging campaign. They praised Mann for her stand against the 'good ole boys' in

Albany and her fight to open the back rooms of political deal-making to public scrutiny.

The Observer Dispatch didn't endorse either candidate. They listed the platforms that each candidate espoused and praised the good fortune that the voters had in being able to pick from two good candidates. Having endorsed Mann in her previous two elections, Temple took this neutral stance by the paper as a positive gesture.

The Utica papers endorsed Mann, again citing her efforts at making government more open to the public. However, they also praised Temple as a new star on the horizon. A man who talks straight, is bright, and has a sincere interest in turning the state around financially. They finished by stating, "We hope Jay Temple will stay active in politics and will run again for public office. We need more people like Temple in politics."

The weekly papers throughout the district endorsed Temple. They cited his business, legal, and community service experience as well as his fresh approach to government as reasons why they endorsed his candidacy. They said that Temple was issue-oriented and was well-versed in the financial problems of the state. They believed that he was best qualified as a voice for change.

They also noted that Mann had fought for the right cause, open government, but that she had been ineffective during her six years in the Senate. "She has not gotten a single bill that she has sponsored passed by the Senate."

The lone local weekly not to support Temple was the Hamilton News.

The editor endorsed Mann as the pro-choice candidate who was not afraid to speak out on the issues. He went on to say that Temple was pro-life, pro-business, and another in a string of good old boys sponsored by Senate Republicans to get rid of Mann, a Democrat who had held their feet to the fire.

Temple wondered what influence these endorsements and editorials would have on the campaign.

Also appearing in the papers the week before the election

479

were letters to the editor supporting candidates or criticizing them. It was evident that some of these letters were politically induced.

The chairman of the Onondaga County Democrats wrote a blistering letter which was published by the Syracuse Gazette against Temple. Not unlike the editorial in the Hamilton News, the letter indicated that Temple was a wealthy insurance executive trying to buy the election. Temple was accused of being against the working man and the poor, against the pro-choice movement, and lacking in any kind of meaningful experience that would qualify him for the New York State Senate. It concluded that Temple had run the dirtiest political campaign ever seen in Onondaga County and that the voters should reject Temple at the polls.

The timing of this letter to the editor was also interesting to Temple. It appeared in the Gazette the Monday before the election. Any kind of damage control would be too little and too late.

* * *

Temple spoke at the Canastota Rotary Club at noon on Election Day. He reminisced about the experiences that he had during his race and talked about the need for change if New York were ever to pull out of the downward spiral that it was in. He outlined his proposals for changes in state spending, law enforcement programs, and the need to set spending priorities to funnel more money into education and health care. He concluded with a call for more individuals to become actively involved in the political arena. "Only by all of us taking an active part can we ever expect real change to occur!" Temple thanked his audience for the invitation and received a standing ovation in return.

On the way back to Syracuse, he stopped at a little restaurant in Chittenango for a cup of coffee. He had discovered this place in his many travels to and through this hometown of

480

the author of The Wizard of Oz.

Sandy Small owned the restaurant and had liked what she had seen and heard of Temple.

"Hello, Mr. Temple."

"Hi, Sandy. How about calling me Jay?" He smiled at her. She was another in a long line of nice people that he had met along the campaign trail.

"It's okay with me. So what will you have, Jay?" she laughed.

"Hot tea with milk and some of your famous mincemeat pie."

Sandy brought the order back to the table and asked, "You going to win today?"

"I don't know, Sandy." Temple looked at the clock on the wall. It had the face of the Scarecrow from The Wizard of Oz on it. "I'll know in about seven hours."

"Well, good luck. I don't know if I've ever met a politician like you before. You're okay." She was sincere in her compliment.

Temple smiled at her. "Thanks. Win or lose, that's what made this race all worthwhile!"

He finished his tea and pie, said goodbye, and climbed back into his van for the trip back to his headquarters. Now it was time for the results of ten months worth of effort, planning, campaigning, listening, debating, asking for contributions, and running through the emotional gamut that was all a part of the political process.

He thought about all the people who had helped out along the way. Win or lose, how many would he see again after the election. He promised himself that he would make an effort to thank everyone and to try to maintain the friendships that had developed throughout the past year.

It was three-thirty in the afternoon by the time Temple arrived back at his headquarters. The parking lot was filled, so he parked in the restaurant lot next door.

As he walked into his headquarters he was greeted by a

cheer from the some fifty people standing in the main room. Laney Gardiner ran over to him and hugged him. She smiled and said, "You're winning! You are ahead by two hundred and eighty-six votes!"

Temple was astonished. He didn't expect to get any results until the polls closed. "You're kidding! How do we know that?"

Before Gardiner could answer, Temple was surrounded by people shaking his hand and congratulating him.

Steve Adamson, the reporter from Channel 4 confirmed that he was leading. "We have three percent of the returns in. Voting machines that have had to be shut down. You're leading by two hundred and eighty-six votes." He held up a microphone. "Can we get a comment from you about your current lead in the New York State Senate race against Senator Mann?"

Temple became aware that camera lights had been on since he walked in the front door. He looked at Adamson, "I'm very happy to have the lead at this point. But with only three percent of the vote in, it's still too early to predict the outcome.

"I would like to say how much I appreciate all the work so many people have done to get us to this point."

Cordis pushed through the crowd to shake Temple's hand. He was excited and obviously very happy with the latest news. "Remember, I get to take the Senate Plates off her car and put them on yours!" He shouted as others shook Temple's hand as well.

At five o'clock that afternoon, Temple was still holding the lead by almost a thousand votes. His headquarters was now packed with people and reporters.

After his twelfth interview in less than two hours, he asked his assistant, Patrick Fitzgerald to try and keep the interviews down to one an hour unless there was a big swing in the vote. Fitzgerald stood about six feet four inches and was imposing enough to accomplish the task. He also had a good degree of tact.

Mike Flynn, a reporter for the Gazette who Temple

482

considered a friend, was allowed past the 'Fitzgerald line.'

Flynn asked Temple, "How does it feel to be the first politician to take the lead in a race with Senator Mann?"

Temple smiled at his friend. "Tell me if the 17th Ward results are in and I'll answer your question."

"Good point." Flynn knew as did Temple, that the 17th Ward was a huge block of votes in the City of Syracuse and that it was predominantly Democratic.

The Ward Leader for the Democrats there had a great get–out–the–vote machine. She had delivered big for Mann in the past and Temple's hope was that he could build enough of a lead to offset that vote when it came in.

At six-thirty, dinner was served to over two hundred people who had filled Temple's campaign headquarters. Some thirty-two women, who had worked with Pat Temple on mailing her "Do Me A Favor" letter, had also helped make casseroles, salads, and desserts to go along with the cold cuts and soda that the committee had purchased for the Election Day celebration.

People were in high spirits. They wore straw hats with Temple bumper stickers on them. They wore Temple buttons, held Temple balloons, and some even carried banners around touting Temple for Governor. The media had a field day covering all the excitement. It was the culmination of everything that Temple's workers had hoped for.

At seven-fifteen, a group of fifteen campaign workers arrived from Rome. Temple greeted them and asked them how things were going in Rome.

Allan Gant, the assistant to Rome's mayor, smiled broadly, "You won! Rome has gone for Jay Temple!"

TV and radio reporters quickly picked up on this latest development. With fifty-six percent of the vote in, Temple had the lead in a traditionally Democratic stronghold. Rome would go to Temple.

Temple and his friends were jubilant at this news. If he could win big in Manlius, DeWitt, and Cicero, he could offset Mann's expected plurality in the City of Syracuse.

* * *

Senator Mann had made the rounds of the polling places, talking with poll watchers and fellow Democrats throughout the day. At six o'clock that evening she slipped away to a restaurant on the north side of Syracuse for dinner with Joel Samuels and Tork Johns.

After they had ordered their dinner, Mann turned to Samuels. "I'm a thousand votes behind. Am I going to pull this one out?"

Samuels looked at his protégée. She looked tired and concerned. He smiled at her as he cupped his hands over hers on the table. "You'll win by four to six percent. Syracuse will send you back to Albany."

"Are you sure?" she asked. She had never been behind before, and she was tired. The last few weeks had turned into a blur as she criss-crossed her district seeking votes.

"Count on it," Samuels reassured her. "Have I ever let you down?"

"No. But then I've never run against a Jay Temple before."

"Well, after this race, you never will again. You'll have beaten a tough campaigner, with no skeletons and lots of money. They'll never find another politician with those credentials."

She looked at her campaign manager. "So you're finally admitting that Temple's a good politician."

Samuels looked back at her with a knowing grin. "All right. So I may have underestimated Temple in the beginning. Who would've guessed that a no-name could go the distance like he did. As far as I can tell, he really had all amateurs working his campaign. Matter of fact, I think it was the pros that blew it for him."

"What do you mean?"

"Word has it that Ophidia and your friend Senator Valli were the ones that cooked up that postcard fiasco. That lost our Mr. Temple some votes."

She sat back in her chair. "He carried Rome."

Samuels acknowledged her with a nod. "Yeah, but he lost some ground. He also lost votes here because of the smell to the whole deal."

Johns interrupted. "I think Laura Ann beat him more than he lost it." Johns was always the staunch supporter.

Samuels looked at Johns. "That, my friend, is always the imponderable. What really were the ingredients for victory or defeat? In this race, we may never know."

At eight o'clock, Mann, now joined by her daughter and husband, entered Democratic Party headquarters to wait out the results of the election.

She worked the room, talking to friends and foes alike. Politicians often are jealous of one another, and Mann was no exception. She had those who thought she could do no wrong and those who thought that she couldn't do anything right, both within her own party. But politicians have a way of bonding in public and for tonight, the party was bonding. They all knew she was in the race to watch. Every time a voter update came in, all eyes focused on her race.

It had been bleak early but now the gap was closing. She had been down by a little over a thousand votes but now was within four hundred votes of the lead. It was the most exciting race of the night.

Chapter XXXIII

Election Results

The polls closed at nine o'clock. Unlike national elections, state and local election returns come in quickly. There are no time zones to deal with and the voting booths are tallied immediately after the close of the polls. Though not official, each party has its own poll watchers who take the totals and call them in to a central point. The votes are then tallied and a winner declared.

Temple had agreed to let the DeWitt Republicans use his headquarters as their central reporting place. DeWitt would be an important town in any victory that Temple would walk away with. It was one of three heavily populated areas in the Onondaga County portion of the 48th Senate District. Temple needed to win big in DeWitt to offset the expected Syracuse vote from the seventeenth ward.

It amazed Temple to see how quickly the results of ten months worth of work played out. At 9:15, DeWitt had its totals. Temple had received forty-eight percent of the vote to Mann's fifty-two percent.

Shelly Roberts was the Republican Town Leader for DeWitt. She and her husband had worked hard for Temple and couldn't believe the results as they came in.

Howard White and his family had joined the Temple headquarters party for what he thought was going to be 'the upset of the century.' White had been jubilant each time a new preliminary report came in showing Temple ahead. Now, as he looked on in disbelief at the DeWitt numbers, he decided on a

486

new tack. He quietly gathered his wife and son together and left the Temple headquarters through the side door.

Shelly turned to her husband with the weight of the world on her shoulders. "I have to tell him."

Her husband nodded and patted her hand.

Roberts got up from the Table and walked back to where Temple was talking to his wife and daughter. He turned and smiled at Roberts. He could see the results in her eyes before she spoke.

"Jay," Roberts paused. This was one of the hardest things that she had ever had to do. She really liked Temple as a person and she blamed herself for what she was about to say. "We have the final tally for DeWitt. It's not good."

Jay looked at his loyal volunteer and knew what she was going through. He felt a little sick inside, too, but didn't want it to show. "Part of politics is taking the good news with the bad. How much did we lose by?"

"Four percent. You got forty-eight percent of the vote in DeWitt. I'm really sorry." Shelly Roberts eyes filled with tears as she shuddered.

Temple put an arm around her shoulders. "Shelly, you did everything I could've asked for in DeWitt. Look at it this way. When I started, my name recognition was around three percent. To take it to a positive forty-eight percent in ten months is a great accomplishment. I owe you a debt of gratitude."

She looked up at him sensing what he was trying to do. "Thanks." She walked back to the table where her husband and a few DeWitt committee people were packing up their papers to go to the County Republican Rally at the Sheraton Hotel.

Temple didn't have much time to dwell on the results in DeWitt. Chauncy Allen, the town Republican leader in Manlius, along with his aides, Kerry Heathrow and Ira Sterling, stopped by Temple's headquarters with their results. Manlius had gone for Temple fifty-seven percent to Mann's forty-three percent. It was 9:20 in the evening.

Temple thanked Allen for stopping by on his way to the

County Republican Rally. He also thanked him and his assistants for the hard work that they put in on his campaign.

As Allen was about to leave, Channel 7 reported that with sixty-four percent of the vote in, Senator Mann had taken the lead by six thousand twelve votes. They also reported that they were now projecting Mann as the winner.

The reporters at Temple's headquarters immediately sought Temple out for comment. Fitzgerald was really tested but was up to the task as he held the reporters at bay while Temple, Cordis, Roth, Yondle, and Gardiner went over the numbers. Robert Anderson helped Fitzgerald with the reporters telling them that Temple would have a comment as soon as he confirmed the numbers.

Jim Summers was on the phone with the NYSSRC verifying results as they were computer tabulated in Albany. All district computers fed their numbers to Albany, and there they were totaled and the results plotted against voting demographics from previous elections. At 9:45, Toby Hagan got on the phone with Summers, Cordis, and Temple.

"Jay. Unfortunately we are projecting your race to result in fifty-two percent of the vote going to Mann and forty-eight percent going into your column." Hagan waited.

Neither Cordis nor Summers could speak. Jay looked at both, and then asked Hagan. "You don't have any reason to doubt this projection?"

"No. We have examined where the votes have come from, and with eighty-six percent, you can't make up the six thousand vote difference in the areas of the district left to report.

"I will tell you this. You ran a hell of a campaign for your first time out of the box. I think with what we have in the computers you could win the next time." Hagan knew where Temple got hurt. He had seen the drop after the Ophidia TV commercial and again after the Ophidia postcard. He could never divulge this information or he'd lose his job. But he knew that Temple had been on the right path up until these two tactical errors and that the race had been close enough that without them,

Temple could have won.

Temple closed the phone call. "Toby, thanks for all the work you and your people did for me. I haven't forgotten how you went to bat for me early on when we needed some money to get this campaign going. Good luck."

"You too, Jay. If you do decide to go again, let me know."

Jay thought about this. It was too early to make those kinds of decisions. "Thanks, Toby. Goodbye."

Temple turned to his waiting staff. Ed Thatcher, Mary Tarkings, Mary Price, and Fred Childs, his Syracuse coordinator, had joined the others. All were very somber.

It occurred to Temple that these people had given their hearts and souls to him throughout the campaign. They had high hopes and expectations. His loss was their personal loss as well. He wished that he could have done more, if not for himself, then for them. But it was time to face facts and Temple could not change anything that had already happened. He put on his best front and smiled at them. "I have to go out there and make a statement. Before I do, I want you to know that I will never forget you for all that you have done. It sounds too simple to really say all that I should say," he paused as he looked into the face of each one of them, "but thank you very much." He forced a breath or two down and then turned to go out into the main room of his headquarters and give his final news conference of the campaign.

* * *

A cheer went up at Democratic Headquarters as the crowd watched Channel 7 report Laura Ann Mann as their projected winner in the 48th Senate District race.

Mann heaved a final sigh of relief. This was confirmation of what she had been told by the 17th Ward Leader moments after the polls had closed. They had again given her an insurmountable lead of over six thousand votes. Rome, Manlius,

489

the southern towns of Onondaga, and parts of Madison County, all places where she had won big in the past, had all gone to Temple. But her block in the City of Syracuse, together with Cicero, and surprisingly, DeWitt, had again returned her to office.

A stream of well-wishers passed by her as she sat near the front of the room with her daughter and husband. She smiled broadly and thanked everyone of them for their good wishes.

Tork Johns brought her a mug of beer and smiled at her as she winked at him. "Thanks, Tork."

Kevin Mack of Channel 7, along with several other reporters, asked her if she would make a statement.

"I'd be happy to, but I want to wait until Mr. Temple has conceded the race." She put them off very diplomatically. She wanted to see how Temple would handle this defeat. She wanted to know if he would be coming back at her in two years. She wanted to be sure that whatever happened tonight, she would have the last word.

Samuels leaned over to one of his friends, pulled a large cigar from his mouth and said, "She doesn't know the size of the race she has just won. That girl can write her own ticket now!"

* * *

Three soldiers sat in the second floor office of the Armory. They were watching a small black and white television. The news reporter had just given the results of the 48th Senate District race and projected Senator Mann as the winner.

The Captain looked at his two subordinates and commented, "We lost a good man."

The Sergeant nodded. "He'd have been an ally."

The Captain agreed. "Yeah." He thought a second longer before his military training kicked in. "Get me the file on our number two choice."

The Sergeant looked at the Captain for a brief moment,

490

resigned himself to the facts, and got up to get the Assemblyman's file.

* * *

The Sheraton was filled with people celebrating election evening. Winning was part of it, but for most being seen and seeing was the major attraction.

The Onondaga County Republican Party had rented the ballroom and a few suites on the second floor for the party faithful.

While most of the committee people milled around on the ballroom floor or watched the large screen televisions, the party leaders met on the second floor for free drinks and a chance to relax before going down to the main ballroom.

Arthur Gaines just shook his head as Channel 7 announced its projected winners. He turned to Ken Mathews and said. "I told Temple that his stand on abortion would kill him. He should have come out either for or against it. Lansing was against it, and he won. White was for it, and he won. Temple made a big mistake not taking a position."

Mathews had raised a lot of money for Temple and knew Temple well. He had been an inside adviser for Temple and had been through all of the issues with him. He said to Gaines, "Well, you know, he did state his position pretty clearly. He said that he couldn't make the decision to take a life, but that he also didn't feel that he could make that decision for someone else."

Gaines looked at Mathews in disbelief. "Who understands what that means? The voter just wants to know will you vote for or against an open abortion law. They don't care what your answer is, just that you have one. I think the abortion issue lost him the election."

The Congressman had his own suite on the second floor of the Sheraton. He, too, watched the election night coverage with a few close friends.

491

Tim Sullivan, his public relations man, turned to him after the Temple-Mann results were announced. "That's too bad. Jay ran a great campaign."

The Congressman nodded in agreement. "Temple ran a heck of a campaign. I think that two years from now he'll beat Mann and have a long tenure in the New York State Senate."

Larry Kent, the Congressman's campaign manager, had a different view. "If Temple runs again for the Senate, Mann will consider other options."

Both men looked at Kent. The Congressman asked, "What do you mean?"

Kent took a drink and continued. "She'd have lost this race but for a few screw ups in Albany. She's smart enough to know that. We won tonight but by a lot closer margin than we had hoped for. In this Congressional District, you are never going to pull away with the vote. It's too diverse.

"Mann's not going to want to face another grueling race with Temple at fifty-fifty odds, only to go back to a Republican–controlled Senate. She might as well face close to the same odds in a race for Congress with the hope of joining a Democratically–controlled House of Representatives.

"If I were her boy Samuels, that's what I'd be telling her."

The Congressman listened to Kent's theory. He'd have to think about this long and hard.

* * *

The Senate Majority Leader's office was a spacious marble and polished wood room with carved columns and beams, mahogany furniture, and a twenty-four foot long conference table tucked neatly into one alcove off to the side.

Senator Manto was celebrating the reelection of all of his Republican colleagues along with three new Republican Senators. Joining him for his private celebration were Arnold Ophidia, Toby Hagan, Senator Valli, Senator Giles, and a handful of

492

secretaries and aides who had worked on the campaigns for the NYSSRC.

Manto looked at Valli and Ophidia. "Nice job, gentlemen. The NYSSRC was a very wise decision. The state committee is practically bankrupt, but we came through this election with flying colors. You are to be congratulated."

Valli looked at his boss. The NYSSRC was his brainchild. A separate fund raising arm from the state committee, it could take advantage of the power of the New York State Republican–controlled Senate. Valli hoped that his committee would propel him into the majority leader's seat at the right time. He said, "We did exactly what we had to with ninety-nine percent success."

Manto thought about this and said with some regret, "Yes. Too bad about Temple. He ran a close race with Mann. I thought he had her number."

Ophidia laughed. "We had her number. We could've beaten that bitch if the guy had listened to us. He didn't want to take off the gloves. I don't think he has the stomach for it."

Valli looked at Ophidia and asked, "What about next time? Can we position the guy for a successful rematch in two years?"

Ophidia really didn't care for Temple. Temple had snubbed him and now it was payback time. "That guy couldn't get elected dog catcher! He's not a politician. Running for office is just another form of community service to this guy. Politics is a business. If you don't treat it that way, you're finished before you start."

* * *

Temple walked out of his back office and into the main room of his headquarters. Camera lights went on immediately, recording his steps toward the area that had earlier been designated for his acceptance or concession speech.

Volunteers shook his hand, smiled, cried, or offered

493

words of consolation as he approached the bank of microphones taped to the podium.

He stepped up to the podium, smiled and said. "First and foremost, I want to thank everyone here tonight for all your hard work and effort in what I think has been a great experience for all of us. I know it has been for me.

"This race has been between two candidates who have different approaches and different perspectives on the issues. Both of us talked about what we felt were important to the voters. I think that at this point, people know what we both stand for, and they have made their choice at the polls.

"But beyond the politics, I have found out something else about the people in Central New York. We are a very friendly, open and accepting community.

"I've met people from all walks of life, all ages, and from a variety of political persuasions. They all have certain things in common. They love their families. They worry about crime, drugs, and the economy. And they all have hope and expectations for the future.

"I believe that long term, the politicians in Albany and in Washington will hear what the people want and need and will respond to those needs.

"On a more personal level, there are so many people to thank, I hardly know where to begin."

Temple looked around the room filled with friends, family, volunteers, and reporters. He continued, "Ted Cordis took on the Herculean task of campaign manager. We did everything from marching behind racing pigs to coordinating a campaign strategy together." Temple looked directly at Cordis and said, "Thank you for everything."

Temple then went on to thank each of his primary workers individually. "Patrick Fitzgerald was our Irish workhorse. No job was too big or too small for Patrick. Whether it was putting up yard signs, licking envelopes, driving the mobile headquarters, or keeping my son, Tyler, company, Patrick was always there.

494

"Mary Price was another tireless worker. She and Mary Tarkings coordinated our volunteer activity, our mailings and our phone-a-thon. At this point, I want to thank both of you and give you your lives back! They've spent the last eight months giving every spare moment to the campaign.

"Laney Gardiner is a very special person. She staffed our headquarters from morning till night. She also helped coordinate volunteer activity, made phone calls for our fund raising effort, acted as an additional hostess at our special events, and often went on the road with us for parades and appearances." Temple looked at Gardiner, smiled at his loyal volunteer, and said, "Thank you."

He then focused on Dave Yondle. "Dave Yondle has been a longstanding friend who finds more ways to raise money than any other person I know. Dave's crowning achievement this year was our dinner at the Hotel Syracuse. A lot of people doubted that we could pull this off but not Dave. He stuck with it, and it turned out to be our biggest single fund raiser of the campaign.

"Thanks, Dave." Yondle nodded, forcing back his emotions as he listened to his friend go on.

"Kevin Roth is another longtime friend who kept our finances in the black and met all the reporting deadlines of the campaign. Kevin, I appreciate all your hard work but especially your good counsel during the campaign.

"Kevin and Jim Summers were my 'kitchen cabinet' during the campaign. When I needed to bounce some ideas off of someone, both of these friends were reliable and ready listeners. I'd like to thank you both.

"There are so many people that I need to thank, and will in the weeks ahead. Ken Mathews, Don North, Doctor Carey, Tom Mosby, all key people in our fund raising efforts.

"Friends like Bob Anderson, Tony and Joan Falo, Allen Benair, Ed Thatcher, Jim Trout in Chittenango, my secretary, Gloria Bryan, Calvin Wendt, Allan Gant, Mary Catallana of Rome, they all have put their personal lives on hold while they

495

went out and campaigned with me.

"Finally, I want to say a special thank-you to my family. My Mom and Dad flew up here to be with me tonight, and I appreciate their being here. My daughter, Amy, flew home from college to be here also. It's important to have a family who cares around you at times like this. My sons, Tyler and James, have worked the campaign trail with me and I think learned a lot about people and politics." He looked at his two sons and laughed. "Are you guys ready to run for public office?"

James shook his head indicating that he wasn't about to pick up where his dad had left off. Tyler just lowered his head in embarrassment.

"The person who really bore the entire weight of this campaign for our family is my wife, Pat. She worked hard on every little detail of the campaign. Whether it was baking our favorite chocolate cake for us while we worked or marching in parades, appearing at special functions, getting mailings out, calling for volunteers, or setting up our headquarters, Pat was there.

"On top of all the political activity, she found time to maintain our home and take care of our family. The limelight of any campaign is always focused on the candidate. But I think the toughest job belongs to the spouse of the candidate. No one ever fully appreciates the hard work and emotional roller coaster that the spouse endures.

"Pat, thank you and I love you."

Temple's wife wiped away a tear and joined her husband at the podium. Temple's children also came up to the podium to be with their father.

Temple finished his speech by saying, "Thank you all!"

Sally Notholm rushed forward at that point to ask Temple a question. The camera lights were still on.

"Mr. Temple. Do you think the dirty politics and name calling in this campaign had anything to do with your losing?" She fired the question at him without flinching.

Temple looked at Notholm for a long moment and

496

concluded that he should expect nothing more from this reporter. He answered, "Sally, Senator Mann is a tough, hard working campaigner. She is probably the best politician in this area when it comes to delivering a thirty–second sound byte, and she works the media better than anyone else I know. I think she won this election because she is THE politician."

Steve Adamson stepped forward and asked, "Mr. Temple. Will you be back in two years to run again for the Senate?"

Temple looked at Adamson and smiled. "The only thing I'm thinking of running for at this point is my home and family! I've missed them, and it's time for us to be together."

Temple's friends all pushed forward to shake his hand one more time before he left. There were still over a hundred people in the room and Temple made it a point to thank each one personally and to share a remembered experience with each of them before he left his headquarters for the last time.

Dan Crawford, the news anchor at Channel 7, was watching Temple on the studio monitor as Temple was shaking hands with the people at his headquarters. He turned to Karen Lastri, his co-anchor person and said, "Now there's a guy I could vote for."

Chapter XXXIV

Epilogue

In the weeks that immediately followed the election, there was still work that had to be done.

Temple's volunteers took down all the yard signs, cleaned the building that Temple had rented for his campaign headquarters, and packed up all the campaign material that had gone unused.

When they were finished, Cordis met with his inner circle of workers from the Young Republicans. They were disappointed that all their work had not paid off. He told them, "We didn't win, but we gained a lot of experience on how to run a campaign and how to raise big dollars for a campaign. We have an organization now that other politicians will want to use. This gives us power. I think we are in good shape for the future."

Temple met with Yondle and Roth for a final review of their campaign finances. All bills that had been received had been paid. There were no outstanding debts, and in fact, Roth reported that they had a little over twelve thousand dollars remaining in the campaign account.

"We've come a long way since that first meeting in my living room." Temple laughed. "Remember how everyone was convinced that you couldn't run a viable campaign without debt?"

Roth remembered.

Temple had three options. Keep the money, use it for his next campaign, or donate the money to others. He decided to contribute a small portion of the money remaining to the campaign funds of the Congressman, the County Executive, and a couple of other candidates who were in debt after their campaigns.

The major portion of the surplus from his campaign, he donated to a variety of local charities. It was his way of giving something back to the community from his campaign.

The Congressman looked out the window of his office. He had won reelection by a narrower margin than he had hoped for, but he had won. In politics, that was all that mattered.

His campaign manager interrupted his thoughts. "We need to start thinking about the next election."

He knew that this, too, was part of the game. You'd think that there would be a break, but there isn't. You have to analyze your strengths and weaknesses and try to build on one and lessen the other.

His public relations man spoke up. "Mann's already giving signs that she is thinking of taking you on next time. She says that you are out of touch with your constituents."

The Congressman heard both of his friends. A car passed below his office window. It had a bumper sticker which read, 'Temple For Senate.' 'Name recognition,' he thought to himself as he turned to answer his key workers, 'name recognition.'